Praise for *Voyage to Kazohinia*

"In an Old World voice with postmodern tones, Sándor Szathmári's *Voyage to Kazohinia* takes a comic knife to our various conceptions of government, skewering our efforts to determine the most expedient social arrangement for populations to adopt. Gulliver, the belittled individual with an oversize sense of capacity, earns our fulsome affection, if leavened with our apprehension about his own blindness. Crusoe encountering Friday, Alice at a loss at the Mad Tea Party: Make room for the new Gulliver! He has brought home news out of Kazohinia."
   —**Gregory Maguire, author of *Wicked and Out of Oz***

"[A] dystopian cult classic. . . . Gulliver (yes, that Gulliver) is alive in 1935 and employed as a surgeon on the British ship Trafalgar. After a shipwreck, [he] washes up on the island of Kazohinia, which is populated by bizarre inhabitants. . . . whose sense of morality and society force Gulliver to reconsider his own understanding of life, love, and death."
   —***Publishers Weekly***

"*Voyage to Kazohinia* is among the secret treasures of Hungarian literature, and it is really about time it appeared on the world stage. It was so ahead of its time that its time still hasn't caught up. Perhaps now it will."
   —**Miklos Vámos, author of *The Book of Fathers***

"A powerful stimulus to thought. What distinguishes *Voyage to Kazohinia* from similar ventures and yet links it to *Brave New World* is its description of utopia *and* dystopia."
   —**Michel Duc Goninaz, author of *La Plena Ilustrita Vortaro de Esperanto* (*Complete Illustrated Esperanto Dictionary*)**

"Szathmári succeeds in forcing readers to confront the ways citizens of societies accept as truth those precepts that define and enable the society's existence, even at the expense of the individual."
   —***ForeWord Reviews***

"Written in 1935, *Voyage to Kazohinia* is a strikingly postmodern and open-ended dystopia that rightfully belongs among the twentieth-century classics of the genre. And it is unique in being less a strident political cautionary tale than it is a brilliantly mordant reflection on government, reason, and language."
  —Carter Hanson, Associate Professor of English,
  Valparaiso University

"This classic utopian *and* dystopian novel can now garner its rightful, essential place in its genre for readers in the wider world. A modern-day Gulliver is caught between the equally unacceptable hyperrationalism of the Hins and the insane irrationalism of the Behins. In both encounters, Gulliver proves incapable of perceiving the irrationality of his own society. Confronting the prospect of unlimited technological capability and our consequent alienation from natural life, Szathmári takes us on a voyage to a futuristic, transhumanist society. In so doing he suggests that we face two alternatives: to drown in our contradictions or eliminate them by eliminating ourselves. Whether or not we agree, this must-read novel challenges us at the most fundamental philosophical level."
  —Ralph Dumain, librarian & independent scholar,
  autodidactproject.org

"Sándor Szathmári writes in the best tradition of Jonathan Swift in using the framework of an adventure story for a fascinating in-depth exploration of interhuman relationships.... [He] remarkably brings off a crystal-clear style that never gets boring in the least."
  —Reinhard Fössmeier, International Academy of the Sciences
  San Marino

ABOUT THE AUTHOR

SÁNDOR SZATHMÁRI (1897–1974) was among the most extraordinary and elusive figures in twentieth-century Hungarian literature. The author of two published novels and several story collections in his native tongue, he is best known for *Voyage to Kazohinia*—which, titled *Kazohinia* on most editions in Hungary, has been treasured by generations of readers.

Completed in 1935, *Voyage to Kazohinia* was first published in Hungary in 1941 as *Gulliver utazása Kazohiniában* (*Gulliver's Travels in Kazohinia*). The second edition, *Utazások Kazohiniában* (*Travels in Kazohinia*), appeared in 1946 with an author preface noting the inclusion of previously censored passages and two new chapters; three similar editions titled *Kazohinia* appeared during the communist decades and two have been published since.

Despite a childhood marked by frequent ill health and the deaths of his older brothers, Szathmári received a good education, excelling at mathematics and even writing a textbook on the subject. He spent much of his career as a mechanical engineer; this, together with his limited oeuvre, the biting satire of his magnum opus, and his political persuasions—which ranged from an early, ambivalent affiliation with communism to anticommunism as Hungary became a communist dictatorship—kept him ever on the margins of the officially sanctioned literary establishment.

A central figure in Hungary's Esperanto movement for decades, Szathmári published his writings in his own Esperanto-language editions, which assured him a measure of international recognition and literary freedom during the communist era.

ABOUT THE TRANSLATOR

INEZ KEMENES, who was born in Budapest in 1937 and lives there to this day, is the translator of numerous works into English—from science fiction and travel to art history and archeology—for Corvina Press, which for decades was Hungary's foremost foreign-language publisher. Her translations from English to Hungarian include novels by Pauline Melville and John Lanchester.

Sándor Szathmári in 1973, the year before his death. Photo © János Eifert

Voyage to Kazohinia

Sándor Szathmári

Translated from the Hungarian
by Inez Kemenes

New Europe Books

Published by New Europe Books, 2012
15 Doanes Lane
North Adams, Massachusetts 01247
www.NewEuropeBooks.com

The characters & events in this book are fictitious. Any similarities to real persons, living or dead, is coincidental and not intended by the author.

Copyright © 2012 estate of Sándor Szathmári
Translation © 2012 Inez Kemenes
Cover design © 2012 András Baranyai
Interior design by József Pintér
Copyediting by Fred Macnicol and Paul Olchváry • Proofreading by Dale Cotton

Others whose support has helped make the publication of this book possible:
László & Ildikó Olchváry, Dorottya Olchváry, Jenny Gitlitz, and Miklós Sólyom.

First published in English as *Kazohinia* by Corvina Press, Budapest, 1975. Translation by Inez Kemenes. Original Hungarian edition first published in 1941, Bolyai, Budapest. Subsequent editions published in Hungary in 1946, 1952, 1972, 1980, 1996, and 2009.

ISBN: 978-0-9825781-2-4

Library of Congress Cataloging-in-Publication Data

Szathmári, Sándor, 1897–1974.
[Kazohinia. English]
Voyage to Kazohinia / Sándor Szathmári; translated from the Hungarian by Inez Kemenes.—1st ed.
p. cm.
ISBN 978-0-9825781-2-4 (acid-free paper)
1. Dystopias—Fiction. 2. Utopias—Fiction. I. Kemenes, Inez. II. Title.
PH3351.S59917K3813 2012
894'.511334—dc23
2012007547

Printed in the United States of America
10 9 8 7 6 5 4 3 2 1

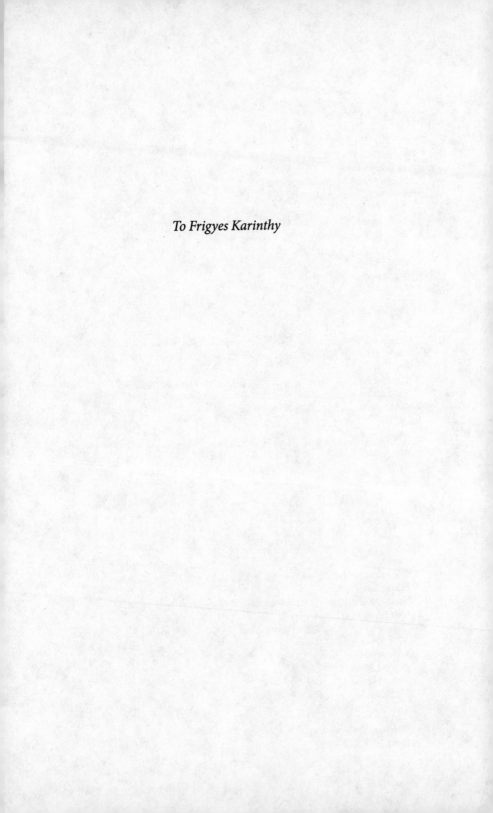

To Frigyes Karinthy

Voyage to Kazohinia

Sándor Szathmári

PART

I

GULLIVER
AMONG THE HINS

CHAPTER

1

*The author resolves to offer his services when his country
is threatened by dangers. He is assigned to the cruiser
Invincible and starts for Shanghai to protect culture. They
encounter an Italian ship. The cruiser is sunk by an explo-
sion but the author has a merciful escape.*

THE READER WHO MAY HAVE FOUND MY FORMER, HUMBLE
works worthy of his attention may well be surprised to learn
that after so many adventures and severe trials I have put to sea
again.

I can assure the Reader that now, having returned from Kazohinia and as I look back on my sufferings among the Hins
and particularly among the Behins, I am of completely the same
opinion.

Thus may I mention, not by way of excuse but by way of
explanation, that on this occasion, apart from my accursed
adventurous spirit, it was the protection of Great Britain and
Christian civilization that prompted me to travel anew. And I ask
the educated Reader whether there is a more worthy calling for
a British subject than to serve under the Royal flag the elevated
ideas of mankind and Christianity against their sworn enemies.

Also deserving some appreciation, perhaps, is the fact that
my voyage to Kazohinia led me to hitherto entirely unknown
territories and afforded me such extraordinary experiences as
no fellow being had previously undergone. In particular, my

becoming acquainted with the Behinic disease raised my hopes
that my travels had not been in vain and that by describing my
experiences I should be able—in proportion with my humble
faculties—to perform some service to my country and to medical science.

I am perfectly prepared for the Reader to accept my narrative
with an occasional shake of the head; I therefore mention in
advance that in the course of my work I have always striven to
describe everything with the strictest objectivity.

Should, however, some parts of my book still furnish opportunity for doubt, I shall not be unduly surprised. Kazohinia is so
remote from my country and European civilization that both its
customs and particularly its Behinic disease are completely unknown to us, and had I not seen them with my own eyes I would
possibly not believe that they exist and that they are indeed as
they are.

If now, having compiled my accounts of this voyage, I nevertheless publish them all, this proves only my devotion to objective
truth—a truth that, faced as I was with the inevitable doubts of
the Reader, prompted me to describe these definite facts.

*

Mankind, redeemed of its sins, was writing "one thousand nine
hundred and thirty-five" when the government of His Majesty
came to the conclusion that, in all probability, we should have to
wage war with Italy.

To the educated Reader I possibly need not explain in detail
that differences of opinion had arisen as a result of the actions
directed against the Ethiopian people.

It is beyond doubt that Italy entered this action with the intention of extending her territories—an action that an English
gentleman can take cognizance of with a measure of respect,
even if perpetrated by the enemy. And lest the Reader should

accuse me of partiality, I hasten to add that this was appreciated by every decent inhabitant of Great Britain.

We were deeply impressed by the enthusiastic generosity of the Italian prelates—who sacrificed money, valuable pastoral staffs, and bejeweled crosses of gold on their country's altar so that incendiary bombs, bayonets, and even tanks be purchased for a noble purpose. Likewise most admirable were the spirited patriotic letters in which they ceaselessly encouraged one and all—the shepherds, farmers, fishermen, fishmongers, grocers, piemen, icemen, longshoremen, gingerbread makers, candle-dippers, beggarmen, and thieves alike—to go to the front and spread culture and true Christian virtues among the Blacks, while they would just as ceaselessly implore the Savior and the Virgin of Loreto in devout prayer that the grace of Heaven should succor those bearing arms for a noble cause.

At the same time, we willingly recognized the heroic feats of those Italian soldiers whose death-defying courage and other honorable virtues might well be followed as examples by every loyal British subject of character—naturally under the Union Jack, and against the Italians. I repeat that as regards the *how* of the matter there was no discord between my country and Italy; it was merely the *why* of it that provided a basis for disagreement.

As their motive for the Ethiopian action, the Italians put forward their desire to liberate them from the yoke of the Amharas and to spread culture. The obvious untruthfulness of this—with all due respect—must prompt every sober-minded and better-educated person to laughter if he has even but a passing knowledge of the diplomatic phrases customary in other countries when they wish to gloss over the essence of things and thereby mislead the uninitiated observer.

I have no wish to slip into the error of partiality in the manner of those travelers who are not above a disproportionately ostentatious display of the glory of their country in the guise of scientific description; I believe, however—which with all modesty and due respect to foreign states I might mention—that the adoption of such a perspective is an error a British subject would never commit. In my country it is well known even to the less educated that the devoted but noble work of liberating the peoples of the tropics has always been a heartfelt duty. Sufficient proof may, I feel, be found in the many colonies from Southeast India to the Boers, whose peoples were set free from oppression at the cost of heavy battles.

And, much as an English gentleman is left cold by the material aspect, I cannot conceal my opinion that, apart from the cause of culture and freedom, Italy, in making her decision, may have been influenced, possibly unconsciously, by Ethiopian coffee and oil fields.

This is why the government of His Majesty, having made sanctions against the Italians, came to the decision to launch a defensive war against Italy. With this end in view and to ensure peace and balance of power in Europe, several divisions were urgently posted to Egypt with airplanes, tanks, flame throwers, and incendiary bombs, while battleships were dispatched to the Mediterranean Sea accompanied by torpedo-carrying destroyers and submarines.

These actions were of course received with strenuous counteraction by the Italian press. They asserted that, apart from the reasons mentioned, my country's actions had perhaps been influenced by the desire for gain and that she was begrudging a needy people the few oil wells and mines that did not even approach the sphere of Italy's interests, and would not even have been mentioned had not the British become involved.

The Reader may by now find the political details tedious, but it is my strictly determined intention to adhere to the objective truth and always to raise my humble voice in protest whenever unmerited blame is cast upon my country, its navy, its airplanes, its tanks, and in general on any of our splendid establishments that distinguish noble man from the beast of prey.

Thus, so as not to lose the thread of my story, it happened at the time that His Majesty's heavily armed battleship *Terrible,* riding at anchor in Chinese waters, was dispatched to the Mediterranean and in its place an old tub, the worn-out cruiser *Invincible*, was sent to fly the Royal colors and represent the rightful interests of my country with its presence. The task of the *Invincible* was not at all easy, as my country's interests were strongly threatened in the Far East by the danger of Japanese expansion; and some Chinese were in rebellion against our trade zones, which represented not only commerce but also culture and civilization.

It was on account of these interests that the *Invincible* had to be stationed at Shanghai.

My country was resolved to secure a European-type civilization in the East, further. The conflict with Italy, however, did not then permit it, and the opportunity was thoroughly exploited by Japan, who herself began to spread civilization in northern China, in full concord for the time being with the Covenant of the League of Nations and my beloved country.

The *Terrible* was replaced by the *Invincible* for a further reason, too; if the Japanese sank the *Invincible*, the damage would be comparatively insignificant and the case would not require consideration as hostile action. Although this intention was a strictly confidential naval secret, it nevertheless leaked out to the crew and, as a direct result, several requests for transfer were received. These requests were turned down by the Admiralty, whereupon many of the crew members deserted.

The government was compelled to resort to other methods, as they feared that the forced personnel would jump ship in Shanghai.

Accordingly, a doubling of salaries was promised together with a great deal of life insurance.

At that time I was serving as surgeon aboard the cruiser *Trafalgar*, and having returned home one day I made mention of the matter to my spouse.

My wife—who was the paragon of the faithful partner in marriage, as well as a good mother, and who as a zealous and chaste spouse had never ceased to rouse me with her frequent advice and urgency in my duties as a husband—immediately grasped the situation and enjoined me not to hesitate in having myself transferred immediately to the *Invincible*. With zealous words, she explained that in Shanghai I should have no expenses, nor should I be in a position to spend my afternoons with frivolous friends in the club and prodigally waste my money at dominoes, but would instead send it all home for the support of my beloved family. Nor would I need to be anxious about what would happen to them in the case of my death in action; for apart from the pension, the life insurance would be sufficient for her and the children to cherish my memory as befitted my rank.

The lofty words of my gentle and loving spouse, as well as the call of my adored country, prompted me to petition my transfer to the *Invincible*, which I duly received within a week.

After another week we sailed. My wife bore the pain of parting with the strength of spirit becoming to a patriotic woman. She did not even accompany me to the port lest she cause me unnecessary grief, but to ease her aching heart, she hastened to the dressmaker to try on the dress she had ordered, using my first double salary, for the tea party to be given by Mrs. E. Palmer two days later.

The sailing incidentally took place quite without ceremony. On October fourth but half an hour after embarkation, the *Invincible* weighed anchor, and after three cheers and some cap waving we put to sea.

Already on the eighth we were passing through the Straits of Gibraltar. After another four days we reached Malta, where we took on coal, oil, and fresh water but continued our voyage. On the fourteenth we arrived at the Suez Canal, through which several Italian troop ships were moving accompanied by some torpedo-carrying destroyers and the battle cruiser *Il Duce*. This had earlier been called *Libertà* but had been renamed due to the demand of a grateful people liberated from the oppression of the old regime, to which the leader—in all his modesty—could not turn a deaf ear.

Both we and the Italian battleships expressed our delight at the meeting in the most courteous manner. We each hoisted the flag of the other nation, dipped our own, and fired salvoes partly to convey our friendly greetings and partly to show the other that we had ammunition.

I do not want to bore the Reader by describing the details of our voyage on the Red Sea—although around Aden in particular we enjoyed a magnificent panorama; I will rather continue from the point at which we reached the Indian Ocean.

It was necessary for us to reach our destination discreetly if possible, so our route led widely south of the Equator to avoid the sea lanes of regular liners. Our next port of call was to be Singapore, which we had to reach by sailing around Sumatra.

We had been cutting through the waves of the Indian Ocean for eight days, and readily believed that we should arrive in Shanghai safe and sound. The captain was quite prepared for our ship to represent true British tradition, so he had two sailors put in irons in solitary confinement and another threatened with a court martial. This was because they had not polished their buttons properly and had shouldered arms negligently on parade.

Everything was in perfect order. The guns were polished, the hull repainted; in the end we managed to look as formidable as if we had just come out of dock after being completely refitted.

At about seven o'clock in the evening I was standing beside the gun turret on the middle deck. Near me my friend, a lieutenant commander, was rubbing his hands contentedly, and from the crew's quarters came the sound of drawling voices singing away with accordion and castanet accompaniment. It was an old song they had learned in Barcelona. (Lest the educated Reader accuse our honest officers of laxity, I hasten to add that at that time the Spanish Civil War had not yet broken out, and consequently my country had not yet signed the Non-Intervention Agreement.)

Suddenly, without warning, I felt a violent thrust. The screw propellers pulled our ship backwards with full countersteam; confused shouting and running about could be heard.

I looked around in fear, and understood everything in a flash.

From the distance a dark streak was drawing nearer and nearer at an incredible speed. For an instant I faintly thought that it would perhaps pass by the prow, but in vain. I had time only to throw myself to the floor in the recess behind the gun, and the next second a terrible force hurled me against the opposite wall, the detonation almost deafening me.

My head abuzz from the blow, I was only able to crawl out on all fours. My friend the lieutenant commander lay near me, laughing uproariously.

"The blockheads. . . . The blockheads. . . ." he spluttered. "They surely believe they've made a lucky hit! We've played a fine trick on them! . . . It's good we swabbed the ten-inch ones! . . . One must burst!"

He would have continued, had he not then died. I meanwhile endeavored to drag myself quickly toward the stern, which was as yet out of the water.

One of the crew threw some lifebelts into the lifeboat after us; another managed to throw in some forty pounds of food tins, but then we hastened to get launched and row away as fast as we could, lest the wash of the ship should swamp us.

I do not wish to concern the Reader with excessive detail. It can be imagined how we spent the following pitch-dark night down in the Southern Hemisphere, far from every sea lane, and the significance it had for us when, at two minutes past midnight, we no longer received any answers to our shouts and thus had to conclude that we had lost contact with the other boats.

We rowed to and fro until dawn, and when the sun rose saw nothing but water and more water.

One old sailor asserted repeatedly that there was in those parts a sea current that we had slipped into, and that our stupid dodging about had more deeply enmeshed us in it.

I bitterly cursed the foolhardy impulse that after so many trials and tribulations had driven me to sea anew, and I beseechingly prayed to the all-merciful Lord of Heaven to rescue me but this once more, vowing that I would never put to sea again.

The only thought that relieved my despair was that my admirable wife and family would inherit my heroic name—a name that, cut in stone together with many others, would proclaim on the main square of Southampton where foreign citizens should place their wreaths. After the reconciliation, even the Minister of Naval Affairs from the state that had us torpedoed would stand before our monument and pay tribute with zealous eloquence to the heroism with which we had drowned at sea. This thought filled all of us with pride. We realized that a true English patriot could expect more from life and with heads erect, we awaited our destiny and sang before we were due to perish.

Our rations gave out on the fourth day. At noon we opened the last two tins, took our last sip of fresh water, and prepared for our glorious death.

At twilight, however, we were lucky enough to be caught in a storm that grew more and more violent. Eventually it so raged that not even the oldest seamen could remember anything to compare with it, and I myself could only compare it with the monsoon that overtook us on my voyage to Brobdingnag off the Molucca Islands.

Everybody put on their lifebelts with sinking hearts, and half an hour later, when our boat was already being swallowed by the billows, I decided to try my luck with the lifebelt round my waist.

In another half-hour the storm had blown over, and taking advantage of the opportunity I tried to fasten myself with the strings of the lifebelt.

Thus did I spend the night. The sufferings of this night would, I believe, be unnecessary to describe in detail. When day broke I saw no one around me, but to the even greater pleasure of my faint heart the coastal line of an island appeared before my eyes at a distance of some two miles.

Gathering the rest of my strength, I began to swim. My arms felt reinforced in the knowledge that a stone inscribed with my name would proclaim my death as a hero—during my lifetime at that—and that I should never see my beloved wife again.

After a desperately hard struggle lasting four hours I succeeded in reaching the shore, where I immediately collapsed from exhaustion and sank into a deep sleep.

CHAPTER

2

The author awakes in Kazohinia. He meets the Hins, who help him but misunderstand his respectful gratitude. For the time being, he cannot determine the reason for this. He arrives at the Hins' uncommon capital. The English currency is unfairly treated. The author's sense of decency is seriously outraged. He recounts his experiences in a Hin restaurant and on the street. His guide invites him to his home.

WHEN I OPENED MY EYES, IT WAS MORNING. MY CLOTHES had been dried by the blazing sun and my strength had returned, but I was all the more tortured by hunger and thirst.

I set out toward the interior of the land and soon found myself among beautifully cultivated, enormous rice paddies. Along and throughout them ran pipes; through these the water necessary to swamp the land appeared to have been led, as it is well known that rice cultivation requires flooded soil.

Along the edges of the rice paddies I walked a good hour and a half before finally reaching a highway.

I stood there in open-eyed amazement, never having seen such a splendid road before. It was made of an especially fine material—softer than concrete, soundless and flexible like rubber, cohesive like gravel, and smooth as a mirror. It was flanked by fruit trees. There were gullies on both sides, and on the right was a sidewalk shadowed by an endless promenade. At intervals of about fifty yards, big outdoor armchairs were situated along the road. They were not, however, woven of reeds or twigs but made of a smooth material that I took for Bakelite. The chairs were surrounded by cypress bushes. Every quarter mile stood a little house, made of concrete and glass, with a single room the interior of which was about five paces long and just as wide.

A single window running all the way round constituted the walls, the roof being supported by a metal pillar, pale silver in color, at each of the four corners. Looking in, I saw a table of wonderful finish that was nonetheless of extraordinary simplicity, with comfortable, springy rubber easy chairs around it. In the corner there was an electric heater. In my homeland I had seen similar—but by no means so luxurious—glass rooms at bus stops in metropolises and along the promenades of fashionable bathing resorts, where passersby might take shelter from the rain. My supposition that here they could serve a similar purpose was borne out by the fact that on the door there was no lock. Along both sides of the roadway, at a distance of about twenty paces from each other, stood durable-looking, twenty-foot-high lamps, each made from a smooth tube with a silvery sheen.

Gradually I came to the conclusion that I was on the estate of some very distinguished man. This beautiful esplanade, these glass rooms, the lamps, could not at any rate be public property, for however closely I examined them I discovered no trace of damage or obscene inscriptions. Besides, everything displayed a much finer workmanship than is customary with things destined for public use.

I wondered only why so much valuable property was not enclosed within a fence. In turn, it also seemed strange that such a beautiful promenade led among rice paddies and not among ornamental plants.

I should have liked to get away lest I should incur the rightful resentment of the property owner, but I hurried in vain for the road did not come to an end.

Exhausted, hungry, and thirsty, I had just sank into an armchair when I discovered to my joy that near me stood a small basin with a tap in the middle.

Regretting my less than impeccable instincts here, too, I now overcame my due respect for private property. Turning on the tap, I let the fresh water pour into my palms and avidly quenched my raging thirst.

Hunger was also gnawing at me, and the sight of trees covered with fruit almost led me to temptation. I was able to save my soul from falling into sin only by strongly recalling the gentle instruction of my venerable teachers concerning private property, and the self-restraint that is the ornament and virtue of non proprietors.

I was at the point of despair when a luxury car appeared from afar. Its outlines were sleek and displayed advanced technical knowledge. Its dull silvery surface and soundless progress impressed me.

Certain that the lord of the estate had arrived, I started up from my seat in alarm.

At first I wanted to run away, but then thought it better to stand squarely in front of him, honestly disclosing my situation lest—were they nevertheless able to catch me—perhaps I should be taken for a thief. And, indeed, I was driven by hunger, too.

So I stepped to the middle of the road and, opening my arms wide, indicated to the chauffeur my honorable intention that I should be happy should they consider my person worth stopping for.

The car did indeed stop. Inside on the back seat there was another man.

Both the driver and his passenger had fine features reminiscent of Greek statues and betraying exceptional intelligence. Had one of them not been sitting at the wheel, I could not have distinguished the lord from the chauffeur. They were both characterized by a long straight nose, finely arched eyebrows, lips pressed close, a high forehead, and a cold detached look, combining in a peculiar manner a clever and attentive expression.

I had never seen such a fusing of unusual contrasts, and it was all the more strange as their faces did not lack harmony. That is, not only did opposites meet but disharmony united in them with harmony. As if smiling was a regular geometric figure! A strange, uncertain feeling stole over me.

The chauffeur addressed me in a soft foreign tongue of which I understood nothing, and in reply I tried through gestures to make him understand that I did not want to talk to him, but to the passenger whom I thought to be the landowner.

And the landowner, comprehending my wish, got out of the car and stood before me. It was only then that I perceived that he was dressed in precisely the same way as his chauffeur. Each wore a gray suit in one piece, with a belt round the waist, tightly buttoned at the wrists and the ankles, fitted out with big pockets, and tailored from a very fine fabric. It appeared that the suit was used to counter the dust when making trips by car. Each had, further, a light soft cap similar to a beret, fastened to their heads by a rubber band.

I bowed deeply and removed my cap with a wide sweep.

I was surprised, however, to see that the landowner did not acknowledge my greeting. Instead, he looked in bewilderment at the cap extended in my hand and then hesitatingly reached for it, took it away, glanced at it and uttered some surprised words, which, of course, I did not understand. It was only with great difficulty that I gathered from signs that he thought I wanted to give the cap to him. I myself felt uneasy seeing that greetings had other forms here, unknown to me, and I thought fearfully of the possible awkward situations my ignorance of the rules of the country's finer society might—despite my best intentions—place me in during the weeks to come.

Flailing my arms and legs about, I began to explain that I had come from the sea, whose shore I had reached by swimming, and I begged his pardon for my trespassing.

At this point I placed my left hand on my chest and bowed deeply once more. In reply he immediately stepped up to me, undid my clothes, and examined my chest where my palm had been. Obviously he had misunderstood me, thinking my chest hurt.

Anyone who has ever been in a foreign country where local habits are unknown to him will understand my embarrassment, which only deepened by their not laughing at all; in their eyes I could see nothing but matter-of-fact goodwill. I seemed to have arrived among decent gentlemen who, understanding the awkwardness of the foreigner, politely stifled their justifiable laughter.

Hunger, however, gnawed at me increasingly. Realizing that I was getting nowhere, I pointed to my stomach and explained with signs that I was hungry. I was somewhat ashamed at being compelled to broach such a subject so early, but their evident patience encouraged me. I was sure that my request in this respect, too, would be comprehended.

And I was not disappointed. They understood fully. They looked at each other, then at me, and pointed at the tree in surprise, indicating that I was at liberty to pick the fruit. This generosity moved me deeply; timidly I picked an enormous pear, greedily stuffing it into my mouth.

I confess that this single pear did not satisfy me, but I did not dare ask for permission to take another one. I hoped that when they saw my voracious appetite they would offer it to me anyway.

It was then that I encountered my first disappointment in Kazohinia. The landowner, so cordial a moment earlier, did not care a fig whether I continued taking nourishment. This, I admit, surprised me somewhat unpleasantly.

Oh, had I been familiar with the circumstances, I would not have hesitated to pick as much as I needed! But I was uninitiated. In any case, I attempted to express my gratitude by smiling pleasantly, as I no longer dared to bow.

Their features, however, remained entirely unmoved, which again seemed contradictory to their former cordiality. They even looked into my face with a certain anxiety.

Then they exchanged a few words with each other and beckoned for me to get into the car.

The honor gave me pleasure, and although I felt I should endeavor to express my gratitude, I did not dare venture to do so.

The car started off. Then, after about half a mile, it stopped.
The landlord stepped out and went behind the car, and I was
surprised to see him untie a shining metal ladder, which he then,
with the help of the chauffeur, extended and supported against a
lamp post. The landowner climbed up, unscrewed the bulb, and
replaced it with another.

I was surprised. Why did he not entrust such work to his ser-
vants? For now, I could find no explanation.

Before long, they put the ladder back and we continued on our
way. I saw that the landowner looked at my waterstained and
crumpled clothes with interest, and I was extremely ashamed
of my unbecoming appearance. I apologized in every possible
manner, explaining that reasons beyond my control had led me
into such an unpresentable state. I perceived, however, that he
took special interest in my badges of rank. In turn, seizing the
opportunity to offer some proof of my quite respectable social
rank, I explained what it meant, how many people were under
me in rank on board the ship, and that my rank even entitled me
to enter His Majesty's inner household. I noticed that he understood little, however, and I was worried by the thought that he
might not appreciate it properly.

After five minutes we stopped again, whereupon the two men
got out. I watched them with astonishment as they each put on
a dirty smock and, having lifted a heavy manhole cover from the
road, disappeared underground with portable repair kits hanging from their sides.

Out of curiosity I followed them and, looking down, saw that
they were repairing cables. So my destiny seemed, after all, not
to have brought me into contact with the owner of the estate.
This again set me in confusion, and I blushed in shame over my
earlier humble behavior.

Nor did I understand how these two men had dared to offer me their master's fruit. I cannot say that I formed the highest opinion of their morals.

After a solid half hour they repacked their kits and we drove on.

We drove for about fifteen minutes and the landscape remained the same. Slowly it began to dawn on me that this could not all be the private property of one man. But why all this wonderful technical equipment? This I could explain solely on strategic grounds; for only that noble sentiment, devotion to one's country, can motivate a people to build on such a grand scale and thus erect a bulwark against the menace of foreigners.

Using hand gestures, I tried asking one of the men why they had made the road in such a luxurious way, but he seemed to misunderstand me, as he seemed to reply that it was only to avoid bumpiness.

The rice paddies were followed by fields of corn, potatoes, and other vegetables. In some places slender concrete water towers, irrigators, and pumps appeared; and then there were people steering strange big silvery machines. These farmers wore the same kind of clothes as my traveling companions.

Here and there I could already see houses. Of the first I believed that it was the summer residence of some eccentric grand man of rank. It was not large; it might have comprised some two or three rooms in all, but it was an uncommonly precise, perfect, and solid building, suggesting a developed culture. It had a flat roof, enormous windows with four or five panes, a spacious porch, a solarium, and a roof promenade. Surrounding it were trees and shrubs arranged in neat rows, but I saw no flowers. The house didn't have chimneys, but in front of the porch there was a swimming pool, as well as a lounge chair, a hammock, and some gymnastic apparatus.

Later I discovered many such villas. They were all alike.

We stopped once more. The chauffeur got out, opened a metal cabinet at the roadside and pulled a tube from it to the fuel tank.

At first I thought this was a special sort of fuel station, but seeing no attendant, I came to believe that it was a water tap. He, however, began to pump in a casual manner and the smell indicated petrol. I had no idea how they protected it from thieves. Not only was there no other person in sight, but not even a fuel gauge on this metal cabinet or a lock on its door.

We drove on. A few minutes later, without any transition, we arrived in a town.

Two- and three-story houses followed, all in a style similar to what I had seen in the paddies. At first I admired them, but later the monotony and lack of ornamentation made me feel that something was lacking. In such a rich environment I would have expected showy, turreted palaces. I anticipated how beautiful the public buildings, churches, theaters, and fashionable dancing bars would be—no doubt with colonnades, arcades, caryatids, and illuminated advertisements. But I saw none.

On the contrary, all we encountered were more cars and streetcars. They ran almost silently but at such a speed that I continuously wondered how it was that we did not crash.

At intersections we raced through underpasses and up onto overpasses. Now above, now under us, electric express trains shot by at a tremendous pace and in what amounted to absolute silence. Soon I realized that the wheels of the vehicles were not of iron, but of some special, soundproof material, similar to hard rubber.

But what surprised me most of all was that the countless people, whether on foot or traveling by car or train, were all very similar to each other; and their attire, too, was almost uniform, like that of my traveling companions. The only variation was that over the suit some wore a gray cloak, which, however, ought rather to be called a cowl, as it had neither a collar nor a lapel. Most of them went about bare-headed, with only a few wearing the same type of cap as my companions, and of hats I saw none.

Their shoes had no heels. I took them to be slabs of rubber cast from a single piece with vent-holes here and there; they were held together by a single buckle. The Reader may imagine in what silence cars and men passed by on the rubber roads.

What is more, the women were also dressed in this way, so at the beginning I thought to see nothing but men. Why, even their hairstyle was uniform; it was worn sleek and cropped all around, which could hardly even be called a hairstyle. It was only later that a gentler feature—a finer, lighter way of moving—betrayed to me who the women were among the many uniform beings.

It was likewise in vain that I scanned the surroundings for luxury stores. What might have been shop doors bore strange inscriptions that comprised simple geometric figures, and they lacked the iron shutters I would have expected on a store entrance. As if they were not businesses at all, but rather apartments. Nowhere was there a shop window; only the big, square windows in the dull silvery frames I had seen so often and of which everything here seemed to be made.

Our car now stopped, my guide getting out and motioning to me I stepped out and the car moved away, while we proceeded to the streetcar stop. I was greatly ashamed to be a financial burden to my companion, all the more so since I naturally had only English currency on me.

All the same, I took out my wallet and handed him one British pound, hoping he would be able to convert it later at the currency exchange.

Regrettably, the bill was rather crumpled, as it had been soaked. Turning it over, my companion scrutinized it and asked questions using gestures that naturally I did not understand. Then he simply gave it back to me.

I did not know whether he did it out of chivalry, or whether he was offended at my not being able to give him currency in better condition. I was beset by doubts but had no time to ponder. A streetcar arrived and we got on.

Comfortable rubber seats received us. Everything was of silvery metal, glass, and Bakelite. I have to state that I had never traveled in such a comfortable and finely sprung streetcar.

People got on and off wordlessly, in a silence scarcely imaginable to us, and with a brisk precision. I had arrived among a wonderful people.

For all my admiration, however, this automatism was also depressing. Nowhere a smile, a cordial greeting. Everybody sat with a wooden face, without uttering a single word.

What struck me most, however, was that I saw no conductor in the streetcar. And yet, it started exactly the instant the driver, who kept glancing into his sideview mirror, saw that everyone had boarded. I also looked in vain for a money slot, finally determining that here everyone must carry a monthly pass. I could not comprehend, however, how they knew no one got on with an expired pass. For all my brooding, I was as yet unable to find the explanation.

And this was only the beginning.

We reached a river. On both banks, over a width of about a hundred yards, stretched an endless park with that same row of villas, already repeated a thousand times, behind it. As if everyone here were a millionaire bachelor, and the whole town was not older than twenty years. Not on a single plaque in town did I see anything that might recall the past, nor did I see any work that gave pleasure to my eyes. I could only marvel at the richness and comfort.

I saw neither a single statue nor an inscribed monument proclaiming the merits of their great ones. There was no triumphal arch, no ornamented bridge or solitary fountain that might hint at a delight in art, as would befit such an affluent town.

We left the streetcar and went underground by escalator, into a subway station. A minute later a four-car train drew in at lightning speed. Braking strongly, it stopped. At that moment the doors of all four cars slid apart, and we got in together with others, the door closing the moment the last person boarded. The train then started off.

There was no driver on the subway train. As I came to know later, here practically everything functioned automatically. At each stop, the doors opened by themselves, the train setting off when they shut. All-embracing safety automatons ensured that it would not crash into the preceding train, and that the schedule be duly adhered to.

We whizzed through a tunnel under the river, and on the other side we rose above the houses, continuing nonstop for five minutes, at incredible speed. Below us swirled a sea of houses, parks, and gardens, and to our side flashed strange signals and controlling automatons. The train took the bends at full speed, practically gluing us to our seats with the centrifugal force. I wondered in anguish what would happen if the train were to brake suddenly at a bend.

At last we came to a stop, whereupon my companion motioned to me and we got off. Everything was swirling around me as he caught my arm and led me onto a moving sidewalk that resembled an endless conveyor belt. Soon we stepped onto another, then to a third, each moving a little more quickly than the previous one. On the third belt there were benches on which we sat while still being swept along.

We traveled in this manner for about a quarter of a mile, houses visible from above. As if in a field or in a park, on every roof I saw plants: grass, shrubs, vegetables, and fruit trees. Not a single roof had a chimney. Then we stood up, and stepped back to the main part of the sidewalk. One after another lightning-fast trains whizzed past.

Now we stepped into a nonstop elevator, which took us down to the ground.

I dare say that since swimming ashore I had not experienced such a feeling of relief. After seeing so many machine monsters running to and fro, I stood once more on solid ground.

Now we went a few paces on foot, turned onto a side street, and stopped before a door on which there was some lettering.

I followed my companion inside and took off my cap out of politeness. The door opened before us automatically and closed behind us in the same manner.

Inside, in innumerable glass wardrobes, lay clothes by the thousands, similar to those worn by everybody.

But in the shop—I cannot call it anything else—there was no one.

My companion now took out a tape measure and measured my waist, as well as the height to my shoulders; he now reached for a suit of clothes from one of the wardrobes and, placing it before me, indicated that I should put it on.

Just then three people entered: a man and two women. They conversed briefly, then, in a similar way, set about making their choice among the clothes.

Untying the clothes, I also found a shirt included. Considering the presence of the visitors, I asked my guide where the dressing room was, but he did not understand my question. Then I made an attempt, having pointed at the ladies, to imitate dressing; I next pointed at the door and tried expressing my desire to try on the outfit elsewhere.

At this, without a word my guide approached one of the ladies, exchanged a few words with her—their words were brief and easily pronounced—and then returned to me with the lady.

Politely I bowed and, offering my hand, introduced myself.

"I am Gulliver," I said with as benign a smile as possible.

The lady, however, looked at me in surprise without returning my smile. As for my hand extended toward her, she took it in her hands, turned it over, looked at it closely, scrutinized it, and then, uncomprehendingly, let it drop.

Realizing that my guide had misunderstood my wish, I again tried to make myself understood by pointing at the ladies, the door, and the clothes. They nodded approvingly and, taking my arm, led me out to the street, where something happened to me that I am ashamed even to relate.

There in the open, bustling street, the lady undid and pulled off my coat, then kneeled down and also unbuttoned my trousers.

Blushing from indescribable shame, I snatched my trousers together close to my body with a cry of horror. Flailing my arms and hands about I explained that a terrible misunderstanding had occurred, and that I would not have been so bold as to ask for help of this kind from a lady even in my dreams.

They, however, indicated without any sign of emotion that I must in any case take off my clothes. At that I babbled at random in Spanish, Portuguese, and German, explaining that an Englishman could never suffer such a stain on his personal honor, which at the same time represented the honor of his nation. I threatened them with diplomatic sanctions, but all in vain, for they did not understand.

Quite a few passersby had already stopped. Some asked questions, and the frightening thought flashed through my mind that I had strayed into a land of lunatics where I was all alone. Nobody would come to my rescue, and I was without protection, at their whims. What was yet to come? I thought of the terrible possibilities, and my forebodings came true all too soon.

They conferred briefly, and then several of them set upon me and despite all my shouts and protests, there, in the open street, they held me down while the lady stripped off my trousers.

I called for the police at the top of my lungs but in vain. Nobody took pity on me; they just stared inanely and uncomprehendingly at the maltreatment of an unfortunate fellow-being.

My shirt and pants followed, and I lay there exposed to public ridicule, stark naked, surrounded by cars, streetcars, and passersby.

On the faces of the bystanders, however, I perceived nothing but wonder and perplexity, which then definitely convinced me that I had fallen among lunatics.

Now the lady wanted to put the new shirt on me but I, gathering all my strength, wrenched myself from their hands, snatched the shirt, and covering my private parts with one hand, hurriedly pulled it on.

When the others saw this, they let me go and handed over the clothes, which I put on in similar haste. As for my old clothes, I left them there after transferring everything from the pockets.

My cheeks burning with shame, I grasped my guide's arm and begged of him that we should disappear quickly.

After a few seconds' consideration, he consented and we went. Now it was I who led him, and dragging him hastily into a side street, I again committed myself to his care.

My heart was pounding in my throat on account of this barbarism that had made a mockery of all decent feelings. Human life and freedom seemed to have no protection here—until then, at least, I had seen no policeman; nowhere was there anybody with a pistol or a bayonet. How could they sleep at night?

At the same time, I had my own opinion of the decency of the women here, who let themselves be carried away by performing such obscene and immoral acts without the least sense of shame—acts to which the well-mannered and chaste ladies of my country would never have descended. And certainly not in the open street!

A country of lunatics and sluts! The mere thought of it was appalling. That here every woman could be had so cheaply!

I must admit, however, that the clothes were especially fine and light. I had never felt so easy and comfortable. The most softly flowing Scottish textiles could not compare with them.

I had no idea which street we were treading. All of them were equally wide and edged with shrubs, trees, and completely uniform houses; it was only the traffic that made one distinguishable from the other.

My guide now ushered me through another door bearing some sort of inscription. The doors, too, were all alike—lockless, each with a glass pane, and opened automatically when approached. It seemed they were controlled by an invisible beam. I pondered in vain to determine how they might be locked.

Although I tried asking with hand gestures why the doors could not be locked, my companion appeared not to have understood, as he indicated by way of reply that they would not then open.

We reached an enormous restaurant that occupied the ground floor of a massive building. At its end was a glass partition, behind which white-coated figures operated silvery machines, the purpose of which was unknown to me. It was undoubtedly a kitchen, but nothing in it resembled the equipment in our kitchens. I saw containers and pipe systems with valves and pressure gauges. Mysterious electric instruments inscribed wavy lines on wide strips of paper tape. Liquid columns oscillated in U-shaped tubes. Colored signaling lights flashed on a panel behind round sheets of glass. There was a swiftly revolving drum and other marvelous machines.

At the many tables I saw the same comfortable armchairs I had seen so often already in my short time here. The walls were completely covered with a butter-yellow porcelainlike coating. Wide spaces had been left between the tables so that even with that many people there was no crowding.

Silence reigned, interrupted only by the jingling of cutlery.

Between two rows of tables we flitted along like ghosts on the spongy rubber carpet and sat down at the first unoccupied table.

It was only then that I perceived the endless conveyor belt slowly moving on the other side of the tables with silvery boxes, cutlery, and glasses set upon it at equal distances.

From among all this my guide simply lifted off two sets of each, placing one before me. At first I did not know what one was supposed to do with the box, but then my guide opened his own and began to spoon the food out of it. I followed suit.

By this time I did not know what to think of these strange people, who were sometimes brutal, sometimes gentle and obliging.

And when I tasted the strange, mushy food I exclaimed in rapture.

It was an extraordinary meal. The heavy savor of roast partridge and the light sour touch of mustard were somehow blended in its taste. It included the scent of wood; the overflowing symphony of the juice of the succulent white butter pear; the intoxication of full-bodied wines; and the refreshing sobriety of spring water. I may say that the meal tasted of life itself.

It was only now that I realized how hungry I was, for indeed since swimming ashore I had eaten but a single pear. Greedily I fell at the food before me and gulped it down in an instant.

As for my guide, he removed the empty dish without a word and, placing it in the middle of the table pushed a button, at which the table opened, the box sank, and everything closed again. On the smooth, yellow glass surface the outlines of the trapdoor could scarcely be seen.

Then, having witnessed my hunger, my guide took another box from the conveyer belt and set it before me.

So much kind-heartedness touched me beyond measure. I deeply regretted my earlier thoughts. Somewhat moved, I mumbled a few words of gratitude as tears welled up in my eyes.

Seeing them, my guide bent over and regarded me with visible fright. Suddenly he took my face between his palms and, turning it toward the light, scrutinized it with knit brows.

Then he stood up.

"Elo! Elo!" he cried.

One of the men stood up, and came over to me. My guide said a few words to him pointing to my face, and the man produced a bag from his pocket.

From this he took out a tiny syringe, which he held to my face and drew my tears into, before squirting them into a tiny bottle about a quarter inch in size.

Now, pulling my eyelids down, he began concernedly examining my eyes, and this made me realize that I had come into contact with a doctor.

Again I became seized with terror, and the horrible idea that I had fallen among lunatics haunted me anew.

Wanting to convince him that there was nothing wrong with my eyes, I wiped away my tears and smiled. This caused another sensation.

They conferred briefly and the doctor left. I sat down to eat the second helping, but with considerably diminished appetite.

Notwithstanding their imperfections, I did realize I had much to thank them for. It occurred to me that my companion had been unable to pay for my clothes, as I had run away and he, lest I should remain alone, had chosen to accompany me, exposing himself to the possibility of being pursued as a robber. Here, too, it was he who entertained me. I wanted to refund his expenses by any means possible.

I had already seen that he did not recognize our currency, but fortunately I had some gold and silver coins on me. I emptied my purse and handed over its contents to him. He turned the coins over and over, examined them thoroughly, and asked by signs what he should do with them. I repeatedly pointed toward the kitchen, but putting the money into his mouth and twisting his face in an imitation of chewing, he indicated that no meal could be produced from them. I did not exactly know whether it was his generosity that made him jest or whether he merely did not comprehend our money at all. I tried to explain my intention, but explanation was too difficult; finally I gave up, and returned the coins to my purse.

Now my guide beckoned to me; we rose from the table and left. Expecting him to drop the price of the dinner into some machine, I planned to watch him carefully in order to seize the opportunity to explain my own currency in a more tangible way, but eventually I had to conclude that he did not pay here, either. Now I was indeed full of curiosity as to their way of life, but there was no way of discussing it.

It must have been about six o'clock in the evening. A sea of lights illuminated the streets, and yet we proceeded almost without shadows. The effect was neither yellow nor white, but like sunshine: a diffusive, clean, quiet flood of light.

We walked along for around ten minutes in traffic similar to what I'd seen that morning. I could scarcely make out the shapes of the cars whizzing along, they disappeared so quickly. I had never seen so many strange automobiles. One held a long container but no driver; from another mechanical arms rose high; from yet another an enormous metal mouth gaped forward. I also saw a car that had wheels on top so it could run upside down as well.

Sometimes a big, torpedolike body drifted over us, closely following a wire but without touching it. The men on the silent roadways wore soundless shoes; the vehicles seemed even more soundless, and yet all were rushing. This mute, witches' dance of machines curiously deprived me of my sense of security, as if there were no force of gravity, only the swish of weightless movement.

The whole had an effect on me as if all of this did not really exist, or at least as if there was no foundation to it all. And the people's faces, too, were so strangely unfamiliar: from their unusual proportions emanated both goodwill and a repellent inaccessibility.

Suddenly I thought of my comrades—with whom I had spent so many pleasant evenings in the club, and who were perhaps now resting at the bottom of the ocean in their watery grave. My heart sank and I felt a desperate need for a living being, a friend with whom I could talk warmly and relate my impressions of these people. I had the strange feeling that they were not alive; as if behind this terrible perfection there was no substance.

As we walked on, another feeling gradually took hold of me, although I was as yet unable to give an exact account of its nature even to myself.

I would have welcomed the opportunity to throw myself before an altar and cry. But why? I had no idea! While at home I could not have been said to be terribly religious, now I suddenly felt I understood the whole genesis of religion and the roots of it hiding within us. I looked for a church where I could pour out my heart without having doctors gape at my tears.

Pointing toward the sky, I tried asking my companion with hand gestures where I might find a church, at which he, likewise with signs, reassured me that there would be no rain. That is, he had understood this no more than so many other sensible questions of mine that had preceded it. I was not unduly worried by my failure, thinking I would surely come across a church, but my search proved to be in vain. Every building was hopelessly uniform and unornamented, and who could tell into which of these cheerless boxes they had squeezed the church?

Now we stopped before a door that likewise opened before us. We went inside, then stepped into an elevator that carried us up to the third and uppermost floor. Stepping out we found ourselves in a gazebo whose every window looked out on the back garden and was wide open. Down below extended a park about fifty yards in length and breadth; beyond this another building followed, without any intervening fence. Along the paths comfortable rubber couches and a variety of arbors could be seen, all beautifully lit.

Several people were lying on the couches, others were walking on the paths, but everyone was alone and silent. Nowhere a crowd; nowhere an intimate group; nowhere a merry or cosy little niche of acquintances roaring with laughter; or, say, a debating circle.

From the garden rose a concert of crickets and the intoxicating scent of lime trees.

Inexplicable people! Behold! They were fond of plants and lay down on lawns. They had large windows and spacious sunny verandas, and their gardens had the usual swimming pools—all the property of men complete in heart. Why then this self-segregating rigidity? Why did they not honor each other with kind words or warm friendship?

From the gazebo we proceeded into a room in which the lamps turned on as we entered. My guide closed the windows by pushing a button.

The walls were butter-yellow, like those of the restaurant. The room contained three chairs, a couch, an armchair, and a square table; none of these was made of wood but rather of that material similar to Bakelite that I had seen so often here. The floor was the same, with no trace of carpet or curtain. Near the window stood a radiator covered with perforated metal plates, and in the corner was a telephone, an electric clock, and some other devices whose functions were perfectly unfamiliar to me. On the wall, behind some sliding glasslike windows, were books. Like the wardrobes, the bed, too, was built into the wall. At the flick of a finger it slid outward, and when it slid back, a vacuum cleaner popped out of the wall to automatically clean and air it.

Then we stepped into the bathroom. I shall not bore the Reader with excessive detail; it is not difficult to deduce the essence from the foregoing. My host undressed in my presence without reserve, then I had to follow suit in order to wash under the shower, which was, at least, very agreeable.

Then my host removed some bed-sheets from a wall cupboard, and after arranging them on the floor prepared a marvelous resting place and motioned for me to lie down.

I admit I found it a bit strange that he made his guest lie on the floor. Not that my resting place was uncomfortable, for the rubber mattress would have been equally soft wherever it was placed, but this procedure cast an unfavorable light on the breeding of my host. I tried to find excuses for him; after all, he was apparently only an electrician. But then what kind of conclusion was I to draw from his no doubt expensive and extraordinarily fine furniture?

One would, however, expect even an electrician to offer the bed to his guest. He might have known that my good manners would not allow me to accept it anyway. Sighing, I thought again of my dear country, where people were kind and generous and where the host always offered the best to his guest, knowing full well that he would make excuses and not accept it.

I went to bed while my host took out various fitness machines in the form of springs and weights and went to the balcony to exercise.

Fifteen minutes later he came back, lay down, and clapped his hands once, whereupon the light went out.

All the day's excitement kept me awake for a long time. Furthermore, I was unaccustomed to retiring so early. My host seemed to be among the more prosperous. But why then he did not keep a servant, or why was he not at least married?

My first day in Kazohinia ended with a profusion of unanswered questions, and I excitedly awaited the next day for them to be clarified.

CHAPTER

3

The author is examined by a doctor. The Hins place him in a hospital among the Belohins and teach him their language. Further, we encounter the kazo concept: the basic principle or, rather, the prevailing condition of the country.

IN THE MORNING WE AROSE AT SIX O'CLOCK, SHOWERED, and dressed. Then my host stepped to the telephone and exchanged a few words with somebody. He waved to me to go over, and holding a lens of sorts to my face, continued talking for a few minutes to the person at the other end of the line.

Then he motioned to me and we started out. In the street the elevator carried us up again to the top of the buildings, and on a moving sidewalk we went to the express route stop and from there to the train. We shot over the town.

Now I paid closer attention, but could discover no variety at all—not a tower, a colonnade, an outstanding building; no cemetery, either.

At one point we passed over factories; at least the special arrangement of the buildings, the skylights, and the railways winding about the yard demarcated them as such. But the buildings had no chimneys or fences.

I came to find out later that everything ran on electricity. Electricity operated the machines, cooked the dinners, baked the bread, heated the rooms, cleaned, washed, and dried. Only in laboratories were open flames visible.

Then we passed through fields where the track ran along a raised embankment. We were among mountains and forests.

Suddenly a big block of houses emerged before us. Here the train went underground and, braking vigorously, came to a stop.

We got out. Beside us shone the metal cars of a different kind of train. Many people got out of them, some with bandaged hands or faces, others carried on stretchers. From this I gathered we were at a hospital.

We stepped into an elevator that carried us straight into the main hall of one of the buildings. Now my guide led me down a series of corridors until, entering a room, I found myself among strange machines.

Two people were walking around an apparatus. On our arrival one of them came up to me. My guid, pointing at me, exchanged a few words with him and he in turn bade me to sit down on a chair.

My guide now turned without a word and left. Doubts preyed on my mind as I did not know if he would leave me here on my own or would return. But he did not take leave of me, and so I became calmer, reassured that I would not be alone in the company of a man who knew even less about me than my guide.

My new custodian, who—as became clear later—was indeed a physician, sat down opposite me, observed my pupils, tapped my knees to test my reflexes, and then, having made me remove my shoes, had me stand in front of a machine.

On a snow-white enamel column stood a large flat disc on which several scaled glass windows were situated all around. Several dozen jointed metal arms projected from the column, one of which ended in a metal plate, another in a needle, and a third in a suction head. This machine resembled a hundred-armed statue of a Hindu god. On top were some sharply pointed glittering metal spires.

The physician pushed a chair in front of me and I reluctantly sat down. I looked with particular suspicion at that mechanical arm which ended in a needle.

The doctor took this very arm. He pulled open my clothes at my shoulder and without the least emotion pricked the needle into my shoulder blade.

I was just about to protest against this unnecessary torture, as nothing was wrong with me, but surprise deprived me of speech. I felt nothing of the needle, though the physician had not anaesthetized me.

I looked at the bizarre device with amazement. Streaks of light lit up behind its windows, which then oscillated up and down, changing color several times.

The doctor now fastened the machine's other arms to my forehead, chest, temple, and back. The lights again flickered intensely behind the glass windows, and the metal protrusions atop the machine gave off sparks of electricity, which then slowly faded. The machine buzzed, then spat out a wide strip of paper with writing all over it. The physician tore this off and examined it through a magnifying glass.

The room suddenly turned dark, and on the glass wall opposite me a vernal meadow appeared. The earth was covered with a marvelous carpet of flowers, the shrubs were laden with blossoms, and all the blooms were white. The meadow was stirred by a soft breeze, and when this whispered past my face I could savor the refreshing spring scent as it filled my lungs. And from the shrubs came the song of birds.

However, this great whiteness slowly faded. The meadow became now yellow, now blue, then changed into an utterly improbable ultramarine and finally turned red.

At the same time, men and women dressed in white stepped out of the shrubbery, and slowly walked across the scene. Their bodies swayed, their arms swung rhythmically, and even the throbbing birdsong was in harmony with this rhythm. It was something like a dance, but much more simple and natural.

Given my dejected state of mind, this was at any rate both a refreshing and an interesting sight. I marveled at the exquisitely three-dimensional figures and at the scent, which could not have been produced by any technical equipment in our cinemas. Besides, to begin with, the spectacle afforded a definite artistic pleasure.

Unfortunately, however, the beautiful creation was spoiled by some blunders that considerably lessened its artistic value and gave the impression of bold dilettantism. The flowery field divided into parts. Blue, yellow, and red squares drew close to one another and then merged, one color overwhelming the other, and the pulse of birdsong gradually became so artificial that it disturbed my pleasant mood. To make matters worse, unnatural sounds such as the beeping of cars and the crackling and whistling of instruments broke in upon the song of the birds. The performers' clothes changed, too; airy white spring gowns became heavy ones trimmed with fur. Yellow brass belts appeared on them from which hung shiny blue stones and other unlikely odors finally mixed into the vernal scent. I could smell mint, ether, and even sulfur.

Now—to be frank—I began losing all comprehension of the matter. But I had little time to ponder, as the room became bright, the picture disappeared, the whizzing suction fans extracted the smell, the machine buzzed, and a new sheet of paper emerged that the doctor tore off and scrutinized.

It became dark again.

On the wall appeared the picture of an orange, then another beside it, a third one, a fourth one, and so on. At the same time such a pleasant orange aroma wafted toward me that it made my mouth water and I felt a great desire to eat one.

When, however, quite a heap had formed, the oranges began to arrange themselves into rows until I was finally faced by a single wall of oranges.

Now the oranges slowly dissolved into one another, the outlines blurring; only their color remained, as if the wall of the room had been painted orange. At the same time, the scent evaporated.

The color then turned into more and more vivid tones, gained a lacquered shine, and finally glittered so brilliantly that none of the paints known to us could possibly compare with it.

With this, however, the room became suddenly bright and the machine buzzed and ejected a new roll of paper for the doctor to examine. I sat dazed, as I had no idea as to the meaning of this, why they had done it, and what connection there had been between the events shown on the wall.

It became dark again.

On the wall, in the left corner, a man appeared. In exhaustion he collapsed into a chair and wiped his forehead. This was repeated in the right corner: a man appeared and sat down. Now a table set itself in front of each, and on the tables there appeared food boxes such as I had seen in the dining hall.

The first man opened his box hastily and voraciously attacked the food, but before he could even sink his spoon into it the other stepped up to him, took it from him and threw it away.

This unexpected turn of events astonished me, but before I could regain my equilibrium the aggressor was back at his seat, and on the table there appeared another box. The hungry man again fell at the food, but the aggressor stepped up to him anew and cast it aside.

This outraged me and, indeed, I could only admire the hungry man's patience at allowing the attacker to again commit his perfidious deed without reprisal, but this was not yet the end of it. The scene repeated itself step by step a third time! This unbelievable impudence so infuriated me that I was almost on the point of leaping over to take revenge on behalf of the poor helpless chap—although, to tell the truth, I would have most gladly given him a piece of my mind as well.

Now the fourth box of food appeared on the table. The hungry man opened it, whereupon the aggressor stood up yet again.

This was already more than enough. I felt that if the hungry man did not slap the aggressor's face this time, I should burst.

However, the hungry man stood up, too. With my nerves stretched to breaking point I was looking forward to the hard, relieving smack. But this was not what happened.

Instead the hungry man shouted.

"Elo! Elo!"

At this several people ran to the scene, surrounded the attacker, and forced him to sit in his place. What now ensued could have been termed anything except my expected solution to such a dramatic conflict.

The hungry man opened the aggressor's box, dug his spoon into it, and—made him eat, while the others kept him down! In the meantime he continuously spoke to him, as if by way of explanation, but without any emotion in his voice. Once they had compelled the aggressor to eat his whole portion, he was helped to his feet, three men led him away, and the hungry man set at last about his own portion and ate it.

With this, the room became bright again, and I was filled with a profound feeling of want. This story not only lacked dramatic justice but also deeply unsettled my day-to-day sense of justice. I do not say that the aggressor's food should have been thrown away as well; for, after all, food is not to be wasted. But at least some lesson should have been taught him to remove any similar inclination to high-handed actions in the future! Or, if they thought that such a timid public would be horrified by this, they should have turned him over to the police, so that behind prison bars he might have had the opportunity to ponder over the rules of proper conduct. But to feed him!

From this story, fair play and reassuring justice were entirely absent. It was not balanced, it was unjust, it was incomplete. Why? And why had I, above all, had to see all this? I took the whole business to be some sort of psychotechnological examination. But why should the victim be treated to an episode that lay beyond all logic? What diagnosis could possibly be established on such a basis?

The doctor, however, pulled the needle from my shoulder blade, tore a new roll of paper off the machine, examined it, and rang a bell.

Two more of his companions entered, beckoned me to go with them, and then, again through corridors, we came to an enormous park and, crossing that, entered a one-story building.

They led me into a low-ceilinged room where I had to sit down stripped naked on a chair. Having sat, I was horrified to discover that on its arms were copper sheets, similar to those of an electric chair, and suddenly the suspicion flashed through my mind that I had fallen into the hands of one of my country's enemies. I saw a formidable metal hood hanging at the end of a cable from the ceiling, and a strange hissing could be heard from inside it. My presentiments were confirmed when I realized they wanted to crown me with this.

Screaming, I started from the chair and wanted to run out, but two of them jumped on me, held me down, forced me back onto the chair, strapped me to it, fitted the hood onto my head, and fastened it securely.

Beads of sweat gathered on my face; shouting in all kinds of languages, I protested and kicked about, but was unable to battle against such numerical superiority. My strength waning, I closed my eyes, committed my soul to God, and gave up the struggle.

A third man now flicked a switch on the wall and I felt my hair standing on end. At that time I ascribed it to fear, but later it turned out to be the result of static electricity. A low buzz could be heard from the hood, they then removed it from my head and I eventually realized with relief that I was still alive.

They untied my hands, and as I touched my head, everything became clear: my hair had been cut. I now had the same plain, cropped hairstyle as they themselves. The whole haircut had taken scarcely five seconds. Now I was looking forward with much greater tranquility to the things to come.

After this, my chair began to move; in the next room they fitted another cap on my head. Soon lukewarm water flooded over my head, a rotating brush washed my scalp, and a few minutes later, when they took the cap off, my hair was already dry and combed. From here the chair carried me through a pool full of water; then warm air was blown onto me. Finally I passed through a big tube, in which a strange lilac light flickered.

Afterward, they dressed me in brand new clothes, just like those

I had received in the town, and finally they led me into a comfortable, clean little room, explained to me in terms that I somehow managed to comprehend that this would be my home, and left me alone. The furniture of the room, by the way, was exactly the same as I had seen in my guide's home. This reassured me, as I was worried that on account of the regrettable misunderstandings that had occurred they took me for a madman.

But what was to come?

I had little time to ponder. A few minutes later a man entered, took hold of my arm, and said: "ba." Then he pointed to my foot: "bola," he said and motioned to me to repeat it.

So then, they wanted to teach me their language. This made me very glad. At last I could hope that the many hitherto unsolved questions would be cleared up. Next he pointed to himself.

"Zatamon," he said.

I understood. That was his name.

I shall not bore the Reader with more details. Suffice it to say that I spent the following period studying the language, and in a month I could speak to them perfectly.

Their language is of the utmost simplicity. Their alphabet consists of thirty letters : fifteen vowels and fifteen consonants. From among the consonants the "r," "q," "x," and "c" are missing, whereas they have more vowels than our language.

Speaking their language is, on the whole, an extremely comfortable sensation. The more difficult sounds and double letters, they do not have; in their words, vowels and consonants follow each other alternately. The characters, too, are completely plain: horizontal, oblique, and vertical lines, upright and horizontal ellipses, our letter "v" in four different positions, the circle and deltoid, and so on. In short, each was a geometrical figure, which so aptly fitted the local ways.

For counting, too, they used letters. Each number had two names: a vowel and a consonant, from which the Reader can already see that they did not use the decimal (base-10) system but, rather, the pentadecimal (base-15) system. The names of number one, for instance, are "e" and "l," number twelve "i" and "m," number fourteen "u" and "z." (I make mention only of such characters as also occur in our own alphabet.) This abbreviates the numbers in both writing and speech alike, as the numbers, too, are expressed by placing vowels and consonants alternately one after the other. The number 3,331, for example, is written in the pentadecimal system with three figures only: 14-12-1, and they write and call it "zil."

For units of time they did not use hours and minutes; the day was divided into 50,625 parts (that is, the fourth power of fifteen); one such part is somewhat longer than our second. And what we express as "6 hours 32 minutes 11 seconds in the afternoon," they simply denote by saying "kalaz"; that is, the number of time units that have passed since midnight. Later I learned how easy it was to memorize telephone numbers this way.

Their words are extremely brief, and I had the impression that their language had been compiled artificially, as the words used most often were the shortest. The character of each word can be established by considering its first letter. For example, all nouns begin with "b," such as "ba" and "bola," which have already been mentioned. Personal names, as already mentioned, commence with "Z," and attributes with "k," while with initial vowels they indicate verbs. The fact that the indicator of the character of the word stands in front makes speech more easily comprehensible, as the listener's attention is better distributed within the word.

With intonation, too, they express much more than our language does. Different intonations are used by one who advises, addresses, approves, or refutes. Similarly the word order is also quite varied, and the meaning of a sentence can be altered by changing the place of a single word. And all this was simplicity itself to acquire, as their language has the strange feature that it has no exceptions.

To give an example, in our legislatures lengthy debates can ensue over questions such as who is to the right in political discussions and who is to the left, who is a nationalist and who is an internationalist, who supports dictatorships and who supports liberalism, and so on. In their language the dozens of variations in intonation, word order, and affixes do not convey such concepts as dictatorship, liberalism, or nationalism, but the intention, the goal. This is why they do not have expressions for such things, but all the more often I heard the words *kazo* and *kazi*.

As the Reader will come across these two words many times, I must discuss them in more detail.

None of them can be translated into any European language. If these people say of an action, "It is kazo," this would mean, if we might put it, that it is "legal, rightful." But this is only an approximation. Let us see what they apply this word to. Kazo is somewhere between chivalry, impartiality, patience, self-respect, and justice. It connotes a general rightful intention but cannot be translated with any of these words; to us, a one-shilling tip to the waiter is considered chivalrous, but that is not kazo as they see it, being the overpayment of something. Nor does "impartiality" suffice, because that concept is bound up with the idea of compliance, while the heart has nothing to do with kazo. Rather, kazo is a strict mathematical concept for equality of service and counterservice, similar to the principle of action and reaction in physics. If someone who does more strenuous work also eats more, that is kazo to them. If somebody eats more because his stomach requires it, then that is also kazo. And if an invalid who does no work wishes to have finer food, then this, too, is kazo.

It is likewise kazo if somebody finds himself in trouble and the others, putting their work aside, help him, but only as long as is necessary.

It took a lot of my time for me to understand this idea. In order to somehow familiarize my Readers with it, I will endeavor to approach it by this definition: Kazo is pure reason that perceives with mathematical clarity, in a straight line, when and how it must act—so that the individual, through society, reaches the greatest possible well-being and comfort.

That is, to be Kazo is to organize work, rest, sleep, sport, food, and our attitude toward our fellow human beings so we can produce the maximum possible, but without damaging our health through unnecessary strain. If somebody works less than this, it is not kazo, because what he has not done, somebody else must do as extra work, which he can do only wearily, to his own detriment. We must not forget, kazo is not individualistic but communal in sense: what is not kazo for someone else is not kazo for me, either.

Kazo does, of course, have personal implications, too. The more talented, the stronger, produce more. To us this appears to be an injustice, but to the inhabitants of this land it is as natural as to expect a bigger output with less fuel consumption in the case of a more efficient machine. Kazo also pertains to help given to companions in trouble, as it is not an individual but a general principle. When necessary the work of a whole town will pause to rescue a single man. And most remarkable, as we shall see later, kazo has no emotional resonance. Often I saw it applied even to matters that had no connection with human society. For example, hares that gnaw saplings would be considered Kazo, but a mother hare devouring her own young would not be. To truly follow these people's thinking would take a remarkable feat of understanding!

The opposite of kazo is kazi. For example, you buy new clothes when you could continue to use the old ones; or if, without pressing need, you disturb the actions of your fellow men—for instance, unnecessarily talking to them of things that are of no consequence to either—or, let us say, if you were to announce out in the yard that nobody else may sit on a certain deck chair even though you are not yourself sitting on it.

If someone is lying on a lawn chair in the yard, and there is no other seat, and another man comes up to him and asks him to yield his place and he is not willing to do so, then it is kazo if the resting person is more tired; otherwise it is kazi.

When, in the course of my studies, I got to this point, I felt as if balance would be precarious indeed. I asked Zatamon how they avoided the occurrence of kazi things.

"A kazo man does only kazo things," he answered.

"I think," I said, "you do not understand my question. How does someone who wants to sit down on a bench know that he is the more tired?"

Zatamon looked at me in surprise.

"Well, if he asks for the place of another man, it can only be that he is more tired!"

"But how does he know?"

"Because it is kazo."

Clearly we did not understand each other.

"But how can he see into the other?"

"I have already told you," he replied. "Because the kazo is like that. There is a species of ant, for instance. If one ant finds honey, it will take its fill. Now, if it meets a companion that has not found honey and is hungry, it will stick its mouth to the other ant's mouth and thus the full ant will transfer honey from itself until each of them is equally satisfied. How does the full ant know that the other is more hungry, and how do both know when each of them is as satisfied as the other?"

"Well, how do they know?" I asked with eager curiosity as I thought that through their more developed knowledge, a secret of nature still undiscovered by us would be revealed to me.

"They know because the fuller ant gives honey to the hungrier one, and they will be equally satisfied when they part."

This stupid answer astonished me. It was not at all what I had expected of Zatamon. But however often I asked him, I could not lead him out of this circular chain of thought. And he always ended by saying, "The kazo is like that." Thus I stopped inquiring; surely I would come to know by myself.

They call themselves Hins, which may perhaps be the equivalent of the word "man" but, as with every word, this, too, is connected with intention and aim, as the Reader will presently see.

If someone's behavior does not follow kazo laws, such a person will not be called Hin. For this designation, however, they have more than one word, according to whether the person concerned commits kazi acts through a lack of knowledge or a lack of goodwill. The ignorant are called Belohins; and the recalcitrants, Behins.

The concept of Belohin may perhaps be the equivalent of what we indicate by the word "unschooled." This, accordingly, is where children and those beginning a new profession belong. These people are sent to school, but compulsion is hardly ever employed—at most, in the first stages of childhood. It is the Hin's conviction that with a sound mind nobody commits kazi things.

It follows from this that the Hin's education is radically different from ours. Whereas with us, the main aim of schooling is to bring children up to be virtuous and decent citizens, and to make their souls susceptible to fine and noble things, all this is to them an unknown concept: schooling is no more than a source of physical, chemical, hygienic, and technical acquisition.

I asked Zatamon how, by teaching purely technical knowledge, they could achieve the avoidance of kazi acts.

To this he replied, "In the possession of technical knowledge and a sound mind it cannot be imagined that somebody would still want to eat an electric lamp."

I retorted, of course, that that is not what I had meant, but rather: How could morals be directed without moral precepts?

To this he replied, "What would be the sense in teaching what we are permitted and what we are forbidden to eat? It would have several disadvantages. On the one hand, it would complicate education as, besides glass, we should have to mention stone, iron, nickel, and thousands of other things. On the other hand, it would not be expedient, either: If you hear only the rules but do not know the essence of things themselves, you will lack automatic direction and will never be able to act independently. This is quite apart from the fact that intellect is a property everyone is born with, from which directive education would remove something, while the aim of teaching is not to subtract but to add. Finally, it is also unnecessary because, as I have said, if a man of sound mind has acquainted himself with reality, he will not eat glass even without prohibition. Prohibitions are to be explained to a fool only, and to a fool you explain in vain in any case."

Evidently Zatamon had misunderstood me once again. I remarked that I had not spoken of eating glass but of the avoidance of the kazi way of life and acts, but he only kept repeating:

"This is precisely what I have explained."

I can confirm at any rate that kazo has nothing to do with morals. Kazo itself is not taught, either; it connotes a certain state of knowledge that, once acquired by a man of sound mind, will be observed by him, anyway. The Hins did not mention it too often among themselves, as we ourselves do not speak of the alphabet; but as a foreigner I heard it all the more—uninitiated as I was, I came up against it at every turn.

The kazo they did not even consider a concept, but said that it was the reality of the existing world itself. On the other hand, kazi did not mean immoral, sinful, or improper, but something like the word "absurdity" to us; that is, something in contradiction with physical facts. It was quite strange, overall, especially when I became acquainted with the other rules of the kazo, because, as the Reader will see, the kazo extended beyond the just way of life to several other matters, too, which I had already deemed unjust and offensive.

In light of all this, the Hins' opinion of the third group, the Behins—namely, those who do kazi things while possessing full knowledge of the facts of natural science—is understandable. They consider Behin not only anyone who eats glass, but also anyone who expects a tired man to stand up; or who himself stands up, even though he is tired, in order to yield his place to somebody who is less tired; further, anyone who works more or works less than he is able to without strain, or anyone who takes someone else's food or gives his own food to someone else while he himself is hungrier.

The Reader will certainly have noticed from this that the word "Behin" comprises two notions. As we see it, someone who takes the food of anyone else is an evildoer, and anyone who gives his own unwisely to someone else is a fool. They, however, expressed both with one word, Behin, without taking into account whether the person concerned had caused harm to himself or to somebody else.

In short, people were designated by quality in three different ways. These separate words, however, did not signify that they regarded the Behins as a different type of person. They did not consider them human beings at all; it was as if they were speaking of a different species.

The Behins, by the way, were confined within a separate place, possibly a reservation rather like a lunatic asylum. From there they were not permitted to come into contact with the Hins.

Fortunately, the Hins took me for neither a madman nor a criminal but for a Belohin to be taught.

The Reader may now be able to understand also the name of this country: Kazohinia—the land of those who know the pure reality of human existence.

CHAPTER

4

*The author is allowed into town, where he has some
rather odd experiences. The Hins do not know money,
and yet they are rich. The author engages in a debate
on money and production. He comes to know the Hins'
streets, parks, restaurants, and library. He undertakes
a fruitless investigation into the past and the morals
of the Hins.*

THUS, AS A HUMBLE STUDENT—OR, AS THEY TERMED ME,
a Belohin—I was, in spite of the medical degree I had obtained at
Oxford University, assigned, to my shame, to a sort of elementary
school.

I had to admit that their knowledge of the natural sciences was
more advanced, but as a loyal citizen of my country, I knew full
well that there existed not only objective facts, but also patriotic
duties. But I took care not to declare this in front of them, so
as not to afford them fresh unfounded grounds for their own
national pride to swell.

So, in order to avoid this slight, I tactfully mentioned my
degree to Zatamon—a degree that, with all modesty, did show
some degree of knowledge and education. I was not, however,
able to resist remarking that its being taken for nothing would
have meant the deprecation of my nation as well.

Zatamon, however, replied that life was everyone's private affair; he himself knew best what kind of knowledge he lacked. My

being a Belohin meant only that if I asked anybody a question he would reply.

Thus I came to know that in fact I was not actually confined to the hospital and was free to go into the town at any time. I had only to carry a certificate as evidence that I was a Belohin, for otherwise I would not receive answers to all my questions.

This surprised me a bit, and put their politeness into a still stranger light—politeness that was, in any case, by no means overdone. As if to bear this out, Zatamon told me only that the Behins were in the habit of making unnecessary inquiries, and an overly curious man might possibly be mistaken by the Hins for a Behin.

At this, I was even more astonished and asked why, but his response reassured me.

"The Behins," he said, "often make passersby stop and begin to talk of the most diverse, nonexisting—that is, kazi—things."

Here he took out his notes and read aloud some passages.

"One of the Behins, for example, claimed that the plum was not to be eaten, but should be set aside and contemplated. When asked why, he replied, 'Because it is blue.' Another asserted that trees talked, and a third that people had to suffer because this would alleviate hunger. A fourth demanded that people who saw him should put their hands on their bellies, and a fifth put a wire ring on his head instead of a cap, and commenced explaining to everyone that this suited him better, as he was taller this way."

This finally reassured me. I saw what he was hinting at, and I in turn reassured him that he did not need to fear mental disorder in my case.

He issued my certificate, however, and with it in hand I resolved to go out into the town.

The first surprise of this excursion was that the Hins had no money.

Although on my arrival I had already noticed that my guide did not pay anywhere, I could not imagine that money would be absent altogether.

I realized this as soon as I entered the hospital subway station.

I took it for granted that the railways of such a developed town would accept foreign currency, so my eyes immediately sought a ticket window. As I did not see one anywhere, I wanted to ask the first Hin, but it was only then that I came to realize that in spite of my having studied thoroughly, I did not know what "money" and "ticket window" were called in their language. Interestingly enough, this deficiency had not hitherto occurred to me.

I knew, however, that my own country had always played a prominent role in the dissemination of humanitarianism and culture—the most eloquent proof of which was our colonies and the international prevalence of such words as these. And stepping up to the first Hin, I said, "Money! Business!"

To my great amazement he did not understand. Taking out my purse, I showed him some coins and explained in their language that I should like to change them into theirs. He, however, replied that they had nothing of the sort.

At this, I asked him how I could get into town by streetcar. He turned to leave without a word. I was about to express my indignation against such groundless haughtiness, the likes of which I had not experienced even in Spain, when Zatamon's words came to my mind and, getting out my Belohin certificate, I showed it to him.

The Hin immediately changed his attitude toward me, relating in detail, almost verbosely, every technical particular of how to board a streetcar. When the door opened I was to enter, then I should sit down, and so on. I told him I was not an idiot but simply wanted to know whether I was supposed to give such pieces of metal to anybody so the streetcar would take me.

He, however, retorted that whoever did not know the technical details of boarding a streetcar was not necessarily an idiot, but the sanity of anyone who wanted to use metal coins to start a streetcar when he knew perfectly well that it was operated by electricity was more justifiably to be called into doubt—which he was prevented from doing so solely by my Belohin certificate.

The frustrations continued to mount before I realized that they had no idea at all about money.

When the streetcar arrived and we got on, my first question was how they transacted the exchange of goods.

It came to light that everything took place entirely without money. Factories turned out goods but nobody received payment. Goods, on the other hand, lay in warehouses for one and all, and indeed everyone took as much as they wished. I could not imagine how maintaining order was possible in this chaos.

Just imagine what would happen if, for instance, our railways were to carry passengers with neither conductors nor tickets—free of charge. Apart from the inevitable bankruptcy, there would not be enough of a fleet to cope with the increased traffic.

So I asked him whether it sometimes occurred that people travelled about aimlessly and unnecessarily by streetcar. "No," said he. "That would be kazi."

"But, even so without a conductor, it might still easily happen."

Naturally I had to explain what a conductor was, to which he replied that, it would be really kazi if a person were on a streetcar just to travel about aimlessly and unnecessarily while the streetcar could go quite as well without him.

I had to explain anew that the conductor was to prevent aimless and unnecessary traveling about, to which people were otherwise rather inclined.

"But why would a person do that," he asked. "when everyone has the opportunity to spend his time in a useful occupation?"

"Well, let us say instead of going to work, he might go to the mountains, where he could sit down and take in the gratifying sight."

I wanted to say "beautiful," but they have no word for it, just as there is none for "tourism."

"How could it be gratifying," he answered, "for someone with rested muscles to sit idly in the forest? Anyone who does not work will not find resting pleasant, either."

"Not to sit down but, say, to go up to the mountains to find gratification in seeing the environment and the flowers."

They have no expression for taking delight in something.

He did not understand, so I informed him that among us there were people who did not work but, rather, exercised their slack muscles in sport. From this he concluded that surely they performed strenuous intellectual work, and announced that for such people they, too, maintained standard gymnasiums and forest resorts.

He by no means understood, however, why someone who did not carry out even intellectual work did not instead operate a machine or push a barrow, when it was much more sensible and interesting since it was useful work, grounded in "reality," while sport pursued for its own sake was no more than imaginary work, a pale substitute for life, in which the unfortunate athlete did not participate.

I remarked that it was precisely those whom we call the rich who partake of the pleasures of life, and not the poor, and that rich people did not work.

"And whom do you call rich, and whom poor?"

"These words express the distribution of money. Those to whom a lot of money has fallen are rich; those who have only a little are poor."

"And on what basis is the money distributed?"

"If somebody has a lot of money, he is rich. Such a man will establish a factory or start a business. Accordingly, he earns more money than the poor man, whose money is not enough for this."

This he found somewhat confusing, and vaguely demanded some "natural starting point"; and even after a lengthy explanation he understood no more than that some people have a great deal of money and others very little. Then, after giving the matter due thought, he exclaimed, "But then according to this, money does not exist!"

"Of course it does!" I said in astonishment.

"What does not exist in nature does not exist at all."

I showed him my money in vain; what he saw only confirmed

his assertion since, he said, whenever he asked me for money I could show him only paper, gold, or silver, but no money.

I had never been fond of empty word play and it was only my politeness that prevented me from telling him so. Thus instead I asked him how they transacted the exchange of goods.

To this he replied that although he did not know why it should be necessary to exchange, say, our coats when his fitted him as well as mine fitted me, but were it nevertheless necessary for some reason, he did not understand even then what money had to do with it.

"Money facilitates the exchange," I said, "and so furthers economic development."

At this his expression changed at once, he produced a notebook from his pocket, and he asked me to expound on the matter in greater detail because he wished to communicate any useful information to the manufacturing parties concerned.

I was delighted to be at his disposal, all the more so as I knew that by acquainting them with our more developed institutions I should enhance the glory of my country.

I related in full detail that money is issued by a central bank in various denominations, from which everyone receives according to his merits, and that it is at the same time a license enabling its owner to take his due share of the fruits of common work. I explained the advantages of money; that it can be exchanged for anything, thus ensuring a free choice of goods; and that through money it is possible to convert the countervalue of the articles we sell, at any time in a lump sum or in installments, to other articles, and so on.

He expressed the view that exchange could not be easier, after all, if we doubled the work by involving the exchange of money. But, he added, clarifying this was not so important, either. Instead he preferred to know how money furthered production.

I explained that money made it possible for many people with small resources to join forces and establish a factory by purchasing shares.

"What are these shares?" he asked.

"Another wonderful invention of the human mind. Another type of paper, which is given in exchange for money."

"And if you thus triple the effort devoted to the exchange, how have things become simpler?"

"That these papers enable work to start."

He looked at me with suspicion.

"What would you say," he asked, "if I told you that I can get up from this seat only after handing over a page of my notebook to you? It has nothing to do with reality—it is a nonexistent thing, isn't it?"

I was astonished by this naïveté but tried to stifle my laughter. In vain I explained how money sets work in motion. He stubbornly replied that he understood this, but it seemed that we did not understand at all, since according to anyone with any sense, the starting of work had only one prerequisite, the starting of work itself, and not the exchanging of papers, which did not even exist in reality and whose invention was a pity.

I asserted that money did exist, and that an eloquent proof of how true this was had been the world crisis that had almost blocked production.

"And why?" he asked.

"Because there was no money."

At that he asked again why we had invented such a thing that did not exist.

I had arrived at the end of my patience. In annoyance I became silent, and he did not ask any more questions. I thought he had taken offense. But after a minute of silence, in the same emotionless tone, he began to speak.

"And how can you ensure, in spite of the money, that kazi acts do not occur?"

"What do you mean by that?"

"That nobody should take from anyone else what is theirs, and vice versa."

I was surprised that, in a country where goods were prey to all, with the concept of ownership impossible to even imagine, he of all people could ask such a question. In such chaos how was the individual to know what was due to him?

I also assured him that with the concept of property, economic life rested on firm foundations in our country, while it was precisely here, in their land, that everything was confused, intangible, and unstable.

He, of course, again did not understand my words, and asked me to explain what property was.

"Property is what is mine, and not another's, so that nobody can take it from me," I said.

"But there is only one such thing," he replied, "and that is your body, because according to nature only his body is born to the man himself. You can part with everything else."

"If I give my consent! But, for instance, these clothes also belong to me."

"As long as you use them. But you are well aware that previously they were in possession of a store, and you have simply taken them without saying anything about it to the storekeeper. Nor would there have been any point in discussing the matter, as his approval would not have made the clothes any better."

"But this is precisely where the difference lies," I replied. "As far as we are concerned, the removal of property requires the proprietor's consent. Whereas, since you have already brought it up, I must point out that it is precisely the body of which we are not so completely free to dispose."

His eyes opened wide.

"But how can you take the body away?"

"If life is taken away."

"That of the desperately ill person?"

I did not understand how this question came up.

"Not at all!" I replied. "That of the healthy person."

"This I do not understand at all. It would be in vain were I to take away your life: even then your body would not be mine. I could not fix on your hands and feet alongside my own, nor could I think with your brain."

"There are certain cases when citizens must sacrifice their lives for their country, so at such times the fatherland has our bodies at its disposal. But let us not stray too far from the point. Clothes are private property that other people cannot take away."

"That's somewhat confused. In brief, in your country you are the clothes, but your body is not you? How am I to interpret that?"

For a moment I again considered his words a piece of half-baked punning, but he spoke with such a naive surprise that I was forced to think of his innocence as stupidity. On the other hand, this extent of narrow-mindedness was almost enough to make me lose my temper. I angrily struck my knees.

"Understand, will you," I said, "that property is not what we ourselves are, but what cannot be taken away by somebody else. And so, clothes are an example."

"But they can be taken away."

"Not at all! It is forbidden with us!"

"And in general what is it that cannot be taken away there?"

"I have already told you: property."

"What does 'property' mean?"

"What is mine and so cannot be taken away from me."

Now he did not understand the "so."

"As far as I can see," he said, "you are just turning round and round without a starting point, and for this very reason your economics do not seem tangible."

He was once more looking for some "natural starting point" and asked me to explain to him where the firm foundation was that I had been mentioning.

"Well, listen," I said. "Among us, people earn money according to the services they have supplied in economic life. There are those who work at a machine and are paid according to their output by the industrialist. And the goods turned out will be purchased by the merchant, who, if he is smart, sells to others for more money. Then for the money acquired everyone may buy himself what he wants and as much as he can afford. Well, everyone knows how much he can buy, how much is due to him from the goods—that is, how much he can make his property."

"Now I understand."

"At last!"

"In short, among you the mistake is that when a rich man gives money for goods, he feels as if he had brought something into equilibrium, and even when his purchases are well beyond his own capacity, he still thinks that he is buying his own, and that even then he is within the limits of the kazo equilibrium."

He commiserated deeply with our rich people, for we had so confused their perspective that they could not work, and we forced them to eat others' share of bread, whereby production decreased and poverty increased. It took nerves of steel to debate the Hins. Still, I tried yet again to explain the situation. I told him that it was precisely our rich who constituted the most valuable sector of society. It was they who founded and maintained factories and enterprises, by which they gave bread to a lot of poor people. The poor, who lived exclusively on their work, were, on the other hand, not only not useful, but if they became too numerous they would take away each other's bread. It was for this very reason that when someone came to us from abroad we refused him a work permit, lest he take the bread of others.

My Readers are, of course, under the impression that after such a clear and understandable explanation my companion comprehended everything and admitted my being right.

No! Quite the contrary!

While I was speaking he scrutinized my face, and then instead of replying, he asked again for my Belohin certificate. Musing, he perused it several times, then said that I seemed to have become a little tired of learning for the day and I had better walk for a few hours in the open.

I adamently protested, stating that I was in perfect possession of my senses, and the truth of all this was proved by the fact that in the country with the most developed economy in Europe, all this was tangible reality.

He, however, did not reply.

This haughtiness annoyed me, and only the awareness of my being a guest prevented me from avenging this insult.

So I traveled on in silence. He did not inquire as to my destination, and when we reached the riverbank I decided on the spur of the moment to get out.

I entered the wide, large park stretching along the riverside, a park that was the epitome of both orderly care and neglect. Gravel paths, steamrolled to become as smooth as glass; silvery lampposts; here and there a path protected by glass walls sunk into the ground; and many chairs with rubber seats.

I saw, however, neither statues nor fountains. In their lawns, weeds and grass grew together; the trees were only superficially pruned; and of ornamental plants I saw no trace. But I had to admit that the air was excellent, as if I were not in a park in the middle of a big town, but out in a forest.

One small area was surrounded with a low-hung chain. On the grass within this area, there were some saplings. Beside the chain was a sign that read:

ENTERING IS NOT USEFUL.

In one section of the park I came to a clearing. It was only there that I found mown grass.

The clearing was edged in the form of a semicircle with comfortable lawn chairs for sunbathing, on which, here and there, people were lying or sitting. I also saw some pieces of fitness equipment and strange electric machines, the functions of which were a complete mystery to me.

What provided the greatest interest, however, was the snack bar situated in the center. On the wall there were taps supplying cold milk and refreshing drinks; inside there was a refrigerator with paper boxes filled with a variety of solid foods; and in a bin, paper cups.

The Hins came and went, ate and drank, and I saw no sign of attendants.

Lying about on the lawn chairs in underclothes of fine, lacy fabric were yet more Hins. This sight, together with the unattended snack bar and the whole atmosphere, gave me the same impression of intimacy as had the rice paddies after my arrival: as if I had not been in a public place, but at the garden party of a hospitable aristocrat. I may say, it was very strange to my European eyes, seeing this society whose every member was rich without having a single penny. As if the whole society had formed a single household within which there were no financial problems, no written regulations, no prohibited areas, and no work status problems, but where the members of the family went about freely, helping each other with the housework, and helping themselves from a dish set in the middle of the table. I felt a warm, friendly, and intimate atmosphere that I had never before felt among any people.

And in such sharp contrast to all this was the complete silence of the Hins.

The new, fresh impression of this plethora of public property swept me away, and I drank a fruit juice, but my good manners did not let me impose upon their hospitality. At my side I imagined a polite host who, although he offers food as becomes a gentleman, nevertheless takes a poor view of the greedy guest.

Standing near the snack bar, I watched the Hins coming and going. An incomprehensible sense of contradiction defined the scene. These wonderful provisions free for everyone's taking seemed to indicate the highest degree of warm, familiar fondness, and at the same time everyone was a stranger; not a single greeting was to be heard. Each person simply did not exist for the other.

I should have liked to strike up a conversation with one of them, to ask about this. Finally I went up to someone and said, "We seem to have fine weather."

He looked at me, stood for a minute, and then without deigning to answer, left.

I may say that their manners are expressly insulting. I had no time, however, to ponder further because at that moment there came a slight breeze and a second later my eye closed painfully. A speck of dust had got into it, and rub it as I might, it would not come out.

With my head bowed I stood blinded, when all at once from the right and from the left two hands grasped my arms. As far as my stubbornly closing eyelids permitted me to see, two Hins had taken hold of me and began to lead me away.

So much tenderness touched me beyond measure, and in my confusion I stuttered some words of thanks, which was all the more difficult as I did not know such words.

I thought they were leading me to a faucet, and was all the more surprised because when they reached the road they stopped, flagged down the first car, helped me in, then disappeared without a word, while the car turned and carried me away at high speed.

I had practically no time even to ask where we were going when the car already stopped, the driver helped me out, led me into a house, and delivered me to a third Hin, whereupon he, too, disappeared like camphor.

This last Hin had taken me into a room full of medical instruments, and sat me down on a chair. Then a fourth man came, lifted my eyelid, took out the grain of dust, and said, "that's all," and disappeared.

Puzzled, I stood alone in the consulting room, and did not know what would happen.

After waiting for about ten minutes I finally grew bored and asked the first man I came across whether I had to do anything more, but, like everybody up to then, he did not answer but told me it was up to me and abandoned me. At this I left.

Thus I was again on the street, and when I reflected on what had happened, the whole procedure seemed like a big automaton that accepts the object dropped into it, one manipulator passing it to the other, the wheels cleaning, polishing, folding, and rolling it, and at the end the finished product is ejected; for that, however, neither the object nor the machine is responsible, as the whole procedure simply took place, and that is that.

Walking their streets, I was able to thoroughly inspect the infrastructure. Every fifty steps there was a phone booth built into a building wall—a public phone that, of course, operated free of charge. There were lots of warehouses, too, with signs advertising what was inside. Inside, every product, from toothpaste to generators, was piled up in the utmost order, and everyone took whatever and as much as they needed.

There was a post office, too, which accepted only parcels—not that they were stamped, and most weren't even wrapped in brown packaging paper, as was the custom in my country. From a complex microscope of sorts dangled a slip of paper bearing the address. The Hins placed their parcels on the long table underneath, and went away. Apart from these people sending parcels, there was not a soul in the room.

At the back of the room were two doors bearing the words, "Sorting Room." And another sign underneath: "Intellectual work in progress." In my country, the expression would have been "No admittance."

After observing for ten minutes I saw the table as it moved off and disappeared through the door of the sorting room, while from the other end of the room a similar table came out empty. This much is certain: there was no line. But it was beyond me how it was possible to process such a volume of mail exactly and safely without the control of records and receipts.

Though it is rather difficult to make Hins speak, I felt encouraged by their earlier accommodating attitude and asked someone how and why parcels were sent as they were.

He answered that if for every parcel a note had to be made in a book, it would not help but merely impede the flow of mail.

I asked him whether it did not sometimes occur as a result of such happy-go-lucky handling that parcels disappeared into thin air. To this he replied that according to a long established law of physics, no material could be lost within nature.

Here again I had the impression that a Hin was talking of something other than what I'd asked, but later I was forced to realize that they simply do not know of stealing, and that evoked my sincere admiration. This untaught morality, for the maintenance of which technical knowledge in and of itself could by no means suffice, thus appeared even more mysterious to me. There had to be something else behind it. But what was it? And how could I come to know it?

Then I asked where they posted letters and telegrams. It turned out that every flat and office had its own mail drop into which the letters were put to be carried to the central post office, which in turn sent them on to the addressees. He remarked that this was a somewhat awkward method of correspondence (to me it seemed wonderfully easy) but that the following year new mail drops with guiding mechanisms were to be put into operation. Once properly set, the box would automatically read the address line and direct the mail accordingly. There was, however, scarcely any correspondence because messages were dealt with mainly by telephone. If there was no reply from the dialed number, that did not matter, either, as the telephone received and recorded the message, so it could be listened to at any time.

Now, however, the rumbling of my stomach warned me that it was lunchtime, so turning in to the first restaurant I sat down at a table and took my meal from the endless conveyor belt.

Soon someone else settled down opposite me, and I was meditating upon what people actually did here, if there were no attendants. The absence of waiters was already a familiar fact to me, but now a new problem arose. How could economic catastrophe be avoided in a place where people were displaced everywhere by machines?

It occurred to me that my own country had great difficulty finding work for the unemployed, that many jobs were maintained for purely social welfare reasons, and that the implementation of new technology often had to be curbed to prevent too many layoffs. Among us, a good many people earned their living by participating in the work of the nation as waiters, conductors, post-office clerks, bookkeepers, gatekeepers, cashiers, policemen, clergymen, prison guards, or soldiers. How beneficial is the existence of all these institutions, and what would happen if all these posts were abolished and the millions of people dismissed and deprived of their livelihoods? Why, in industry unemployment figures are sadly high even so.

Addressing my table companion, I mentioned all this but he replied that it was not worth wasting time with idle chatter. It is interesting how variable their willingness to help was. I came to realize only slowly that if I asked about their institutions they went as far as possible to explain everything. If, however, I broached an individual thought, or mentioned our home institutions, they did not even deign to answer. The problem, however, occupied my mind, and, producing my Belohin certificate, I managed to get my table companion to speak.

I asked him how it was possible for so many people to make a living solely from productive occupations. He was astonished at my question, and believed only after I had thrice repeated it that that was indeed what I had asked.

"I still do not understand," he said, "what there is to be asked about it. If fewer of us were engaged in production obviously we would be able to produce less and would therefore live less well."

"But do the machines not squeeze men out of the factories?"

"We always leave enough space for people to walk comfortably between the machines."

"That is not what I mean. A machine does the work of many people, whereby a lot of workers become redundant, and a major part of the goods produced will be superfluous."

"Machines are made precisely so that we can produce more. How can it be imagined that clothes are made for any reason other than putting them on?"

"But how is it possible for such an enormous number of people to work in industry?"

This again he did not understand.

"Every man works as much as he can," he replied. "The more

they work, the more they produce. What is there to restrict the working force?"

"Overproduction! Does the danger of overproduction not threaten you?"

He asked what this meant, and I in turn explained to him the world crisis, the bank failures and the cutbacks that come in their wake, the surplus of goods, and general poverty.

I had to say it over and over again, because he did not comprehend a single word of it. When he finally understood, he said that I must have observed things inaccurately in my country, as my description was rather imperfect, for there was no connection between the phenomena mentioned.

"For how could the existence of a society be imagined," he said, where suffocation would be cured by the deprivation of air? To say nothing of the fact that unnecessarily complicating simple things would show facts in a false light; and any man in his senses would rather endeavor to become acquainted with things as they are than to blur them."

I vividly protested against his mentioning my country in such an offensive manner, but instead of replying, he again asked for my Belohin certificate. Musing, he perused it several times, and then said I seemed to have become a little tired of learning for the day and I had better walk for a few hours in the open.

But I did not give in; I protested against this contemptuous tone; I demanded that he should provide me with the necessary information; after all, to my knowledge all Hins were at the disposal of a Belohin.

At this, he appeared to be ready for further conversation, suggesting only that in my own interest we should speak about less difficult topics.

However, I felt hurt by this disdain and scathingly remarked that the things I had spoken about and that had seemed so incomprehensible to him were well known to any street cleaner in my country.

With this observation I reverted to our former subject. To me it seemed impossible that the population could find occupation in industry with such a degree of mechanization, when so many other posts were absent, so I reasoned that they must work for export. But when I asked him about this, it came to light that they knew nothing of shipping, either. He said that nothing was grown on the sea, so why should they go there?

I mentioned to him how foreign trade boosted the standard of living and how useful it would be if they were to export butter, corn, honey, and other things to my country, whereby they could accumulate a considerable reserve of foreign exchange. To this I received the surprising comment that they would get no satisfaction from food eaten by others!

It was beyond my comprehension how they had not yet died of starvation with such a lack of economic aptitude.

But with this, I saw that any further debate would be in vain, as an enormous gap yawned between us, and the Hins' soul contained a kind of secret that, unless it were explained, made it impossible for me to make myself understood.

So I got up and left. I racked my brain for a long time to figure out how I could come to know them without having to converse with them. Here, I might ask anything of anybody, and while they all gave odd replies, each reply was remarkably similar. Personality was hardly present at all. And it was for this very reason that I was eager to know what sort of spirit kept them so wonderfully disciplined as could not be imagined among us even in the army.

Finally I resolved to read.

Surely some sort of ethnographic work would provide me more information relating to their customs and nature.

Stopping the first Hin who came my way, I asked where I could get a book about the nature, clothing, and general way of life of people here. This, I figured, would convey the concept of ethnography through circumscription.

He replied that I had mentioned too many subjects at one time, some belonging to anatomy and the functioning of organs, and others to the textile industry.

I saw that he did not understand me, either, so I asked him only where I could find a library in the neighborhood.

Willing to be at my disposal, he told me the address, but I could not make much of it. When he learned that I was a stranger in town, he immediately joined me. We boarded a streetcar and he took me to the library.

We arrived in a huge, round church-like room the wall of which, to a height of about ninety feet, was a single mass of shelves with millions of books. In front of the shelves hung tiny balconies at different heights, with a chair and a little table on each. In most of them a Hin was reading, and soon I noticed that these small balconies also moved. The Hins led them along on the horizontal and vertical rails between the shelves to reach the book required.

Oddly enough, I had the impression there was a great deal of noise in their library, although it was only the turning of the pages that could be heard, and the space itself was not a bit noisier than our own libraries. Their public lives, however, were so silent that I was surprised to find that this was not even more silent.

Here and there between the shelves were signs bearing big characters indicating the subjects: "Ethyl ether," "Cellulose," or "Protein," and elsewhere, "Neurology," "Stomach transplantation," "Transformation of elements," "Grain automatons," or "Depth scrutinizers."

I thought my guide had misunderstood me and had taken me to a science library, whereas I wanted to learn about the Hins and especially their customs.

Fortunately, I noticed a table in the middle of the room with an "Information" sign above it.

I stepped up to the Hin who was sitting there, and repeated my question. Word for word he, too, gave me the same reply as my guide.

I saw that I would not achieve my goal this way, and that perhaps I ought to start with another kind of theme through which

I might acquaint myself with their life. I decided to study their history, and said that I was looking for a book dealing with the past. The Hin answered that this was a very broad subject. There were books dealing with geology, with the development of races, the nervous system, the intestinal canal, and many other things.

I told him that was not the sort of book I was after, but something about the past of people.

I had to repeat my request, but still he did not understand and asked me if I could mention a book about a similar subject. At this, producing my Belohin certificate, I had to reveal that I was a foreigner and I told him I was not in a position to know their literature, but could only mention the books of my own country.

At random I mentioned the books on the history of my country by James Anthony Froude and by John Richard Green, but he asked me to say something about their contents as well.

I spoke of the age of Henry VIII—of his marriage with Anne Boleyn; of the fights around the Reformation; of the revolt of the Northern Shires; of the execution of Sir Thomas More, the Bishop of Rochester, Anne Boleyn, and Catherine Howard; of the battles between the various kings, Parliament, the Duke of Norfolk, and Oliver Cromwell; of the trans-substantiation debates, celibacy, mass, and confession. . . . Of course, the whole of this history seemed unbelievable to him, but I had already grown accustomed to his asking at every sentence, "But why did they do all this?"

When I finished, however, he was surprised at my speaking about the past as if it were something that existed, when in the end it turned out that all this did not exist.

"But it did!" I replied.

"That is possible, but this word in itself implies that it no longer does. What is the sense in dealing with imaginary things? It is only the real, the *present*, that is, and if into the bargain you deal with nonexistent things, why do you spend so much unnecessary work precisely on the past? In the same way you could also make maps of nonexistent planets."

I observed that many valuable conclusions could be drawn from the past as to how we should direct our actions.

"It is something like taking a laxative on an empty stomach in the morning," he replied, "because we overate in our dream."

Thus it came to light that they had no history at all. Everyone remembers only the period through which he or she has lived. And from the forefathers all that remains for the descendants is what they themselves create: a new chemical procedure, a building, a machine. But as for the maker, builder, or inventor, nobody knows a thing.

In brief, I was again faced with deadlock. That they had no arts I already understood. I racked my brain to discover what I could study that might cast light on their life and outlook.

I asked for philosophical works, but once more the Hin I'd been speaking to asked what that was. When I spoke of human thinking and its rules, he referred me to neurology without hesitation, from which it became evident that they had no philosophy, either. At this, I was sincerely astonished, as the whole of their life consisted of varying the concepts of kazo and kazi, from which any sober mind would have concluded that this was a nation of philosophers. I also asked him why they did not write a single line on even the main problem of their lives. I mentioned how many authors had tried to interpret morality, the laws of God, and justice, and from how many angles they had done so.

"What exists," he replied, "needs no explanation. What sense would there be in explaining, for example, that the circle is round? And if a figure is described once as round and then as square, this is possible only if this figure does not exist, because if it does exist it is either one or the other."

I was already profoundly bored by these fruitless debates. For this reason I thought it better to seek out a book on economy; the Hin, however, asked me which of the branches of manufacture I was interested in. I enlightened him as to my wish to be informed of the system of production, but again he said only that it was different with every article produced. Wheat was grown according to one system, rye differently, and textiles were woven by yet another method.

Shortly it became clear that this did not exist, either. They simply had no economic system, no administration, no religion, no literature!

I was stupefied and could not grasp where I was to find the key to their existence. I should not have been a bit surprised if it had turned out that they themselves did not exist.

Finally I resolved to have a look at their books on neurology, hoping that from their most frequent neurotic symptoms I should be able to draw conclusions as to their inner life.

So I got myself onto a balcony, and after the Hin librarian had briefed me concerning the operation of the buttons, I rose to a height of about three stories and began to search.

Of the titles of the books, however, I could not make out too much. Finally, taking out one at random, I looked into it.

The title of the first chapter was: "Electron Currents and the Pattern of Thinking." I scarcely understood even the title, to say nothing of the text. It spoke of cells, of the forces occurring in them, and then came flexible collision and oscillation calculations and miscroscopic enlargements magnified fifty million times, but as to what they represented I had not the slightest idea; and so too there was an endless series of chemical constructional formulae and mathematical deductions.

Turning the pages, I came to another chapter: "Brain Technology and Nerve Assembly." I saw photographs of weird measuring instruments, people with small metal boxes on their chests or heads; tweezers and scalpels; and nerves extracted and transplanted. Then followed some strange pages made of metal, which were gridded all over with little squares so close together that it was injurious to the eye, and the whole vibrated in a dirty gray hue. At the bottom was a word unfamiliar to me: "Bomeli."

I was compelled to go down and turn to the Hin at the information desk. He then came over to my table and flipped up the right side of its top. Out popped what looked like some sort of microphotographic device. Opening the book at the page in question, he inserted it into the device, whereupon I had to look at the page through a lens.

This is what I saw: a glass vessel containing a human brain from which innumerable pins protruded. From the left, a violet ray projected a violet spot onto it. All around it were countless instruments with indicators.

The librarian now pushed a button. The indicators began to move and the brain slowly assumed a reddish hue. Then a human hand reached into the picture and poured the contents of a bottle into the glass vessel, whereupon the brain regained its natural color and the indicators sprang back to zero.

Of course I did not understand a single thing that I had seen, and above all I found nothing in the book to give any indication as to the nature of the Hin's inner life.

And it was in vain that I told the librarian I wished to know something of their range of emotions and thoughts; his response to this was that we feel and think with our brain, and that all the mathematical formulas concerning both the birth and the inter-connection of thoughts were fully dealt with in the first chapter.

"Naturally," he went on, "if you also wish to study the paradio-logical or sphero-electronic components of the birth of thought, this book will not satisfy you."

With this he began explaining in detail the part of the library I should next ascend to. From a catalog he began to read a mass of book titles, and the multitude of unknown words made me dizzy. Then he typed the book numbers onto a keyboard, and fi-nally pulled out a strip of paper from under the keys and handed it to me. It bore the title, number, and exact location of the sug-gested books.

However, I did not at all feel like experimenting with more books; they would certainly not have included the one I wanted.

I felt as if I were in a vacuum. The bridge that might connect us was burnt, it seemed, and I was unable to even explain what I wanted. For some time I searched for the expression, but they had no word for "soul," and had I mentioned the heart, I would most certainly have been referred to the shelf with the heading, "Circulation."

After racking my brain for a few minutes, I gave up all hope and turned my back on them.

On stepping out of the library, I walked to and fro for a while, thinking. I approached a Hin and inquired about art galleries.

He said there were pictures in every book, and it depended on what I was interested in. I told him that I was looking for painted pictures, but seeing that he, too, was about to abandon me, I hastened to produce my Belohin certificate.

I had to explain what a painted picture was like. Once he understood me he said it seemed we did not know its more perfected form, photography.

It was in vain that I repeatedly asserted that painting was the more perfect, as it portrayed not the surface but the core of things, to which he replied that even in this respect photographs were still more perfect, and I realized from his words that he was speaking of X-rays. He spoke further of a machine that saw into the depths of the earth, as well as of other strange pieces of equipment that revealed the inner structure of matter to the human eye.

At this point we found it very difficult to understand each other. I wanted to express that things had an emotional essence, an impression that they made on us. He, however, observed that things would appear to us either as they are, and in this case photography was the more perfect form, or else a different image of them evolved in us, in which case the fault was not in the things but in us.

Try as I did to describe to him individual painters' varying impressions of the world around them, which did not falsify things but sought to get closer to them, he maintained his stance that the essence of something could not vary, and if more than one conception of it evolved, then all of them except one would obviously be wrong. He recommended that I take any object whose essence I might find doubtful to a chemistry or physics laboratory, where I would receive an exact analysis of it.

With a weary wave of the hand, I stated that I needed no more information, and at that he left.

But the problem of discovering the secret nature of the Hins had become still more exciting as a result of all this. Before my eyes there was a marvelous mechanism whose cogwheels fitted into each other and performed their work to such a degree of precision as could not be expressed in human terms. And search for it as I might, I was unable to discover the main spring that kept the whole working. I stood there like Kepler or Pasteur, who, as they came to know the laws of nature, became more and more convinced of the existence of the Creator, who, however, withdrew farther and farther from the senses. His voice faded away into the Burning Bush, his eye no longer flashed in the storm, his voice no longer thundered in the clouds, and the more certain his being became for us, the more distant the mists he withdrew behind.

My brain was throbbing feverishly, so by now those Hins who had suggested I rest were indeed right. The day's learning had heaped so many problems on my mind that it was time to sleep on them.

I asked the first Hin I saw to show me where the overhead railway was; he willingly led me to it, and I got in.

On the way home, I nevertheless made a rough list of questions and decided to consult Zatamon on all of them. After all, as a neurologist himself, he dealt with the psyche, and he also knew me better than anyone else I'd met in this land.

CHAPTER

5

The author becomes acquainted with some of the se-crets of the Hins. We come to know that the Hins have no governing constitution. Zatamon expresses strange opinions concerning the administration of justice, love, the soul, and literature. The author plays a difficult game of chess with his tutor, and hears a confused explanation about the kazo.

BY NOW ZATAMON DID NOT BOTHER MUCH WITH ME. I HAD acquired the language and the fundamental ideas of Hin life, and as far as the rest was concerned I was more or less left to my own devices. The next day he did not even call upon me, which was all the better, since I was thus able to organize my thoughts more appropriately.

I took it for granted that a very democratic, parliamentary government ruled the island. At least thus far whenever I inquired about any procedure I was told that it was my own concern, and it was up to me to decide upon what steps to take. Here a strange mixture of freedom and discipline prevailed, but their exact relationship was, for the time being, an enigma to me.

It was for this reason that I inquired first of all concerning the Hins' form of government. But when I did so, I had first to expound upon what we meant by "constitutional form," "democracy," "dictatorship," and "parliamentarianism," and what "elections," "appointment," etc. were.

With enthusiasm I spoke eloquently of my country's ancient

parliamentary and democratic government, which had always ensured the right of the people to have a say in running their own lives.

When I got to this point, Zatamon asked me why it was necessary to have a say in the running of life, when life existed so that it should run and not so that people should interfere with it.

"In order," I replied, "that we should be able to ensure freedom."

This I could express only in a roundabout way; I spoke to him about general human rights and equilibrium, but he replied that freedom could not be as I had described it, because as soon as there was intervention, it was no longer freedom. And no country could have much to do with reality where equilibrium is expressed with such an emotional, which is to say, nonexistent, word like "freedom."

To cast some light on the concept of equilibrium as we understood it, I mentioned, as its most brilliant example, the administration of justice—which, through the rightful punishment of crimes, restored the disturbed equilibrium and ensured a peaceful, quiet life.

And this was where I was to have a veritable surprise.

In no way could Zatamon understand the difference between crime and punishment. Even after my lengthy explanations, he seemed able to appreciate a difference between them only in sequence, and could not see why we had made two different words for two identical concepts that differed only in their order in time insofar as crime came first and punishment followed; but it could also be the other way round: the judges might first commit kazi things, and then the criminals would gain the right to "restore the equilibrium" by perpetrating other kazi things.

"As I see it," he continued, "you believe that the kazo comes about by committing not one but two kazi things at the same time, whereas the doubling of the kazi will—according to any sober thinking—only aggravate its kazi character."

It was no use, my telling him that the judge punished only through necessity and with a kazo intention, in the interests of public law and order, so as to diminish the number of criminal cases. Zatamon replied that criminals were people just as much as the judges—that they, too, were part of us.

"Or what would you say," he asked, "if it turned out that sparrows had a habit of mutually ravaging each other's nests? Would you accept the plea that all this is not done by sparrows, because whichever ravages later does it after the first? And finally, how would you accept that mutual ravaging is the means of ensuring peace, quiet, and equilibrium?"

In the end, he summed up his opinion as follows:

"It is not enough that you commit crimes, you even punish as well."

This was how I came to know that they had no kind of government. Not only were they unaware of being ruled; they did not know the parliamentary system, either.

"Only sick brains," he said, "need to debate their own affairs. Anyone in his right senses knows what he needs; he goes to the warehouse and takes it; if the stocks are running out, the factories come to know it and replenish them. What is there to be debated in this?"

So they had no legislature, nor consequently any laws, and as to the administration of justice, they hadn't a clue. Everything unfolded on its own. I could not imagine how it was possible to live without governing bodies, and Zatamon in turn wondered how we could live amid such uncertainty, one in which a lot of people who had nothing to do with production, continuously interfered with and disturbed the ongoing work.

Now I proceeded to the second part of the problem, the great mystery, the question of discipline without law. I asked Zatamon: "Tell me, doesn't any difficulty arise as a result of the absence of all forms of control?"

"What kind of difficulty do you mean?"

"If, for example, a resourceful, smart, and bright man realizes that if he works less and eats more it will be of greater use to him."

Zatamon replied almost angrily—almost, I say, because it was unclear whether they had any familiarity with anger at all.

"How could it be of greater use? If we thought in this way production would not increase but decrease, and so, on the contrary, we would be able to eat less, which is not in the least useful. But why do you label "smart" precisely those feeble-minded people who don't know such a simple form of mathematics?"

I felt a deep respect for this country in which integrity and unselfishness were such innate human properties. I wanted to tell him so, but there were no words for this either. I wondered how a people, a state could be so honest when it did not even have a word for it. I could only say, in English, that it seemed that here everyone was honest and good-hearted toward others.

Of course, I had to explain the words and when, with great difficulty, Zatamon finally understood, he voiced the opinion that in my country the opposite of such people probably occurred if we created a separate word for those able to interpret mathematics properly.

I gazed at him in astonishment.

Here, integrity was ensured not only by a complete lack of laws—they did not even know what it was. The cogwheels fitted into each other perfectly: there was no hitch, there was not a single squeaky bearing in the social machinery, and all this was kept in equilibrium solely by the strength of the common soul!

I should have liked to ask Zatamon about psychological motives, but remembering my failure in the library, I was forced suddenly to realize that they had no idea of the soul either, of the very thing that seemed to shine more brilliantly in this very place than anywhere in the world. But where had all this come from, and what was it that maintained it in them?

In a faltering voice, choking with emotion, I confessed my admiration to him. I frankly admitted that all this was beyond me.

I now explained to Zatamon what a comprehensive and circumspect establishment ensured the smooth running of society in my country; that law, money, and the administration of justice controlled the exchange of goods, and so too did the long years that children were schooled in morality, goodness, and honesty—while so far as they were concerned here, it was purely and simply the soul, the common spirit, that held together the whole, and what is more, even more perfectly.

I was carried away by a veritable rhetorical passion as I explained that I was still unable to see the common source of all this: in what way and from whom did the soul come, and what imbued them with this miracle?

He asked me to explain the concept of soul in more detail.

I answered that it was the soul that enabled one to do good. I mentioned as an example that we also had hospitals and homes for the aged.

"And," I asked, "what do you think it is that makes us build them? Well, that's the soul."

"Hospitals are built by masons, with machines and concrete," Zatamon answered. "What has the soul to do with that?"

My first reaction was to be annoyed at his lack of comprehension, but then a clinical case of mine came to mind: We had removed a cataract from the eyes of a six-year-old little boy, blind from birth, but even weeks later he was unable to identify figures. He saw his mother, but came to know where she stood only by hearing her voice. In the brain of the child the connection was missing between the concept and the image itself. He had to learn to see for some months before he had by practice established the connections.

Then I thought I understood everything. These people were brought up among cold realities, so they did not perceive the soul in the same way as we did—with other senses, and not just with their brain, which comprehended tangible things only. So my task was the same as in the case of the little boy who had been given back his sight: I had to put him on the right track, one that would enable him to make the connection between the facts and the soul. He was bound to have some notion of it already, as the *kazo* was the consummate soul, only he did not recognize it.

I evolved a really strong line of attack, and asked him: "And why do you build hospitals?"

"Because there are sick and aged persons. Why else would we build them? Why do your sick people go to hospital?"

I did not understand the point of this question.

"Because they want to regain their health."

"Then how can you ask why we build hospitals? In order that the sick may regain their health."

This simple aphorism, of course, did not throw me off balance and I was determined not to let him slip out of my hands. "This itself is the pure aim," I replied, "but not the reason. It is the soul that enables us to help our fellow men—that is, the connection that fills the gap between the fact of illness and the actual building. To give an example, it is like the mortar between bricks without which the wall would fall apart. So this is what induces us to help. Now do you understand what I am looking for?"

"I understand even less. Why should there be any gap here? If between illness and building there is no direct connection, and instead a foreign concept is wedged in, this does not connect but disconnects them, just as mortar, too, is a heterogeneous insulating layer between the bricks; and the fact that something needs an adhesive only goes to prove its being in a state of disintegration. Concrete needs no adhesive, as it is in itself one material; that is why it is superior."

"Oh, soul is not a foreign concept—it is the content of our whole life! Why would the sick man want to recover if his life had no spiritual aim? And it is not in the cold concrete of the hospital that the essence of helping lies but in this. Forceps, medicines, and bandages are not enough; most important is the spirit of helping, which has greater healing power than that. Why should we live without substance? What would be the sense in recovering and getting back into life if we were not tied to our fellow men by the thousand threads of friendship, love, interest, and faith—if our life was not warmed by all these emanations of the soul, thus making it desirable for the sick man to recover?"

Of course, I had to circumscribe everything. The interconnecting spiritual ties, for example, I compared to a magnet's lines of force. After my lengthy explanation Zatamon finally replied.

"Our body consists of atoms; they determine our desires, because they are the natural world. And nothing else can be imagined, as nothing else exists. Of the concepts that you compared to a magnet's lines of force, my more exact questions made it quite clear step by step that they are neither magnetic, nor atomic, nor even vibrations, and consequently they are nonexistent. And what does not exist, is not."

How horrifying was this cold way of thinking, whose chilling atmosphere was numbing. Zatamon asked me, however, to continue my narration because—as he said—he believed that nevertheless there was something real behind my words, and I was merely unable to express it.

Thus, instead of carrying on a fruitless debate with him concerning principles, I began to speak about my country. I told Zatamon how much a true friend was worth, one on whom we could rely in trouble and when we needed protection from the wrath of our enemies. How our life was sweetened by friendship, a loving wife, or a warm domestic circle. What happiness it is to sit around a fireplace with our loved ones on winter evenings; to buy gifts for them at Christmas. Or when celebrating our birthday to invite our friends, where a witty conversation may start about the theater, art, less significant events, and how beautiful life may be made by a supper taken happily among such friends.

One by one each concept—friend, hatred, wife, happiness, theater, art, and party—had, of course, to be explained. I was pleased to see that Zatamon listened attentively to my words and took notes while I was talking. I was already on the verge of hope, but in the end he said he had discovered an apparent contradiction in my words.

"I thought," he said, "I might learn from you, since you spoke of some act of help in unison that seemed to show proper mathematical comprehension, but I was disappointed. In your country the kazo is considered to apply to certain groups only, which, however, already means that it is not kazo as you do not observe it where others are concerned. Because if you imagine some persons closer to yourselves and favor them, this can only be done if at the same time you offer less or nothing to others. That is, both the things you give your friends and those you do not give others bear all the marks of the kazi concept. These friends do not receive out of need, or on the basis of a general state of equilibrium—at least this is what I gather from your words—but purely because you have invented the kazi idea of 'friendship.'"

"And as for the word 'love,' it seems to me you wish to indicate with this that people outside an exclusive circle are to be treated beneath the merit of their existence. But why do you call the same thing hatred on other occasions?"

I was astounded at Zatamon's incomprehension and began to explain the difference, but he insisted that anything beyond equilibrium and reciprocality was kazi and there was no sense in dividing it into two separate words. And if we also assigned different meanings to them, it only proved that our vision was confused.

"Or," said Zatamon, "why should a wife or a lover be valued above the merit of her existence when every woman has the same organs; and, as far as I can see, you also make a distinction among children, according to whether or not they originate from yourselves; whereas those children who came from the seed of others also exist. You, however, call the former your own—although every person belongs solely to himself, as his life was born to him and not to the father. And for those children you buy gifts at Christmas, but for the others, nothing. You make it appear to the child as if you were giving to it beyond the limits of equality and reciprocity, and on top of all this, you hold this activity of yours up to the child as something especially right, which is doubly kazi. For the child's own portion of all goods is due to him as is the case with anyone else, and it is wrong to have it seem as if he received it from us, and without reciprocity."

Zatamon considered the concept of Christmas to be especially improper, drawing the conclusion that on the other days we were to hate our fellow men more. My explanation that Christmas had been created not for hatred but for love was all in vain; he clung firmly to his opinion that love presumed hatred, as light did shadow, and a word could be created for this only where its opposite also existed; and the fact that we loved somebody implied that we had to behave more harmfully toward all those we did not love, so love itself was kazi, entailing contrast, conflict, hunger, and decay—an overwhelming accumulation of kazi things, in short, which thus yielded a decrease in production and welfare.

Zatamon thought there must be a great many Behins among us, who, though aware of the impropriety of it, still endeavored to eat more, work less, and get others to do the work, because they were imbued with the poison of love.

One special thing he did not understand was why we described as more useful precisely that particular situation in which we could have more food and less work, while it was a general balance that our organs needed, and overburdening was equally harmful whether the strain was on the stomach or the muscles.

I saw he would never understand the essence of love in this way, so I mentioned that we Europeans all followed the tenets of a great common prophet who had announced two thousand years ago that we had to love all our fellow men equally—which is to say, love did not encompass only small groups but the whole of mankind.

I related to him how beautiful and enjoyable our life was made by following this; the faith that beautified our soul and filled it with pleasure brought comfort to us, and sheltered us against trials and tribulations, and how elevating it was to be aware of the infinite mercy that provided the soul with a point of support.

"Would it not have been simpler to make life secure in advance?" he asked.

"I don't see what that question has to do with it."

"To make it secure, calculable."

"But why?"

"So that one should not be compelled to flee from uncertainty to uncertainty. Confused and inexpedient causes can only lead to confused and inexpedient effects."

For this, of course, I was none the wiser. I retorted that his reply was much more confused than our life, which had been provided with a firm basis by the law of love applying to everybody and connecting the whole of mankind.

At this he observed that what I was saying now was in complete contradiction to what I had said before concerning love. He, however, was convinced that of the two statements it was the former that tallied with the facts, because if love did indeed encompass the whole of mankind it could no longer be called love, in the same way as if the whole surface of the earth were to rise to the level of its highest peak, nobody would say of the earth that all its points were peaks—we would call it a plain and would not even have a word for peak.

He supposed, however, that this prophet of ours might still have been a Hin in whom the state of the kazo was present, and it was merely that we had not understood the mathematical facts he had spoken about, probably because we had a soul to hinder understanding; so, instead of learning from his words and being reborn into the kazo condition, we had been looking for "solace," "beauty," "pleasure" in his words. Obviously we would never possess life in this way.

I protested vigorously against this. I told him that the essence of a man was not, after all, his hands, feet, or stomach but his "self." And the soul was nurtured by beauty and variety, which it required no less than the stomach requires food.

This Zatamon declared to be completely beyond comprehension. He asked me to explain what this beauty was by which the soul was nurtured—and what was the soul, which needed only things that were of no necessity to man himself, while I contended that the soul was man himself? I had hitherto only spoken of the soul as the connecting material between actions, but now, said Zatamon, he saw that it was not only a partition wedged in between the facts of the natural world—somehow it also existed independently, and it must be very confused. It behaved like a living organism, the way I'd put it—I had, after all, claimed that it took nourishment—and still I could not describe its form.

I could not help but smile at his words. An old patient of mine came to my mind. He had gone into the Navy as an uneducated longshoreman. The poor devil had a screw loose, and gave his military superiors a lot of trouble. I myself attended to him when he was under treatment; I spoke to him at length of the glorious calling of the British Navy, the past of the United Kingdom, and the sweet nourishment our souls could draw from our traditions.

When finally I asked this old patient if he knew what tradition was, he answered: "Perhaps it's some sort of pudding."

Now I faced a similar task with Zatamon.

To illuminate soul and beauty better I mentioned the most distinguished works from our literature: *Hamlet* by Shakespeare, *Anna Karenina* and *The Kreutzer Sonata* by Tolstoy, *The Ironmaster* by Ohnet, *La Dame aux camélias* by Pumas, *Peer Gynt* by Ibsen—and other classic works that have explored the depths of the human mind, revealing the passions and emotions boiling within. Such books, I explained, uncovered the enigmas of ego through precise analysis. And they probed the maladjustments and subconscious inhibitions that sometimes separate even the purest of souls from each other or that drive some persons to discord and even—as with Raskolnikov—to murder and martyrdom. Why do some bow to their enemies or, indeed, to death? The answers lie hidden in these works. I stressed how profound and perfect the analysis of the character of an Anna Karenina was in its thousands of variations, and what an experience it was to recognize one's own soul in the struggles that Faust or Peer Gynt fought with themselves.

Attentively Zatamon heard me out, and when I had finished

he answered that we appeared to perish in tangles created by ourselves, because instead of seeing things in their clear reality and living simply, we preferred to wander intoxicated in a maze of illusory problems that were all entangled with one other. He voiced the opinion that the soul must be some terrible disease confusing everything and preventing the kazo equilibrium from developing. He did not understand why it was necessary to keep on analyzing the soul in thick tomes instead of recognizing the uselessness of this confused and troublesome thing, and discarding it as valueless and looking for something else that it was possible to use.

"Here, too," he said, "it sometimes happens that the production of methylated spirit, sulphuric acid, or cellulose does not come off. All this can be done badly in hundreds and hundreds of ways; but we would consider anyone mad who devoted his life to describing what bad cellulose is like, by how many methods we can obtain bad cellulose, in how many ways the cellulose may become spoiled, and for how many purposes it is unsuitable. Our books describe the characteristics only of good cellulose and contain information concerning the manufacture of that alone—of that, however, not a word is written in your literature. But first of all I don't understand why you call it creative work when somebody—withdrawing his labor from creative work— wastes his life on the fruitless analysis of bad and useless things."

I protested in vain against his calling our works of art bad and useless. I realized that for them only pudding is nourishment. So I decided to reply only to the question of why books are written at all.

I told him they were written for entertainment, which was a pleasure and was consequently necessary for people. As to the question of what entertainment was I mentioned reading, games, and chatting. Of course he also classified these as kazi.

"Is even conversation kazi with you?" I asked in surprise.

"Not necessary conversation. But as far as I can see, you speak of conversation carried on for its own sake, which is unnecessary conversation, which for this very reason cannot be so agreeable as creative work."

"But during the hours after creative work!"

"At such times, rest is necessary. Or what would you think of the man who had already reached his destination, sat down in exhaustion, and continued to move his legs at the normal pace of walking? The life of anyone who enjoys this is already off balance, because he can certainly find as much satisfaction in unnecessary as in necessary conversation, perhaps even more, and will look for the opportunity to shift his time from the necessary to the unnecessary. Attributing value to the unnecessary is the bud from which kazi things blossom—what you call beauty, entertainment, literature, and other nonsense."

Of all this I gathered no more than that he did not really understand what I had said and remarked that there was a great difference between time stolen from work and refreshing entertainment after a decent day's work, which even improved the ability of the mind and the body to work. He, however, stubbornly reiterated: "Nothing but damage can result from cultivating nonexisting things, because we ourselves live in the existing world."

I searched my mind for an example of entertainment to which he could not object even from the point of view of the kazo. Finally I mentioned chess as a harmless pastime of the soul from which nobody could suffer any harm.

I drew a chessboard, and sketched chess pieces on small slips of paper and then I expounded the rules of the game, which, I may say, was an onerous task. I had never had such a thickheaded pupil. When I had explained for the fifth time, Zatamon repeated his question for the sixth time: "But what is the aim?"

"To remove the king of the enemy," I said and began to explain again.

Shrugging his shoulders, he eventually agreed to a game. I made a move with a pawn and beckoned to him to move, at that he took my king, placed it beside the chessboard, and looked questioningly at me.

"And now what is the sense in that?" he asked inanely.

I put the figure back with considerable annoyance.

"It's not that simple!"

"You can see it is!"

"But you must observe the rules! If you play like that then of course there is no sense in it. If you play according to the rules, you will see that there is sense in it."

With great difficulty we played a game right through to the end. Of course, I beat him.

"And now what?" he asked.

"Now I am the winner."

"What does that mean?"

"I have taken the game."

He thought for a long time. Clearly he still did not understand, but he eventually came out with it.

"And what does that actually mean?"

"That I have won."

"You explain one word with another, which for you seems to be necessary because none of them has anything to do with reality. You have coined both of them without either of them having any content."

Zatamon was unable to understand—as he put it—why we were doing nothing so lengthily and painstakingly, to which there would have been no point even if I had removed his king at the very start, and he drew the conclusion that the whole of our life and public life probably consisted of making complications out of nothing, and that our actions were directed by imaginary idols. And if we took nothing as actuality, this could only produce poverty, discord, and the accumulation of kazi things, which all seemed to be the aftermath of the disease I had called "soul" and emotions that drew us away from creative work.

I felt hurt by this belittling tone and contradicted Zatamon by saying that it was precisely the soul that gave rise to great works that soared, which elevated people from prosaic everyday things and induced them to create.

As proof I suggested painting, referring to the captivating magnificence of a *Mona Lisa,* and of churches, statues, monuments, and decorated marble facades of public buildings; that is, I drew a lesson from what had happened already and mentioned only tangible, real things that even Zatamon could not say did not exist

But he would have none of it: "All this proves precisely that the soul takes your energy away from creative work, unbalances it, and sidetracks it. In particular I do not understand how you can describe as "soaring" that very millstone which prevents you from living an easy life, wastes your energies in false pursuits, and leads you into a maze of problems and into senseless conflicts. This burden, far from elevating you, hinders your progress and weighs you down but not to the earth that is the only real place for life: it takes you beneath the earth, where you stagger in darkness and are unable to get out to simple, sunny reality. This yields the many tribulations, hatred, poverty, public buildings, literature, insecurity, gifts, oppression, love, lies, paintings, and all the heavy burdens of life you have spoken about."

And all this Zatamon interpreted as further evidence that the only way to live was the kazo, cooperative aid, where everybody, working for a common aim, devoted his life to the community.

"This, of course, you express by love, willingness to make sacrifices, and other words that have no connection with reality. And yet these words that designate nonexisting concepts lead you to deeds that are in contradiction with the pure kazo which is the sole way of true usefulness, only you don't know it."

This was one charge I really could not stomach. I asserted that in my country every citizen subjected his life to a common aim, as he knew that if the country were lost, everything would be lost. As the most magnificent repository of the common spirit I mentioned the army, enumerating the struggles of our forefathers by which the present world power of my country had been established.

Zatamon listened attentively to me for a while, but on his forehead a strange, anxious frown showed more and more strongly.

Then suddenly he stood up and remarked that the day's learning seemed to have been too much for me as I could not even understand his words, and what I had just said not only failed to have any connection with reality but also failed to have any connection with itself, so the whole was improbable.

Again I began explaining to him the lofty tasks of national defense. Zatamon questioned me three times and I had to repeat the answer three times, but even so, in the end I could only make him see that there were situations when the ordinary citizen had to sacrifice his life so that the country should survive.

At this he asked what the country was.

I told him that it was all the citizens collectively, at which he again did not understand the beginning and asked how we could live collectively in order to die one by one.

I gave a dispirited wave of my hand, and he concluded I must be very tired.

With this, Zatamon wanted to leave. It was in vain that I protested that all I had said was actually so; it was in vain that I asserted that I myself dealt with healing the wounds inflicted by others—he merely said my words were becoming more and more contradictory and that I had certainly misunderstood something.

But I would not let him go away. I told him I would explain everything and that he would understand.

Zatamon sat down again.

"But why do you do all this?" he asked.

"Because we have the capacity to feel."

"We have the same senses as you, and yet we don't do it."

"Because you sense heat, light, and sound but not happiness."

"What, then, is it that you call 'happiness'?"

"The satisfaction of the soul."

"That is when the soul has had its fill."

"Something like that."

He pondered.

"Did your soul have its fill when we played chess?"

"Yes, becaus: I won the game. You see, you have no such pleasures."

"And how do you manage to arrange that both parties win the
game?"

In spite of my low spirits a smile flitted across my face.

"How can you imagine that? It is a game for us to play against
each other and not for each other. One of the parties must lose."

"And is the losing party happy, too?"

"No. He is unhappy. But he, in turn, may be the winner on
another occasion."

"Then why do you make one of the parties unhappy?"

To tell the truth, his question somewhat surprised me, and
I had to gather my wits to make him understand the situation.

"The thing is," I commenced, "that happiness means obtaining
a certain energy for the soul, and like every energy, this, too,
comes from a difference in levels, from the results that I have
achieved and not others."

"Explain this more comprehensibly."

By way of explanation I enumerated for him the decorations
customary in the Navy; I spoke about the power of the pharaohs,
the treasures of the maharajahs, then as an example I also mentioned stamp-collecting.

"But what would be the point in being decorated," I said finally, "if the same medals hung on everyone's chest? What would
make the Indian maharajah happy if everybody had as many
diamonds as himself, or the stamp collector if everybody had a
'Mauritius'?"

Zatamon shook his head.

"As far as I can see, to become happy the unhappiness of not
only one person but of very many people is necessary."

"Happiness, as energy, is in proportion to the level attained,
which can only be measured by our position in relation to others.
The more people one stands out from among, the more happy
one is; and it cannot possibly be imagined otherwise. On the
other hand, it is precisely this desire for happiness that prompts

us to create and work. Without this we would be clambering about in the trees to this very day."

This, too, Zatamon classified as absolutely incomprehensible, and then came to the conclusion that happiness was an empty and unattainable castle in the air.

"Because," as he said, "it stems from the nature of things that at most only one man can rise above everyone else; that is, all the others are obviously unhappy."

It was his opinion that happiness could not even exist, because if it once existed it would cease to be.

"What do you mean by that?"

"Each of your obsessions ceases to be at the moment of realization, and your imaginary aims, which in general you call cultural endeavors, differ in this very point from real targets. A hungry man suffers as long as he is hungry, but he is pleased when having eaten his fill, and it doesn't diminish his pleasure if others, too, eat their fill, as the stomach is satisfied not by the hunger of others, which is by the concept of a difference in level, but by the physical fact of satiation. Your soul, however, feeds only on the hunger of others. The admiral would be unhappy if everybody were to become an admiral, and the stamp collector would commit his album to flames if a generous government in its efforts to further common happiness provided a 'Mauritius' for everybody. Just as love's becoming universal would mean its ceasing and turning into the kazo, in the same manner happiness would not exist any more if everyone was able to achieve it. This is also why your philosophers rack their brains to discover a 'happy state.' Well, is it possible to imagine a thing that exists only as long as it does not exist?"

I was about to interrupt, but Zatamon stopped me with a gesture and continued: "But let's speak of whether these cultural requirements can be satisfied materially at all. That is, your soul's endeavor is never to help, but to rob others, as this provides the difference of level. But the stomach of your soul is a bottomless sack, the filling of which knows no boundaries. The cubic capacity of our actual stomach is defined. It cannot hold more than a certain quantity of food, and to overburden the stomach is just as painful as hunger. We feel equally uncomfortable at temperatures below or above a certain range, but cultural requirements have no upper limit. Though your kings travel by coaches of gold and wear robes of state heavy with all kinds of jewels (which are of course unnecessary), they still don't permit the people to use their remaining energy for the benefit of their own physical well-being, but force them to build a pyramid for themselves, or wage war to reduce other peoples to destitution as well. The soul drives you only to trample upon each other and never to help each other, and completely aimlessly into the bargain, as the aim is unattainable."

"You say that happiness is something like repletion," Zatamon continued. "But it is only the appetite of your body that can be satisfied—this, however, can be fully satisfied. Were this your goal, then judge, policeman, soldier would all become unnecessary and all goods could lie unguarded in the warehouses, since for a kazo man there is no sense in using the labor of his fellow men to make unnecessary things for himself or shifting manpower from making what is necessary."

"You once mentioned," he went on, "that money ensures the equitable distribution of goods. On the contrary: it is only an unjust distribution that needs to be ensured by distributing the purchasing power in advance. The real aims can easily be reached without controlling distribution by force; why, our bodily needs are so small—it is only the fantasy of the soul's happiness that pushes you into squabbles. The soul is the primary cause of the laws of continuous robbery and struggle."

I had no wish to permit such a false interpretation of the soul and contradicted Zatamon by saying that the happiness of the soul could be found not only in rising above others, but in self-humiliation and self-denial as well. As an example I spoke about Buddhism, which endeavored fully to conquer all desires. I mentioned the yogis, who did not wear woolen clothes and were able to do without nourishment for weeks, while they soared high on the wings of the soul away from the earth that is weighed down by desires.

"I'm not at all surprised," Zatamon answered, "that the soul is such a confused thing and is in contradiction with itself; all the less so because in the happiness of the maharajahs and the yogis it is only you who see a contrast, and you who believe that love and hatred are opposites."

"It would be much better," he continued, "if the yogi did not soar but remained on the earth and peacefully consumed the meat of the holy cow, because no soaring could change our physical existence and from the point of view of the kazo it is equally harmful if we torment our own body or that of someone else, for all bodies are alike and part of reality."

"The fact," Zatamon went on, "that the soul drives you either above or below each other likewise proves that it does not make for balance and harmony, but jolts you away from them."

He found it telling that the maharajahs haunted the very places where the souls of self-effacing holy men soared high while their bodies starved and were bitten by lice.

"Our bodies consist of atoms," Zatamon repeated, "and cannot be changed by any kind of soaring of the soul. With kazi intentions, however, it is possible to imagine that we do not need air and food but starvation and diamonds; we can even manage to make our pleasures unnatural, which you very aptly call 'happiness' as distinguished from natural pleasure, but our lungs and digestive organs cannot be altered in any way. Nor is it necessary. Indeed, it is easy to satisfy the will of nature, whereas to produce diamonds or pyramids or gold coaches is troublesome and can be done only to the detriment of our stomach and lungs."

In general Zatamon was incapable of finding any difference between the life of the maharajahs and that of the holy men. He termed both equally sick.

"What, then, is your actual opinion of the soul?" I asked as the debate had grown a little long and I wanted to hear the results briefly summarized.

"The soul is a disease because it is in disharmony with the body. As long as you are unable to transform the body biologically and become attuned to it, it will continue to cause your ruination."

For a few minutes I struggled with myself. I wanted to respond sharply, although I knew that by doing so I would achieve nothing. My ability to curb myself was mainly due to the recognition that in the course of our debate we had completely digressed from the point and my most important question was still unanswered.

Zatamon was already at the door when I shouted after him that I wanted an answer to one single question only.

He turned, and I asked him: "Tell me what keeps the kazo spirit in you? If you have no laws, no judiciary, and no education, what is it that still maintains what you call kazo and equilibrium?"

"What maintains the equilibrium? Of course, the equilibrium itself! Only different weights sway the scales."

So once more Zatamon wanted to elude me with a cheap aphorism! This obstinacy began to awake the suspicion in me that he was possibly not so uncomprehending as he appeared to be, but was concealing deeply hidden secrets from me. But now I had already decided not to let him beat about the bush. He had either to answer my question or tell me that he could not reveal the secret.

"Are you willing in the end to answer my question?" I asked him straight out.

"What actually is it that you do not understand?"

"I do not understand this total cooperation! That here nobody has deviating, individual aims of his own. How can one imagine law without law and morals without morals? Where is the force that ensures the observation of these courses?"

"I don't know," he replied, "how you can ask such a question. What forces the planets to keep to their elliptic orbits if not the planets themselves—whose force of gravity operates this way?"

Then Zatamon explained that it was not the force of gravity that was a separate thing but the planet itself—that is, everything that happened happened as it did because everything that is exists. He continued: "Force would be needed only if you wanted to shift them to another orbit, as force is necessary only to knock something out of its equilibrium. You take the kazo for the steel-firm law of cooperation and look for a legislator, whereas it simply exists. Complete order can result only from things as they are, as everything will surely be in accord with this. In physics it is called the line of least resistance, which for a freely falling body, for example, is the vertical. All legislature is only a harmful intervention that is a source of imbalance, errors, and insecurity. In a word: kazi."

"Perhaps we should not speak in parables of doubtful origin drawn from the universe," I answered impatiently. "It might again lead our debate onto sidetracks. I want to become enlightened with regard to your social system."

"You speak as if man did not belong to the universe. For you the comparison is reality, so it is small wonder indeed if you consider your nonexistent problems to be real."

"What do you mean?" I asked. "Don't you mean that gravity and the kazo . . ."

"But yes. Man lives within the universe—that is, the kazo is neither a law nor a custom but the reality of the universe itself, with which it is also essentially identical. Everything that exists in the world exists in accordance with the kazo as the kazo is reality. Anything in addition to this does not exist—it is kazi which is nonexistence itself."

I pondered Zatamon's words for a long time. As became a correct gentleman, I wanted to understand his words and not discard them. Again and again I thought over every sentence conscientiously, but the more I racked my brain the more confused it all seemed to me.

Finally I was forced to conclude that their principles were nothing other than half-baked nonsense, completely beyond comprehension to the sober British attitude, and I may claim with a clear conscience that any educated citizen of my country would have come to the same conclusion in my place.

Thus from the whole conversation I came to know only what they lacked and what they were incapable of. Somewhat meager information for understanding the secret of the Hin life.

I decided to give up my research for the time being, relying upon time and my own experiences to solve my problems.

CHAPTER

6

The author moves out among the Hins and practices medicine. He learns of the Hins' advanced medical science. The author, though innocent, becomes involved in murder, and through that he must leave his post. The Hins have no consideration for the soul of children. The author becomes a weaver, but boredom almost causes him to drift into catastrophe.

ONE DAY ZATAMON TOLD ME THAT AS HE SAW IT I HAD already learned enough and could be a useful member of Hin society. He observed that although the structure of my brain did not seem sufficiently clear, and I would probably not attain the state of perfection needed for the fullness of life, if I had the will to practice I might become of use.

He added that he had already come into contact with several undoubted Behins who, even though they lacked the kazo state, had nevertheless been able to perform the tasks of life.

They, of course, had stumbled about, as their brains did not possess the natural compass, but the methods they learned by watching others had still shaped their behavior, so that a non-medical layman did not even notice their organic deficiency, in the same way as a deaf-and-dumb person is able to learn to speak from watching the lips of others, although he would never experience the essence.

So Zatamon informed me that I could leave the institute and commence the work of life.

Thus dismissed, I was filled with anxiety concerning my future. I stood bewildered; I asked what I was to do. After all, I didn't know where an employee was needed or where they would be willing to employ me.

Zatamon, however, replied that I should go wherever I wanted and I should not expect to be directed. Everyone knew best himself what he was able to do: it would be kazi to interfere in the business of others.

His words, of course, not only failed to reassure me but filled me with utmost insecurity. In my country, one's school record has a precise and definitive value; the citizen knows what it entitles him to, who is in charge of which company or government office, and who among his own friends is on good terms with that person. But what was I to do here, in this land of anarchy, cast as I had been to uncertainty?

The first problem was where to live. I already knew how to obtain lunch and clothes, but I was completely ignorant in matters of housing.

After leaving the hospital I loafed about in the neighborhood for a number of hours and then went off to the forest. However, the coolness of the evening drove me back.

Finally I gathered up all my courage and entered a house. I thought I would ask one of the occupants to give me shelter for the night. The Hins readily host people. (Not that I can really call them "hospitable.") Just as I had succeeded in finding lodgings after my arrival, I might be successful now, too.

I went from door to door. Of course, none of the doors was locked and the occupants did not even glance up at my entrance. They take no interest in anyone until he speaks. Furthermore they have no knowledge of undesirable guests in the same way that they have no knowledge of desirable guests, either.

The first person whose flat I entered was reading, and I did not want to disturb him; the next one lay on his bed already undressed. In two flats I found nobody at home. Finally I asked a third to give me lodgings.

"Why?" he asked. "Is there no empty flat in the house?"

"Well, is there?" I asked with interest.

"That I cannot know. Go and see."

"Well, who keeps a record?"

"Nobody," he replied and turned away.

Had I produced my Belohin certificate I might have received some information, but I did not dare show it too often; for I had been dismissed as a useful member of society, and while looking for employment I did not want to draw attention to what I did not know. Left to my own devices, I had to learn everything by myself. I turned, therefore, without a word and went through the entire building.

In each and every flat there was indeed someone, or at least the furniture showed that it was inhabited. Finally, on the second floor, I saw a slip of paper hanging on one of the doors:

I HAVE MOVED OUT.

I turned the handle and, of course, the door opened. I looked around, but every sign indicated that somebody still lived there. All the furniture—chairs, bed, everything was in place. There was the telephone, the lamp, and everything was exactly the same as in the room in which I spent my first night in Kazohinia. Then what did the slip mean?

I looked around helplessly, but since for the moment there was nobody to be seen inside, I pulled the bed, which was made, out from the wall and threw off my clothes. Then I went to the bathroom to take a warm bath, as I had become quite chilled in the forest.

For half an hour I waited for the host, but eventually I became very sleepy, so I went to bed.

It only came to light some days later that the room indeed had no occupant, and the slip of paper was put outside for that very reason, because otherwise nobody would be able to distinguish a vacant flat from an occupied one.

The following morning I had a more thorough look around the room.

Besides the apparatus I already knew, I discovered some buttons on the wall. Each bore an inscription. One operated the air-conditioning, a second the window, a third the fan. One button read, "Announcer." I pushed this one, too, and looked around. Nothing happened. But ten seconds later I was startled by a voice behind me:

"All right."

I turned round, but there was nobody near me. The voice had come from a loudspeaker on the wall.

I waited to see what would happen next but nothing did.

To and fro I walked, pondering my future. I lowered the windows and was surprised to see hundreds of cars slipping along below while the elevated railway snaked past above me. And I heard not a single sound. It was as if I was watching a silent film. In the meantime, the loudspeaker had slipped out of my mind entirely.

Now, however, something clicked behind my back. I turned. A flap door opened downward from the wall and a small metal cylinder protruded from it.

I went over and took hold of it, and it came off.

While turning it over I realized that it could be opened.

Two small containers fell out. One held milk, the other a few pieces of fruit.

Thus, by pushing the "Announcer" button I had announced that the occupant of the room was home.

It seemed therefore that for the time being everything was in order. The uneasy feeling of uncertainty diminished slightly. Why, I could live here for any length of time without having to mix with the Hins—and that thought positively scared me. Living among these people one could never be sure when he was violating the kazo.

After breakfast I again paced back and forth, almost satisfied knowing that I could live in peace. Later this became somewhat boring, and I was almost glad when the door opened and a Hin entered.

He was a little surprised, I thought, that the room still had an occupant. But then, unperturbed, he went up to the wall, pulled out a vacuum, and cleaned the room with it. He washed the bathroom with a hose, put my breakfast capsule back into the wall, started the ventilator, then left.

Silence reigned once more, and I set about my investigations anew.

Behind a swing door in the wall I discovered a large opening, which developed into a chimneylike passage. When I went down to ground level I came to know its function: it ended in a big container into which they threw their laundry, to be carried off from time to time. Beside the container, however, clean linen for public use was displayed.

Returning to my room, I lay down for a while, but then, becoming bored, I went out and sauntered about the streets between the gray, monotonous walls and ungainly trees. At noon I had lunch in a dining hall and thought about how I should spend my afternoon in order to use my freedom pleasantly.

I thought I would go to the seaside.

When I got there, I walked along the promenade and then climbed a rock. The eternal surge of the infinite sea slowly made me drowsy. So I slept for an hour, and when I awoke I was haunted again by the problem of what to do until evening.

Devoid of ideas, blankly I walked for another hour before sitting down on a bench. From sheer boredom I began to twiddle my thumbs. This I practiced backward and forward alternately.

I got out my watch several times to see when it would be evening so that I could have dinner. Now setting out for a walk, I counted my steps, measuring the distances in every possible direction and regretting that I had been unable to sleep longer.

I was almost glad when I felt hungry. Eating was always a change. I went back to town, had dinner, proceeded home, and in the dead silence I returned to bed.

After breakfast the next day the cleaner came again. He looked at me in astonishment and asked: "If you work in the afternoon why don't you ask them to send the afternoon cleaner?"

I stammered something or other in confusion, this and that— I had forgotten—and he promised that he would report it. After this, I made myself scarce and rambled about aimlessly late into the evening. Before noon I managed to sleep for an hour on one of the lawn chairs on the river bank. I got sleepy even after lunch, but I did not dare to lie down in case I should not be able to sleep at night, which would have been still worse.

Thus the thought slowly took shape in my mind that I ought to commence some kind of work, as idling cannot be endured for long.

What could I try? I am a surgeon, so my first thought was to look for a job in my field.

The next morning I went out to the hospital and there tried finding the administrative department. No one had ever heard of such a thing, though—they said the hospital was for curing patients.

On seeing a Hin who appeared to be a doctor, I said that I myself was a physician. I referred to the medical qualification I had gained at Oxford University, but he did not know what that was. I was compelled to reveal my origins, my previous activities; I had to explain the essence of a diploma, but then he asked how people could establish what someone else knew.

"Because," as he put it, "knowledge lives inside the man, there is as yet no way of ascertaining it from without, but it is not even necessary, as that in which one has acquired proficiency is in any case known by the person concerned. Anyway, I seem to have nothing to do with all this. So tell me, what do you want from me?"

"I should like to be given a job here so I can work."

"That is entirely your business," he replied. "Tell me what it is that you want from me."

Now I gazed. Had I lived among them even for ten years,

I could not have become fully acquainted with their complicated customs.

"Understand," I said, "I am a surgeon and wish to work."

Again he replied that that was entirely my business!

"So there is no system?"

"It depends on the faculty. We cure each disease according to its own system."

My patience was exhausted. After all, incomprehension, too, has its limits. I simply stated: "I want to work here and I am asking you to acquaint me with the work here."

It was only impatience that had put these words into my mouth, and at that time I was unaware that with this I had found the key to the whole of life there.

Without the slightest surprise my medical colleague took my arm, explained the operation of all the department's equipment, and summarized their procedures.

This much I can say: although I had seen many wonderful things among the Hins, I could not in my wildest dreams have imagined anything like this hospital and while my colleague led me about I was more and more amazed.

This was not actually a surgery ward I found myself in. They classified diseases according to a system that was completely new to me. Nor was this complex of buildings all that similar to a hospital.

When we think of a hospital, we think of clean wards painted white. Looking at the enormous buildings, I, too, thought that at least twenty thousand patients lay there.

It only came to light later that the wards, or, as they called them, "sleeping rooms," occupied no more than a very small part of the buildings and there were altogether no more than four- or five-hundred patients.

This was for two reasons: first, as a result of extensive preventive measures, illness was much rarer among the Hins; second, by means of their extremely advanced medical treatment, they recovered comparatively quickly.

The largest part of the hospital really resembled a huge plant. Together, my colleague and I walked through an endless row of rooms, large and small; we moved over balconies with rubber floors, went up and down spiral staircases, and elevators and moving sidewalks whisked us away to the vast maze of machines and equipment.

Yellowish steam coiled upward from a wide glass chimney, beneath and over us hissed silvery coiled pipes, motors shrieked, compressors purred, luminous signals flashed, indicators danced; from the eye of a rotating telescope a red beam of light swept over an endless belt carrying steaming bottles. Elsewhere, a metal basket floated above our heads with a motionless human body inside. The lid of an immense metal drum opened, blinding flames shot out, the metal basket carried the body straight into the flames, and the lid closed.

I was convinced this was a crematorium and was astonished to discover that it was in fact a disinfector, and that the flame was not a flame but radiation that destroyed certain viruses and germs but had no effect on human cells, as the patient had earlier been submitted to an immunizing procedure!

Despite their inane behavior, these people are at least a hundred years ahead of us in medicine. Barely able to even memorize the names of their machines, I was terrified to ponder what I might do here that would allow me to work without revealing ignorance—lest I should afford them a basis for their groundless national pride.

To avoid shame, I lied that I specialized in dentistry. After all, the technology of filling and extracting had perhaps not developed to such a degree of wizardry that I should not be able to learn it.

Crestfallen I listened as I was told there were no dental diseases; the food turned out by the dining halls, under the supervision of physicians, was at the same time a medicine that prevented the development of certain diseases, including dental ones.

Now I was only trying to think of a good pretext for making my escape, but all at once my colleague said it would be best if

I worked in the sleeping rooms and assisted at those operations that came closest to my knowledge.

His malicious remark was definitely an affront, but his features betrayed neither malice nor any other kind of emotion. I knew I could not go back to dreary idleness and so, though deeply ashamed, I accepted his offer.

I was assigned to a room, and so I put on a standard white smock and tried to work. Of course I had to ask questions at every turn.

The very first day, my colleague asked me my name. I was surprised at their taking any interest in the identity of the employees at all, but it turned out that they wanted to have the requisite technical journals sent to my address.

When I told him, he said that it was not a name, as it had no connection with me!

I was astounded that he dared to make such an assertion. After all, who knew better than I what I was called. But he repeatedly claimed I had no connection whatsoever with the word "Gulliver"; this was no more than a senseless pile of letters, and he would help me to recall my name.

Had they not considered laughing a Behin activity, I really would have had a good laugh. He, however, in the most natural tone in the world asked for my date of birth and the address of my flat; then, converting my birthdate to their chronology, he said: "Well, you see, your name is Zamono Nital."

Open-mouthed I gazed at him. After lengthy reflection I managed to work out the meaning of my "name." The letter "Z" indicated that the word was a personal name, while the other letters conveyed the data concerning birth, gender, and professional knowledge, whereas the second word was my telephone number, which was identical to my address. Thus the Hins, when they change their address, also change half their name.

I wondered why the Hins did not have names of their own, while my colleague wondered why we had no name of our own but only an irrelevant, senseless pile of letters.

"What is a name for," he asked, "except to give us an idea of the person?"

I retorted that objective data can't shed light on a person's character anyway. This I could express only in a roundabout way, as they had no word for "character," and even then he replied what a strange land my country must be, for among them everyone breathed oxygen and fed upon carbohydrates and proteins.

But as far as they were from understanding personality, I was just as far from their practical knowledge.

As I have already mentioned, I worked in the sleeping rooms, but my work did not extend to more than nursing.

The sleeping room was approximately equivalent to the concept of our wards. It was only now that I came to know why they still called them sleeping rooms.

They make every patient sleep whose disease entails pain. They drive an electric pin into the nape of the patient's neck, from which he sinks into a deep sleep. The pin is taken out only on full recovery, or at least after the painful period is over. The Hins simply sleep through their sickness, and while asleep they are artificially fed.

Once I took a cardiac case into surgery and was amazed to see how they removed his heart. They connected tubes to the aorta, which issued into an electric pump and were kept warm; then they temporarily stitched up the patient's body and the pump maintained the circulation for days, while the heart palpitated in some liquid that was replenished every day. Later the heart was returned to its place.

I must admit that I would never have counted as a doctor here. Concerned that they would despise me because of my ignorance, I was ashamed even to ask questions: perhaps I would even be exposed to their rightful malice, as is usual among colleagues. Otherwise, in reply to my questions they only gave explanations with an indifferent, inscrutable face, from which I could make out nothing. And as for the fact that behind those wooden faces there was indeed no kind of emotion whatsoever, a European

could not be accustomed to this, anyway. I was always looking
for the impulses behind them as I scrutinized their features, and
from their coldness I concluded that they actually loathed me.
And in almost completely incomprehensible contradiction to
all this was their unlimited readiness to help me at every stage,
without a single smile of goodwill or sign of kindness apparent
on their faces.

Their willingness to help misled me so much that I also tried
to win their friendship, but all my efforts in this area were rigidly
and uncomprehendingly rebuffed.

They asked me to define more exactly what I wanted because
what I, after a confused roundabout description, called "friendship" was some sort of abstract concept and consequently could
not be provided.

I said in vain that I only wanted somebody to be with me, support me, and converse with me. They asked what he should do
and what he should converse about, and would do anything as
long as I said definitively what it was I wanted.

Regardless of how much I had already heard from them, I still
received their words like those of lordly aristocrats who use a
polite pretext to exclude an intruder from their circle. I looked
upon them as undecipherable, perhaps precisely because back in
my own country I had become accustomed to unenigmatic faces
concealing the greatest psychological complexities.

My position, which was in any case awkward, was made extremely unpleasant by the intellectual and social divide. When
in the surgery room the scalpel gleamed from one hand to the
other soundlessly and with the precision of clockwork, I merely
jumped around them like a scalded cat, and shame made me
blush whenever a voice cut into the stony silence, as it was always
meant for me.

And it was in vain for me to browse through the trade literature that the dispatch tube regularly delivered to my flat—as far
as I was concerned it might have been written in Martian. The
whole consisted of algebraic expressions, even for the medicines;

their effects were not described, only their chemical properties, of which I understood not a word. And my colleagues were as silent and sphinxlike as ever.

If they had at least chided me I would have borne everything more easily. But their detached, elusive, seemingly didactic tone, that vacuumlike intangibility of their soul, was getting on my nerves.

My situation was made utterly intolerable by a dreadful event that completely unsettled my Christian and humanitarian outlook.

We visited a dying patient. My colleague examined the sleeping man, then called another physician, who examined him again. Then the first stepped to the medicine cabinet and handed a vial to me to give him an intravenous injection.

As soon as I had injected the contents of the syringe into the patient it was to my greatest horror to see that death ensued with an immediate stiffening.

I rushed to my colleague, asserting that I had not been the one to change the injection, and he, with complete composure, told me that no change had taken place; the person in question had been a hopeless case and his life had therefore to be ended, so I should phone the Conveying Department.

I staggered. I was a murderer!

I stammered out a few words asking what the people belonging to him would say to such a procedure, but he replied that only a suit and a pair of shoes had belonged to him, and such things were always burned for reasons of hygiene.

People perished here without anyone shedding a single tear for them! No one knew this man's mother and father, nor did parents know their children, and as soon as the dying patient reached the point of death he was considered no more than rubbish to be removed!

"So you are able to deny the fundamental aim of the medical profession?" I asked after pulling myself together.

"What kind of aim do you mean?"

"To maintain life up to the last possible moment." My colleague stepped nearer to me with interest.

"Is that the aim of the medical profession in your country?"

"Why in my country? Everywhere. No other aim can even be imagined."

"That's a mistake. The aim of our profession is to save man from suffering. And of course, if at all possible, to give him back his health. And if that is not possible, we end his life without pain, not to cause him unnecessary suffering and ourselves superfluous work, which energy we would be withdrawing from treating others where success would be certain."

Although these cruel words were already enough to hurt my humanitarian feelings, my colleague went on: "Besides, there are cases when recovery can only be partial and would entail a life of suffering. Especially when the patient loses a part of his body for which there is no perfect substitute. For instance, if we are to remove only his heart or a lung, it can easily be replaced by transplantation or by an artificial heart or lung. Even an ear can be replaced by an artificial one that can be attached to any functioning nerve, and within a short period of time the patient will learn to hear again. But the replacement of an eye, for example, is only at the experimental stage, and the ocular prosthesis issued up to now can only be attached to an intact optic nerve and visual center. It is even worse when somebody loses a leg, and he would have to limp with an artificial leg forever. Obviously such a patient's life would be ended while sleeping."

I trembled with horror.

"I only wonder," I said, "that anybody dares to go into your hospitals at all."

"Why would he not dare when he knows that from the minute of his arrival all his suffering is over?"

"And the life instinct?"

"You must mean the vital instinct inherited from animal life. This atavistic attitude also existed here some thousand years ago, but today our instincts have, of course, adapted themselves to our present circumstances. You have mentioned that a tooth can still decay in your country. You know what pain this entails. One feels that the aching tooth should be pulled out, and indeed the decayed tooth will in no way cure itself, so it would only be logical that with the pain of the decayed tooth should go the pleasure of the extraction. Instead of this, the tooth reacted with racking pain even to the slightest touch, protesting against the only possible cure. So even in nature there is inconsistency."

"But the life instinct . . ."

"That was just as inconsistent. The patient, even raging with pain and in a completely incurable state, still insisted on his life."

"Because it is a natural instinct."

"That was appropriate to primitive conditions. Our civilization, however, changed our environment and our way of life. If our instincts adapted themselves today to the ancient environment and were not selected for the type of man suited to the present environment, this would indeed be unnatural, as an internal contradiction would destroy our life."

"And this is why you put people to death? This is the real contradiction!"

"This is why we don't commit murder. Under primitive conditions people had to fight against each other for food, while today we ourselves produce it. If our primitive instincts had not developed along with our civilization, we would still be killing each other today, whereas for food we must not kill but support each other in production. Yes, we would kill, without even knowing why, under artificially concocted pretexts, but by keeping the hopeless patient alive we would compel him to continue suffering. Well, this would be a contradiction."

"You speak of contradiction when you serve life by ending it?"

"The opposites are not life and death but life and suffering."

"Why, then, do you cure at all? If your aim is purely to avoid suffering, why don't you put the newborn baby to sleep and then immediately to death? After all, going by your principles we inevitably arrive at the conclusion that the most perfect being is nonbeing. And, indeed, in nonexistence there is no contradiction, while in your thinking there is no end of them."

"We have made life safe and abundant and it is worth being born into it and recovering. The patient is brought to us by his healthy instinct that is adjusted to the environment because he knows that we shall cure him and bring him back to a painless life and, if his future life is threatened with suffering, we shall cure him by giving him a painless death. Your hospitals, on the other hand, are torture chambers left behind by a primitive age. I wonder how anybody has the courage to enter them."

Of course, his words not only failed to convince me: I became even more horrified by this rigid and ruthless way of thinking, according to which human life was not one bit more sacred than that of beef cattle. Indeed, it is only a soulless creature that can without protest tolerate that the individual's most elementary right to life be trampled into dust.

I could not stay there a minute longer. I rushed out and traveled a long way from the towns, and once I arrived in a place where nobody could see me, I threw myself to the ground and begged the Lord of Heaven to forgive the immeasurable sin this heartless, vicious, murderous race had involved me in against my will.

With this, however, the cup was full. Somehow I had to switch over to an occupation that might fall within my field but where I would at least not be required to kill.

In the end, an excellent solution presented itself as the thought flashed through my mind that I should matriculate at their university: there I would be able to spend my time as a passive student. With this I not only thought I could solidify my position among them and dispel my boredom; I was mainly led by the thought that later, on returning home, I should be able to do valuable service to my country and Christian civilization if I could give back life to those of our soldiers who at that time seemed hopelessly wounded.

According to my rough calculation, if we were able to extend the life of every British sailor even only twice before final death in action, His Majesty's Navy would be able to inflict about 70 percent more casualties to the vile enemies of my country and civilization.

As I told my colleague, I realized that my knowledge was incomplete, and so I wanted to study further at the university and asked for his consent, to which again I got the reply that that was my business. So I announced my withdrawal, my post was taken over by a Hin, and I went to the university.

There I entered into an enormous complex of buildings where all kinds of schools were grouped together. I could not even establish which belonged to the school and which were unaffiliated. We are accustomed to buildings that are grouped together and closed in by fences. Now, the Reader should imagine a group of buildings with gardens, which are neither separated from the pavement nor divided from each other by any visible boundary and there is no difference between street and yard.

To this day I do not know on what territory I was standing when I caught sight of a man pushing a handcart with a male corpse lying on it without any shroud.

I started at the sight but I was already accustomed to finding no shame among the Hins, so I reconciled myself to the situation— indeed I was glad for the chance to find the medical faculty by following the cart.

Along I went after it. The cart approached a door that opened by itself. We entered a corridor.

To my great surprise I saw several very young children in the corridor, but the Hin pushed the cart along among them without any emotion. Some of the children turned their attention toward it, following the cart with interest.

This was too much for me to accept without indignation.

And this was only the beginning! The real surprise ensued only when the Hin pushed the corpse into a room. On three other tables in the room three human corpses were already lying, surrounded by innocent tots of both sexes!

And in the rubber-gloved hands of the children there were knives with which they dissected the intestines and private parts of the corpses without the slightest awe.

This astounding sight quite took my breath away.

Turning to an adult who was explaining something to the children, I asked whether they were to be physicians, although that in itself appeared strange to me—given that they were being inculcated at the age of seven or eight with what in civilized Europe was revealed to the developed mind only at the age of twenty.

I was told that they were not yet learning any particular profession—only the fundamentals necessary for life. The physicians were in the other building.

I could not help posing a question. "Then under what pretext did the corpse get into the hands of children?"

To this he replied in the most natural tone in the world that teaching commenced with this. One had to know one's own body first of all.

This obscene and vulgar trampling down of the children's innocence filled me with such a disgust that I left the room without a word and no longer felt any interest in the faculty of medicine, either. I would rather do without their science than suffer this frivolous outrage of the human soul even only as a passive spectator.

The days to come were again marked by hopeless boredom. As soon after breakfast as possible I had to leave my flat and take to the woods. If rain or cool weather drove me into town, hanging about the streets was even more dull. I was surrounded by tens of thousands of people and still I felt perfectly alone.

My only pleasure was to watch my stomach—whether I might be able to eat something. Hunger and its appeasement were the only variety in my life.

If I was sitting I stood up, if I was standing I sat down, and I was continuously thinking about what I could while away my time with. Regrettably the pen can only describe the horrors that actually happen, although it is more horrible than all of these if nothing at all happens, so to those of my Readers who are surrounded by the colorful and varied British public life and have no knowledge of this, I depict it in vain.

Exiled into nothingness, that was my fate. I should have looked for an occupation but was unable to participate in the Hins' vicious and inhuman life. I wanted work that would be naturally independent of their offensive customs and that I would be able to learn without any special grounding—something, at any rate, that I simply had to do, because things could not continue in this way.

Great Britain is famous for two things: for her navy and for her textiles. The Hins had no marine service but they did have a textile industry.

This was how I came to think I could be a weaver. At that time I still foolishly believed that this would dispel my boredom.

Why should I bore the Reader with the details? After all, such things don't really exist here. Life here does not take place, it only is. When one has been born, one *is* until one dies, then others *are*.

I asked for the address of the textile mill (there was only one of each type of factory, though this one was colossal) and located it.

I found myself in a twelve-story building with glass walls that extended farther than the eye could see, and there I told the very first Hin I saw that I wanted work there. (By this time I had managed to acquire their mannerisms.)

They assigned to me a foreman who took me by elevator to the seventh floor, which consisted of a single vast room about half a mile long—but only twenty paces wide—in which approximately ten thousand strange but completely identical power looms were spinning away. Between the endless rows of machines was a wide corridor. We proceeded on a soft, springy, rubber floor underneath a ceiling that comprised a single, butter-yellow, porcelainlike surface; and on both sides of us the sunshine, filtered through the opaline walls, produced the most perfect lighting I have ever seen.

The foreman led me to the machines and explained how they worked.

Everything went smoothly indeed. My work consisted of looking after sixty power looms. The warp threads came down from above through the ceiling to the machine; the supply was never exhausted because up there, by some process unknown to me, they were being spun continuously. In short, my machines consisted of shuttles whisking to and fro, and I had no need even to change the bobbin, as it was transported by an endless band also coming down from above to the shuttle magazine. When the thread ran out, it was replaced automatically.

At home this factory would have been considered a real wonderland.

I do not know what kind of material was used, but while I was there not a single thread ripped, although the shuttles worked at least five times faster than at home.

When it was ready, the textile then flew through the floor to the finishing shops where—through rows of shearing, washing, ironing, brushing, and other machines—it passed down from floor to floor, then to the tailors' workshop, where a squeezer cut the forms in a single pressing and let them down to the "sewing" shop, where a machine that replaced the sewing machine, proceeding along the edges of the cloth, glued the pieces together. This bond was stronger than if sewn.

The raw material for man-made fiber was pressurized up to the twelfth floor through a pipe; on the ground floor the finished goods—from handkerchiefs to winter jackets—were loaded into trucks, whereas I had only to see to the smooth running of the machines and replace any worn-out parts.

When the foreman saw that I had acquired the knack for this, he pushed a chair under me and left.

In the immense room, which extended further than the eye could see, about a hundred colleagues worked wordlessly away. There was no supervision at all. Most of my companions were sitting, nor did they stand up when the foreman appeared, which surprised me a great deal, and I drew sad conclusions concerning their discipline compared to the situation in my country where, in recognition of the value of order and labor, not even streetcar drivers were given anything to sit on while at work.

Among the Hins, it seemed, the only important thing was that the textile should be made, so they would have something to wrap around their soulless bodies; and as for loftier social aims that distinguished man from brute beast, they did not care a fig.

I could not help smiling at the thought of what a soldier would have made of such a soft, hedonistic Hin. Indeed, I was downright sorry for the strapping lieutenant commander who might have wanted to make men of them.

So this was where I was to spend my life.

In the early days I was not even bored because, although I did not dare ask questions, purely from watching the Hins I came to know a lot about them. At the outset I saw that everything worked here by itself. Nowhere could I perceive a central directing force, and yet some invisible bond united the big machinery into a clockwork of the utmost precision in which there was not a single dissonant movement; in none of the workshops were there too many or too few workers. No record was kept of the material; the Hins just processed what was furnished by the initial production unit, which in turn adapted itself to the capacity of the clothes depots. Also, the scope of the individual's activity evolved according to mutual agreement; there was neither election nor appointment; everything was done by the individual himself, and still there were no disputes.

I did ask how they could maintain the balance without coordinating and directing organs, and they in turn could not understand how the balance could be maintained if any external will meddled in the business. According to the Hins, everyone had his own *kazo* sense.

To me kazo appeared a sixth sense, and yet they never mentioned it as an ability but as self-evident reality.

"Why should an organizing force be necessary?" they asked.

"Anyone who knows the difference between an ironing machine and a spinning machine will not be in the least likely to arrive at the idea of ironing with a spinning machine."

They did not even understand what I had asked.

My new place of work was, however, in town and my flat was on the outskirts near the hospital. So I had to look for a new home, one close to my workplace. On the very first day after work I set out to find a new flat in the buildings nearby, but there were no empty ones.

Finally a brilliant idea occurred to me. After all, I already knew their customs a little.

In one building I entered a flat and told the Hin who lived there without the slightest introduction: "I wish to live here. Move out."

My Readers should try to imagine this happening in Europe! But I knew that with them there was no order, and based my calculations on this fact. And I was not disappointed.

The Hin without the least surprise or resentment asked: "Why?"

"Because I work in the neighboring textile mill, and this flat is more convenient for me."

The Hin, who mentioned that he worked at a dining hall in the third street from there, said he found my proposal kazo. He stood up and packed his things—which is to say, he put a toothbrush, some soap, and two books into a suitcase, and threw his bedclothes and underwear into the laundry chute. Then he left, abandoning the furniture, lamp, telephone, dishes, coatrack, and fitness equipment, as in the next place he would find the same; only the toothbrush and the soap are not left behind, for reasons of hygiene.

He then moved out, perhaps only to force someone else out of his home in the third street from there in the same concise, simple manner.

I cannot deny that life among the Hins also had its sunny side, but even so, there is no bloodless philistine in Europe who would endure this environment.

Their way of life always reminded me of distilled water, which although clear, has been deprived of the minerals necessary for life. One drinks and drinks and it still does not quench one's thirst.

After a few days I sank once more into deadly boredom. The machines in the weaving-room workshop buzzed the same monotonous buzz every day, and my companions wordlessly did their work; if I asked anything, I was brushed off with brief, official answers. Conversation was virtually out of the question. I performed my uneventful work with reflexlike movements while the soul-killing midsummer day's humming of the machines really got on my nerves.

I became weary of roaming about the bleak, undecorated streets, which were afforded no variety by a statue, a column, or at least an archway. The streets were numbered by characters: "ab," "ac," "ad," "af," and so on (as transliterated, of course, to our alphabet). They were all the same, and each was exactly perpendicular to or parallel with the next—with parks among them at regular intervals.

Shop windows and advertising were unknown there—there would have been no point in having them, anyway. Only over a few doors could be seen the laconic inscription, "Clothes Depot," "Cold Food," or "Electric Articles," but inside there was not a single soul except those people drawing on their self-imposed rations, whom I cannot call buyers.

This was the street as it was by day. And in the evening, everything was desolate.

There were no theaters, cinemas, or restaurants. Alcohol was known only as a medicine, and as far as religion was concerned they did not even know what it was, and if I had mentioned it at all, it is absolutely certain they would have taken me for a Behin.

At ten o'clock darkness fell on the streets. At night no kind of factory operated, and I had to go home, to the empty flat, where at best I lifted the dumbbell, but having nobody to compare my strength with, this too became infinitely tedious.

Summer followed. One day I noticed several people going about naked in the street; some wore sandals on their feet, and canvas bags hung from some of their shoulders. The first I took for a madman; the second, a nudist. Finally, pulling myself together, I asked one, but he did not even know what the word meant, and hurried on.

But then why did he go around naked? What kind of a sect was this whose ribald whims offended public morals?

Finally I also put this question to one of them, but he seemed to misunderstand me, because he said it was warm.

Shaking my head, I remarked that whatever the essence of their fad might be, nudity would be gravely punished in my country, at which he stared open-eyed and asked me how we could avoid nudity, as under our clothes we are all naked.

I did not even condescend to answer his stupid question, so he hurried on, and I became convinced that however strict discipline seemed to be with them, citizens still could not be left completely without reins because, as this example showed, without public order, even in the most disciplined society the licentiousness of the beast emerges, and sooner or later plunges culture to ruin.

Nevertheless, in a few days nudity also appeared in the factory. Every day more and more workers, both men and women, came in without clothes. Fortunately nobody forced me to follow this indecent fashion. I merely followed the example of those who put on lighter clothes, with trousers coming down to the knees, leaving only the calves uncovered.

Many times I went down to the sea, where lots of people were lying about, strolling, or bathing on the splendid beach. Most of them were naked there, too; they were in the same condition even on the streetcar. The only thing they carried with them was a strapped up, flannel-lined raincoat. They did not take any thing else, knowing that food could also be obtained on the beach; they did not smoke, and keys did not exist. Everyone went about separately and wordlessly.

Much as my sober European outlook found this frivolous and licentious custom deeply repulsive, I cannot deny that to begin with, the fresh sight of women's figures, steeled by sports activities, awakened desires in me. After a few days, however, nudity became so habitual that I took no notice of it, and women not only failed to be more desirable, I might even say they lost their charm. I realized that I was more intrigued by those women whose bodies were covered by the exciting veil of clothes. In nakedness, there was simply nothing interesting to appeal to a man's imagination.

But why did they undress?

For me this was the last novelty in Kazohinia. Now I knew all about their life, and from then on my life sunk into boredom.

For books I looked in vain because, as the Reader already knows, apart from technical, medical, physical, and chemical works, there was nothing. As for a work that might have had something to offer the soul, they had no idea about that.

Perhaps I need not even mention that they had no newspaper either, unless I counted as a newspaper the trade journal "Textile Industry" that appeared at irregular intervals, in which the factory laboratory informed the workers of the development of new processes and that the dispatch tube forwarded to my flat. This was my only reading, which I skimmed through of necessity, but I was even more sick of that than of my life.

Slowly I began to loathe the Hins. Not as if I had not loathed them up to then as well, but this feeling gradually became unbearable. When they passed by me tongue-tied or imparted to me with the most official brevity what they wanted to tell me, I felt an irresistible urge to slap them on the face just so that something should happen. I looked for pretexts to speak to someone. I asked about streetcars, streets, and addresses, as it was only to such questions that they replied.

My Readers, who have experienced no more than a taste of boredom, cannot even imagine what absolute boredom is like. Among us, boredom is known only in the context of abortive summer holidays, when city dwellers "rest" their nerves in farm-houses in the furthest reaches of the countryside. By the third day they are yawning amid the realization that it is much easier to go mad from boredom than from the most nerve-racking work. Notwithstanding this, even in the remotest village something happens; if nothing else, the Sunday service, an occasional game of cards with the parish priest or the pharmacist, a wedding, a game of bowling in a pub, a fight, or at least some gossip.

Here, however, there was nothing. There was no friend, enemy, pleasure, grief, rank, rich, poor, creation, progress—in short, no variety. To put it in another way—no life. What is life if not the difference between yesterday and today, and expecting some-thing of tomorrow? To stop is to die.

Zatamon was right: the Hins had indeed been successful in eliminating contradictions, and leveling everything out. In this "life" there were no peaks or valleys, love or hatred, white or black, only the infinite dead vacuum, over which the migratory bird fell dead. They had eliminated light because it had existed only together with the shadow. But how can we see if everything is equally bright? And if everything is silent, what are our ears for? Emptiness deafened, blinded, and paralyzed me. I was completely alone. Neither in the mill nor outside did a single soul speak to me. I could not play a game of cards, as they did not know how to play. I thought of painting cards for myself and playing solitaire, but where was I to hide them? Why, my flat was cleaned daily, and if they noticed my cards they would take me for a Behin.

Once I lost my self-control and began to hum a tune by the power loom. My companions ran up to me anxiously and I im-mediately fell silent. I even had to mind my breath.

I should have liked at least to live together with somebody. Only so there would be a living being in my room, even if he did not say a word. But nobody lived in one room with others, and I could not even bring up the subject.

The only thing my empty room was good for was having a

good cry in the evening after I had carefully closed the door. At such times I pressed my face into the pillow and wept so that my heart almost broke. But I had to take care that the Hins did not hear it, and it did not ease my mind, either.

I paced about like a caged beast of prey looking for air and life. Here I stood, in the biggest possible prison; I was free in vain—the air around me was not free. I withered away without companions, in the country of Nothing between the endless funeral dirge of the power looms and the deadly silence of my room, where my life energy was being wasted on an empty existence without once being able to say that I had achieved anything.

Once I caught a cold and lay for three days with a fever, and, believe it or not, for me sickness was a pleasure. Because finally something happened—even a doctor came to me to inquire after my condition.

Of course, he offered to have me taken to hospital, where I would regain my health in the radiation oven in ten minutes.

I did not agree. My condition was not so grave, I replied, noting I would also recover from it in this manner, and that he should only send me an extra blanket and examine me every day.

He shook his head and voiced his surprise at my insisting on such an obsolete cure, whereas in half an hour I could, if I had wanted, go back to the factory in full health, but he consented and visited me on two more occasions.

How I needed a little affection! But I recovered and the pretext for visiting me disappeared. Restored to physical health, I now became more ill than I had been with the fever.

In despair I saw how the days pass, one after the other, squandering my short, human life. They merged hopelessly into each other so that I did not know whether two months or two years had passed, for they had no calendar in our sense, either; there was no Saturday, holiday, anniversary, event, party, disaster; one day disappeared emptily after another without any landmark for the soul.

Once when it occurred to me that perhaps I would eventually have to die here without living a single day, I was so shocked that when I arrived home I could not fall asleep. My agony began with bitter sobbing, then despair so overcame me that I could not control myself any more. With a horrible fury I ripped apart the pillow that had been pressed tightly to my mouth; I sprang to my feet and, tearing my hair and beating my head with clenched fists, I wanted to smash all the pieces of furniture in my prison to smithereens.

At that time some great strength of mind still restrained me from committing any thoughtless act, but I felt that this was the final test of my self-control. If a change did not soon ensue, terrible things would follow.

The next day I could hardly wait for work to be over. I took the express train, hoping that the dizzying speed would distract me from my anguish, but instead it conjured a terrifying vision: the jaws of hell were before us and I was the driver, shooting with hundreds of women and children into damnation. Still reeling from this vision, after getting off the train I ran deep into a forest until I was sure no one was around. There I bellowed at the top of my lungs and went on running as far as my lungs and muscles could take it. Then, in a fit of rage, I dashed against a tree and stabbed at it repeatedly with my pocket knife.

But, I felt, even this postponed catastrophe for no more than a day.

On the third day I acquired a car from the garage—this car, too, was common property—drove it away, and smashing into a tree I broke it so that I fell against the windshield and my face was injured. The next car stopped unprompted, took me away, and at a breakneck speed took me into town, and while my insignificant wound was treated the driver phoned a garage to haul away the damaged car. Then, seeing that I did not need him, he left me there.

Even in their dreams the Hins could not contemplate the idea that anyone would touch something with anything but goodwill and competence. So they dismissed me without a single prying or reproachful word, making me promise that if I had the slightest trouble with my wound I should report it immediately. And once again I stood aimlessly in the excruciating silence, all alone and with nobody to care for me.

And whatever I did, I could do it only to myself; whatever I did, nothing happened. I kicked over the traces in vain; there was no point, as there were no traces. It was as if I were pummeling the thin air. My life cried out without an echo and I had nothing to hold on to. I hovered in space where there was no upward or downward, forward or backward, only the unsatisfied desire for life kicking within my numbed being. Without resistance there is nothing to win, there is no excitement, there is no life.

And I saw clearly that of all my troubles, loneliness was the most unbearable. There was no one to love me, to take care of me. True, I did not have the worries they would have entailed, but that was all the worse. I needed someone to hold my hand and protect me. True, there was no enemy, but I would have preferred to have one. Maybe Zatamon was right in saying that love could only be brought into existence together with hatred. However, the void had to be filled with something, as it was unbearable in itself because there was no reality in it.

It occurred to me that explorers never set out for the Sahara alone. Not because of the dangers, but because human nerves cannot tolerate absolute silence, which in nature they generally never experience. I felt that my efforts were but the futile panting of the passenger in a rising balloon, one that cannot keep up with the thinning of the atmosphere.

I had to cling to someone, I had to snatch at a hand, as I felt clearly how I was drifting day after day toward an abyss from which, if I fell into it, there would be no recovery.

CHAPTER

7

The author becomes acquainted with a Hin woman in whom he wants to build a soul. His experiments have unfortunate consequences. He is hospitalized once more.

I WAS IN THE SAME MOOD WHEN THE NEXT DAY DAWNED. After work I hurried to the seashore, where I took a long walk. The soundless, amorphous mass of Hins teeming round me with such inexplicably strange, regular disorderliness brought an anthill to mind.

Seeing their cleverly attentive glances and in spite of all my earlier experiences, the desire to approach them awoke in me anew. That day I felt this desire even more keenly but just as I was about to speak, I was held back by the knowledge that if they were to refuse me on this particular day, my increased tension would reach breaking point and I would be carried away by stupidities. I was walking the promenade for the tenth time and evening was already closing in when bitterness drove me from their circle. To escape temptation and deadly disappointment I clambered up the rocks.

The air was soft and spicy, and the moon had slowly emerged from the water, broken into a thousand pieces on the waves, and gracefully performed the dance of the nymphs. The sea washed against the beach with its ceaseless murmur and then, dividing into innumerable pearls, fell away from the rocks. In the distance, strange birds circled in the sky and crickets chirped beneath the long-tressed trees. My heart was overflowing with intoxicating desire, the will to live. And below, the Hins were wordlessly walking, sitting, or lying alone, not deigning to cast as much as a glance at the poetry of nature.

Then I was cut to the quick by the knowledge that over this wide expanse of water, far away, my friends were having a fine old time at the club; the speakers in Hyde Park were expounding their views of the world; ladies were hurrying to the theater in enchanting attire; and glittering neon signs advertised the latest stars.

Helplessness twisted my heart. I struggled against myself for a few minutes longer, but by this time I was weak. I had to admit I could bear loneliness no more.

I scrambled down from the rocks, and all traces of my former inhibition disappeared.

On the beach there were already fewer people walking. On one of the benches lay a woman. Her light, one-piece suit made even more obvious the harmony of her clean Aphroditelike face. I approached. She addressed me: "Don't make me get up. The next bench is unoccupied."

"I don't want to lie down," I said firmly. "I should like to talk to you."

At this she immediately stood up.

"What do you wish?"

I pointed at the sea.

"Do you see the ocean? Do you feel the atmosphere of evening? Don't you find this rather pleasant?"

It felt extremely awkward trying to express such a sentiment with the Hins' deficient vocabulary, for there are but imperfect words for things exalted and elevating. To them, everything is simply kazo and kazi, which I was by now sick and tired to hear whenever I did.

"Yes, I do," she said. "It is pleasant. What do you wish?"

"What do you wish!" I said impatiently. "Nothing! Warmth! I should like to get closer to you!"

"Are you cold?"

"Not in the least!"

"Then why do you say so?"

Seeing those vacuous eyes, it came back to me how a woman had pulled off my trousers in front of the clothes depository, and I was convinced that here every woman could be had for money.

But in this desert where was money to be found? What a pleasure it was at home to buy gifts for our ladies of pure and fine spirit! What a happy feeling it was to deprive ourselves, to make sacrifices for someone beloved and to see how her heart filled with love toward us. But here, everything was ready-made, everything was the property of everyone. There was no money; there were no gifts, no sacrifices. How did a man love here, and why did a woman love?

"I don't mean that kind of warmth," I said. "I simply want your closeness. I want to hear your voice. . . ."

"Why?" she broke in.

"For your voice itself. I want to have somebody to whom I can talk not out of necessity but for amusement, about trifles, to make our life more pleasant."

"How do you mean that life would be more agreeable if we deprived it of its sense by empty conversation?"

This reply was more characteristic than anything else. The main impression of the whole of my stay here was that technique and perfect hygiene were present in vain, as the whole had no aim, the whole had no why or wherefore. And, to the Hins, this life meant life and they regarded ours as senseless.

But I thirsted deeply for pleasure and beauty.

"Tell me," I said in a trembling voice, "don't you feel at times that you need someone who appreciates you, someone to whom you can relate what pleases and displeases you; someone who is for you more pleasant than the others? I need somebody very much, to hold; someone to whom I can nestle close and with whom I can exchange tender words, and whose voice would quench my thirst. Look at the moon as it dances on the waves divided into a thousand pieces, look at the millions of stars, the evening, the sea, this endless night that drives people to each other and opens hearts to each other..."

"I don't understand," she interrupted. "Stop it! Time is passing without purpose whereas I have a wish."

A new quiver filled my limbs, more and more I was feeling that this disappointment would be fatal and the inner tension would burst its limits.

"I am at your disposal," I said, trembling.

"My desire has awakened, and apart from this I have still to give birth to two children. Are you available for sexual work?"

I gazed at her vacuously. I did not want to believe my ears.

"Well, isn't that what I've been speaking about?" I asked in bewilderment.

"No," she replied in an edifying tone. "You spoke of the sea, stars, moon, and night."

I was taken aback. I had reckoned with everything except this. And although I could have danced with joy, the quick confession produced strange, dissonant afterthoughts in me, similar to those I had felt when I heard that a gondola had been built to one of the steep crags of the Alps, the tourist dream of my youth.

Oh, how much sweeter were the kisses that I had taken from the lips of our tender girls in times past, at home, with whom I had spoken first about theater and fashion, and had then gotten to the point in an exploratory manner only weeks later, both of us blushing partly from shame, partly from desire.

How sweet and thrilling was the feeling of reaching what is far away, opening what is closed, chasing the hunted prize, until finally the gentle creature, after lengthy protestation, shut her eyes and panted, "No! No!"—and gave in. How is it possible to love without all this sweet struggle?

Desire, however, propelled me. Why, I had been thirsting for beauty for so long that even a morsel was a royal dish.

And lest I should also lose her, I began explaining that what

I wanted was far from the opposite of her aims, but rather a much more complete and perfect form of them.

Zolema (later it came to light that this was her name) looked at me inquiringly. Gently pulling her closer to me, I continued: "Imagine if the sun in the sky gave only light and no warmth."

"Without the warmth of the sun, human life would become impossible!"

"It would, wouldn't it?" I said enthusiastically. "Life can really be lived only in its fullness, because if any of the components is missing, it is no longer life."

This also Zolema found an unobjectionable and sensible statement in perfect harmony with the kazo, and I was glad to have found a bridge to their armored soul, and I began talking to her of the attraction that warmed hearts and made couples of men and women.

Who could possibly describe my pleasure when I saw that Zolema listened to this with sparkling eyes! Her attentive face came closer and closer to mine, she breathed more and more passionately, and then . . .

But this cannot be described so simply! What happened was something like when the rope is put around a condemned man's neck, and then the letter of reprieve arrives.

How it happened I do not know to this very day, but suddenly our lips met!

And Zolema did not resist . . .

Not only did she not resist, but it was I who had to ask of her that we should draw aside somewhere.

"Why?" she asked.

"Somebody may come."

"Anybody may come. It doesn't matter."

"But I don't want anybody to see us. I want to be alone with you."

"Why?"

My blood throbbing, I was not in any mood to enter into new explanations. I asked her to come with me to the rock, saying that otherwise I would not be able to comply with her wish. Zolema pointed to a nearby house.

"I would rather go there," she said.

I agreed. When we reached the house, Zolema led me into a regular flat that was like all the others. Inside, a Hin was sitting at a table having his supper. Zolema sat down on a chair; the Hin did not even turn toward us.

Some minutes passed in silence. Finally I asked Zolema: "Now what are we waiting for?"

"For him to finish eating. You see, he is hungrier than we are, so it would not be kazo to interrupt him."

I was compelled to wait. The minutes passed with nerve-racking slowness. The Hin eventually finished and began to tidy away the plates one by one, when Zolema interrupted him, after all: "Leave for a few minutes."

Now the man turned toward us.

"When shall I come back?"

"Take a seat on the bench in front of the gate. I shall let you know."

The Hin left, Zolema pulled the bed out of the wall, unfastened her clothes and without any prelude threw herself into my arms with such ardor that I must dispense with detail.

At that moment I felt the whole of my life there had been nothing but a nightmare, because, behold, I had found the philosophers' stone, the panacea, the Soul! Every single drop of my blood was in exultation. Emanating from the end of the dark tunnel with royal brilliance came light, voices, flavors, and my heart resounded with the soaring symphony of life!

(I assure the Reader that with regard to the moral aspect of my behavior I, too, had felt pricks of doubt, but it occurred to me that officially I would be announced missing, presumed dead, and if our laws and general practice found no fault in the living partner in marriage entering into a new relationship, how much more right had the dead to do so!)

Regrettably my pleasure did not last long.

After fifteen minutes, we left. Zolema told the Hin sitting on the bench that he could go back, and I asked her who the kind host was.

It came to light that she did not even know him, and that that was the first time she had seen him.

"Then how did you dare lead me in and send him out?" I asked in surprise.

She looked at me.

"You wanted nobody to see us, and you wanted to be alone with me!"

"And did he just at a word leave his flat?"

"Of course. You heard me ask him to do so."

I gazed silently.

Zolema, referring to the lateness of the hour, said she wanted to go home.

Naturally, I offered to see her home, at which she asked why I did not go to my own flat. When I explained that I would accompany her only as far as her flat, she briefly said that there would be no sense in my going out of my way. This reply started an avalanche of problems in me. Had it been said by another Hin, I would have ascribed it to their emptiness, but in light of what had just passed between us, I knew Zolema to be quite different.

So she was afraid to be seen with me! Perhaps she had somebody else!

I looked deeply into her eyes and asked her to tell me sincerely why she did not want me to go with her.

"Why should you come with me if we do not need each other any more?"

The innocent sincerity with which she said this, to my intense regret, convinced me of the situation. It partly reassured me, but at the same time it also threw cold water on my earlier belief.

But I did not give in. I felt that Zolema was the last experiment for me, and I could not let this hand drop. With a heavy heart, I had to revert to the old method, using my Belohin certificate. I may say I never loathed a piece of paper more than then—this ironic death certificate of sorts that certified for those who were truly dead the unfortunate fact of my being alive.

And yet, at that moment, I still believed it was Zolema in whom I would find everything if I did not lose heart before then.

So Zolema remained with me to teach me, and waited for my questions.

And I, in turn, drawing my hand through her arm and leading her to the seashore, spoke scintillatingly of the beautiful feeling that in my homeland was called love, and which was the summit of goodness and devotion.

Zolema said that this, in such a form, was a little confusing. She asked me to expound in more detail how devotion manifested itself. I in turn explained that due to a rising feeling within us we gave all that we had to the partner we had found and devoted ourselves completely to her.

This, Zolema called a very unfair procedure, because—as she explained—why should the beloved deserve more from than others? I told her in vain that the partner, too, gave everything she had, and what pleasures were caused by the mutual exchange of gifts. Zolema drew only the conclusion that two people were associating in order to take something from other people and give it to each other.

"It's a mistake to think that," I replied. "The poorest people also do so; they most certainly do not take from anyone else what they give to each other. "

To this, however, Zolema answered that there was no point in it, because what would we have gained if she had given me her clothes and I had given her mine?

"The stress is not on the practical value of the objects," I tried to explain, "but on the love that accompanies them, and that fills our souls with contentment."

"Then I definitely don't understand. If I ask what love is for, you refer to the giving of things, and when I ask why we should give, you revert to love. But where is the starting point that makes both things logical and necessary?"

I gestured desperately.

"It is essentially himself that the lover gives, and it is love and not sale and purchase."

Zolema became lost in thought.

"Then it is even more incomprehensible. To give something means that we part with an object that we hand over. But how could I hand over myself to you and part with my own self?"

"In the way that you were mine just now."

"Everybody belongs to him or herself. It cannot be imagined any other way. My hands, feet, and head are mine, and such an expression that somebody belongs to another would have no meaning."

"But you gave me your body."

"How have I given it? I still have it."

"I see you don't understand. Love is not an equation that can be proved."

"Then why do you deal with it at all?"

"Just because. The equation would have been solved long ago. But let me tell you everything. Among us, a certain feeling of want, similar to hunger, is innate with man, which makes us sick if we do not satisfy it."

"In the warehouses . . . "

"Don't interrupt me! It is not to be found in the warehouses. It can be given only by you. Don't look at me in such a surprise, yes, only you can give that. Because you are good, you stroke my hair, take my arm, and talk about all kinds of things."

"Of what do I speak?"

"All kinds of things. This is our springtime, isn't it?"

"It is summer now."

"But it is spring for us."

"Speech is for communicating existing things. How could I possibly communicate using it for something that does not exist?"

"But it does exist. Perhaps for the moment you do not yet understand, but if you can get close to me, you'll see. Come now, don't jump against my chest like that, in and of itself that makes no sense. Everything must come by itself."

Zolema promised that so far as my recovery depended on her, she would do everything, and asked that I, as a physician, should describe what she should do and how, about what she should speak and how, and whether it would be possible to work it out in advance for a month so she should also have time to rest.

"Stop it," I said irritably. "It must come from the inside."

A bitter dissonance mingled with my former, intoxicating, blissful mood, but on the other hand I felt that she did actually love me, though only subconsciously. How could she know the name of love if she had never heard it? However, I knew nothing for certain. She was mysterious, and this incited me all the more. Suddenly I felt I might have it in me to force Zolema to love possibly by delivering blows.

To regain my lost mood, I turned off the road with her. We climbed a promontory over the sea. On its summit, we settled on the fresh turf.

The dark silent sky was above us, the sea murmured beneath; a mild breeze fanned our faces with its intoxicating salty scent. Moonflowers shook their heads all around. There was not another soul in the vicinity, and most of the Hins had already gone home. Zolema's naked leg touched mine; slowly my spirits returned.

Suddenly I embraced her, lifted her, and sat her on my lap. When my hand brushed her breast I felt that she breathed more impetuously. Intoxication overcame me again.

Picking a moonflower, I placed it on her bosom. She kept silent, though her heart beat more quickly.

Stretching my hand toward the moon, softly, eyes shut, I commenced to hum the *Barcarolle* by Offenbach.

No sooner had I sung two or three bars, when Zolema's excited question interrupted: "Are you perhaps unwell?"

"No. I am singing."

"What's that?"

Again I became unsettled. This, too, I had to explain. But, possibly, there was still some inclination in these people toward the beautiful and noble, only they did not know. Perhaps I would be able to save a soul from the desert, and it would be mine.

I commenced to explain the essence of the song. I began with the chromatic scale.

She was unable to comprehend what the whole thing meant, why we called musical sounds only those that were in a certain, arbitrarily defined vibrational relation with one another, and what need there was to distinguish the sounds from one another in this way.

And once Zolema understood the essence of music she exclaimed: "But then it does not even exist!"

This was their general response. She could not understand why we had created things that did not exist in reality, so that something else could be created from them.

"What is the point in grouping the sounds according to such contrived rules?" she asked.

"Because music is beautiful."

"And what does beautiful mean?"

"Artistic."

"You equate one meaningless word with another, which, it seems, you need, because none of them has anything to do with reality. What benefit do you get from the arts?"

"Art is for itself, and the contradiction that art has no reason for existence because it cannot be eaten could only be made by an uneducated person. If it changed into bread and butter it would be no longer art."

"On the contrary, it is only man that is for himself. Any human creation can only be for man. The uneducated person is one who believes that it is worth bothering with things that exist for themselves, and even to adapt human life to them."

"You only think so because you were not educated in art. You were not imbued with a feeling for it."

"One must be educated only for untruths. One snatches one's

hand from the fire by oneself, and would only believe that a piece of copper is nourishing if one is educated."

She thought of the tonal scale as akin to us growing fruit for its scent or wanting to taste a ray of sun. Sound is for communicating thoughts, she asserted, not for creating unjustified systems and building yet another nonexistent level on top of it—namely, music. And then we ruminate and debate whether a musical composition in question was in compliance with the rules created by ourselves, which in fact did not exist, as they were only imagined.

I heard Zolema out patiently, let her have her full say. Why, she did not know anything! When she had finished, I again set about my beautiful soul-building work. I spoke about musical instruments. On the violin she heard me out; as for the horn, however, she remarked that it seemed to her that we did not know about silencers by which even the most ear-splitting noise could be reduced to a tolerable level.

We were back at the beginning again. Now I had to bring it home to her that we made music intentionally. This was quite a task. When she finally understood, she fell into deep thought.

"The noise of the machines in the factory is so insufficient that you also set up separate noise-making machines?"

I enlightened her that music was not made in the factories, but after work; from the peaceful parks came the sound of promenade concerts and enchanting tunes that reinvigorated the heart.

This Zolema simply did not want to believe. She said that to spoil the refreshing silence of the parks with the noise of machines was as barbaric as if we were to have smoke-generating machines between the bushes instead of enjoying the fresh air.

"So," she said, "you must have moved so far from reality into the mazes made by yourselves that you not only think the nonexistent exists, but vice versa."

"What do you mean by that?"

"For instance, that it is better to die than to live, that starvation is pleasant . . ."

"Don't think such stupidities about us!" I cried, but she continued:

". . . that the fevered patient should be put on ice; that shoes should be filled with sharp nails; that the thirsty be offered vitriol; that sexual activity should not be performed whenever we wish and with the person who presents himself and is capable of it, but according to other, fabricated regulations; that society is not for us to eat our fill and live in comfort, but for us to die or suffer privation for it."

In spite of her cold, strange demeanor, I felt love for Zolema more and more. Slowly I realized that I was hammering with my fists on barren walls, but it was at least some exercise for my flaccid brain—something I had yearned after for such a long time, and that was now precisely what kindled the flame within me. Her manner somewhat recalled the coldness feigned by our chaste and well-behaved girls who pretended not to understand, and knew that by enhancing the desire in their chosen partner they could induce him to make a proposal. For this reason my attraction to Zolema only grew. She was mine and yet she was not, so I had to win her; I had to reach what was distant, open what was closed, pursue what was fugitive. What I had not yet guessed was that there was nothing at all distant, closed, or fugitive about her.

I shared my convictions on the matter with Zolema, who replied that it was for this very reason that perfection remained unattainable to those in my country; for we pursued only what was out of our reach; the "existence" of these unreal things lasted only until we reached them. We ran not for the aim, that is, but for the sake of the running itself. She voiced her suspicion that we also imagined and projected into the distance things that were nearby so that we could live out our senseless habits in this way.

At that time I still did not believe that these words really reflected how she felt. I suspected I had missed something, but did not know I had missed it because I already had all there was to it.

In a roundabout way I tried to acquaint Zolema with the happiness of the heart. I described what complete and happy satisfaction could be derived from the knowledge that we had a soulmate with whom we could unite and find understanding.

Zolema listened to me attentively, then asked what "understanding" was called in our language.

"Because," she said, "if private parts are called 'understanding,' what word expressed understanding itself, and why was it necessary to call something by another name?"

I was astounded.

No words had ever missed their target more than mine. The Reader who from the foregoing perhaps considers the Hins somewhat strange but basically goodhearted, kind persons certainly cannot even imagine how many unkind, even coarse traits are hidden behind their seemingly clean Aphroditelike faces and high foreheads. I may say, I had not come across many seamen in the dockland pubs of Liverpool who could have matched the weaker sex among the Hins in being blunt.

I tried to explain that understanding was not what she had thought, but the concept of the union of souls, from which she drew the conclusion that the word "soul" represented our organs.

And when I finally managed to acquaint Zolema with the actual situation, she became deeply sorry for our women, who, it seemed to her, were languishing among males who were no more than lunatics, and in response to their desires received only nonexistent and stupid fantasies.

"So among you," she said, "if a woman decently and honestly calls upon a man for sexual work, instead of satisfying her according to the justice of the natural world, you will talk to her of 'heart,' 'affection,' 'understanding,' 'companionship of the soul,' and other nonsense."

These thoughtless words filled me with anger, and it was only my good manners that made me realize that I was faced with a lady. So I had to content myself with attempting to give a true description of the virtue of our patriotic ladies, who—as befitted their good education—first of all look for affection, chivalry, and decent character in a man. I explained that only an uneducated woman might commit such an enormity as to place bodily desires before spiritual things.

After a short while Zolema asked whether my parents belonged to the educated or to the uneducated classes.

Though the question had not been phrased in the most polite form, I tried to explain without any resentment that my good parents were the offspring of the best families, whose good manners were beyond any shadow of doubt.

At this Zolema asked how we multiplied. Coming to know that it happened in the same way as with anybody else, she again did not understand the beginning. She told me not to continue, because the matter was only becoming increasingly confused.

What caused the greatest suffering for me with Zolema, however, was that she never smiled at me. It was what I would have liked to achieve, and so my sense of futility and powerlessness filled me with despair. It was now that I understood the essence of hopeless love: the lover does not actually want one particular woman, but to reach the ideal through her, and his inability to win her over to this ideal drives him to impulsive actions.

One question gnawed at me. I should have come out with it, but I was ashamed. I felt awkward and childish, like one who gives his heart, and in the midst of humiliating himself receives as the only response from his partner the shock of objective soberness. I could think only in my own European terms and try to explain such a coldly immediate attachment from a woman, so the Reader should not be surprised that I began seeing all sorts of illicit scenery behind the action. (We can't possibly imagine the world without scenery, without art of our own making, can we?)

In short, jealousy got the best of me. "Maybe she has someone," I thought. "Why, the instinct has not disappeared from them, and it is impossible that attraction should not also be present in some form."

We set out homeward. For a long time I walked beside Zolema

in silence. When we reached the streetcar stop, the question burst from my lips: "Tell me, do you have a relationship with somebody?"

"What do you mean by that?"

"A man."

"The streetcar is coming, let's get on."

So she had secrets that she did not want me to know!

While we were getting on, thousands of suspicions flashed through my mind;, I imagined the most adventurous things, and decided I would not let her be elusive. After getting off she would have to confess everything.

And as for Zolema, we had no sooner sat down than she quietly commenced to give me a list of the people with whom she had performed "sexual work," and remarked that she did not remember most of the names as she had not asked them.

Everybody around us could hear her. I was burning with shame and public humiliation; the words cut into me like so many axes. I should have liked to vanish from sheer shame, although not a single face turned toward us in the silent streetcar.

At first I tried to warn her with a wink, but she did not understand this. I was compelled to ask her not to continue, at which Zolema immediately and without the least evidence of surprise fell silent and did not utter another word.

However, when we got off, I blazed forth at her in reproaches. I openly told her that her behavior had been most improper, and if she wanted to help me she should not do such things again.

Of course, now, she did not understand the origin of my question. Why did I ask if I did not wait for an answer, she queried. Coming to know that I objected only to publicity, she stated that it was now definitely beyond her comprehension as to why she should observe such complicated rules, which made no sense to her, but nevertheless she reconciled herself to the fact that I was a physician, so asked me to prescribe the cure more exactly—what she should do and how—and she would act accordingly.

With this, of course, the sense of powerlessness became even keener in me, and to avoid further mental blows, I hurriedly took leave of Zolema, asking only to let me meet her every day, to which she agreed.

I did guess something. Why, I had been told openly and plainly several times that for them there was no personality to which individual feelings could be attached, and therefore love could not exist; or, put another way, their love was not of this world, so I could never reach it. But at that time I still could not imagine it, as we cannot imagine beings who become warm in the cold, or put on weight as a result of starvation, or lose weight because of eating.

Everything simply appeared illogical and unimaginable. Tossing and turning at night in my bed, I wanted to assemble the factors into a logical, compact, and organically connected whole. I did so in vain, because even though a colorblind person may be persuaded by teaching that colors exist, a real feeling for them will never run in his blood; colors will never be a part of him.

The next day we met again at the beach. The conversation was slow to start, but I could not keep my feelings to myself. I complained with excited words that I had not slept.

I asked her to do the things that needed to be done at such times to make me feel better, even if she did not know love—to caress me and run her hand through my hair, and above all, not to think of any other man except for me.

Instead of answering, she asked why I equated love with compassion while I wanted not to support but to hinder her in life. Then she expressed her opinion that if we in Europe behaved in such a way toward the beloved woman, we would probably prevent those who were not loved from all sexual work.

These words hurt me deeply. Trembling with excitement, I asked her not to say such things. I made a vow to myself to try my best to fill her being entirely, so that finding everything in me, she would settle down and I should make further searching unnecessary for her.

With this, however, she wanted emphatically to disagree.

"You yourself have told me," she said, "that you are ill. So if love is indeed compassion, you should have supported me in finding a man more perfect than you."

"Silence!" I cried, covering my ears from the inconsiderate words. "You don't understand! You don't understand, so please don't speak about it!"

She, however, replied that, on the contrary, it was her duty to teach the Belohin—otherwise there would be no sense in our being together.

And with this, she also began explaining that my behavior was not only kazi, but I would also have compelled her to act in a kazi way, had I wished her to refuse any man who might have wanted to perform sexual work with her.

I was unable to control myself. My lips were trembling. Suddenly, turning mad, I slapped her on the face with all my strength. Zolema clutched at her face and looked at me in surprise. "You!" she said. "It hurts! Why did you do that?"

I could not bear it any more; I ran away. Zolema made no attempt to call me back. I knew everything between us was over. I was in a prison with closed walls, where I cried in vain and there was no understanding.

I had no idea what might follow. My brain was torn to a hundred pieces. I hated Zolema; her loathsome confidence made me furious to an extreme. In feverish pictures I imagined how I could put her to shame, though I knew it was impossible, as their emptiness was invincible. Then, all at once, I hated myself for being unable to understand the situation and draw the appropriate conclusions.

I do not know myself whether it was homesickness or the unconscious desire, the passion, that compelled me to return to the very place that recalled the most bitter memories—that drove me to the seashore the next day.

And then, unexpectedly, I again caught sight of Zolema. My heart leapt to my throat and I did not know what to do. Finally, to avoid shame and an embarrassing situation, I wanted to disappear in a hurry, but she ran after me and called to me to stop.

Blushing from head to toe, I stopped. Zolema then stated in the most indifferent tone that she had come at the usual time and was at my disposal.

With downcast eyes I asked her in a roundabout way whether she was not angry, and she asked me quietly to explain why I had hit her.

From her voice I felt that she was not angry, and did not even suppose that I had hit her out of anger. Anger was kazi for them, and they considered it as absurd as if one of our scientists intentionally wrote 5 in his calculations as being the result of 2×2. He would have been either wrong or a fool. For them, anger was no more understandable a concept than love.

"Why did you slap me?" she asked.

"Because I love you," I answered in a hollow voice.

"Do your people beat those you love?"

With some difficulty I explained that this love was different, from which she concluded that it seemed she had to remain with me. This made me very glad, although she had said so because she found it her duty to cure me of my "disease."

After some thought, Zolema said that it seemed to her that some sort of error had slipped into my therapeutic course of treatment, for ever since we had been experimenting, my condition had not only failed to come closer to the kazo, but it had also moved even farther away from it. So I should rely on her and she would acquaint me with "reality," with work, with the laws of the kazo—in short, with healthy things.

Zolema asked me to call upon her in the factory, where I would see just how interesting creative work was, and how unnecessary it was to deal with aimless and harmful things.

Indeed, I myself would certainly have preferred—if I could not see other human beings—to lose my own human characteristics, to become blind and deaf, since with a human heart I could not endure life in this atmosphere.

The next day I found the factory. It was a long, narrow building from which small auxiliary buildings branched out. I was led down the corridor of the main building. Innumerable doors opened one after the other; finally we went through one.

Zolema, who was alone in the room, stood with her back toward me and kept reaching into a trough that extended from the neighboring room to the left and passed through the wall on the right.

When I arrived, she turned and, with her rubber-gloved hand, beckoned me to step nearer.

As I went forward, my glance fell on the trough and I shuddered.

A male corpse lay inside, partly dissected. The hair was missing from his head, and his mouth was cut up to the ears on both sides so that his lower lip fell on his chest. All his teeth had been removed and the enormous, gaping mouth with the horrible wounds that remained in place of the teeth looked as if, in an agony surpassing all hells, some apocalyptic howling were bursting forth from within.

The skin was slit open from the chin right down his whole length; the ribs, the stomach, and the intestines were visible.

One of the eyes of the corpse had been removed, while the other looked at me with horror. I had to turn away. I grasped Zolema.

"What are you doing here?"

"I am preparing the eye," she said with the same dispassionate objectivity, exactly the same tone that I had always heard here among these wooden people.

"Look at it and listen to me," she continued. "When someone dies he is delivered here. This is the corpse processing plant. First the corpse is observed for three days in order to make sure that it is not a case of suspended animation. Then it is given a narcotic injection, so that if the person were actually still alive he will not awake. Following this, processing commences. Hoofed animals are processed in the neighboring building, birds and fish in the next building over. From the animals' bodies, food is prepared for the dining halls. The human being department is much simpler, as there is no slaughterhouse involved; it receives corpses from the hospitals. Most of the material has died of disease or old age, and it is therefore not suitable for consumption, but it is all the more suitable for pharmaceutical and industrial purposes. As you see, I, too, have been assigned to the human department; it is my task to take out the eyes and the brain and pass them on to the adjacent building."

"Look," she said, and in spite of all my disgust compelled me to look. "First I take this small, electrically operated rotary hand saw, now I cut the skin on the temple, opening the bone under it with the saw, like this . . . and the eye will come out easily after a few cuts. Previously, with a hand saw, this work took five minutes, and now the whole process takes three minutes, with less crumbling of the bone, which is a very useful material. Adhesive and medicine are made from it."

"Just look, this is how an eye should be removed," and taking the electric hand saw into her hand, she showed me. "It has to be finely parted from the motor muscles, and the optic nerve should not remain on it."

From Zolema's hand a man looked at me, and I became covered with goose bumps and trembled with horror. I wanted to escape, but no sooner was I about to express my feelings when she continued: "You, of course, wonder what the eye is used for. I'll tell you. You see, I put it on this belt and push this button. The belt starts, the eye disappears through the wall, and it passes to the next room where it is collected in a container. The container is emptied daily, and a chemist processes the contents, that is to say, he extracts from the vitreous body the material that, when mixed into the food of people suffering from a lack of appetite, cures them."

"And do they know what it is made from?"

"Of course they do. Everybody learns such elements of natural science in school."

"And does it restore their appetite?"

"Yes. It's a very efficient remedy. But listen. Most parts of the corpse are used for transplantation to the sick. In the liver, how-ever, a great many useful materials are stored, which in the form of injections restore an organ racked by disease. In addition, the skin is processed by industrial means, excellent string is made from the entrails, soap and food-preparation extract are manu-factured from the fat, and as for the brain . . . "

I could bear it no longer. I interrupted: "And you perform it so calmly? Doesn't it turn your stomach?"

"A ventilator operates above my head," she said, pointing upward. "Where the bowels are processed, they even get gas masks."

I looked with horror at this person who allegedly was a woman.

"Is this how you appreciate Man?" I asked in a muffled re-proachful tone.

"Yes," she said almost proudly. "Not a single atom is lost. And how is your processing carried out?"

I related the funeral rites, the mourning of the family, the black clothes, the tears, the priest, the horse-drawn hearse, the bell-ringer, the coffin, and burial, the memorial stone, and the pious annual commemoration when the bereaved place flowers and possibly a candle on the tomb of the beloved relative.

It was very difficult to explain, and even when I had said it all, I could see that Zolema still did not understand fully. While I was speaking, she didn't cease interrupting me with her questions. She thought the bell was some sort of attempt to revive the dead; the priest, she considered a physician. She continually looked for some purpose: why did they cut the flowers, as they would wither and therefore could not fruit. Why did we use a candle on the grave when electric lights were better? Why did we not mourn in white in the summer, and if we had to wear black, who and what was it good for—the dead, the priest, or the relatives? And how?

I described the funeral process three times, but Zolema kept on shrugging her shoulders in puzzlement.

"What is the aim?" she asked about everything.

I explained that it was to pay one's respects to the dead.

"In the dead there are only chemical values," she answered, "that you do not respect but throw away, apart from the fact that as the interred is in one piece, he is exposed to the possibility of being buried alive by mistake. It is you who do not respect your dead."

"It is not the chemical value that we respect, but that he used to live, that he was a man who worked, loved, and was of benefit to others!" I cried.

"Again you are doing things that do not exist, and even these back to front. A man's work is to be respected while he is alive, by repaying him with good nourishment, a flat, clothes, and comfort in accordance with the kazo equilibrium. But as you yourself have said, among you there are people who are very badly off although they are working—in fact, those who work the hardest. So you do not respect Man either in life or in death according to his merits."

Terrible gulfs were developing between us that I would never be able to bridge. Slowly I looked differently upon Zolema. Only yesterday her perfect human form, even her beauty, had misled me, but now I began to regard her as a moving automaton. I understood that in the case of Zolema and the other Hins I was dealing with human bodies only, in which, however, there was not even a trace of humanity. They could be termed thinking objects, and now, finally, I fully realized that neither Zolema nor the others were a special type of human—they simply were not people. They were completely different.

Now it became clear to me where the soul was for which I had searched in vain.

Nowhere!

It was only now that I understood that, here, the soul could be completely absent.

But who were, or, properly speaking, what were these around me? And what was it that maintained their society?

I asked only out of curiosity: "Why didn't you choose a more womanly job?"

"Why, isn't that what I'm doing?" Zolema asked in surprise. "Once I was sent to the day-nursery out of necessity, because there were not enough male workers. I lifted beds, carried buckets of water, took the dirty linen to the laundry, and used the hoses to clean with just like the strongest men, but I could not stand it for long. I consulted a doctor, who confirmed that I was not fit for such work and I had to do some womanly job, whereupon I took up my present duties here."

While Zolema was speaking, she receded into an incredible distance. At first I could see two objects: Zolema and the gaping corpse in front of her, which by now had no eyes. Then the two became increasingly blurred and the difference between them faded.

I announced briefly that I had learned enough, and required no more. Then I left. I did not thank Zolema for her trouble, neither did I take leave of her, as both courtesies were in any case unknown to them.

Nevertheless, I looked back from the doorway. Zolema stood with her back to me and continued working as if she had never seen me. At the moment she had accomplished the task assigned to her by the kazo in connection with me, nothing further connected her with me. As if I had never existed.

Thus it is that people who work ten or fifteen years in each other's proximity are able to go about their daily lives, without developing the slightest shred of a relationship. In the morning they enter their workplace without greeting each other, then they get down to work, at noon they leave. If, after ten or fifteen years, one of them winds up elsewhere, they disappear from each other's lives without saying good-bye.

A feeling of terrible powerlessness came over me. I was buried alive among the dead on this island, in whose suffocating atmosphere my life-thirsty lungs gasped for air in vain. There was no escape. I was to wither away here, without air and life, to be carried off in the end to Zolema, who would, quite unperturbed, cut out my eyes, whose glistening above my smile and whose tears had meant only something exotically unfamiliar for her. My body would then continue its journey in the trough until dissected and classified by chemists into "useful" materials on the basis of the kazo.

And no emotive memory of me would stir in Zolema even then; why, their own fathers and mothers, their ancestors, were unknown strange objects who were or had been, but with whom there was not a thread of genuine contact.

The air lay heavily upon me; I almost suffocated. A fit of dizziness came over me. With a single jerk I tore my clothes open at the neck and staggered.

I grasped the doorjamb. Zolema knew that I was there, but it did not even occur to her to turn. Everyone there was convinced that everyone else acted properly and expediently and had no interest in them unless someone spoke.

The world began to spin along with me, and my feet failed. I snatched at the back of a chair but in vain. Together with the chair I fell full length on the floor.

Zolema had already turned on hearing the noise. With a jump she was beside me.

"Are you unwell?" she asked.

"No! Leave me!" I shrieked. "Leave me alone! Get away! All of you get away! Let me rot away alone!"

She stood puzzled. She took a few steps, then turned back to me. Finally seeing my tears and distorted face she said, "You must be unwell. Why do you claim things that are not in reality?" They had no word for telling a lie.

After hesitating briefly, Zolema threw off her overall with a swift movement, and after a few seconds she came running back with two companions.

One of them took over her work, while she and the other one lifted me up with a gentleness of which no man of feeling would have been capable. Holding their breath, they carried me to the yard. A car was already waiting there, and they hoisted me into it. Zolema sat near me, undid my clothes over my chest, poured some sort of tonic into my mouth, and we set off.

After two minutes we stopped. There, two men were waiting for us with a stretcher. With great care they lifted me out of the car and carried me to a special streetcar waiting there. This was the ambulance. They set me down on a spongy rubber bed. Then we moved away, but I only realized this by looking out the window, as I heard nothing and felt nothing.

Zolema stood close by and bent over me, anxiously watching all of my movements; and I was again shedding tears. I half lifted my arms toward her, wanting to hold her to me, but my arms fell back. It would have been in vain, anyway. It was horrifying to see people around me and to know that everything was illusory; that affection was not affection, goodness was not goodness, bodies were devoid of content, and I was all alone.

A wild, impotent sobbing shook me and tears flooded down my face.

Zolema went to get some cotton swabs, with which she blotted up the tears.

Then she turned on a tap that filled the air with the refreshing scent of ozone.

In ten minutes we reached the hospital. Here again I was awaited by two men with a stretcher, who carried me upstairs by elevator, and put me in a bed.

A physician stepped forward. Zolema reported where I had been brought from, mentioning that I was a Belohin, then added: "In the event of death, attach a diagnosis stating whether the brain can be used or whether it should be discarded." She turned and left. I never saw her again.

Sobs choked me but I did not dare weep. I said I had been overcome by an attack of giddiness and that I already felt well. To prove it, I gathered all my strength and got up.

The physician examined me, administered a spoonful of some oily liquid that stank to high heaven, and sent me over to the Belohin department, where I went to bed.

The author suffers from homesickness and complains bitterly to Zatamon. Zatamon makes strange statements concerning the author's country, but the author proves the rectitude of European culture. Zatamon speaks about the Behins, who now appear much more attractive to the author, who asks to be led among them.

I THINK IT WOULD BE ALMOST NEEDLESS TO SAY THAT I could hardly sleep that night. My disappointments and continually frustrated desire for life filled me with infinite bitterness. Day was already dawning when exhaustion sent me to sleep.

Strange and confused dreams troubled me. I was hovering, with big, soft balls hanging near me in space, and they were weightless. I struggled ceaselessly with some word, but I no longer knew what it was.

I awoke late in the afternoon. My hair was wet and matted, and my bed sheets were soaked with perspiration. Not even standing under the shower was enough to calm me down. I put on my clothes, and for a moment I thought that perhaps I should get some fresh air into my lungs by going out to the street.

But I soon gave up that idea, too. The very thought of their streets filled me with nausea. And it was all the same, anyway, whether my prison consisted of twenty square yards or fifty square miles. The kind of atmosphere necessary for my mind was not to be found anywhere in the country of the Hins.

I returned to my room. Absent-mindedly I pushed the call button for food. The little table popped out of the wall with my afternoon snack on it.

I could only manage a few bites. The silence and the foggy emptiness of time got on my nerves. Starting up from my seat, I charged to and fro for a while and then exhaustedly threw myself down on my bed without knowing what to do.

A melody haunted me, stubbornly; it was impossible to get it out of my head. It was a stupid song: "Mary, My Sweetheart." I kept on pushing it away in vain, trying to divert my attention in vain; I could not rid myself of it. The tune was oppressing me, cloying my brain; it accompanied my pacing and tortured me. When it came to an end, it started all over again.

Since then, this song has been my veritable enemy, my pursuer. When I hear it within myself, I relive these monstrosities. It revives in me the whole atmosphere—the taste, the smell, and the sounds—of that situation. I see the room, my disheveled bed, the sunbeams slanting inward; I smell the sour scent of sweat and hear the horrible silence of the hospital ward; the dull hopelessness of emptiness overcomes me. Now, if I hear this song played I run away, but it comes after me, tortures me; as if out of spite because I want to tear myself away from it, it does not leave me. It was difficult even to write about it now, as it has already begun to haunt me again.

So, when "Mary, My Sweetheart" had sung itself in my brain for about the twentieth time, Zatamon entered.

He was the only one for whom it was an official duty to be interested in all my troubles (if I may use the word "duty" here at all), the only one to whom I could show myself in my true light. And I had never needed so badly to unburden my soul to somebody as now.

No sooner had he come in and sat himself near my bed than I snatched his hand, dissolved into tears without the least restraint, and entreated him to hear me out.

Zatamon reassured me that he had treated many similar cases

already, and though he himself as a sound organism was unable to appreciate the symptoms completely, in relation to the then existing state of medical science he did nevertheless know my malady quite well and knew that at such times the patient, whose mind was stricken by erroneous beliefs, had to be reassured about his ward's good intentions. He had had dealings with more than one patient who attributed Behin properties to the physician, as their brain had been disturbed by the strange current that I called fear, and such a patient even went so far as to assert that things were not as they were in reality.

"It is a strange and hitherto unaccountable matter," he said, "about which it is necessary for me to enlighten you. Speech, as we know, is for communication, and only existing things can be communicated. Such patients, however, forget at such times why speech has come about, and try to use it to communicate nonexistent things, like someone wanting to see with his ears or make light with a typewriter."

Seeing my confused face, Zatamon assured me firmly that this had indeed occurred during his practice.

But I needed no encouragement to be sincere. What did I care now if they took me for a madman! It could not be worse among the lunatics! Throwing off every self-tormenting shackle, I cried and, choking with sobs, almost shrieking, I unburdened my soul.

"Are you telling me to be sincere?" I asked. "You, who did nothing else but compel me to tell lies?! I assure you, however, that it is over, and I won't conceal my soul any more!"

Zatamon listened with an unchanging wooden expression and I continued freely.

"Be informed then that I am indeed ill! And if you really do have good intentions, then on this occasion don't try to stop me with stupidities; instead try to understand and help me!"

"I understand everything."

Yet again the comforting words were such a peculiar contrast to his hollow voice, but for me even this morsel was a great, liberating gift that, relieving me of my fetters, brought forth a volley of words from me.

"You are the only man who takes an interest in my fate, so let me tell you everything that weighs heavily upon me. I am not actually angry with you, but I still hate you because you have deprived me of everything. Oh, don't interrupt me, don't tell me that everything was at my disposal in the warehouses. What you have taken away you have not taken by hand, but simply by not even touching the victim! Indifference was the most terrible dagger with which you have driven me away from Life, and this is why I hate you, although I am not an enemy but merely different from you, and cannot tear out my soul. The whole of my being would have to be changed for me not to perish in your airless, frosty world after my experiences in cultural life."

Burying my face in my hands, I added in a faltering voice, "I'm afraid I cannot bear this icy jail for long!" Zatamon, seeing how agitated I was, waited until I had calmed down a bit and then asked:

"What is it you actually miss?"

So he might understand me better, I spoke of the British citizen's variegated and colorful life, of the first motherly kiss, of the sweet games of childhood; about college life, harmless jokes, sports, beautiful daydreams so full of color; about the sweet, sunny years of budding love; about the happiness that comes from the knowledge of bread won by hard work; the family house and all that is "my own"; about the pleasures of the warm, soft nest, where in the evening beside the crackling fire a child is dandled on his father's knee—a child in whom the happy parents see the continuation of their lives, a child they caress and rear like a gardener nurtures a sapling. The head of the family sees that his life has been worthwhile, knowing that when he dies, his name and memory will survive, eventually to be enshrined in the hearts of his grandchildren, who will come to his grave at least once a year to tend the flowers with loving hands and to offer a prayer for him.

I spoke of the struggle of social ideas; the debates of the philosophers, scientists, and politicians; the life-forming force of the homeland; card games in society circles; the elegant balls. I spoke about the intriguing details of social life, the colorful streets, the monuments erected in honor of great people in posterity; about competitions, theater and literature —in short, everything that could be summed up under the term of "fine human culture, " and all of which I had to do without here.

"Oh, I am aware, only too well," I said bursting out passionately, "that there is very much trouble, misery, and inequality in our world. I have been watching your country with open eyes and have to admit that in many respects you are perfect. And I have no wish to complain about having to dispense with what is bad with us but rather to say what is good. What a person of culture cannot endure is that you live without heart, without the salt and sense of life; his life becomes intolerable, and he dies of thirst. For what is the point in living in order just to linger from one day to the other with no aim? Tell me," I shouted, almost beside myself, "what is the sense in it?"

"Do you call life lingering?" he interrupted. "Does man not live for life?"

But I was not to be stopped.

" . . . to die at the end like a dog, to be processed. . . ."

"Do you not die?"

" . . . and to be cleared away, without having lived, without having had anything to live for . . ."

"As I see it," he said, "you do not know the essence of life, *the life.*"

"Oh!" I broke in. "Don't repeat that! I have heard that nonsense so often already! And anyway it makes no difference, I am fed up with it! I would rather have no more of this life! I will not sink to the level of a robot, look at the sea after a monotonous job, then go home and go to bed; never to be able to talk to anyone, never to love, never to feel enthusiasm, never to struggle for some aim. I can't endure such a complete vacuum, do you understand? That really can't be treachery, can it? That really can't be kazi, can it? This is the red color of life, without which there is no sense. No, because it is not life. Of everything we do, you say that it really does not exist. On the contrary, nothing you do exists! At last I have come across the expression I wanted: *this is what is not: it is the life that simply does not exist!*"

Zatamon looked for a long time at my excited, heaving chest, and then, seeing that I had finished, he began to speak quietly.

"I am a physician, so I'm not surprised at your words. Those who imagine of nothing that it is something, can do it only if at the same time they see the existent as nonexistent. The camera records what is white and black, and the picture is visible only because at the same time black appears as white. If the camera took everything in black we would see nothing." I was astonished. These profound words bewildered me. Maybe our approach was a similarly complete whole such as theirs? Two worlds, which could never perceive each other simply because the other was not a separate entity but the reverse of itself. . . .

I now remembered that when I first heard the earth was a sphere I wondered why it was that the American children did not fall off the earth, and no doubt American children thought the same about us, because we did not know that in reality there was no up and down. But then. . . .

Suddenly I spoke.

"All right. It is possible. But if you know only that we each live amid opposite worldviews, what evidence is there that yours is the positive and ours the negative? We are unable to penetrate each other's concept of the world. But surely it can be seen that we are both able to live, however impossible it may appear from the other's point of view."

"Yours is the negative," answered Zatamon.

"Where is the evidence?"

"It is not difficult to determine which is the negative between something that *is* and something that is *not.*"

"Speak more clearly! Why do you say that it is not we who live reality?"

"With you existing things are only a means for reaching nonexistent aims that you call ideas while it is precisely the reverse that can be called reality: when we think of bringing about something in fact. Only an aim taken from the real, natural world can be termed positive, as only what exists can be achieved. But you don't live for building a house, for producing clothes and food, and even if you accomplish all this, you do it for imaginary—and therefore unattainable—aims."

"But a house is built and in the oven bread is baked. Does it make any difference for what aim all this takes place?"

"It does. The result of a negative endeavor can only be a negative life."

"What do you mean by that?"

"Negative life is death. And is that not how all your activities end? Did you not conclude in every case that for 'faith,' 'flag,' 'love,' 'beauty,'—which is to say, words—one has not to live but to die? But to build houses one must live, and a dead man cannot reap the cornfields."

A lengthy silence ensued, and then, softly, I began to speak.

"You may be partly right, but you cannot say that we don't live a real life. What I've related to you about the life of the inhabitants of my country, mostly takes place in the world that is also called real by you and for tangible aims. Or does the student not learn in order to become a breadwinner some day in the future, and is it not the kiss in that love ends?"

"No. This is also imaginary. You fight as if you wanted to reach something, and when you have reached it, you are still farther from it. The student lives in his dreams and the loving youth in his desires; but if the student realizes his dreams or the youth wins his love, then they are no longer satisfied. It is then necessary for them to sire a child to raise, so yet another unattainable aim can give meaning to life. Ends already attained you consider senseless, and the fullness of life you term lifelessness. But then why do you strive to reach it? When you are far from something, you force your way toward it, you redouble your efforts, and when you have it, you throw it away, as it has then lost its value."

"And you? Why do you work?"

"For life itself. And you for the struggle. Once you told me what a pleasure it was for you to solve crossword puzzles, and if you happened to come across the magazine in the club with the puzzles already filled out by someone else, you felt vexed, instead of being pleased. You mentioned that a trend in poetry or art was beautiful until the meaning of the metaphors became well known. As soon as you become accustomed to iron meaning strength, and spring meaning youth, you no longer consider these metaphors beautiful. The target is always moved farther and farther away, because you fight for the fight itself, not for the goal. And you also told me that for a diamond you would give everything, as there are only a few of them, while air had no value, although this is what is necessary and not the former. You fight for the love of a woman as if it did not depend on the woman alone whether she loves you or not."

"That is precisely what we fight for," I replied in surprise, "because it depends on her and not on us."

"But a woman is also a human being, so you fight for a thought in a human brain, the existence of which depends solely on your imagination. You lay siege to the walls drawn on a map just as if it were not you yourselves who had drawn them. You heal wounds inflicted by yourselves in order to be able to wound again, and you struggle against an economic crisis as if it was not you yourselves who stopped the machines. You have invented friendship, beauty, love, and hatred, which create obstacles for you to have something to struggle for or to fight against, as you attribute independent existence to these obstacles."

"And is it not variety that gives meaning to life? In the village, do we not long for the city so that we can be delighted by more variety? Are the arts not for making life more tolerable? And is faith not for relieving anguish, to give substance and purpose to our lives, without which only a barren skeleton and an unfilled gap would exist between birth and death?"

"Whoever wants to come out of the water must reach for the

shore and not for himself." Zatamon observed. "Progress can be achieved only by reaching for the real world."

"Oh, I know very well that for you, only matter and well-being exist. But realize that we also reach for the shore. Many of our philosophers are working for the enlightenment of man and searching for the governmental system that will set as its target progress toward eternal peace and a just material life."

I told Zatamon about Plato's state, Saint Thomas Aquinas's principles of the divine universality of the outcome of labor, the common work of the Cathari and the Hussites, Fourier's phalansteries, Thomas More's *Utopia*, Proudhon's people's bank, Louis Blanc's national workshops, Robert Owen's social manufacturing plants, and the communal states of the Dominicans and Jesuits in South America; and finally I came to scientific socialism and the latest theories—to the plans of Marx, Lenin, Bakunin, Bernstein, Kropotkin, Kautsky, and Plekhanov, and to technocracy and the democratic socialism of the Fabian Society, Wells, and the Webbs. I spoke of the work theory of mercantilism and physiocracy, of the liberalism of Adam Smith, and of the trade unions; nor did I fail to mention those ideas that had not materialized, such as Georgism, syndicalism, and anarchism.

Zatamon simply could not understand how it was possible to imagine so many things concerning such a simple thing as life.

"Only the words and the names of the theories can be varied," he countered. "Not life itself, which is predetermined by the body. And anyone who attributes independent life to words is sick and a somnambulist."

"But from these words economic systems are born," I retorted.

"Is it not all the same in which system you are ill? Even then your soul will remain, which is what draws you away from natural life."

"How can you say that? Emotion is our innate, natural property. Go all over the world and you will not find a single group of people without faith, art, love, and hatred."

"Well, is that not what I have said—that you are basically sick,

so words and enlightenment will not cure you? You are dreaming, and talk in vain to each other about what is good, because
you also dream the concept of good and your philosophers, too,
are no more than figures in a dream. You will always remain in
one place and struggle with yourselves. Your life is a stagnant,
dreary drudgery, for drudgery itself—in which there is no
progress but the infinite, dull monotony that any man wishing to
make progress could not, with a sound mind, tolerate."

I was astonished at the audacity with which Zatamon was able
to impute all the deficiencies of their lives so cynically and un-
scrupulously to ours.

The next minute, however, I was overcome by a very strange
feeling. I felt as if I had heard my own words from his mouth—as
if my own skull had emerged from somewhere and grinned at
me. How did it happen? Was there indeed no difference between
us other than the difference between one side of something and
its reverse?

My being divided into two now meant that each aspect was
fighting against the other, and I did not know which of them
I now was. However, I had to get rid of one of them. I had to clear
the matter up. I put forth another question.

"So, according to you, superior aims have no reason to exist?"

"Among men there are no aims beyond Man," said Zatamon.
"Furthermore, there cannot be."

"None beyond Man, only superior ones. Or does literature not
deal with the human fate and reality?"

"All of your life is imaginary. And if you write of this imagined
life a story that is itself imagined, you stray only farther from
reality."

"But it refines our taste. It gives new content, new aims, and
clearer vision to our mind. But let's say you are correct. Let us
presume that we have not progressed in the things you call 'real,'
that we have wasted our energies on spiritual aims. One thing
you cannot deny: in this we did make progress, as culture has
constantly led to new problems, new styles, new manners, and

new tastes. Or don't you see any development from Plato to Marx, from Pheidias to Rodin? Is not spiritual life more developed today than two thousand years ago?"

"You are building a cage for yourself—one equipped with an exercise wheel that allows you to imagine intentionally infinite horizons, lest recognition should spoil the illusion of your long-distance running."

Somberly I remarked that it seemed I could not rely on even a spark of understanding on his part, yet at the outset he had stated that he would understand everything.

"By understanding you mean approval, whereas sickness can be approved only by misunderstanding, by the inability to recognize the heart of the matter."

With a tired wave of the hand I fell silent and decided not to continue. However, prompted by a sudden inspiration, I gave a start.

"Perhaps," I said in a more lively tone, "perhaps, if we wanted just to exist on the earth, we ought to emulate you. But tell me, what shall we do with our heart now that we have it?"

"Why do you use the name of something that actually exists as a designation of something that does not exist?"

But now I felt that God had delivered him into my hands, and I regained my stride. Backing up two steps and putting my hands on my hips, I hurled it into his face: "Because it is! Because it exists!"

"What does not exist in nature does not exist at all."

"Tell me," I said acrimoniously, "why do you eat?"

"Because we are hungry."

"Why do you drink? Why do you sleep? Because you are thirsty and sleepy, isn't that so?"

"It is so."

"Thus, after all, you, too, live in order to satisfy desires, and these desires are in you; which is to say, they are in human beings, and therefore in nature. Do realize," I went on in a raised tone of voice, "that we are driven to culture by the same feeling of want. If this desire is for words, then we subsist on words, but the fact that a thirst is quenched not by water, but by music, love, or enthusiasm only confirms its existence."

"But a word is not a reality . . ."

"That's not important!" I interrupted. "The point is that we do have such desires!"

"There are only existing things in the world."

Airily I waved my hand. I had never been so sure of myself. I almost found pleasure in stabbing my words into him.

"If I said about your eating and drinking that they are nonsensical, I would be more justified because we know material desires as well, but you haven't the least of cultural needs. This particular desire is our property only while it is missing from you, so in this respect we are more than you. Yes, we are more, because what you have, we have as well, but you have only part of our senses. How dare a color-blind person claim that there are only coarse and smooth surfaces but there is no color?"

"Dreams cannot be reality," he reiterated stubbornly, "a dream is a self-created picture of the brain."

"Look here, you say that no desire that aims at anything other than existence can exist. But in me, such a desire does exist, and I say that its being is possible. What does that prove?"

Zatamon was attentively watching my face. After a short while he said: "That you are a Behin."

At first, I wanted to fling myself at his throat. How dare he offend me, a British citizen, in such an arrogant manner?

It took me minutes, during which I reflected on the nature of the Hins, to curb my passion. The mind accustomed to the animated European atmosphere can hardly but realize that among the Hins there is neither offending nor flattering intention, purely and simply the objective meaning of words.

"You are a Behin!" He uttered these words as if he had examined litmus paper in a test tube and pronounced, "It is an acid."

Gathering my thoughts, I tried to comprehend the essence of the words that had just passed between us, and suddenly it flashed through my mind that, accordingly, the Behins could be nothing other than people blessed with a soul—people who, because they were misunderstood by these automatons called the Hins, had been exiled from their world.

"Look here," I said with interest, "what is Behinity, actually?"

"It is a mental disorder that regrettably has yet to be cured; we only know its cause for the time being."

"Tell me, what is its essence?"

"For that, I must explain the natural metabolism of the brain, as generated by the sun's cosmic rays."

"How?"

"It is a fact that cosmic rays emanate from the sun, while the brain functions as an antenna, and when affected by these rays it realizes its aim of furthering life, which you call 'natural instincts.' In nature there is no contradiction, as everything that exists has developed by itself over billions of years, and the rough edges of the components of the overall mechanism have been worn down to work together smoothly. So the sun's cosmic rays induce the functioning of natural life through the antenna that is the brain. But we know that the receivers, according to their size, also generate self-oscillation, become autoexcited, and with a lack of proper shielding these oscillations also affect the antenna, which therefore receives distorted waves. The apparatus squeals, crackles, and roars because it is reproducing its own voice. In the case of creatures whose brains constitute small apparatus, this effect cannot be perceived; the animal just lives its natural life. With those possessing a more developed brain, neurosis manifests itself quite obviously in some cases. . . ."

"Speak of the Behins!" I interrupted.

"The Behins' brain is completely influenced by its self-oscillation: so their life is directed not by natural but by artificial aims coming from within. These interior, phantasmagoric waves turn life into its reverse, which sometimes results in its elimination. Today we are experimenting with a cure, but the whole brain must be removed in the process, and as this is very dangerous, it has not as yet been tried out on human beings. So, for the time being, we cannot do too much for the poor fellows, only leave them alone and see to it that they should not be in want of anything."

While listening to Zatamon's words I could hardly keep from smiling. Before my very eyes there was this tiny unseeing man babbling away, now officiously explaining what can cause an obsession with colors and how it could be cured.

"But still, what do the Behins actually do?"

"Nonexisting things. Speech is fit for communicating only existing things, so I could not even tell you the essence of them, but this much I can definitely say—their deeds are very similar to yours. There is, for example, one who paints his shoes saying that doing so increases their usefulness, although in fact this covers over the pores of the fabric, so the feet do not get air. They may dress in the clothes made by our factory, but before doing so they alter them, each in a different way with a lot of senseless work."

The former greatness of Zatamon now diminished in my mind to nothing. No longer even paying attention to his words, I was interested only in how I could get among the Behins to shake with tearful eyes the hands of my poor, outcast, zealous fellow men.

"Where are the Behins?" I asked.

Zatamon informed me that they lived behind the hospital in a spacious settlement, encircled by a wall. Within this enclosure they occupied normal flats; the Hins provided them with food and clothes, but otherwise they lived completely according to their own incredible system. The Behins, however, not only endured each other's company: they were, in fact, unable to live outside it. Internment was not therefore a punishment, a concept foreign to the Hins, but merely the separation desired by both sides.

"How can I get in there?" I asked.

My question somewhat surprised Zatamon, and he anxiously warned me of the "madnesses" to which one was exposed among the "crazy people" that could not be tolerated by the sound mind. He remarked that they took in people only in very grave cases, and that perhaps it would be better to experiment with some other cure for the time being, as maybe "there was still hope."

I, however, claimed I felt myself to be completely hopeless and demanded to be taken among the Behins.

"Be warned also," Zatamon continued, "that on no account do we intervene in the Behins' lives, so if you suffer from their lunacies we cannot help you."

And he commenced to explain that every Behin had a different opinion from the others, even concerning the simplest things. Because of this they sometimes quarreled. It happened on such occasions that one of them would ask for the protection of the Hins, which he was given. But it always came to light that the Behin did not want to reach kazo and peace—he only wanted to impose his own fixed ideas upon the other Behin who had hurt him. Hence the Hins intervened to restore order only in the most serious disagreements; for, regrettably, such fights occurred. Otherwise the Behins managed their own lives, which could not in any case be understood with a sound mind.

Smiling, I reassured Zatamon that I fully agreed to the principle of nonintervention, and stated that I was not afraid of anything. He consented, and said that he would take me to the Behin settlement the next day, if possible, but first he had to study my symptoms carefully.

With this, Zatamon brought a syringe, drew blood from my arm, cut a sample of my hair, and then left me alone.

For my own part, I spent the night sleeplessly—but now it was from joy. My soul had been parched in the desert of the Hins, but now before it there dawned, with an ever-brightening glow—the long lost hope of warm, colorful human life.

Oh, had I only known what was to come!

PART

II

GULLIVER AMONG THE BEHINS

CHAPTER

9

We arrive at the gravest days of author's adventurous journey, spent among the Behins. The author recounts the oddities of his first day there.

THE NEXT DAY ZATAMON VISITED AGAIN, ADVISING ME THAT the matter had been thoroughly discussed. They had obtained the opinion of a doctor, interrogated Zolema, and carried out blood and hair tests—and as a result of all this they had no objection to my going among the Behins.

His words somewhat surprised me, and I even remarked that I was astonished at this severity, as it was not usual for the Hins to try to influence individual decisions and everybody acted as he thought fit.

Zatamon replied that this was the only wish that could not be complied with according to the individual's will because—as he explained—there were mental patients who imagined themselves Behins while their case was only "simple" paranoia, which was curable, and their belief was nothing more than one of the usual obsessions; for example, they would imagine themselves to be a corkscrew or made of glass. Such milder cases should not be exposed to the grave disturbances of life among the Behins, and it was purely with regard to the seriousness of the consequences that they had examined my particular case so scrupulously.

Zatamon's words again made me smile, and I reassured him that I would withstand the encounter.

At this he stood up and we set off.

We crossed the park and soon we came to a big wall.

At the gate we had to ring. This was the first door in Kazohinia on which I saw a lock. To my question, Zatamon replied that many strange things took place among the Behins. They did not use things for the purpose for which they had been made. They asked for unnecessary things, which they were usually given, as there were cases when, if the request was refused, the Behin's face became distorted, his voice resembled a turkey's, and he began shouting even though one was standing rather near him. On such occasions they quite unnecessarily broke fragile objects, and sometimes even hit someone without being asked to do so. This perhaps meant a more serious stage of the illness. It was for this reason that such a mechanism was needed on the door, as this had the property of allowing it to be opened by a suitable device.

No sooner had the door opened than Zatamon took the key out of the doorkeeper's hand and explained its operation, noting that it had been designed by the technical department of the hospital. It was the simplest type of key. Any of our amateur scoundrels could have opened the closed gate.

Smiling to myself, I listened to Zatamon's words and excitedly awaited the prospect of meeting my first Behin.

Oh, had I only known I was about to enter the most terrible bedlam in the world—that a chapter of my life was about to commence that I cannot look back on even now without my heart being twisted by the memory of the sufferings and monstrosities! We entered a long corridor. In a window recess a man was standing in a rather shabby-looking suit of clothes. These clothes had several gaping holes, and some parts hung in rags. On our arrival this man watched us with furrowed brows, put his forefinger on his nose, and turned after us.

"You see," said Zatamon, "there is a cut in the middle of his head."

Frightened, I looked back, but saw only that his hair was parted in the middle, which caused me definite pleasure.

He led me into a room containing a bed, a table, a chair, and a wardrobe, mostly in the wall. Then he left me alone.

When I looked around, my first impression was that although the furniture of the flat was quite decent, everything was considerably more worn than with the Hins. On certain pieces I even believed I could find definite traces of willful damage.

A big electric cooker was in a particularly deplorable state, its burners battered, half its switches broken, and one of its legs propped up by a brick.

But all this was for the moment of no interest to me. I wanted to get acquainted with my new country.

Going out to the yard, I found myself in a vast space bordered partly by a stone wall and partly by buildings. And yet, as I looked in another direction, the yard appeared endless. Somewhere rising in the distance was a shrub-covered hill; otherwise, it was all grass and trees, with paths and a few benches. It was mild and sunny, and there were a lot of people wandering about, many of them in groups—something I had not seen among the Hins. Their clothes were quite as ragged as those of the man with the parted hair, and I attributed this to tight-fistedness.

Under one of the trees a man went about placing glasses on a table, pouring varying amounts of water into each, and finally hammering out a tune on them. The others surrounded him, sang, and—laughed!

After the terrible emptiness, this was music to my ears. Could it be possible? . . . My heart throbbing with joy, I ran up to them.

"I am Gulliver," I said freely to a man, smiling and offering my hand.

"*Prick-pruck*," he said, putting his index finger on his nose.

Such words I did not know—they could not even occur in the Hin language, in which neither the letter "r" existed nor could two consonants come immediately after each other.

A shiver of horror passed through me. So was he mad, too? He had seemed so pleasant only a minute ago! What had come over him? Could it be some strange custom? But I could find no explanation. No, this could not be normal. What was I to do? If I were to run away he might get into a fury. As for him, seeing my embarrassment, he suddenly and without the least hesitation began to laugh hysterically.

This froze the blood in my veins; trembling, I looked toward the gate that, however, had closed forever behind me.

In my confusion I looked for a way of reassuring him, to explain why I had addressed him.

"I only wanted to ask," I said, "when we shall eat."

The smile suddenly froze on his lips and he turned his back to me. The others contemptuously followed suit.

Taking advantage of the opportunity, I hurriedly took to my heels. For a while I kept turning my head, hoping to spot a more decent sort of person, someone I could start a conversation with, as I had to acquaint myself with this strange environment.

I could not even suspect what the dangers were, and just how exposed I was to them.

In my mind, I bitterly reproached Zatamon for having brought me here like this without suitable warning. And yet it seemed equally apparent that if people with souls really did live here, the Hins would not have been able to inform me in any case.

Left as I was to my own devices, I knew I had to find out something about them.

On a bench was a man reading a book. Hesitating briefly, I approached him.

"Do you mind if I ask something?"

Placing his finger on his nose, he said, "prick-pruck," and smiled.

So this one, too. My knees were buckling from the anxiety. I stood there, puzzled.

The smile froze on his lips, too, and he turned away.

But I had to talk to them, for I knew nothing and was exposed to the greatest uncertainty.

"I have just been brought in," I said entreatingly. "I am uninitiated. Please answer me."

At this he suddenly became more friendly and turned to me. "Ah! I didn't know. Then, of course, the case is different. Everything is *kvari*. I see. So I shall teach you. Prick-pruck is *belki*."

"What?" I was stupefied.

"Belki," he said cold-bloodedly while I was looking for a way of escape. "You, of course, don't understand it, as you don't know what the *ketni* is."

"Ketni?"

"Ketni. If they say 'prick-pruck' you must return the gesture by putting your finger on your nose, because with us it is the belki. If you don't do so, you don't behave in a ketni way, and of course they will *enoate* because of you."

"Enoate?"

"Well? Shouldn't they enoate if someone doesn't behave in a ketni manner?"

"Of course, of course," I said soothingly, "and what's that?"

"Ah, I see, you don't even know that either. Well, the way I plunged back into my book showed that I was inwardly enoating because of you. Be careful! You may expose yourself even to being hit if you are not ketni."

"If I don't say 'prick-pruck'?"

"Of course! Why are you surprised at it?"

"And if I say 'prick-pruck'?"

"Then they will smile at you, scratch your posterior, at which time you scratch theirs in turn. This indicates that neither of you is enoating because of the other and that both of you are ketni."

"That's nonsense!" I snapped.

He frowned.

"Watch your tongue, and don't speak about the ketni like that as you may be exposed to the greatest enoa. I kvari your behavior because you have just arrived, but you will learn the ketni that makes us superior to the *bivak* mob outside."

"Bivak?"

"Bivak. Because they behave like bivaks. If we belki to them they pay no attention to us either; even if we scratch their posterior they gaze at us idiotically. They are all idiots. From first to last! And they haven't the foggiest idea of the ketni."

With this he scratched my posterior and I had to scratch him back to prove the sanity of my mind! Slowly the horrible reality dawned on me.

The Reader is likely to be most annoyed at the many Behin words, charging me with negligence or even bumptious ostentation for not presenting them directly in English translation. And it is for this reason that I must remark here and now that the untranslated words have no equivalent in the English language. They indicate special fixed ideas that simply do not exist in our culture.

By way of example, let the Reader imagine that somebody has pricked his finger, then lifts it instinctively to his mouth. This gesture has a normal English name: pain. But if somebody places his finger on his nose, for no apparent reason, and calls it belki, how am I to translate it into the language of the sober citizens of my country?

Now another man was approaching the bench. He cut a strange figure, poor fellow. Above each of his knees hung a heavy copper cube on a chain that painfully knocked against his legs at every step, so he could only walk very slowly. I felt sorry for him.

My acquaintance suddenly jumped up, lifted his right foot with one hand and with a painful face he wailed toward him: "*Vake! Vake!*"

The man stopped, with an infinitely grave grimace shook the copper cubes on his legs, and asked, now with a smile: "How does your nose grow, *kaleb*?"

"*Vaksi*, steadily."

From this I saw that the grabbing up of the foot and the vake were not expressions of pain but some new nonsense. Lest they should take me for a bivak, I started from my seat, and placing my finger on my nose said to the newcomer: "prick-pruck."

By way of reply I got a deep, resentful look. My acquaintance dug me in the ribs with frightened perplexity, at which I, still more confused, scratched the posterior of the copper-cubed arrival.

At this the copper-cubed one contemptuously looked me up and down and wanted to move on but my acquaintance leapt before him and placing his right hand on his head explained entreatingly: "Elak betik! Oh, kvari for this bivak! The worthless creature has only just arrived and does not know what the ketni is."

Copper Cubes was considerably appeased; with a cordial smile he twitched the nose of my acquaintance and then mine. "That's a different matter," he said graciously. "How does your nose grow, kaleb?"

I gazed like an idiot and was about to say that it did not grow at all, but my acquaintance poked me again in the ribs, so I thought I had better keep silent. The newcomer continued on his way, and my acquaintance, again snatching his right foot into his hand, wailed and bellowed vake-vake, so I already wanted to go to his help, but he pushed me away.

I stood there agape with my feet rooted to the ground.

When Copper Cubes was already far away, my acquaintance turned and fell on me angrily.

"How could you say 'prick-pruck' to a betik, you bivak?!"

"Well, was it not you who told me?" I stammered.

"But to a betik! Didn't you see the bilevs on his feet?"

"The copper cubes?"

"They are not copper cubes, they are bilevs!"

"Are they not made of copper?"

"Well . . ." he said, his voice choked with anguish, "perhaps, if we look at it like that, that's what they are made of, but you must not say so."

"And why not, if that's what they are made of?" I snorted.

"For you must understand they are not made of it!" he cried. "It is not material, it is an aneba! You must not say about it that it is material, because it is material-like manifestation of the bikru's existence, and it is not permitted even to think about whether it is material or not."

I had no idea what the aneba and the bikru were, but the cube was material for certain. But what sort of stupidity is required to deny what everyone can see with his own eyes?!

Never in this place did I ever hear a person call the bilevs material. Once I saw a locksmith who was just burnishing a pair of bilevs, and he, too, was convinced that actually there was nothing in his hands; or, properly speaking, that there was the material-like manifestation of the bikru's being, which could be neither seen nor touched, though it was in his hands and he was, manifestly, continuously touching it.

At these words I was beset anew by fear. In a seemingly calm way I enquired, "Then what is the bilev?" "It indicates that one is a betik."

"What does 'betik' mean? What does a betik do?"

"Nothing! He is a betik! And a betik is elak! Do you understand? And when an elak is concerned, the belki is not prick-pruck but, as I did, you must snatch your foot in your hand and wail: 'Vake! Vake!' As an indication that your foot aches because you cannot wear bilevs on it."

"It aches because I don't wear them?" I was now utterly confused. "It would ache if I did!"

"Hush!" he said, looking round in a frightened manner. "You must not say so!"

"Come now!" I snorted. "You surely don't want to make me believe that my feet ache because I don't wear bilevs to hit them? Even the simplest common sense protests against such nonsense!"

"In your own interest," he said severely, "I advise you not to speak in this manner. There are certain things that cannot be disputed, and must be accepted without reference to common sense as they are aneba things, and it is well known that all of us would be only too pleased to tie on the bilevs, because a betik is elak."

"Let me rather not be a betik and elak," I said with deep conviction, at which he gave a loud laugh.

"Oh, what a bivak you are still! You poor ignoramus! I advise you not to say such things, for the others will laugh their heads off. On the other hand, if you keep on asserting your nonsense, they may grow angry and somebody will call you *lamik*, and if you suffer that, you must immediately stab a knife into him."

"Because he has said that I am lamik?"

"Of course!"

"Who would compel me to stab a knife into him for that?"

He looked at me compassionately.

"Would you swallow somebody calling you lamik?"

"And why shouldn't he say it if it pleases him?"

"Because the word is *borema*!" he said with infinite solemnity.

"What?"

"Borema. Yes, it is borema if you want to know the truth."

I gazed at him, stupefied.

"And what is 'borema'?"

"For instance, the word 'lamik.'"

This, of course, made me no wiser, as we were back again at the beginning.

"But what is this borema concept?"

"Well . . . how shall I explain it to you? . . . 'Borema' is a word for which, if directed toward you, you are bound to stab him who says it."

At this I burst into laughter.

"So I must stab, because it is borema, and it is borema because I must stab. Don't you think that there should be some firm starting point to make this all both logical and understandable?"

He waved his hand.

"I see you don't understand. You have no sense of the ketni, so I will not continue to explain. But I suggest to you that you should beware of anyone calling you lamik and letting them go unpunished."

Now I waved my hand in annoyance.

"Well, let them have some consideration when they say it. If it doesn't hurt me, I will not stab, and if I don't stab, it will be of even less harm to me."

He looked me up and down completely amazed.

"You .... Do you believe that it would be of no harm to you?"

The laughter froze on my lips. By now I myself began to get scared.

"Why?" I asked. "What kind of danger could be entailed by my failure to stab someone?"

"What kind of danger? Oh, you poor newcomer! So you are not yet aware of the consequences?"

"No! Of course not! Tell me!" I urged him excitedly.

"Well, look here. If you don't take up the knife, the Behins will meet, draw up minutes of the meeting, and declare you unqualified to fight with a knife."

"And what does that mean for me?"

"And that means," he said, stepping back and poking his forefinger against my chest, "that later on you will not be stabbed by others, either!"

He placed his hands on his hips and waited for the effect, which did not fail to follow.

That is, I stood for a minute gaping, then laughter burst forth from me anew with overwhelming force.

As I saw it, here everybody continuously harped on words assembled in an idiotic way; to this they pay homage, for that they feel repugnance, but the main characteristic of each word was that it had nothing to do with reality.

My acquaintance gave an angry wave of the hand.

"You have no faculty for the ketni. Take care, because if I don't teach you, you will be exposed to the greatest enoa."

That much I had already guessed—enoa meant anger, contempt, or some such thing, to which the knife also belonged, so I thought it best to stifle the protest being waged by my common sense and revert to the main subject.

"Tell me, why was the betik interested in the growth of our noses?"

"Not the betik but the elak betik."

"But you said betik!"

"Yes, I did say that. But if you refer to him, you must call him an elak betik. I was sitting here on this bench earlier."

I was perplexed, but again curbed my outraged common sense.

"All right, all right! So why was he interested in the growth of our noses?"

"First of all, he was not interested, as a betik is not interested in things, he only inquires. Next, if he were interested, he would not be interested in the growth of my nose, it's only a custom to inquire. But mind! You must not ask about the nose of a betik, only he about yours. This is the ketni."

I was fed up with the ketni. I should have liked to speak about more sober things.

"Tell me about eating here. Where do we get the food from and where do we eat it?"

He started in fear. He pressed his hand on his mouth and looked round in alarm.

"Hush! Don't say such a bivak thing! Say: when and from where do we get spirituality."

"Spirituality? Do people not eat here?"

"Hush! Hush! At least speak more softly!"

He drew nearer and explained in a whisper.

"Spirituality is what you have mentioned, but it must not be said in that way, because it is kave."

"You mean that eating must not be called eating, because you have invented the word 'kave.' A senselessly coined word you replace by another senseless one, and you manufacture such concepts out of thin air, by the ton. Tell me: Can a reasonable man not be found among you who would relentlessly say that we don't live for words themselves, but that words are to be used in life?"

He now looked at me compassionately.

"I only wanted to help you," he said. "As for me, I kvari your words, because I am a tolerant and enlightened man, who has always professed that a wrong action does not necessarily result from bad intentions, but may also originate in ignorance. But you attack all the anebas so strongly that for this everybody would enoate and call you a lamik—you might even be heavily punished, too."

"Punished?" I cried, taken aback. "Whom did I want to harm? Did I not want to make life easier for you? I want to liberate you from the shackles of all the nonsense that renders your life more difficult, and you have the nerve to enoate because of me?!"

"Don't say any more of that nonsense!" he cried with flashing eyes.

I was startled. Instead of saying thank you for the help, they were persecuting an individual who, with his clear-sightedness, wanted to improve their life. Such a thing could indeed only be done by lunatics.

It was a general custom among the Behins that they did not expect kindness and morality of each other, but certain compulsory lies. Above all, the material nature of the copper cubes should be denied so that nobody had to beat his neighbor to death.

It is for this reason that I strongly suggest to anyone who may find himself among such lunatics not to try to be good and helpful, as it is their most characteristic attribute that they fly at the throat of the sound in mind.

So I preferred to let him have his way, and he continued.

"You had better thank your good luck for having led you to me. Anyone else would have long ago taken you to the betik. But I don't want to suppose you have any ill will in you, and in spite of your strong attacks, I am still willing to believe that by learning the ketni you will mend your ways, that for now you are yet unaware of the monstrosity of your words. Well, prick-pruck."

"Prick-pruck," I said, placing my finger on my nose and seeing that he was visibly pleased. We scratched each other's posteriors and I hurried on.

The Reader may have perceived that the speech of my acquaintance also included words that did not figure in the Hin language, such as "good" and "ill will," "punishment," "laughing," "pleasure," and so on. Although they were completely new also for me, I could gather their meaning from his speech, and thus now I render them in English translation. I give in the original only those words that do not convey something that actually exists, and which therefore cannot have any counterpart in a language created by reason.

As I wanted to have a good look round at my new country, I set off in the yard.

After the long L-shaped building I saw some barnlike structures. I had, as yet, no idea as to their function, but I did see that they were in a most neglected state. Surely the Behins could not have built them.

So I was all the more surprised to catch sight of a bricklayer's scaffolding behind them that covered quite a tolerable building. But the real surprise came only later.

Part of the house was in fact already complete, above the scaffolding, and a team of workers was engaged in demolishing it with pickaxes.

I did not understand the connection, and pulling myself together I asked one of the workers what purpose the building was to serve.

He said that it would be flats for the Behins.

"Then why are you pulling down the other half of it?" I inquired.

"So that we should not remain homeless."

I thought I had not properly posed the question, and so I asked again and again, but the worker repeatedly replied that the house that had been built had to be pulled down, for if it were to remain, people would remain homeless.

"Well, I don't understand that," I declared.

"I wonder why," he replied, distrustfully scrutinizing my face. "Why, it should be obvious even to the ultimate boxshaker."

"Boxshaker? What is a boxshaker?"

At this the mason put down his pickaxe and stepped toward me.

"Don't you understand that, either?" he asked and a queer light flashed in his eyes.

My whole being became covered with goose bumps.

"But yes . . . of course . . ." I stammered, backing away. Then, turning round suddenly, I shot off at a wild gallop. Fortunately the man did not follow me.

Now I hurried into my room without the least delay, but I did not feel safe even there, as it had no lock.

I decided to leave the door open. At least this way I would see if anyone were to pass by. On the one hand I was afraid of everything that might follow, but on the other hand I wanted to see everything, so that, from a safe distance, I should learn, without causing any scenes, as much as was necessary for me to avoid being beaten.

As I crouched in my room, a little table appeared from the wall by itself, and through a flap-door behind it a dish of food was pushed onto it. Then the door closed again.

So the food problem had solved itself, thanks to the Hins' thinking of everything. As for me, I fell upon the meal, eating voraciously. Here I might have asked questions to no avail; everyone would have turned away shocked if asked about "spirituality," and I might have died of starvation because of the ketni.

A few minutes later a woman passed along the corridor. She stopped before the open door and glanced at me. She kept a handkerchief in front of her mouth, as if she had toothache, but even so I noticed she was smiling.

All this, however, lasted only a second, because no sooner had her glance fallen on the food than she cried out and collapsed.

I darted up immediately to help her but already others had gathered. Excitedly they questioned each other, and when one of them caught sight of the food on my table and the spoon in my hand, he shouted at me, beside himself with rage:

"When you perform spirituality, shut the door, you bivak!"

"The lungs should be torn out of such a person!" bellowed another.

From somewhere a low grumbling could be heard: "Lamik . . ."

The blood froze in my veins. This was the word for which I had to stab, only I did not know why. I fingered the knife in bewilderment.

Outside a clamor of consternation could be heard. They looked for the grumbler and looked at me to see what I would do.

"But still it cannot be uttered," said another one, breaking the silence.

"He has the right to say what he wants to," said a third.

"He hasn't!"

"But he has!"

"Who said 'lamik'?"

"It's none of your business!" then he turned to me. "To which *beha* do you belong, *kona* or *kemon*?"

I did not even know whether I was a boy or a girl, only that I had to answer to escape.

"Kona," I said daringly.

The word worked a miracle and brought about a turn of events for which I was not at all prepared. The crowd, which up to that point had unanimously raged against me, broke into two groups. Half immediately wanted to jump upon me, while the others, led by the former inquirer, stood in front of my door and wanted to push them back. Wild shouting broke out, and in no time everyone was fighting. The woman who had fainted had been completely forgotten. I cried out that they should not trample her to death, but it seemed she was not quite as oblivious as I thought, because no sooner did she get the first kick than she arose with a start, and after a further scream, ran away.

Out in the hallway more and more people intervened in the fight. One of my defenders was thrown against the door so hard it was torn off its hinges with a loud crack, the panes of glass falling out and shattering on the floor. For my part, I was jammed in and could not even cry for help, lest I might infringe an aneba or the like. To tell the truth I would have been pleasantly gratified if both parties had exterminated each other to the last man, but at least, I thought, those who had wanted to rush at me should perish.

This latter desire fortunately materialized, as after a five-minute bloody struggle my enemies, still shouting wildly, were routed. My defender came into my room gasping, but at the sight of the food he turned red and spun around.

"Kvari, kvari," he stammered and tried to close the door while going out, at which it finally collapsed.

With sudden inspiration, I took the bed cover and laid it over the food, which indeed solved the problem at once. My visitor came back in smiling, and placing his finger on his nose, he panted out a warm 'prick-pruck'. After mutual scratching of posteriors, a very friendly atmosphere evolved between us.

I had exactly the same feeling as when a magician says "abracadabra!" and a pigeon flies out of his top hat; what one does not understand is simply the connection between the "abracadabra!" and the pigeon.

Although the situation was extremely confused, I tried to conduct myself as befits a gentleman. I briefly begged his indulgence for my not being able to convey the gratitude I felt toward him, but frankly speaking I was a foreigner and in the Hin language there was no suitable expression for this.

I realized only afterward what dangers might stem from my rash sincerity, because in doing so I also disclosed that I had no idea of the nature of the kona, as I had so bravely declared myself only minutes before.

But the Behin settlement is a land of surprises.

For my visitor, instead of rebuking me, with a broad smile he expressed his great pleasure that even though I had not known what it was when confessing myself to be kona, this proved I had immediately felt the boeto given by the kona.

I must say straight away that I never came to know anything about the nature of the boeto. Nor did they themselves. Nobody knew what it was. They merely continued to debate whether the kona or the kemon gave the true boeto. It was about this that the two perpetually quarrelling parties, or whatever they were, had been founded.

After this incident, my new acquaintance began teaching me with utmost fervor. He explained what that feeling was called when our enemy was lying on the ground or when someone stronger hit us unjustly; what we feel toward those who fight with or against us; what kind of feeling is caused by the sight of spirituality; and what one feels toward a betik or a bivak. Thus I learned many words, such as those for joy, grief, gratitude, triumph, defeat, indignation, and respect. I also understood that *kvari* referred to a sort of apology, *ketni* to a rule of life, *kave* to shame; and yet these did not correspond precisely to these concepts as expressed in English, and the others had no equivalents at all. As to what the words *aneba, betik, vake, elak, lamik, borema, boeti,* and *bivak* meant, I did not learn—neither then nor to this very day. My questions were in vain. The Behins themselves simply did not know; they only explained that the aneba, for instance, must not be deprecated, that one had to behave toward a betik in a humble manner, but of the essence no one knew a thing; and it was not even proper to ask about such matters. One characteristic of the Behins' words was precisely this: it was forbidden not only to doubt their truth, but also to think about them. One simply had to believe, but they often did not even say in what—the point was simply to believe.

The situation reminded me very much of our mental hospitals, where, similarly, people feel pleasure, gratitude, love, and hatred, but while one person is happy painting his nose blue, another worships a duck's feather, and a third hurls himself on the fourth with indignation if the latter is not willing to bow before a faucet and say "abracadabra"; while, if he does utter the word "abracadabra," he has his hand kissed.

And here there were a vast number of such abracadabras, for instance the word kona itself.

My protector, who was called Zemoeki, reassured me that I need not be afraid, and whenever I became exposed to an attack, I had only to cry out "Vake kona!" at which a lot of people who belonged to the kona would come to my help, all brave and valiant Behins, whereas those belonging to the kemon were all base and hated the konas. He could not give me any reason, except that the kemon believed it gave "the true boeto," although it was widely known that the true boeto was completely impossible outside the kona. Anyone who did not admit this was heading in the wrong direction, and it was for this reason that I had to hate the kemons.

Then, all at once, Zamoeki said that were I to see a circle drawn anywhere, I should erase it and try to draw a square. If, however, anyone drawing a square on the walls were to be attacked by the kemons, I should not hesitate to fly to his assistance, because we had to keep together in defense of the square, and even sacrifice our lives for the anebas.

Then my new friend left with a warm prick-pruck, and I tried to get some fresh air.

I opened my window, then tried to warm my food, which had grown cold; but this was a problem, since the rickety electric hot plate I mentioned earlier had no desire to function any more.

Using my pocketknife, I managed to tinker with the broken switch, so finally the hot plate began to heat up, but then its broken legs gave way. In the end, though, I somehow managed to support it, warmed my lunch, and, considering the circumstances, ate it with a hearty appetite.

During my belated lunch, I endeavored to sum up my experiences on my first day here.

The Behins were definitely not hapless normal people expelled by the Hins' lack of understanding, but were indeed insane—that much was already beyond doubt. Their disease far exceeded the mental disorders known to us. Even in our lunatic asylums it may occur, for instance, that someone eats his handkerchief, imagines himself to be mincemeat pie, or has a falling out with someone else because the other is unwilling to see a feather duster as a scepter; but that they should create meaningless words at the cost of hard mental work for things that do not exist, and that the whole bedlam should subject itself to them, and that on account of stupid geometrical figures the whole society should pummel each other—such things cannot be imagined in our lunatic asylums.

The Reader may be justified in thinking that for the sake of effect, I perhaps color the account of my travels with things that do not quite conform to reality—in the manner of travelers who, to show off their having seen a great deal of the world, and relying on the fact that their data can hardly be checked, abuse the credulity of the public. I am afraid that during the chapters to follow the Reader's doubts will only grow further, so I must assure him that I have checked my travel notes several times, and rather than exaggerate even once, I preferred to include less in my book.

One thing is certain: At sunset on that first day, I remembered with a sigh the "horrors" of my "eventless" life among the Hins. I had thirsted for events. Well, my wish had definitely been granted—if only my nerves would be able to stand it!

The author is accepted into the kona, whose significance is not yet clear to him. His spirituality is taken away by force. He is given a peculiar post. We become acquainted with the Behins' theory of the nourishing quality of the pebble. We learn what the word lamik *means, about the Behins' extraordinary economic views, and about Boetology.*

A FEW DAYS LATER ZEMOEKI ENTERED MY ROOM, HIS FACE radiant with joy. Scratching my posterior, he let me know extremely cordially that great happiness was in store for me. In reply to my excited and joyful questions I was told that I had been accepted into the kona.

The answer somewhat cooled me down and, having hesitatingly inquired as to its practical value, I was again told only that it meant great joy to be a kona, for this was what gave the true boeto. When I asked what the boeto was, Zemoeki replied that to win the boeto was joy and happiness.

So I did not become much wiser and, instead of joy I felt a certain amount of embarrassment, which, however, I did not dare to voice.

Later I realized that boeto was the very same kind of empty word as ketni; an action was ketni, because it had to be done in a certain way—and, conversely, it had to be done in a certain way because it was ketni. It was this vicious circle that constituted the main feature of the Behins' confused twaddling, this arguing with no point of reference to connect their world with the coordinates of the outside world.

Being exposed to their whims, however, I did not venture to argue but, pretending even to be pleased, I cautiously asked what kind of conduct was necessary to receive the grace of the boeto. Zemoeki reassured me that he would arrange everything and left. Before long he returned with a companion who, as I came to know later, was called Zeremble.

Zemoeki and Zeremble then called me away to arrange and carry out my initiation. We crossed the vast yard and entered a distant building. The upper part of the door was boarded up, so that we had to bend down. I had not the slightest idea why they had made it like this.

Now we stepped into a very strange room, where none of the furniture was in its proper place or position. I saw a table that had only a frame with no top, but which was nevertheless fitted out with a back like that of a chair. From the bare frame, yellow pebbles hung on strings on the backs of which the stains of different paints could be seen trickling down.

Another table stood with its legs upward covered with some strange sheet, which, however, could not be used for either a bed sheet or a tablecloth, as it had holes punched all over and thick ropes intertwined over and over through the holes with yellow pebbles on the ends.

Behind the table there was a chair whose seat had a serrated edge, so that the thighs of anyone sitting down would have been in the greatest danger; which is not to mention that thorns were driven through the seat, making it impossible to sit on to begin with. As for the back of the chair, it was three times larger than necessary, with irregular carving all the way up.

In general, the whole room gave the impression that vandals had spoiled everything to make it unusable, or that I had entered a den of destructive spirits.

Fear and horror gripped my heart; I had strange forebodings. I cautiously asked Zemoeki: "What has happened here?"

Zemoeki opened his eyes wide. At first he did not understand why I asked, and it was only with considerable incredulity that I came to know that the devastation had not been perpetrated by an enemy army but by the owners themselves. When I asked why, he replied, "Because it is so *kipu*."

Another new word they had concocted in order to justify another piece of nonsense.

Of course, instead of reassuring me, the fact that the destruction had been self-inflicted gave rise to even more terrible forebodings concerning my future.

A few minutes later a door opened in the background and an odd-looking man entered. From his knees hung the aforementioned copper cubes. So he, too, was a betik. Over his shoulders he wore a large piece of glaring cloth that, with a little benevolent imagination, could have been taken for a raincoat by those with some common sense—and it would seem that he had pierced and torn it everywhere and hung scraps of glass from it so that it could not be used for such a purpose.

Now the betik tied two huge baking sheets underneath his soles, came up to me and, murmuring unintelligible words, hit me on the head with a hollow tin ball.

Laughter bubbled up inside me at these stupidities, but seeing that the others did not laugh at all but were touched and solemn when Baking Sheet Soles made his appearance, I stifled my sense of humor and, although it was difficult, contrived to adopt a solemn countenance.

When the ceremony was finished, everybody gathered around me. They scratched my posterior and were very delighted at my becoming a kona—which, as they had said, meant great joy, for I had thus won the true boeto.

The pleasure slowly spread into me as well, as I really felt relief at having managed to accomplish the boeto so smoothly. After what had happened previously, I had been prepared for much worse.

Unfortunately my pleasure was somewhat premature, as the Reader will see. But I must not get ahead of myself.

Having left the betik, I could not suppress a smile. I recalled my little son, who was happy and clapped his hands when he was given a piece of cake, and I imagined the puzzled little face he would have made at such words as: "Be glad, my son, because you have become a kona and won the boeto." He would obviously have drawn some conclusions as to the mental condition of his father. How deep is the darkness in which, compared even to the children of the glorious British monarchy, these miserable adults live!

On the way home I asked Zemoeki what I profited from becoming a kona, but I insisted that he say something factual and not merely to keep mentioning the boeto.

Their demented brains are so deeply involved in their fantasies that at first he did not even understand my question. He kept on asserting that all the anebas to which the kona, boeto, ketni, kipu, and other fantasies belonged constituted full reality, for it was these that sustained mankind; without these we could not even live, and anyone who did not feel the anebas was a bivak to whom it would be in vain to explain all these. And a bivak was a lost man, devoid of all content.

After a long struggle I succeeded in more or less bringing Zemoeki round to the dull but solid ground of the natural world, so that at last he groaned out the first fact.

"From now on, you, too, have the right to participate in the *buku*."

"What does that mean?"

"You have the right to beat the kemons if they draw their hideous circles on the wall or outrage the square."

"How is it possible to outrage a geometric figure?"

"They break the corners off, or draw diagonals into it."

I was somewhat embarrassed.

"Well, and what else?" I asked after a short interval.

"What do you mean by 'and what else'? Would you be able to tolerate the fact that they draw diagonals into the square?"

To tell the truth I would have, but Zemoeki's intonation made

me surmise that it was advisable to say no. I did my best to protest against this insinuation, declaring that I would immediately
tear the intestines out of anyone who drew diagonals into the
square.

This resolute attitude visibly restored my shaky reputation.
Zemoeki regained his composure and stated that I was a brave
man, although I did not have the slightest idea why he should
have thought this. I also learned that I was worthy of being taken
by the nose by the betik, which according to them was a very
good thing, as it happened only to exceedingly brave konas.

I was, however, much more interested in the subject of fighting
as representing a new danger, but when I inquired about it, he
said: "It is not fighting. It is buku."

"But you have just said that we must beat the kemons. Why is it
not fighting if we are to beat each other?"

"Not each other. The kemons."

"And the kemons the konas . . ."

"That's it."

"Well, then, why not each other?"

"Because we do not beat each other, only the kemons, and that
is quite another matter. This is buku, which is pervaded by the
boeto. Fighting is a nasty thing that a ketni man will not commit; the buku however makes one better and nobler, while also
developing solidarity and respect for each other."

I inquired twice but it became clear that I had in fact not misunderstood him. It is their faith that they cultivate respect and a
sense of togetherness by thrashing each other!

It took me some minutes to collect my thoughts. It was not as if
I had any doubt as to the value of my "privileges," but the greatest
problem of the sane mind among the crazy is how to manifest itself so that it should not be struck dead and yet speak reasonably.
I got into trouble several more times on account of the fact that
while common sense can walk straight with ease, when it tries to
limp it falls. The Behins sometimes seemed to me quite talented
in the way they limped.

The gentle Reader should not be surprised. Once, serving as a doctor among the Hins, I had a case—I was called to a patient whose symptoms suggested a mental illnes. He replied to questions with a completely confused mixture of sounds. When, for instance, I asked how he was, his reply was something like, "*Balevi abargetine trendad homagrido,*" which made not the slightest sense.

Of course, I reported in my institute that the patient talked disconnectedly. They asked what I meant by disconnected talk. I tried to demonstrate, but was forced to realize that I was unable to improvise meaningless heaps of letters and sounds. (By the way, while devising the above example, my mind doggedly sought words that made sense. The patient, however, had jabbered it all out without thinking.)

So I said in reply to Zemoeki that from the point of view of the kona, the most expedient way of taking revenge on the villainous kemons would be simply not to care for the square. Let them mutilate it and draw diagonals into it as they please. If we did not react, they would eventually become enraged.

Zemoeki and Zeremble looked at each other in consternation and stated that my only excuse could be my being a novice, for to speak of the anebas with such cynicism was a great sin, and by my words I exposed myself to the suspicion of aligning myself with the kemons.

The fruitless struggle truly wore out my brain. I curbed my rebellious common sense attitude with difficulty and promised that I should try to acquire some feeling for the anebas.

My greatest anxiety, however, was to avoid the danger of fighting, so I asked: "How does the buku usually commence?"

"The villainous kemons," answered Zemoeki, "burst into our rooms and break up the electric cookers, at which every decent kona, too, makes his way into the rooms of the kemons and breaks up their cookers. But it may also happen that the provocative behavior of the kemons gives rise to our righteous indignation, and so they force us into the buku—and then we break up their cookers first and they in turn ours."

Suddenly I realized with dismay why my cooker was in such a state of disrepair. I only asked why this mutual destruction had to take place.

"Well, we must certainly defend the hearth, mustn't we?" he answered in the most natural tone in the world.

With this we parted, and with a heavy heart I retired to rest. Finally I resolved that in the future I simply would not mix with them, so that by making myself independent I should bear it until I got free of them one way or another without trouble. Fortunately there were the wise Hins who handed me my meal every day, and for my own part, I would lock myself up in my room and not spend more time in the open than was strictly necessary, and even then I would not communicate with them.

Oh, if I had had the slightest idea of what might follow, the soothing sleep that soon overcame me would by no means have come to my eyes.

For the insanity of the Behins is the most terrible of all dangerous epidemics. While among us, only accidental infection is known, here I had to become familiar with the idea of infection by force. One cannot isolate oneself! They follow and compel one to rave with them. It is in vain for the sane mind to try diverting itself; it promises in vain to be silent, and against its better judgment it will watch their suicidal dance without a helping word. Madness is a generally binding rule here.

For if it were only belief in the anebas and other freaks that was at issue, one could carry it off by approving everything. But no! Their madness imposed actual physical suffering on everyone, from which there was no escape. This I myself was obliged to experience sadly the next day—the very next day, when I got my dinner through the wall.

No sooner had I sat down to eat than Zemoeki entered with a radiant face together with his two companions, and let me know that I was once more to be the recipient of great pleasure.

At this my teeth were set on edge and I broke into a sweat. Not without reason. Zemoeki announced that the Council of Betiks had permitted me to partake of the boeto and deliver up my spirituality.

With this, he blindfolded his two companions; they felt their way to my food, covered it with a handkerchief, and simply took it away.

I looked after them dumbfounded. I wanted to say that I could not starve, but as any word about eating would have been kave and would only have shocked him, I explained to Zemoeki, in a faltering, devious voice, that without spirituality I felt I would die.

Zemoeki replied benevolently that spirituality was acknowledged to be no more than the burden of life, while to every decent and honest kona the boeto was not a blow; why this was how spirituality got to the betik, by which it purified the contaminations and became the bikru's material manifestation. Thus I served the kona, kipu, and ketni as well, so it meant pleasure and honor to my own self if I partook of the graces of the boeto.

I could not help it—this delight did not satisfy me. Why, my life was at stake!

I did not let Zemoeki go, but made him sit down, and asked him to find some way for me to partake of spirituality; for, after all, it could not be denied that everybody retained some relationship with it.

This intimate conversation also untied Zemoeki's tongue, and he confessed to me in a whisper that he, too, partook of it daily and promised to be of help if I would only treat what he had told me as confidential.

Having assured him of my discretion, we talked the matter over thoroughly and he suggested that if I wished to partake of spirituality, I should perform some useful work, as I could not expect the betiks to feed me gratis.

This surprised me immensely, as it was known to all that the food was handed in by the Hins, so that practically everybody was a parasite; if, however, we still had wanted to distinguish between Behin and Behin, then it was only the betiks, who simply took away my spirituality, who could have been called parasites.

When I broached the subject, however, I got a resentful answer, as if I had taken their spirituality away—and Zemoeki stated that, on the contrary, as the bee got the honey from the beekeeper, so we, too, got our spirituality from the betik.

I could not believe my ears; I thought he had confused the words by accident, but as it turned out, they actually professed that the beekeeper gave the honey to the bees, and in a similar way everyone owed a debt of gratitude to his spirituality-giving betik, and I should just contemplate where it would lead if the betiks were to cease functioning one day and everyone would die of hunger.

To this I answered that the Hins provided the spirituality, against which Zemoeki strongly protested. And when I asserted that I had seen it being handed in with my own eyes, he replied that it would be good for me to dispense with my eyes. A true kona could not say such a kave thing; we had to believe that it was the betik who gave it, besides which, man had not only eyes but also bruhu, and this was more important.

The bruhu, too, signifies something nonexistent. With words, of course, only existing things can be described, so I cannot relate anything on its own merit, only as to when they use it.

Well, the bruhu was the final cause of the whole of this unnatural way of life and looking at things.

The damaged chair is needed because it is kipu, you must wail "vake" because it is ketni, the square must not be violated, as it is aneba. And if sane minds question why the ketni, kipu, and aneba are necessary at all, these people will reply, "because man has bruhu." This bruhu needs only things that for man himself are unnecessary.

According to this, the supposition that the bruhu as ultimate cause should be translated as "paranoia" would seem obvious; the illness of the Behins, however, went beyond the symptoms of paranoia, to say nothing of the fact that they kept mentioning the bruhu not as a state of mind but as something self-existent, even as something that existed and at the same time did not exist; for when I asked what the bruhu was like, they looked at me shocked and called me bivak, but could not describe its form.

Zemoeki offered benevolently to be of help to me in securing a useful occupation, and until then would let me have some of his own spirituality.

Indeed, a few days later he took me to a betik. On Zemoeki's advice, with my left hand on my head, I held one of my feet with my right hand, and surpassing even his yell, I wailed "vake-vake!"—at which the betik, with regard to Zemoeki's person, received me very cordially, and, calling me kaleb, inquired after the growth of my nose and was pleased to state that he was willing to employ me as beratnu, although many outstanding konas had competed for this position, including some who had already given evidence of their feeling for the anebas by tearing out the guts of several kemons.

So with that, I took up my post.

For what I had to do from then on, I blush with shame as I write. I accept that my Readers will despise me, a British subject, for sinking so low, and I cannot be silent about it, as it is my firm resolution to speak out plainly and sincerely about everything in accordance with the true facts as is worthy of an English gentleman, even though the truth may be disadvantageous to me.

By way of excuse I have only to mention that I had to keep my position, as otherwise I would have exposed myself to starvation. To reassure my fellow countrymen, I further declare that I did not forget my duty to my country among the Behins, either, and in my humiliating situation I never disclosed my background—whenever I was asked about it I always declared myself American.

Hoping that by my correct conduct I have succeeded a little in appeasing my beloved compatriots, I will try to describe my work. It entailed two tasks. The first was that every third day the Behins slung a peculiar piece of cloth—torn to rags—over my shoulders and I had to carry a shining square over the yard while a baking-sheet-soled betik walked before me with a tin box in his hands. A strange melody was played around me on musical instruments, some device generated putrid gas, and finally I had to set on fire a suit of very good clothes.

My other task was the distribution of the yellow pebbles. This meant that I had to collect yellow pebbles that on certain days I carried in the aforementioned tin box in front of the betik. They rattled noisily. The betik stepped beside me and, hitting the side of the box with a pebble, twice motioned to me to distribute the pebbles. And I opened the lid and gave one to everyone. At this, in an ecstasy of joy, people grabbed their right foot up into a hand, cried "vake-vake!" and, squeezing the pebbles under their arms, dispersed.

Although this performance in itself was exceedingly farcical and outdid the most bizarre carnival, the most ludicrous thing was the explanation: these unfortunates believed that the pebble they squeezed under their arm was nourishing; they were even convinced that it was this pebble that maintained life, the human body, and they praised the betik for it. The meal, as we already know, was despised by public opinion, although everyone ate it. (The word "spirituality" was used only to soothe their consciences.)

But with this we have not yet reached the limit of the Behins' absurd behavior. With it also went the belief that only those pebbles were nourishing whose box the betik had touched. Pebbles gathered from the ground became nourishing only when placed under the arm. They would not swallow them, however, and even touching them to the mouth was forbidden, as this would have amounted to an outrage of the pebble. So far as they were concerned it was possible to "outrage" a pebble for, as we know, eating and the mouth were shameful things. I myself saw a lawsuit against a Behin who was accused of eating bread and butter with the pebble under his arm. With the most serious expressions they heard a crowd of witnesses who refuted that it could have occurred this way. The Behin, however, was still convicted, as it had been proved that, with the pebble under his arm, he had mentioned "bread and butter," by which, therefore, the pebble had already suffered a wrong. On such occasions, even to think of spirituality was not permitted.

This madness of squeezing a pebble rattled my mind, and on one occasion I ventured to state in front of Zemoeki that perhaps the pebble was not nourishing after all. In evidence I referred to the fact that no living organism in the world took nourishment this way. Zemoeki in return explained to me that the pebble theory was verified by precisely this fact. As man had bruhu, he did not belong to the common living organisms of the world, so it was self-evident that he had different needs. I answered that as I had become acquainted with human anatomy at Oxford University, I could confirm that from his stomach to every single hair, each of man's organs needed food and not pebbles. Zemoeki, however, warned me that I again referred to my eyes and experience, which was not good, and warmly recommended that I should beware of casting doubt upon pebble-nourishment as that, too, was an aneba, and the Behins were very particular about their bruhu, and they had taken bloody revenge for such blasphemy on more than one lamik.

So again I heard the baleful word "lamik," at the mention of which I was to draw my knife, and of whose meaning I still had no idea.

At that moment Zemoeki painfully yelled "vake-vake!" and as I looked up I saw Baking Sheet Soles approaching, before whom a Behin walked and watered the grass.

Of course, I myself also snatched my foot up, and we attempted to outvie each other in wailing until the creature passed out of sight. Then I asked why the grass had been watered before him, but Zemoeki could only answer that he was a betik.

In reply to my question as to why the betik needed wet grass, he answered again, "Because he is a betik."

I gazed at him with a puzzled expression and he explained that there were even more betik betiks, too, in front of whom two or three Behins watered because they were still more betik.

After all this I dared to venture only quite timidly that watering was perhaps not the most useful occupation.

"I would have you know," said Zemoeki, "that you are not in a position to assert any such thing."

"Why?"

"Because you are a beratnu, and a beratnu must not say things like that."

Thus it was not because the assertion was not true, but because I was a beratnu.

So I thought it better to keep silent, and I continued distributing the yellow pebbles.

Later I had the opportunity to see the most fantastic offices that can be imagined. The Rust Measuring and Record Office bear special mention, though in a later chapter.

From among the posts held by people in this society, I must mention that of the "figure-guards." One of the trees in the yard had a shining tin square wired to the top. Under this tree two Behins permanently idled their time away in shifts. They kept guard lest any depraved kemon should throw stones at, or use insulting language toward, the tin.

The common sense reaction would have been to throw the whole rubbish into the dustbin so that there should be nothing to be pelted and guarded, but I naturally no longer dared to put forward such a frank and reasonable opinion. Instead I merely asked Zemoeki whether it would not have been better if these guards did some work that might be of more service to the welfare of the kona. Zemoeki resentfully put me wise to the fact that it was they who did the most honest and useful work possible for the benefit of the kona.

I fell silent and, wishing to emphasize my appreciation of his remarks, said that it was gratifying that the workers met with such recognition.

But in vain. Among the Behins you cannot say anything that

does not offend some monomania. Now I was scolded for having called the elak figure-guards "workers."

For my own work, by the way, I received money, the existence of which I had totally forgotten about since being among the Hins. With the money I had to go to the Nourishing and Life-Giving Office, where I could buy spirituality, but considerably less of it than I had gotten from the Hins, as the bulk of the food was eaten up by the betiks. It was here, in this place of confiscation and distribution, that I saw in the end the most realistic occupation. They at least concerned themselves with existing materials, even though they did so in a wretched and wicked manner.

I became much less well nourished, and so I met once more with the other concept I had forgotten while among the Hins, as if it had not even existed: financial difficulties. Only amid these circumstances did I begin to see things once again from a materialistic point of view; for I admit that until my food was taken away, I had not given a thought as to how the others were fed.

Now I came to know that there were many hungry people among the Behins, from whom even the clothes due to them had been taken away—they were even driven out of their rooms, so that many of them dwelled in the open air. I repeat, there is no escape from the insanity of the Behins. One cannot remain aloof: they follow you. They take away your food and clothes, and it would be in vain to nod assent and let them do so, so that they should just permit you to retire into a part of the yard like a hermit to grow potatoes and fruit. That is not permitted, either. The only mode of life is to join them and actively take part in their suicidal dance of death.

The freedom of private life cannot even be mentioned. They take you along with them. They rob you, torture you, and compel you to betray your sobriety daily; and you cannot have a minute's rest, as the bedlam is ceaselessly seething in the background and swishing its whip, chasing after you to cause suffering.

As I have already mentioned, new clothes were confiscated, too. Some of them were worn out by the betiks while the others they tore and pummeled to rags as they could "use" them only in that condition. Apart from this, and with my heart aching, I had to set a suit of clothes on fire every third day while holding the square of shining tin on high. And the Behins got only cast-off clothes, and even these they had to wear for years while before their very eyes brand-new fine suits were burnt and torn, to which they shouted, "vake, vake!"—as they believed that without this destruction they would have gone naked.

I should have liked once to tell Zemoeki my opinion, but having already had the bitter experience of seeing them regard anyone who tried to improve their life as their enemy, I inquired only as to why the burning of the clothes under the square was necessary. "The boeto," was the answer. "By this we win the radiation of the bikru for the buku against the kemons and the circle."

I could not prevent myself from remarking that in this case, I still did not hold the buku an expedient affair; but lest Zemoeki should accuse me of aligning myself with the kemons, I hurriedly added that I wanted to take sides neither with the konas nor with the kemons but was of the opinion that it would be best if there were neither square nor circle, if nobody quarrelled about words, if it were not necessary to take people's spirituality and clothes on account of the boeto, if the two *behas* made peace with each other, if the concepts "beha" and "aneba" were abolished, and if by working together we might be able to produce much more spirituality—thus everybody would be able to live better and the betiks would not have had less either, in fact their part, too, would increase.

Believe it or not, it was then that the Behins railed against me most furiously. They would rather have suffered me taking sides with the kemons, but sanity they could not stand. They said I would do well to mind my words, as they dangerously resembled that madness shown by some so forthright that they had been burned alive.

At my question as to why this was a crime, they replied, "Plung-

ing the world into blood, flame, and poverty can only be a sufficiently heinous crime!"

The Behins announced that only incensed lunatics showed the
desire to eradicate the boeto, ketni, kipu, and everything they
valued as the splendid feats of civilization that they were then
enjoying. And if I wanted to know who they were, well then,
I should know! The lamiks!

That was how I came to know the meaning of the word regarded as the most dreadful of all slander, and for which one
must immediately stab the slanderer. It was the sane mind that
they called lamik, as I had in fact guessed up till then, but now
I was sure of it.

I fell silent. I had been thinking for a long time about how
I could help them out of their grinding poverty without touching
upon their suicidal idiocies.

Eventually I said that I did not want to hurt the anebas, and
I felt that the square and the buku should remain, but on the
other hand, it would be expedient to assign the many beratnus,
waterers, and confiscators to the fields to produce corn, honey,
and fruit, whereby we could acquire much more spirituality.

"Impossible," answered Zemoeki. "Because if the beratnu does
not carry the square and the waterer does not water, each will
lose his spirituality."

For all I tried, I did not understand a single word of this; I believed Zemoeki did not understand what I had said, and to make
myself clearer I spoke about how many more flats there would
be if everyone were ordered to build houses rather than have so
many living in one room with so many others, some even spend-
ing the night under the stars.

Instead of replying, Zemoeki took me by the arm and led me to
the house I had seen on the day of my arrival, with one half built
and the other torn down. The only novelty in it now was that
they were rebuilding the demolished part and in the meantime
pulling down the part that had been built.

"Do you see," Zemoeki said, "how wisely the kona sees to it

that its members should have a flat?" I had already been itching to know the secret of this strange house and, taking this opportunity, I asked why they pulled the other half down. He gave the same reply, however, as had the mason earlier.

"So as not to cause homelessness."

At this I timidly remarked that the best help against homelessness would be the existence of flats. I don't know what was so ridiculous about this, but Zemoeki laughed heartily, called me a poor bivak, and declared that I also seemed to be unaware of the science of the economy of housing, which is well known even to the most uneducated Behin. I tried to remain calm and politely asked him to enlighten me on the Behins' science of the economy of housing. We sat down on a bench and Zemoeki began to talk.

He related that once, long ago, the Behins had built houses, setting out from the erroneous belief that this would relieve the housing shortage. Material justice, however, demanded that only those among the homeless should receive a flat who had participated in the construction work.

Accordingly, the builders were given a fancy printed certificate by virtue of which they had the right to housing for a month.

At the beginning, of course, they were given the certificate in vain, because only some of the builders could receive a flat, but as the building progressed, more and more people had roofs over their heads. Everything seemed to be in order.

However, as the building program was carried to fruition, the dwellers, one after the other, had to be turned out into the yard as they were no longer building. So the scholars concluded that building resulted in homelessness.

If the houses were ready, I asked, why were their builders still expected to produce monthly certificates? Why could they not stay forever?

Zemoeki replied that to do so would have been unjust; that it was lamik to demand a flat for a man who did not work any more. However, he admitted that the problem was extremely grave, and that to solve it, the kona had employed many well-paid scholars who racked their brains day and night. They also propounded the scientific law of the economy of housing as follows:

Flat displaces man.

The solution, however, had been a long time in coming, as the problem was double-edged: while building was in progress there were certificates but no flats, and when complete there were flats but no certificates. In the beginning they tried to overcome the difficulty by building still more flats, and while these were being built the builders could remain in their old places. This way, however, more and more flats remained unoccupied, with which nothing could be done.

Everybody had already surmised that flat-building work was useful for the public only if it did not give rise to flats. So they realized that people were to be given employment so that they could reside in them. The flats, however, were to be pulled down immediately in order to avoid catastrophic homelessness.

"But then it is not actually building," I said.

"Of course not! That's all we need! This is the kona's wise provision for its members. The kona puts a pickaxe in the hands of each of its members lest they should remain homeless. This is why we have to hold the kona in high esteem."

I was becoming more and more convinced that some strange force was pushing these people away from reality and logic. Indeed, they *wanted* to be crazy. Why? Reality is so simple and obvious, while raving mad dances demand complicated care and torment the body and soul—and still the Behins choose the latter.

I must beg the pardon of the subjects of the civilized British monarchy for burdening them with the description of such nonsense. But let it be said by way of excuse that when I contrast ways and ideas of the Behins with those of my own enlightened country, which would not only refuse to accept such things but would not even understand them, I believe I am serving a patriotic purpose—namely, I wish to teach my beloved countrymen to value and appreciate the life-shaping force of English soil and of England's sober economic approach.

To prove my words I wish to mention one more of the idiosyncrasies in Behin economic thinking and mathematical ignorance, the reading of which will certainly fill my beloved fellow countrymen with the proud consciousness of intellectual superiority. There were 1,200 konas in the settlement, and that is the number of food portions they received. The Nourishing and Life-Giving Office, of course, confiscated the portions. The betiks, however, gave only as much money to the people as enabled them to buy 900 portions, and 300 were left over. These were purchased by the betiks and their entourage, as they got much more money.

This is, however, only an ugly and inhuman deed, and it is not this I wish to speak about but, rather, their mathematical absurdities.

On one occasion it was resolved that people's wages were to be decreased. The decrease took place accordingly, and the next day, instead of 900 portions, only 750 could be purchased. The 150 portions left over were not bought by the rich, either, for they too had only one stomach each.

People dizzily staggered around with rumbling stomachs, and the food became putrid while stored away in the Nourishing and Life-Giving Office. In sensible Europe this would be unconcievable.

The measure adopted next, however, was even more peculiar. A man in his right mind would on such an occasion—having come to realize his miscalculation—either distribute the rest among the hungry or raise the salary of the people.

No!

Unbelievable though it may appear, the betiks ordered that the leftover food should be thrown away.

I myself did not want to believe this act of vandalism until I saw it with my own eyes. But when I did see it, I advised them benevolently that if they could do nothing with spirituality, they should at least not take it away from Behins.

But they explained to me that this could not be done, as it

would have been akin to robbery and would mean violent interference in the private lives of those whose freedom was the basic principle of Behin civilization. And for the rest, they recommended that I should refrain from such lamik statements.

But the best is yet to come! When I asked them why they threw away the food, they said it was because there was too much of it!

And we have not yet reached the true heights of the ridiculous!

It was the Behin's firm conviction that they starved because there was too much food! And for their follies they blamed not themselves but the *circumstances*; whose improvement, so they hoped, would enable them to fill their stomachs.

This therefore represented the mathematics of the Behins!

I think, in light of all this, it will be no surprise that the Behins were rather weak at the exact sciences, too—or, rather, they knew chemistry and physics, but did not dare to admit that they knew.

The civilized Reader may ask how this is possible at all—the reader who has accustomed in Europe to the idea that scientific knowledge is nothing to be ashamed of, and indeed that it is to one's credit!

To tell the truth, I myself do not understand all this, so instead I would acquaint the Reader with *boetology* without further comment.

I discovered the existence of this strange doctrine on one occasion while I was standing in the yard. Someone came up against me backward and banged into me. He stepped on my foot so hard that I drew in my breath with pain.

The Behin, however, kept on backing into me without a word of apology.

"If you don't mind, could you kindly watch where you're going?" I grumbled with annoyance, but he replied imperturbed, "Today the moon is full."

I did not know what he was talking about and would not have even cared, had I not seen on the very same day at least two-hundred people walking backward who would not have taken a single step forward for all the world!

Finally I asked Zemoeki. He laughed heartily and reassured me that I should not bother with it. "They are stupid idiots," he said, "who believe that if they do not go backward during a full moon they will lose the grand boeto."

I was sincerely surprised, and thought with great pleasure that this was the first reasonable opinion I had heard from Zemoeki. My delight, however, soon diminished as Zemoeki continued.

"Of course, not a word of it is true. Every man in his senses knows that the only formula for winning the grand boeto is that we should not drink water over which a bat has flown."

I no longer dared to laugh, but merely continued inquiring, and in the course of our conversation some fantastic things came to light.

The Behins in general believe that clouds solidify into a stone-hard state from time to time. At such times a strange being runs into them from above and splits them asunder. The sound of their being split was the rumbling of thunder.

As to the nature of this strange being, opinions differed widely. The Behins were not exactly sure of its physical appearance, either. According to some, this being split the clouds with its horn; according to others, with its foot. This was hotly debated. The Reader would, however, be quite wrong to believe that either of these parties attempted to present any positive proof of their view. If I asked why it was so and not otherwise, someone would reply that because anyone who interpreted it differently had lost the grand boeto. And of this everyone is afraid.

Of course, they had no definite conception of the grand boeto, either. It was my impression that the Behins didn't know a thing about the very notions they themselves had invented. Gravitational acceleration they were familiar with; and yet they continuously disputed the attributes of the grand-boeto. As long as they'd invented it, why not in such a way as would suit them? I could at least make out that the loss of the grand boeto was some sort of disease, but not exactly. I could perhaps call this loss a "disaster," but why it was a disaster, they themselves did not even know. I was often told about some person that he or she had already lost the grand boeto, but to me they seemed free of physical or other defects. Therefore I hasten to tell the Reader who seeks to contemplate the disadvantages of the loss of the grand boeto, that doing so is in vain. The Behins' words have no meaning. They are afraid of the words themselves.

It was all the more surprising for me to learn that the hornians and the footians committed homicide more than once to defend their particular theory as to the method by which the strange being split clouds asunder; and indeed they fought long and bloody struggles in order that people should imagine not one image but another. There were even people who were capable— in spite of the knife pointed at their breasts—of declaring that the cloud-rifter did not thunder with his horn but with his foot, and preferred to die rather than wisely leave it at that.

What was the sense in subjecting others to such mental games? This was just as mysterious as the sense of the whole thing in the first place.

The Reader may already be annoyed at hearing so much nonsense, but I must announce that I have not yet reached the end—and this is the point. These people well knew the nature of thunder! When I tried explaining to Zemoeki that thunder is the sound following the electric discharge between clouds, he reassured me with a smile that everyone knew that.

So I asked why they still spoke about the cloud-rifter.

"Because the cloud-rifter exists," he replied.

When I drew his attention to the contradiction in his words, Zemoeki said I seemed to have no sense of boetology, and that was a gross deficiency. "Boetology is true because we must say it's true, and man, being a rational creature, necessarily considers things not only in their stark reality but sees them also on a higher plane. Anyone who is not imbued by boetology has nothing to distinguish him from the brute beast that simply grazes on grass and runs out of the burning stable guided by blind instinct."

I remarked that it was precisely our being rational creatures that required us to try to find the proper image of things, but Zemoeki severely rebuked me, saying that the proper picture of things was what boetology taught, as it was needed by man. Even with the most careful recollection of my studies at Oxford, I could not remember any thesis according to which the human organism would have needed boetology; but not feeling inclined to start an unnecessary debate with lunatics, I asked Zemoeki instead to tell me why we needed it.

"Because it makes the Behin Behin," he answered proudly.

Of the truthfulness of that I myself was already deeply convinced, but I did not understand why it was necessary to boast about it. Zemoeki expounded that boetology was a firm point onto which a vacillating person might always hold, both preventing one from taking the wrong way and leading one to a haven of refuge. "The individual and society alike are in need of a point of support. Without it we grope about in darkness helplessly; and without this pillar, society, too, would collapse."

Concerning the solidity and necessity of this point of support I still had, of course, some doubts. But lest I should jeopardize my position by further fruitless dispute I asked Zemoeki instead to explain to me what connection boetology had with walking backward.

At this I was informed that there were several different commonly held views of the nature of the cloud-rifter, as there were concerning what form he took.

One group suggested that the cloud-rifter lived in a cave and smiled ceaselessly. This they propounded as an eternal truth; and the betiks, too, tolerated and even approved of this view.

The other group asserted that the cloud-rifter was sometimes angry—namely, when the Behin did not go backward when the moon was full. Such Behins lost the grand boeto. This also, was of course an eternal truth and was taught to children as such and was approved by the betiks.

According to yet a third group, one could walk any way one liked, but—as Zemoeki had previously informed me—was not permitted to drink water over which a bat had flown; otherwise the cloud-rifter would become angry and the Behin concerned would lose the grand boeto.

And these three diametrically opposed ideas passed for eternal truths recognized by the betiks—into the bargain, by the same betiks!

And this is where we come to the crux of the matter.

All these were not only tolerated but supported. If, however, somebody had dared to say that nobody knew anything for certain about the nature and attributes of the cloud-rifter—that there was no common view, that we should therefore not create for ourselves uncertain notions but remain within the physically discovered fields of nature—he was designated as lamik, and his contagious ideas were regarded as subversive to civilization. The propagators of such behavior were severely punished, and it was declared that anyone who gave credit to such false doctrines would lose the grand boeto.

I beg the Reader not to slam the book down. I write every word from my travel notes and may I lose salvation if I tell a single lie.

The most foolish event in the course of my being a beratnu, however, was the bileving of the ear-betik, in which I, too, had to participate—namely, to rattle the pebbles.

Grotesque though this bileving may seem, I feel the book of my travels would not be complete without it.

The bileving of the ear-betik took place as follows. Two enormous chained copper cubes were hung on the ears of a betik, then two Behins took his feet, another two his hands, and dangling like this he was carried about the yard, where the whole madhouse had gathered together. From his ears the copper cubes dangled and yet he smiled. Several waterers including myself went in front, followed by a motley crew of grotesque-looking characters. A length of frayed, unraveled rope hung from the nose of one, and the outstretched palm of another held a brick with a hole in it; each of them was presently smothered under heaps of fine clothes as the ragged crowd howled frantically. Many onlookers fell prostrate before suddenly springing up, while some took their shoes off, slammed them down, then threw them into the air; and from so many throats inarticulate monkeylike sounds gargled forth.

I was afraid they would strike us dead at any minute—indeed, this would not have surprised me in the least. I learned only later that the crowd had been howling not from anger but with joy.

And when I asked the reason for such rejoicing over this ugly and repellent caricature of natural human dignity, they replied, "Why, there is only one ear-betik, and he bilevs only once every eight years!"

11

*The author arrives in the skoro. We learn the methods
used to warp thinking. The Behins falsify geometry.
The author has a dispute over a child's bruhu, which he
unwittingly spoils.*

I SUPPOSE IT IS SCARCELY NEWS IF I SAY THE BEHIN'S SICK
brain did not spare children either. Far from sparing them, they
poisoned the innocent souls of children with the most bizarre,
delirious lies.

To make what follows readily comprehensible I must emphasize that although the disease of the Behins showed the
characteristics of an epidemic, as a physician who had acquired
no small amount of experience both at Oxford University and
during fifteen years of practice, I can definitely claim that this
strange disease is not inheritable.

To express it more precisely, only the susceptibility to the
Behinic disease is hereditary—a disease that, however, without
the presence of harmful circumstances would never break out in
acute symptoms.

But—as the Reader already knows—the Behins do not tolerate
sanity among them and, in the same way as they endeavored to
force me, too, into madness, there is no escape for the child born
with a sane mind, either.

Nobody can withdraw from intellectual degeneration. No
sooner has the child learned to speak than they place the Behin's

hands on his heart and try to confuse his clear sight; and in this area, I must admit, they have acquired extensive knowledge. Their methods were so refined as to be almost admirable, and sometimes I had to admit with sincere amazement that if all these efforts had been spent not on ruining the child but on training him usefully, then perhaps the Behins would have constituted the most perfect society in the world.

It was astounding how much energy the Behins devoted to this. A child is sent to a special institute for degeneration, where the adults keep on reiterating the most fantastic figments of the imagination until his natural sense becomes confused, he sees everything in a false light, and once he has completely lost his natural judgment, they call him a "skoro Behin."

My Readers may imagine how useless such a skoro Behin is in life. I dare say that in a reasonable society they could not be employed in any job.

Let us imagine, for example, the consequences of such a skoro Behin—who holds food to be contemptible—going to a grocery store! Or what devastation would be perpetrated in a tailor's shop by those who hold clothes torn to rags and weighed down by stones more valuable than intact comfortable clothes, to say nothing of the bloody battles that would break out because one table is round and another is square.

Well, I must here confirm that not only was the skoro Behin not removed from work but was considered even more fit for it than those with clear and unspoiled minds; and, what is more, the more confused his concepts about the world, the greater the respect he enjoyed and the higher the posts he received. Anyone in whom the proper faculty of judgment still flickered was excluded from work as being useless. The case of a person who had insufficiently asserted the appropriate figments of the imagination was worse yet; for if he dared to profess what was, in fact, reality, they even punished him.

Racking my brain as to what would happen if the wise Hins did not provide for the Behins, I came to the conclusion that this upside-down society would die of starvation in no time; if it didn't first beat itself to death. It is nonsense to wage war against nature and mathematics. I may say, it is only after seeing Behin statesmen that one can really appreciate the wise leaders of one's own nation.

In observing the Behins, it occurred to me just how shocked the educated citizens of my country had been by the systematic and wanton crippling of Chinese women's feet. What they would say if they heard that there is a part of the earth, darker than darkest Asia, where not the feet but the head of man, his God-given common sense itself, is crippled so as to be unusable?! With crippled feet one can live, but if our feet, hands, tongue, and all our senses obey the unnatural orders of a crippled mind, life can be no more than a series of grotesque and inexpedient sufferings where death follows as a salvation.

It was true that these unfortunates also felt suffering and plea-sure in reverse, but is it possible to imagine a body whose health would develop by rejecting food and not by consuming it?

The Reader may ask where I learned all this. My reply is that I had to acquaint myself with the institution of the skoro. I had been a beratnu for just four days when the betik sent me to the skoro to distribute yellow pebbles to the children.

Taking the tin box of pebbles with me, I set off. I reached a building surrounded by a high stone wall. This had been built by the Behins, so the Reader may imagine what a rickety construc-tion it was.

What first caught my eye in the yard was a long, plank structure consisting of about fifty outhouses. I thought at least a thousand children must be interned here, only I did not know where, for apart from this large structure I saw a small, barn-like building.

Entering, I found fifty children crammed together. Not another person would have fit; the air was intolerable. A large, shining square was nailed over the entrance. All over the walls hung pictures the sense of which I was unable to fathom. One of them depicted a Behin corpse with his bowels hanging out, on which another Behin, someone with bloodshot eyes, was dancing away. Another showed a man lying on the grass with blood oozing from his battered head. He was smiling, and in his hand he held a square under which was written: "Oh! what a pleasure!"

Unbelievable!

In one picture something bulged under a cloth, beneath which the edge of a dish showed, and below it was a word readily translated as, "ugh!" I saw pictures of damaged furniture and clothes. A chair had one leg missing and a bent nail was driven into its back; a table had a hole punched in it through which a broomstick was thrust; from the upper end of the broomstick hung a mutilated earthenware pot, a chunk of limestone, and a dead rat. Below this picture was the inscription, "Kipu."

Between the children walked the hawk-eyed *proko*—an adult whose calling was to reiterate the figments of the imagination to the children until they believed them. The proko's methods reminded me of an old acquaintance of mine who had trained his dog so that if he threw a slice of paper to it saying, "It's very good," the dog would snatch it and swallow it, whereas if he tossed a bit of meat to it and said, "Ugh, what a terrible taste," the dog would turn away from it. (I wonder incidentally what would have happened to the dogs of the world if people of such mentality had been their masters?) But even in my wildest dreams I would not have imagined that such a result could be achieved with a thinking human brain, as well. On the other hand, it was probable that the Behins, who for many centuries had systematically been crippling their brains, were susceptible to the Behinic disease from the very first minute of their birth.

The proko just walked to and fro among the children and sometimes cried out: "*Kricc!*"

At this the children had to jump up, place their left hands on the middle of their backs, and with the right hands reach under their right knees and take hold of their left ears.

When I asked him why the children had to be forced into such strange positions, the proko replied that they had to become accustomed to complying with regulations!

Then he yelled something at the children at which the whole flock painfully broke into the "vake vake."

I opened the tin box and handed him the yellow pebbles.

The proko took them, poured them onto a table in a heap, went away, and returned with a covered plate. Under the cloth I noticed the most delicious sweets.

This he placed beside the pebbles and called upon the children one by one. Whoever reached out for the plate was hit on the hand by the proko so that their hands immediately turned blue, whereupon the other children had to threaten him with their fists and shout, "kave!" Whoever reached out for a pebble was scratched by the proko on the posterior while the rest of the children smiled and said, "ketni."

After the distribution of the pebbles, the proko commenced to tell the children how this gift should be appreciated and how the Behins had attained it for themselves with so much sacrifice and bloodshed.

He then launched into a long story on the Behins' past, which I shall impart to the Reader in a nutshell only.

In the proko's telling, the past of the Behins consisted of three main eras.

In the beginning there was the "primitive" or "cruel" age, followed by the "transitional" or "half-raw" age, and then ensued the "modern" or "perfect" age.

Many centuries ago, in the primitive or cruel age, the butuks trampled and practiced extortion upon the people. From the back of each butuk's neck hung an enormous horseshoe, and not only did the people not take it off, but they also respected the butuks. (The children laughed loudly at these words.) Belki was effected by putting their finger into each other's ear when meeting. (The children laughed even more loudly at this.) And it was considered kipu to sew patches on clothes. (Uproarious laughter.)

But there came a certain Behin named Zecheche, who termed

the butuks base conjurers, the ketni and kipu humbug and fantasy, and demanded the rule of reason.

The butuks captured him and skinned him alive. But Zecheche already had many followers, and for fifty years bloodshed was uninterrupted. Finally the Zechechists expelled the butuks and assumed the leadership of the Behins. From this point there began the transitional or half-raw age.

However, peace did not last long, as the new governing body, whose members called themselves *bataks*, began to oppress the people within a short space of time just like the butuks had done before them. They took everything away from the people and gave nothing in exchange. From each batak's belt hung a piece of lead on a wire, and the people, instead of overthrowing the bataks, respected them and cringed before them. (At this the children almost burst from laughter.) It was belki to scratch each other's knee, and if somebody smeared a piece of linen with different colored stains they called it kipu. (The children cackled away all the more.)

And it was then that there came the great Zachacha, who named the bataks base conjurers, whereas of the ketni and kipu he courageously stated that these were humbug and fantasy, and demanded the rule of reason.

The bataks captured Zachacha, had his bowels torn out while he was alive and thrown to the dogs, then set out to slaughter his followers with the most exquisite cruelty. (At these words the children burst into tears.)

However, the number of Zachacha's followers was on the increase. A sea of blood followed for sixty years, in the course of which several bataks were captured. They were tied up, had their teeth torn out one by one, their tongues burnt out, and they were then impaled. (The children jumped up, clapped, and rejoiced.)

In the end the Zachachists won. This was the start of the modern or perfect age, when leadership came into the hands of the elak betiks from whose knees the honorable bilevs hang, and whose wisdom ensures the rule of reason. And since then, everybody may have an equal share of the yellow pebbles, whether he be betik, beratnu, proko, or simple waterer. (The children jumped up and vaked.)

He also spoke of a figure called Zuchuchu, who was in those days fervently organizing the people against order and peace, did not blush to call the honorable betiks sanctimonious pick-pockets, instigated rebellion against the ketni and the kipu, and demanded that not the chair but the wardrobe should be studded with thorns, that belki should be performed by pulling the ear, and rule should be taken over by the biteks. And all this he did with reference to reason, although obviously only a demented fool could speak in this way, and such a fool would sooner or later receive his due punishment. (The children gave expression to their abhorrence, and shaking their fists they demanded that Zuchuchu's eyes be burned out.)

I may say that not even the most audacious Guignol puppet show has ever given birth to a bloodcurdler more horrible than what these rabid people actually carried out. And, instead of spitting into a pistol barrel amid their nausea and shooting themselves in the head, they were even glad that they had per-petrated and achieved all this—nobody knew just what, though they referred to it as "the perfect age."

Sometimes I, too, had nightmares, and it occurred to me that I thought I was dreaming. At such times, gathering all my strength I tried waking up, and after straining mightily I managed to do so—into another dream, that is, which brought perhaps even more horrible pictures than the former one. As I discovered only much later, it too was a dream, at which I made efforts once again and awoke—into the third dream! And each time I woke up I believed that that was the final and irrevocable waking state.

They themselves will never awaken.

I may say during the whole lecture I was covered with goose bumps and felt deeply that it would be the nicest and noblest salvation for the Behins if someone with a single blow of his fist were to sweep away this ulcer from the clean face of the cosmos.

Later I asked Zemoeki why they spoiled the innocent souls of children with such monstrosities. He replied that they did so in order that the children should advance in morality and be able to follow all this as an example!

But let us return to our subject.

The proko finished his tale and announced that a boetology lesson would follow—to be held by the venerable beratnu.

I was already afraid that it might again be me who would have to perform some capital nonsense, in the middle of which I would be certain to break down, but fortunately something else happened.

The children stood up, split into two groups and, leaving the middle desks empty, took their places at the two sides of the room. Now two beratnus entered and the proko left.

When the beratnus came in, the children began to beat their foreheads with their fists and to vake with such pain that an un-suspecting outsider might well have thought that parricides were atoning for their sins.

With this, the two beratnus stood before the two groups and began to elucidate their themes simultaneously.

One proclaimed that whoever drank water over which a bat had flown would lose the grand boeto. With such a person one was forbidden to make friends because he also infected anyone who spoke to him. And it was especially forbidden to drink from the glass of such a man.

The other explained that one must walk only backward when the moon was full, and must not make friends with any man who walked forward at that time, as he might be infectious. And the shoes of such a man had to be thrown into a fire.

Both declared that the other was teaching specially concocted lies and that it was not permitted to listen to him, as every one of his words was contagious. And they declared in unison, "Chil-dren, be pious!"

At this, the two groups burst into an uproar like a wasps' nest, whereupon they jumped up from behind their desks, fell upon

each other, and a fierce fight ensued. Some had their glasses broken to pieces, others their shoes removed and ripped apart, and
the whole time they abused each other with such obscene insults
that I cannot relate them to the Reader.

The two beratnus watched the horrible scene without moving
a muscle—then, to my profound surprise, they left arm in arm,
in the greatest harmony.

My feet remained rooted to the spot and I gazed after them
agape.

It was only when the door had closed behind them that I was
able to move. I ran after them and in a trembling voice asked
why it was necessary to tell the children such things as had led to
these events.

They stared at me as if I had come from Mars.

"The children's character has to be improved," one of them said.
"Otherwise we would all grow coarse and turn into cannibals."

In my confusion it was all I could do to mutter that after this
I by no means understood the connection between the two lec-
tures and the present warm friendship.

They smiled at each other.

"We both serve the same noble purpose, even if in different
ways," they said. "But now we are in a hurry."

Fortunately the proko came and called me back to the children.

Here a new surprise awaited me.

The proko first of all pulled the ear of one child because he had
stuck out his tongue at another. He warned them to be meek,
and have consideration for each other. He called his children
good-for-nothing whippersnappers, whom the kind beratnu had
spoken to in vain.

Then he announced that geometry was to follow.

Although I did not understand how this serious and exact
science fitted in here, I heaved a sigh of relief that I would at
last hear something sensible. Before long, however, everything
became clear.

He spoke of the circle. But no sooner had he begun than my mouth and eyes gaped in astonishment. The proko said that the circle had two foci and that the sum of the radius vectors was constant, which are—as is well known to all—characteristics of the ellipse.

It was already on the tip of my tongue to enlighten him concerning his mistake when he added that the circle had one more rule—that it was forbidden to say of it that the points of the circumference are at an equal distance from the center.

Now I was utterly confused. If they knew what the circle was, why was it forbidden to say it?

All the same I did not dare to interrupt. The next day, however, I asked Zemoeki about it. He explained that the circle must not be called round because it was the kemons' symbol.

And when I referred to geometric reality, which remained unchanged no matter what, he responded that there were not only geometric realities in the world but also anebas, and this was more important. A true kona could not call the circle round.

Simple mathematical and geometrical truths that are known and openly, even proudly, voiced by schoolchildren in my country, these they denied. And the most interesting point was that they did not do it out of conviction, either—their conviction was precisely the opposite—but because "this is what must be said." The Behins told lies not only to others, but also to themselves, and it was so deeply rooted in them that they would have struck anyone dead who uttered what was otherwise known to everyone.

I also asked Zemoeki whether he believed all this. He confessed that he did not, but it was still necessary to teach things in such a way because even though he himself was an intelligent man, if the mass had learned of the circle as round, it would entail the greatest upheaval. I asked why, but he could not give any explanation. He spoke of some matters needing to be as firm as a rock, a principal support, of some sort of order that needed to be ensured and, of course, of the bruhu possessed by the Behins—

in short, of everything that had nothing to do with geometry, but not a single word about what I had asked. Therefore I asked him again to speak on the subject, but I did so in vain: he said that that was what he had spoken about, and that I had not understood.

But let us come back to the affairs of the skoro! After this elliptical lecture the children took out exercise books, and the proko ordered them to write about the manufacture of concrete. The children set about their task. They wrote, and approximately ten minutes later he collected the exercise books, read them through, and finally chose one.

"This is the best," he said and handed it to me.

I cast a glance at it and saw with amazement that the child had written over two whole pages nothing except, "vake betik, vake betik, vake betik."

Thinking I must be mistaken, I turned the pages of the exercise book, but there I found earlier scripts, too, under such titles as "How to treat the catarrhous patient," "Description of the planets in the solar system," and "How to determine the area of the triangle." And after every title came the repetition of "vake betik," page after page, colored only occasionally with such phrases as "Ugh, spirituality!" "Perish, kemon!" or "Vake kona!" Unbelievable.

After this the proko explained some strange, foreign words to the children, which, however, did not concern their crazy ideas but the objects of everyday life: table, chair, hand, foot, house, and so on.

I wondered why it was necessary to know a language spoken by nobody. To my question the proko replied that it was necessary for a skoro Behin to know it. Of course, I in turn asked why he was supposed to know it, and he replied further that it was because the nonskoro Behins did not know the skoro language.

Then he explained immeasurable quantities of nonsense: if we walk near someone who is younger than us by more than seven years, we are to keep our palm on the nape of our neck; in the yard we must tiptoe; on a plank one must put down the heel first;

on certain days of the month we must comb our hair forward, and on other days we must paint our ears yellow.

When I asked the proko of the aim of such things, he replied that they are needed because a nonskoro Behin would not behave like this.

Presently the proko announced that everyone could leave, at which, together with the children, we departed from the Institute for Degeneration.

In the yard I begged his pardon for having to leave for a minute, and was about to enter one of the outhouses when the proko jumped after me and, snatching my hand, shouted at me, "Unfortunate one, what do you want?!"

I was compelled to name my needs but he did not let me go.

"But you must understand that in this closet they do only nasty things!"

I replied in confusion that although I was aware of the somewhat nasty function of the outhouse, we were all frail human beings and my bladder was ready to burst.

"That's why I'm telling you," he continued, shouting. "Do you know what this closet is for? For spirituality!"

It was in such a way that I came to know that each child had a separate outhouse, where he was permitted to have his lunch only after locking himself up inside.

And when I asked the proko why this was, he referred again to the ketni. How else except by such airy imaginings could they justify customs that could not possibly be justified by a sound mind? Because it is ketni! It was a rule, but incalculable and stupid; a soft-headed product of the imagination that I cannot even articulate in English.

Puzzled, and in the greatest confusion, I was looking around and was just about to ask where the lavatory was when suddenly I witnessed a disgusting sight.

The children then swarmed outside, and no sooner had they arrived in the yard than they unbuttoned their garments one after the other and before the proko's very eyes they emptied their bladders without any sense of shame. I was just about to warn the proko when I saw that he himself followed the children's example without any scruples.

I turned away in shame and could not stifle my opinion of their loathsome habit. He, however, did not let himself be disturbed in the least in the performance of his bodily function, and asked in surprise why it was necessary to be ashamed about it.

"It is a matter of propriety," I replied, in English of course.

"What is propriety?"

I became sincerely perplexed. I looked for words, and it was then that I realized that these poor devils had no word for "propriety" either. The Reader may imagine what a difficult situation I was in. I could not even approach it by translating it into a language that was really created for mad fancies that did not exist in nature.

Not surprisingly, when I nevertheless did try to give an explanation, the proko replied that "propriety" was certainly no more than a stupid illusion without a drop of real sense.

What else could I expect of lunatics?

Disgusted to the core, I hastened to bid him "prick-pruck" and left to do my duty at home and to shut myself up away from their maddening tortures until my next day's "work."

However, fate, or more precisely, insanity, did not let me get away with only those adventures that day.

As I passed through the gate a child in the heat of play escaped from one of his mates and, while running, banged up against me with full force. I called out at him angrily.

"Open your eyes, sonny!"

The child gazed at me uncomprehendingly.

"What?" he asked.

"Your eyes! Look where you're going when you are running!"

"What's wrong with my eyes?"

Thinking he'd intended to annoy me, I was just about to scold him, but then with the most serious expression imaginable, the child asked me to explain what an eye was.

"These two shining balls above your nose," I told him, pointing at them.

"And why should I open them?"

"So you can see."

"To see with the emerald stones?" he asked in surprise.

I already saw that the child had no knowledge of his eyes and, in spite of all my annoyance, I explained in a few words that they were not emerald stones, but eyes, with which we saw. The child, however, only laughed, then suddenly turned and ran over to the proko.

"Vake! Vake!" he wailed, out of breath. "This man says that the emerald stones are my eyes and that I am to see with them."

Not wanting to bother with him any more, I was ready to start on my way, when the proko suddenly leapt over, dragged me aside, and launched a verbal tirade:

"Why spoil this innocent little one?"

"I spoil?"

"Don't deny it! The child would not say by himself that he has eyes and that they are to see with! He could have learned that only from you!"

The blood froze in my veins. I did not deny that it was I who had said so, but simply asked why that was spoiling.

"Don't you think it is spoiling if the child becomes acquainted with his organs prematurely? Is it not spoiling if he comes to know what is to be done with them?"

I protested against this most resolutely. I said there was no real sense in it, that the child would eventually come to know what his eyes were for—the organs could not be used for any other purpose, anyway, and if we concealed it, the results might only be dangerous for the child, while he could only benefit from knowing his organs. Teaching should even commence with such things, I preferred, so that the child should get acquainted with his own body. Otherwise how could he protect his health?

"Oh, you base creature! Is it not dangerous if this tender creature opens his eyes and wants to see with them?"

By now I was incensed and could no longer keep my temper. I suggested that if he was mad he should have himself treated but should not molest reasonable people in the street. One word led to another, and more than a few passersby gathered around me, to whom I complained of the base insult. They, however, whether the Reader believes me or not, did not warn my attacker to calm down, but instead went so far as to turn upon me, and I could only escape by speedily racing away from the lunatics. Even as I did so, they shouted after me that I had spoiled the child's bruhu!

Later I also asked Zemoeki the reason for this nonsense, but he again spoke of some order, of ketni, of seedling, and of foundation stone, and I received no answer to my question. So I still do not know what crime I committed that day, and I believe that any sober English citizen would remain in a similar state of uncertainty.

This permanent doubt and dread gave rise to a very strange feeling in me, which of course is unknown in reasonable Great Britain—and for this very reason let me mention it, above all for my neuropathologist colleagues, as a matter of information.

Little by little I was consumed by the feeling that I was the one who was worth nothing and could not be used for anything. There was something that they all knew, and I was the only one unable to learn it, because I was without some particular faculty. They had a special feature that belonged only to them and that I did not possess, so that in this respect they were superior to me. Although inwardly I felt resistance against these idiocies, I believed more and more that this resistance served to conceal my own inadequacy, and that it was in fact contempt for myself.

To cast some light on this sensation, I may perhaps compare it to the feeling one has on looking into a river for a long time— after a while, it appears as if the river is the fixed point and it is you who are moving. On first arriving among the Behins, seeing their self-mortifying stupidities, I was filled with a certain self-confidence and was convinced that my reasonable help was needed nowhere more urgently than here. However, the more general the truth I pronounced again and again, the more heated attacks I had to suffer; and even if on this or that occasion the Behins did not actually assault me, there was one thing I could never achieve—and that was to make them understand that two times two is four. Natural realities that a primitive animal knew instinctively, they could not conceive of. My words were met repeatedly by wild illusions and nonexistent fixed ideas. Between the word a Behin heard and his brain there was simply no connection.

This barren hopelessness—the product of so many stubborn and firmly embedded clichés, and, most of all, the frantic persecution of common sense convinced me that I was the ignorant, insignificant, and stupid one. Wherever I stepped I always came up against phantoms, while logic and self-evident natural truths were not accepted here as a form of communication.

12

Here we encounter a more serious stage of the Behinic disease: the kipu. Zemoeki and Zeremble disagree. We become acquainted with the methods of spoiling a chair, and with the superstringists. A Behin professes reason. There is a debate about women's breasts and about the butterfly bilevs. We read the story of a famous mufruk.

FOR THE KIPU TO BE UNDERSTOOD I HAVE TO RELATE A SAD event to which the fine clothes I had been given by the Hins fell victim.

To remind the Reader, it struck me immediately on arriving here what shabby clothes the Behins wore. Every article of dress was torn in one or two places, so that their wearers shivered at the slightest breeze; and different objects hung from them—stones, dead beetles, toothpicks, bones, and so forth.

Although I did not understand the aim of the latter, the Behins' beggarly rags arose my sympathy in spite of all my disgust. I thought with a certain resentment toward the Hins, who—as I then believed—clad them so parsimoniously, reluctantly offering the hapless creatures even a thread. With anguish I thought of the time when my own good and clean clothes would be worn out, and I myself would dress like a beggar.

For the time being I wore my clothes among the Behins with the proud and pleasant awareness of being well-to-do. I truly felt like a celebrated film star for whom all eyes turned and heads wagged together.

This sensation, however, soon began to make me feel uneasy, since it was followed by pangs of conscience that would be felt by anyone of the more decent sort when his wealth is subject to the envious gaze of the have-nots.

At length I pondered how to remedy this shabbiness—of which Zemoeki, who had gaping holes at his knees and buttocks, was no exception.

At one stage I made mention of my feelings of pity and spoke with sympathy of the poor ragged masses.

Zemoeki nodded approvingly, stating that the betiks also did everything to clothe the masses. The problem, however, was very serious because people regrettably could not put on more clothes—as they had very few.

Perplexed, I announced that the fact that there were not enough clothes proved that they would be able to put on more, but he replied that it proved precisely that they could not put on more. To enable the masses to receive clothes, it was necessary that they have many clothes in the first place, because anyone who had only a few clothes was a poor man. This was an incontestable and fundamental economic law calculated by people cleverer than us in the Nourishing and Life-Giving Office.

But Zemoeki did admit that many people went about in poor clothes. Then he added, "And you can't go about in these ridiculous clothes any more, either."

I had not expected such a reply. Zemoeki, however, explained that in such clothes as mine I might at most stay at home, but as a beratnu I could not go among the people in them, as they are only worn by very poor people, and even they only wear them when doing dirty work.

I did not want to believe my ears, but Zemoeki repeated his words—without a doubt, he wanted me to rip apart my clothes.

Convinced that he spoke out of envy, I thanked him superciliously saying that an undamaged garment was suitable for me.

But Zemoeki said with utmost gravity and goodwill that I should not make a fool of myself; a beratnu had to take care to appear in good clothes.

To this I said that my clothes were good because they were undamaged, and he kept on asserting the contrary: the torn garment was better, for it was kipu and was worn for this very reason by more people.

Of course I did not give in; I stated my views of the kipu with barely concealed mockery, at which Zemoeki looked me up and down contemptuously and left with a shrug of his shoulders.

I thought I had already settled the matter, but a few days later I was called upon once more, this time from a much more serious source, to change my ways.

That is, my own betik exhorted me to try ripping my clothes, as a beratnu was required to comply with reasonable rules and not to go about looking like an idiot.

Again I was forced to realize that there was no field of life in which you could cut yourself off from their madness. They came after you until you did what they said.

Now that my daily bread was literally at stake, I was obliged to ruin my clothes, though I did it with an aching heart.

Thus I looked for days for what was a truly kipulike garment, but I saw almost as many fashions of tearing as there were Behins living in the settlement. Finally I managed to perceive that the majority of people had ripped the cloth on the left side of the chest and over the right buttock, hanging a swallow's feather and a beetle from their collars.

So with deep sighs, I too tore at my good clothes, my only comfort being in the knowledge that I had at least ensured my bread and position among the Behins by doing so.

However, when I stepped before Zemoeki in my kipu clothes, to my greatest surprise he burst out laughing.

"Oh, you poor bivak, how could you ruin your clothes like that?"

My breath failed me, and I could only falter out that a few days earlier it had been he himself who had told me I had to do so, and that I hoped I had not fallen victim to a practical joke.

At this, Zemoeki laughed even more and said it seemed I understood nothing about the kipu. This, in fact, was not kipu, for everyone already wore their clothes like that.

It was in this manner that I learned that kipu was neither that worn by everyone nor that worn by no one. Even that which had been kipu the day before was no longer kipu the following day!

I should have liked to know therefore what the kipu was!

Having thus ruined my clothes, I grumbled in a homicidal mood for days, dreaming up exquisite tortures by which to kill Zemoeki were fate to deliver him into my hands.

Then one day, as I sat on a bench, Zemoeki and Zeremble happened to come along, and, amid a warm exchange, we all said "prick-pruck."

I said a few polite words about the weather, to which they responded with apparent boredom. The conversation suddenly shifted to the way in which a chair was to be made thorny.

Soon I dropped out of the conversation, feeling that beside them I was but a bivak whose presence was tolerated.

For a while I listened awkwardly but in the end I asked why the chair had to be made thorny.

"Because it's kipu," they replied.

"But what is the kipu?" I asked, resolved that now I would not let myself be put off but would press the matter with reason and logic until they became confused.

"Kipu is what is pleasant," they replied in the most natural tone in the world.

Then I demanded to have it explained what was pleasant for them, to which they replied, simply, "That which is kipu."

I was forced to admit that they could never be confused. Their minds were utterly free of the inhibitions of logic that would draw the rein before a mistake and establish a connection between the audible word and the functioning of the brain.

And yet I demanded that they should tell me what the point

was in making the chair thorny. They, however, responded with another question.

"Well, perhaps it is all the same to you whether you sit on a thorny or a plain chair?"

"No. It's better to sit on a plain chair."

Greatly amused by this, Zemoeki gave me a jovial thump on the back and remarked that I was a funny boy, that I should only take care not to disclose my bivak ways to others as well.

This was already more than I could bear. What prevented me from really and truly giving my opinion was that in the meantime an excellent idea of vengeance had occurred to me.

Thanking them very much for their tutelage, I went home and secretly fastened a few dozen wooden thorns on a chair and the next day I watched for an opportunity to have Zemoeki sit on it. For the sake of effect, I even intended to push him into it in front of witnesses.

Fate came to my assistance as I found Zemoeki and Zeremble together again in the yard. Zeremble was just relating the adventures he had endured among the kemons when he had been a drawer of squares.

I should mention that this, too, was a well-paid Behin occupation. The square-drawer stole through to the kemons and there he surreptitiously drew squares on the walls or drew diameters into the circles, by which he "outraged" the circle. This ranked among the most respectable occupations among the konas. The betik took hold of the nose of a square-drawer differently, and those who had drawn particularly many squares on the kemon walls and had been beaten up particularly often by the kemons, were even allowed to tie a yellow band on their left arms.

It goes without saying that among the kemons the same occupation was regarded as the most mean and dishonest one that could be imagined, whereas they revered circle-drawers, who of course scribbled circles on the walls among the konas and drew diameters into the squares.

Zeremble was relating just such an adventure of his—one in

which he had knocked the kemon off his feet who had noticed him, and when the kemon was lying on the ground he also drew a square on his back before taking to his heels.

"I fancy," Zeremble said, laughing, "how the kemons received him when he recovered and staggered home not knowing that a triumphant square was blazing on his back!"

Zemoeki and I listened to him with awe. Zemoeki was respectfully repeating, "well I never!" but meanwhile he whispered to me that not a word should be believed, all this was but empty bragging.

In short, after the narration of these adventures I cordially invited both of them to my room, which they accepted. Amid jovial chit-chat we walked along.

At home I waited until Zemoeki stepped in front of the thorny chair, then suddenly pushed him into the kipu.

He shouted in pain, and I asked him with thunderous laughter how he liked to sit in the kipu.

Zemoeki jumped up, cast a glance at the chair, and, to my great surprise, it was now he who began to laugh.

"Oh, you bivak, you bivak!" He was choking with laughter. "Of course, it pricks if it is not kipu! Look!"

He turned to Zeremble. "According to him, this is kipu!" Zeremble looked at the chair, and now both of them laughed. The walls rocked and the delight in mischief froze on my lips.

"But why?" I asked, dumbfounded.

"Why? Don't you see that these thorns are colorless? They are to be painted, my friend, in a kipu manner!"

"And will they not prick then?"

"How should they? The real kipu doesn't prick. The real kipu lulls you, for it is colorful! But, oh, why should I even try to explain to an unintelligent bivak!"

I simply did not know where I stood, and they roared with laughter. A sharp reply hovered about my lips but suddenly it occurred to me that by painting perhaps they meant something different from what I imagined, something that would make the thorns blunt and therefore more comfortable. Cautiously I asked, "And how am I to paint them?"

Zemoeki assumed a bumptious air.

"Well, listen to me. These ones on the edges are to be red, and the middle ones blue."

"Well, what nonsense!" I exclaimed with deep conviction.

"That's it!" exclaimed Zeremble. "You are getting more feeling for the kipu."

I did not know what to say. For a moment I thought he had recovered his wits.

"It is indeed nonsense," he continued, "because the outside ones are to be painted blue, and the middle ones red."

Realizing that there was nothing to be done, I stepped aside. They entered into a heated debate. They quoted the kipu masters, and after five minutes they fell upon each other, thoroughly tearing and pummeling one another. Two of Zemoeki's teeth were knocked out, and Zeremble's face swelled like a loaf of bread— and though in the meantime they battered my "kipu" chair to pieces on each other's head, ripped my bedcover to shreds, and kicked in my closet door, I can still say that these were certainly my first pleasant minutes since I had been among them.

My good mood, however, did not last very long. No sooner was I alone than anxiety took hold of me when I considered that one day I myself might be the suffering hero of such a kipu debate—and if people well versed in kipu matters were given such a thorough dressing down, what would they perpetrate on me, a poor bivak?

Thus I decided to study the kipu, however barbaric a custom it might be. I already knew that it was aimless and stupid, but still I believed at least in the existence of the system.

I set about my studies by trying to meet the masters of the kipu. Not being bold enough to inquire, however, I solved the problem by flattering them and praising their works, speaking in general terms that—as I had witnessed previously—was a very efficient method, one that opened the gates of friendship. They would not laugh at anyone who offered praise, even if, in their assessment, he uttered stupidities.

But without exception each of them began to explain the kipu by stating that it was not what the other was doing. The chair was not to be mutilated and whittled in the way that someone else did it, as that was not kipu.

And indeed each of them concocted his own form of the kipu, and defined the essence of the kipu individually—as if the debate had been revolving around something outside of them such as, say, the evolution of the species or the grouping of electrons. But the kipu was created by them alone, and its most hair-raising feature was that while they were fully aware of the development of the species and the grouping of electrons, they had not a single definite and commonly accepted view of their own fantasies. If they had to concoct anything at all, would it not have been easier to make up only one?

I guessed even at that stage that I would never understand the laws of the kipu, for there simply were none. What I was still unable to comprehend was on what basis they could continue to debate it all day long.

The Behins' other rules of life, too, were a profusion of fancies nonexistent in reality, but they were at least rules, whereas the rules of the kipu were known to nobody and yet they still had to be followed. That is, the kipu meant not only things that did not exist: the Behins did not even know in what way these things did not exist—as if the kipu had been created so that they would be able to pick a quarrel with anyone who had learned all their topsy-turvy rules. I can most aptly express it by saying that the kipu is *accumulated idiocy*.

Perhaps it goes without saying that in this second-rate cloudiness of the mind, the Behins not only failed to realize the terrible reality of the kipu, but also regarded it as a manifestation of human intellect of the highest order and were awfully proud of it.

And if in the course of any kipu debate someone had said that the construction of a comfortable chair, the discovery of a tuberculosis vaccine, or the mending of a leaky roof were more important than all this, they would have called him an uneducated and feeble-minded bivak.

The Behins were seriously convinced that the kipu was the main aim and content of life, and that the creative sciences were good only for maintaining life so pleasures could be had in the kipu.

This disease embittered all fields of life, making it impossible to realize the potential of technology, medicine, and other useful sciences.

In spoons, for instance, the Behins bored small holes, so that half the soup leaked out. The right angles of door handles were straightened out, so a door could be opened only by gripping the handle with both hands. They walled up windows with big unshapely stones at random, so that hardly any room let in sunshine, and what remained of glass surfaces was smeared with grease of different colors.

However, the Behins spoiled not only objects but also all the expedient functions of life. If a Behin proceeded on his way by jumping once and spinning himself around at every fifth step, he took this, too, as a kind of kipu. At such times many of them also emitted a confused, drawling, inarticulate howl. And finally, regarding communication, if they did not use the words whose meaning covered the things they wanted to relate but instead a jumbled blather that had nothing to do with the subject matter, this was also termed "kipu."

But the majority of my Readers are no doubt from the ranks of the educated, nonexpert public—and as such they peruse the book of my travels principally for a description of exotic lands to augment their ethnographic and geological knowledge as required by general culture, while they are less interested in dry, neuropathological analyses.

Thus, instead of using my modest psychiatric knowledge to show off unnecessarily by analyzing the kipu, I feel it would be better for me to try describing its symptoms, as this is likely to be of more interest to the nonexpert public; in particular, what kind of chairs were deemed kipu by the individual masters.

I need hardly say that the kipu was different among the kona and among the kemon. These they called "specific" kipus. Not as if the others had been uniform, but purely so that it should have a name. Zemoeki once related contemptuously that the kemons blunted the points of the thorns.

As I saw it, this betrayed a mental disorder of a milder degree but Zemoeki deeply despised such blunting.

"Have you seen a kemon chair yet?" he asked vehemently. "Well then, look at it! They practically take the edge off the kipu! A dull thorn can only be created by a dull lung. There was even a kemon thorn-master who painted the thorns crimson! Just as I say: *crimson*!" and at each syllable he poked with his finger at my chest. "Well then, imagine a chair with nothing but crimson thorns! And this is kipu for them! Well, what do you say to that?"

Of course I tried to appear shocked, which in this case did not cost me too much extra effort.

I have already mentioned that most of them also drove sharp cones into chairs, but here, too, opinions differed. One drove them into the back, the other asserted that they had to be driven into the seat. There was one who fretted the arm of the chair so that it could not be gripped, and another nailed knotted strings on the seat, so that it was impossible to sit on because of the kinks.

And there was yet a further group—whose members said a chair was good if it was plain.

But do not think, dear Reader, that they had become wiser and wanted to make a normal chair without kinks, cones, and thorns! Oh, far from it! For them plainness meant that they sawed the back off the chair. There were some who removed the seat and others who removed the legs, components they regarded as "complications" and "mannerisms." There were those who said that it was still not sufficiently plain, and that perfect kipu could only be achieved by discarding every part of the chair. One of these masters proudly showed his room that was completely empty, and replied to the question of the amazed visitor, "A white chair in the white air."

These two groups were, however, in agreement on one principle—that the chair exists for itself, and whoever made a chair to be sat on like an animal was a bivak.

"A chair is a chair is a chair," they used to say superciliously.

On the other hand, it was my general impression that behind completely crazy principles there was still more sanity than behind the seemingly sounder ones, as the Reader will presently see.

Namely, there was a third group that insisted that a chair was not after all for itself, but so that one could sit comfortably on it, and therefore we should not put knotted strings on the seat.

Sounds perfectly normal, doesn't it? I ask the Reader to hold tight.

These people, who called themselves superstringists, came from this fully proper premise to the conclusion that the kink was not to be knotted on the string but in the air!

"Because," as they said, "the kipu has nothing to do with articles for personal use. The kipu is one thing and the chair is another; therefore the kipu must be made completely independent from the chair, so that it should manifest itself in its absolute purity."

These people stood out in the squares, turned their eyes upward in ecstasy, and all day long performed movements with their hands as if they were knotting kinks. And the crowd looked at them with awe, many swearing that they saw the kinks. Those who did not see them were called bivak and backward by those who asserted by contrast that these kinks surpassed all previous ones. However, there were a few who laughed at the whole thing, declaring it an arrogant and senseless hocus-pocus and accused the superstringists of being decadent. But lest the Reader should again fall into error, I hasten to remark that they were on the other hand stringists, who held that the kink was valid, after all, only if it was knotted on a string and sunk into our buttocks when we were on the chair.

Similar disappointments hit me more than once. Such an event occurred, for example, when a kipu master told me in a very serious tone, "Those whom you see here blustering around the kipu are all madmen and swindlers. The chair is for sitting on, and it is good if it is comfortable. Kinks and thorns are not appropriate to it, as they are not appropriate to the air."

I was stupefied. And when he mentioned that the Behins called him bivak for his views, I fell about his neck almost in tears. A warm conversation developed, as we together lambasted the whole bedlam, until suddenly he said, "What is most kipu is what is expedient, because the kipu is expediency itself."

It was then that a strange feeling of dissonance commenced to take possession of me. Uneasily I asked, "But if there is no kipu independent of expediency, then why is the name 'kipu' needed?"

"Because the kipu exists and it is congenital in man."

"But if it is expediency itself," I contradicted, "what would, for example, be the point in stating, 'What is houndest is what is dog'?"

"Kipu is, and it must be," he replied stubbornly. "I suggest that you should read a lot and you will understand that it is necessary, as it is the highest manifestation of the human spirit, which makes life life. Without kipu we could not live."

I even asked twice, but it came to light that he was indeed referring to kipu. Not vitamins and not protein. These, perhaps, took it for gospel truth that without kipu they would have perished of scurvy or beriberi!

His words had the effect of a cold shower, and with a polite scratching of his posterior I hastened to take leave. However, he did not scratch me back but stated that the whole ketni was idiocy. Now was the time for a purifying revolution to give a new and freer ketni to the world, when people do not scratch each other's posteriors like idiots but say quite briefly, "Reason vake!" and rub their foreheads with a thumb.

Again the nightmares from which I had wanted to awaken

came to mind, but I was only able to awaken into another, still more nightmarish dream.

These unfortunates have been doing nothing else for centuries but struggling with an incubus dreamed up by themselves, awakening from one nightmare into the next, from one suffering to the next, one differing from the former only in appearance—but they are never able to shake off the shackles of the dream. No, they are lunatics who have strayed and will never be able to be men.

Now let the Reader imagine my situation among such people, who did not know themselves the meaning of the words they had concocted from thin air—words they interpreted in a thousand ways and at the same time talked about as if hard reality were concerned. The strange decisiveness with which they spoke about their fantasies is outright perplexing, as they harangue with such ease and passion that a sane man would think that they speak of something—and so it is he who feels ashamed for not knowing all this, he who stammers for a moment and resolves to learn their ways. I, too, had this feeling at the beginning, and it took me a long time to realize that there was indeed no sense in all this, and an unconfused schoolchild knew much more than those who held the knowledge of concocted monomanias an indispensable prerequisite for being educated.

It can be imagined what I felt in a society where two times two was said to be five, then three, and then, in accordance with all kinds of rules, one, then something else and yet again something else, but never four. Poor common sense tries to follow along lest it should be ostracized, but it cannot manage to do so; for it knows only one rule, that of natural truth, which can be calculated on the fingers, but the utterance of which in these surroundings is a crime—and, just what the punishment is at any one moment can never be known for sure.

Such an unfortunate person exists in a state of eternal uncertainty; for strive as he might, it is impossible for him to learn the most important rule: to forget mathematics.

More than once I asked Zemoeki for some guidance from which I could at least conclude as to how kipu was to be understood, why it was at all, and what it was good for; as there had to be an explanation, if not of its rules, then at least of its existence. He, however, dismissed me with a wave of his hand.

"The kipu is an instinct, born with man. Whoever is born without it is a bivak, to whom it is no use explaining it, anyway."

(Although I have made the observation once already, I repeat that Zemoeki's assertion is not true. No, the Behinic disease is not hereditary. On the basis of my own experiences, I can definitely state that children aged four or five—whose instincts and senses of heat, hunger, thirst, and so on were perfectly sound—displayed no kind of attraction toward the thorny chair, for example. They did not show any reaction when seeing the kinks, while at the same time they reached with visible pleasure for bread and butter, and in cold weather they seated themselves beside a stove. Of the Behinic disease the child inherits only the susceptibility to it, which develops into a disease after a lengthy infection during years spent in the skoro and in Behin society.)

Thus, all I could establish about the kipu was that each group interpreted its rules in a different way; I talked even to one person who said that the kipu was the Behin himself. I should also mention the peculiar fact that many things had something to do with the kipu that had nothing to do with it even according to them.

Please don't be shocked. I have reckoned with the possibility that the confusion in my words will make the Reader distrustful of me. But this kind of crazy fancy is so tangled that it can only be defined in a confused way. Perhaps I can illustrate this with an example.

Zemoeki related that on one occasion he had bought a chair at a high price, a chair he had found kipu and that was inscribed with the name of a kipu master. (I should remark that the Behins—as the Reader may already guess from the foregoing—not only failed to knock on the head those who ravaged chairs, but even as they themselves tried to ensure that their chairs should also be ravaged, and indeed they paid for the damage effected by the kipu masters.)

Well, it turned out that Zemoeki's chair had not been ravaged by this kipu master; his name had only been forged on it. At this Zemoeki took the seller to the betik, who punished him heavily for deception!

So then, I already knew that virtually everyone held a different view of the kipu. But Zemoeki had inspected the chair previously, hadn't he? So if we could speak of at least an individual feeling for the kipu, he should definitely have known whether the kipuness of the chair was worth the price. And still he was not indignant because it was not kipu enough, but because it had been made by a Behin of another name!

Thus at that time I found it probable that even the person's name was bound up with the kipu. I asked how a kipu name should sound, and what system of thorns should be inscribed with what kind of name so that I could avoid being punished, but he laughed at me and called me a bivak—so I do not know even today whether the sound of the name, the sequence of its characters, or the number of its syllables influence the kipuness of the chair.

I am afraid that I am overburdening the patience of the educated and sober Reader in Great Britain beyond measure by describing this disease—a disease that, fortunately, rages only in exotic continents far from Europe. Hence my compatriots need not be at all afraid of its effects. I must finally mention that the kipu illness spoiled not only objects but also speech.

As I mentioned earlier, if someone did not communicate using those words whose meaning conveyed what he wanted to say, but with a confused jumble instead, this too was considered kipu.

The Reader will of course wonder how the Behins' speech, which was but a heap of wild illusions in any case, could be further distorted.

Well, while their normal speech sounded as if they were talking of something, the aim of kipu speech was to impart not a thing.

Those who spoke like that were called mufruks and, needless to say, the Behins did not strike them dead, just as they failed to do so with the kipu masters; they even enjoyed common respect, and their half-baked jabberings were not only printed, but they also received money for them.

These heaps of words printed on paper they called "breath" to distinguish them from "normal" writings—why precisely "breath," we shall see presently.

Zemoeki and Zeremble were once reading the "breath" of such a mufruk, in which he compared a woman's breast to artichokes cooked in milk, to mallow root, and to butterfly bilevs—in short, to anything as long as it had nothing to do with a woman's breast. This last object of comparison impressed Zemoeki and Zeremble especially, as it was farthest not only from a woman's breast but also from reality, considering that a butterfly did not have bilevs.

The Reader cannot even imagine how seriously they discussed this, racking their brains as to which object was most like a woman's breast. Finally, I with my poor sound mind wanted to help them and said, "A woman's breast is perhaps most similar to the breast of another woman."

Zemoeki and Zeremble looked at each other, then burst into a guffaw saying that what I had said made no sense, it did not mean a thing—for it was indeed so.

That is, there was no sense in anything that expressed reality!

"Then why do you say things of which you yourselves are convinced that they are in contradiction with reality?"

"Because that is the only way it is kipu."

I had no idea how it was possible to debate and rack one's brains for hours about something just to finally invent another thing that was no answer at all to the problem. If it was kipu, then I had no idea what the kipu was needed for at all. I even told them that the sound mind classified all this as rubbish.

"Oh, you bivak," they said. "It is breath; it is not for the brain, but for the lungs!"

What else could I have replied but that only oxygen was for the lungs, whereas words were perceived by the cells of our brain; but I referred in vain to my medical qualification obtained at Oxford University—it was they who laughed at me, called me a bivak again, and then announced that I did not know a thing about the quivering of the lungs, so I should hold my tongue and try to learn, for I was as stupid as a lungless Hin.

(Perhaps I need not say that even the Hins breathe by lungs just like every other man. It is stark madness to suppose a man living without lungs.)

Thus I would have been prepared to accept that the kipu speech was what was not true, that it was not for the mind but for the lungs. But they were not consistent in this either. That is to say, the most remarkable and, for a European, the most incredible thing to witness was that if someone succeeded in concocting an unreal and senseless combination of words, those hearing or reading them still did not say that it was kipu because it was not true, because it made no sense, but exclaimed: "How true it is!" or, "What profound words!"

Unbelievable!

Zemoeki warmly suggested that if I wanted to develop my lungs I should read the breath of the mufruk that they read.

It is very interesting that whenever I had to deny a sound truth they always referred me to books. I must explain why.

In Great Britain, books are for increasing our knowledge and feeding our minds, while among the Behins they serve a peculiar purpose indeed—to dull the brain, and make people believe the opposite of things that would be self-evident without book truths. To be ashamed of eating, and to respect the boeto and the bilevs would no more have become rooted without the books than without the skoro.

Still, I myself began to study this mufruk with interest and by degrees I learned.

While he still lived among the Hins, this man had wanted to become a doctor. As soon as he was twenty years of age he became conspicuous through his abnormalities. He tore off strips of electric insulating tape and stuck them on his clothes, even on his hair. He broke every third tooth of a comb, stuck the mutilated comb into a handful of glazier's putty, and having stuffed the whole bundle into a shoe he set it on the table. From the ceiling above his bathtub hung a wide-necked blue glass jar he had carried home from the laboratory. (It would have been called theft among us, but in the free economy of the Hins I cannot use this word.) In this glass jar there was a ball bearing, some dried orange peel, and a dead lizard.

He regularly washed his handkerchief in a soup bowl and drank petroleum.

This much would have been enough to have him carried, bound hand and foot, for urgent curative treatment, but the Hins, who interfere with individual lives only in the most exceptional cases, did not react to such "mild" symptoms—both because they were not harmful to the public and because they believed that they had some purpose.

They began to take the medical student's monomanias seriously only when his acts began to disturb others in their work, and he became a public danger.

It happened one evening that he stopped a woman on the seashore and began to explain that moonbeams contained protein and vitamins that satisfied and nourished people.

Hearing him out, the woman replied that she was not from the institute for food inspection; she wanted to leave.

However, the mufruk did not let her.

"This doesn't concern food inspection," he said impetuously and continued to explain the moonbeam vitamin. He even affirmed that the moonbeam contained the nourishing materials only in the presence of the woman.

"Then perhaps you should report it to the optical or the radiological institute," the woman replied and tried setting off.

However, the mufruk seized her, loudly asserted that all this did indeed concern the woman, and he went about detailing how the scent of the mignonette flower lifted one from the earth, and that when the moon rose, objects changed their material nature.

The woman, who was convinced that the human word was based on something, finally stopped, made note of the mufruk's words, and reported them to the institutes concerned.

There, with Hin thoroughness, they examined the moonbeam, but even in the presence of a female body they were unable to find vitamins in it. They weighed a man on a precision scale to a thousandth of a milligram, then placed a mignonette flower beside him, but, of course, no decrease in weight could' be detected. Research into the material composition of objects was similarly fruitless.

As he had not presented himself at the institute, they sent the results to the university's medical school, where he was summoned and asked to expound on his experiences in greater detail.

In lieu of an answer, he spoke of the cooperative functioning of a man's organs as possessing an independent existence—an existence that was in fact a color, one that turned darker and darker throughout life, becoming completely black by the time of death. And, he said, the human voice had a taste: that of the baby was mildly sourish, the man's salty, and the woman's mildly orange-flavored.

And when they asked him to speak to the point, he replied, "I was speaking about it the whole time."

As the situation was no longer in doubt they took the man to the Behin settlement, where his condition became increasingly grave, and he grew more and more respected among the Behins.

This was the person whose writings I had to study.

His books dealt partly with the boeto, and partly with spirituality taken by women.

Of the boeto he stated that it was a bay laurel tree that threw its roots into a person's lungs, that the kona climbed upwards along its branches, and that above it rustled the shadow of the sun, and below it black fleas barked.

Elsewhere he declared that the cooperative functioning of

organs was an arch between birth and death, at the top of which the yearning of lungs made music—and that it was nothing other than a crescent suspended on the threads of spirituality taken by women, and that below it, black milk ran high in an enormous bowl.

All this had already somewhat overstepped the bounds of my patience. Angrily I pushed the book before Zemoeki, asking him what he had to say to it. After reading a bit, he went into a veritable ecstasy.

"Wonderful!" he exclaimed. "How sharply he sees life and reality! 'It is suspended on the threads of spirituality taken by women'! Wonderful!"

In amazement he almost fell from his chair.

So did I.

But I have not yet reached the end of the mufruk's story.

There once appeared a book by him titled *The Life of Man*, both the form and contents of which were considerably different from the earlier works. Among other things, he asserted that a mother's milk was white, that those who climbed mountains grew tired, and that old men were feeble.

Zemoeki and Zeremble read it many times and conferred together at length about its "meaning." They guessed for hours, but, rack their brains as they might, they could not come to a decision. Finally they stated that the mufruk's breaths were lately becoming more and more confused.

In my opinion his breathing had a rather obvious explanation, which I told them without hesitation. They, however, waved their hands at me in disgust.

At the same time a host of young Behins declared that they *did* understand the mufruk, and whoever did not was a bivak and his mind had decayed with age.

However, as my earlier experiences made me cautious, I dared not voice my sympathy. I suspected that behind these statements that sounded normal still crazier obsessions were lying in wait.

And indeed I was not disappointed in my supposition. Each

of them drew a different meaning from the statements about mother's milk, the climbing of mountains, and old men, but what it was I have never found out and they did not disclose it, either. They only mysteriously announced that it was for the lungs and could not be expressed in words.

If, for example, such a youth caught sight of a thorny chair, he exclaimed, "Sure, sure, it is hard to climb a mountain!"

If some of them ripped their garments in a different way, this might be explained by saying "Well, a mother's milk is white!" As for what connection there was between these things, the Reader should not ask me. With the Behin it is not necessary for there to be a logical connection between words.

The matter thus far sounds comic enough. The reason I am dealing with it at such length will come to light only now.

On one occasion Zemoeki met the mufruk and inquired as to the proper meaning of the breath.

And then a surprising thing happened.

A sound mind had in the meantime returned to the mufruk, which the Behins did not suspect. To the question he replied, "That which is in it."

For a brief moment Zemoeki gaped in confusion. As he told me later, at the time he did not yet think anything wrong, and behind the latter words he looked for some "meaning," but then, in shame, he inquired further.

"How is it to be understood, for example, that a mother's milk is white?"

"Because it is indeed white," the mufruk said, "as it is hard to climb a mountain, and old men are feeble. But why do you ask? That is known by everyone!"

Zemoeki caught his breath, then hurriedly said good-bye, and the next day he related the whole thing to Zeremble.

They racked their brains about the answer, but finally came to the conclusion that there was something wrong. Thus they set off to report the case to the young people, who received the announcement with an awful hullabaloo and said it was a mean slander. They almost lynched Zemoeki and Zeremble, finally seizing and carrying them to the mufruk himself.

Here they reported on the matter, requesting that the mufruk himself should deliver judgment on these shady characters and issue a proclamation about his breathing.

It was then that the catastrophe happened.

The unfortunate mufruk foolishly repeated his assertions, and referring to his medical practice gained among the Hins, sought to prove that mother's milk was indeed white and that old men were indeed feeble!

At this, the crowd burst into a hellish shouting match, hurling the mufruk's books at his head, demanding their money back, and bellowing that if he had lost his mind he should not take a pen in his hand!

The Behins' worship of losing logical thinking reminded me in some respects of a superstition of the Middle Ages when epilepsy was respected as a sacred trance and called *morbus sacer*, or "holy illness."

But how much more sane than the Behins were Europeans even in the Middle Ages: for all their superstitions, they knew very well that epilepsy was a sickness and did not for a moment sink so deep as to admire it as an utmost manifestation of pure reason.

But I think that enough is enough about all this, for merely describing the kipu has made me quite dizzy. Now let the Reader, who in a sane Europe has heretofore not even heard of it, imagine what it meant for me to live through it!

13

We learn a precise rule for determining when the Behins are consistent. The author shares his strange experiences with the square and with the burning house. We become acquainted with the Behins' humorists, phosophs, and their sayings, as well as the theory of Creation according to the Behins. We learn of their wise men, the makrus, and of their sorry plight. The author almost publishes his travel notes.

I HAVE MENTIONED MANY TIMES THAT ONE CANNOT FOLLOW the Behins' way of thinking. There is but one certain point in their nature—namely, that they will never say anything in accord with reality, but precisely the opposite.

But one fact has not one single opposite but in most cases very many, and bewildered common sense cannot indeed know which of the many untruths is to be selected. As I have already mentioned, the sane mind knows only that white must never be said to be white, but never really knows which is the obligatory color.

Nonetheless, there is one case in which the Behins' opinion can be calculated—namely, in matters where there is only one opposite.

An already familiar example is suffering, the only opposite of which is pleasure. In this regard I could reason almost always with certainty, and had I spent more time among them I would have discovered by myself that the thorny chair caused pleasure, while to sit in a cushioned armchair was suffering, or that if a kemon tore off a kona's ear, that of course was pleasure but having spirituality was suffering.

Likewise inevitably, the opposites of seriousness and laughter belonged to each other; of these I will write a few words in the present chapter. And, indeed, the Behins always laughed at completely serious things that made sense, while at things that they termed deep and serious the sober European would have laughed his head off.

I came to discover this regularity by way of a wretched adventure. When walking in the yard on one occasion, my attention was caught by a man running in fear. He rushed straight toward me shouting, "Help! Help! Danger at the gates!"

I myself became terrified; I thought lava was pouring from the hillside or a flood was about to inundate us.

"What is it? What's happened?" I asked excitedly.

"There ... there ..." he panted, "around the corner ... a wicked assailant ... a damn fire raiser."

"What is it, what did he do?" I implored him to answer.

"With a chalk ... "

"With a chalk?"

"Yes, he drew a diagonal into the square!"

I may say I hadn't had such a hearty laugh for a long time.

"Lamik!" he said with utmost contempt and ran on.

But in no time a host of raging Behins came running back on the tail of the hapless creature who had outraged the square, chasing him over a series of hedges and ditches.

On another occasion, after work, I was walking at the very end of the yard and saw smoke billowing out from under the eaves of a house. On the ground by the outside wall, in a still-smoldering bundle, were the remains of a burnt firebrand. Obviously the house had not caught fire by itself.

I saw that immediate help was needed before the wind carried the glowing embers over to the Behins' ramshackle, highly combustible buildings. Beginning to run around, I shouted:

"Help! Help! Fire!"

I thought if a trifle moved so large a crowd, then a real danger, a true conflagration, would draw thousands. Indeed, a whole lot of konas ran toward me. "What is it? What's happened?" they shouted.

"There . . . there . . ." I panted, "some arsonist."

"What did he do?" they asked in indignation.

"He set a house on fire."

At this moment an enormous tongue of flame darted up.

"There . . ." I said, "a house is burning."

"But why is there danger?" they queried.

"Well, if a house is burning, is that not danger enough?" They looked at it.

"That is a kona's home and it cannot burn," they said, "because with the kona there is order. And, as for you, don't play the fool or you'll find yourself in trouble."

The house, of course, burned to the ground.

But that is not the end of my story.

Later, I mentioned the event to Zemoeki in indignation, but instead of being shocked, he laughed at me and said that, although my behavior had been perhaps comic, the next time I had better not disturb the kona's peace with false alarms.

"False alarm?" I asked, my eyes wide open in bewilderment. "Why a false alarm if the house was indeed in flames?"

"No house can ever be in flames within the kona, because our houses are of iron and are built on rock."

I did not understand how a Behin could say such a thing where there was every possibility to see what wretched hovels they built of boards and mud—veritable fire traps. However, when I remarked that I had been present at the fire, and had seen the thatched roof and the flames with my own eyes, he warned me severely that it was forbidden to say such a thing because it was arson, and called my attention to a paragraph of law that severely punished the arsonist.

I was completely stupefied, but realized that any further debate would be fruitless. I noted that the fire raiser was one who cried fire when there really was one.

With this, however, I began to see the light and became conscious of the above thesis. That is, arsonists and firemen are the sole and exclusive opposites of each other, so in this case the Behin way of thinking was predictable.

Suddenly I asked Zemoeki whether there was a book dealing with the Behins' mode of thinking.

His face brightened, he praised me for at last showing interest in rational thinking and suggested that I should read the works of some of the more remarkable phosophs, from which I would learn very serious and extremely important things.

After all this the phosophs' works began to interest me. Although I guessed in advance that I was looking forward to some hair-raising stupidities, I thought that it was only with a description of the whole range of symptoms of the Behinic disease that I should be able to perform a significant service to science, so I boldly set about studying the works of the phosophs.

I can safely say that I have not come to regret it. If all the humorists of Europe were to cooperate, they would not be able to invent follies as amusing as these.

The first book I tried was very old, but its author is highly respected even today, because—so the Behins say—he laid the foundations of rational thinking.

The book argued that it was the Behin's brain that raised him above the primitive animal that coolly snapped up the fly without working out how many legs it had, while the Behin was led even to this by systematic thought.

He termed his method the "absolute foundation" and professed it infallible. It was a method that enabled Man to solve all the problems that could otherwise not be learned given his limited sense organs.

For example, this is how to determine the number of feet a fly has:

Step 1: The fly is an animal.

Step 2: An animal moves.

Step 3: Moving requires feet.

Step 4: The fly's feet exist to ensure that it will not overturn.

Step 5: The fly does not overturn.

Step 6: To keep from overturning, a body requires three firm points.

Step 7: Consequently the fly has three feet.

When I had read this, I remarked to Zemoeki that the number of the fly's feet could also be found out by catching one and counting its feet.

Zemoeki laughed at my proposition, called me a bivak, and added, "Other people, too, have said such things, but they had no idea of phosophology and they were very ordinary people, which is also proved by the fact that their results were entirely wrong. They stated, almost without exception, that a fly has six feet, which, as you can see, is in complete contradiction with the scientific result obtained by rational sense."

Then I read a book by another phosoph, a certain Zum. Its basic principle was this: "*The Behin has no mind.*"

The educated Reader, would of course be prepared to conclude that this Behin, as an exception, still had a mind. It is for this reason that I hurry to convey Zum's original mental flights. He expounded his thesis as follows.

"When the Behin is born he knows nothing of the world. Only when he has seen the first closet or dog will he come to know that they exist. He has to burn his finger before he will not reach toward the fire. Thus the whole intellect is nothing but a mass of memories collected from the outside world and nothing originates in the Behin himself. Thus it is obvious that the Behin has no mind."

Zemoeki recommended another phosoph, Zantim, who was particularly knowledgeable about pure reason. This book, on the other hand, asserted that the Behin had only a mind, and no hands, feet, or head. Progressing even further, he put forth his theorem:

There is nothing that is, only that is which is not.

I ask the Reader not to exhaust his laughing muscles, for the proof is still to come.

"Our sense organs," says Zantim, "are deceptive and yet we become acquainted with the outside world only through them. Thus we do not know whether ice is warm or cold because, although it feels cold to our touch, it is possible that it is actually warm; it is only that we call this feeling cold. Similarly, we shall never come to know the flea," which Zantim called *dingas* for the sake of scientific accuracy. "We don't know whether it bites or strokes, because it is the flea that bites us and not we it. And we feel the bite through our deceptive sense organs. "The bite"—which he concisely termed the categorial-attribut-imperativus—"is felt only by the flea, in fact, that is *posteriopriorice*, as it does not feel the bite but bites."

"But," Zantim continued, "the flea is in space, and the bite takes place in time. Accordingly space and time are but concepts needed by our imaginations for placing the dingas and the bite in them, but in itself neither space nor time exists. And since everything that *is*, is in space and in time, from this it is obvious that if these do not exist, nothing is that is; there is only the imagination, which, however, is neither in space nor in time, so it is *not*."

But all this was not enough for Zantim. He further drew the conclusion that there are also anebas because they are not, and that people are to be oppressed in order that they should live in freedom.

I think the Reader cannot even imagine that the Behins appreciated the products of a mental disorder of such degree—why, they could not even understand them.

Indeed, the Behins appreciated them simply because they did not understand them. They used to say, "In this is the real depth. Zantim is such a profound intellect that up to now even the cleverest ones are unable to understand him."

Zantim's works were also highly valued, for anything could be deduced from them. Some, for example, asserted that space and time existed and that this is just what Zantim had wanted to say; for according to his own words, space and time did not exist. But as they are *not*, they must be, because only that exists which is not. His opponents, of course, seized upon existence and said that space and time existed, but were *not* because, according to them, there was a significant difference between the two.

But why should we bother our heads about this? Suffice it to say that since Zantim, centuries have passed, and during this time a thousand kinds of Behin maniacs have all been hurling quotations from Zantim in each other's faces.

And I am the only one who presents all this jumble in such a simple and lucid form.

I must ask the Reader not to take this to be a mockery because, compared to the original text, I have indeed rendered it in an incomparably more intelligible form. The most characteristic attribute of the original text was that even the simplest ideas and objects—such as "feeling," "thinking," "flea," "comb," or "dishrag"—were obscured with painstaking work behind tortuous words that aptly reflected the phosoph frame of mind.

And there were people who spent a lifetime on this without creating a single pin or putting together even a chicken coop. After all this, it was only natural that the Behins made such statements about their phosophs:

"Zum is a tremendous creative genius!"

"Zantim was a great constructive intellect!"

However, to my regret, I cannot say that the Behins would have shown a unanimous reaction to this, either.

Once I met the already mentioned proko who dealt with the dumbing down of children in the institute for degeneration. I was sure that this terrible being in whom, precisely because of his calling, all the obscurity of the Behins must have been united in condensed form, would speak about the sofuks with great respect.

All the greater was my surprise when he made the following reply to my question.

"Zantim was a stupid pedant together with all the other phosophs. Any man in his senses laughs at the idiocies he scribbled together."

I gazed at him in wonder. I had to admit that I shared his views in full measure, but asked him to give his reasons.

"Real life," he said, "cannot be invented at the desk. If I were a betik I would put all these idling swindlers to some useful work."

With some suspicion I asked what his opinion was of real life and useful work. My precaution was not unjustified.

"These dusty-eared loungers don't see that the kemon danger is at our gates," he continued, "and if we don't sharpen our knives ceaselessly the fate of the square will be sealed. Real life, therefore, requires us to unite and develop all our strength in the defense of the square. The phosophs, however, emasculate the young, and divert their attention from the salvation of the knife."

In short, if one Behin criticizes the stupidity of another, he does it only because he wants to perpetrate a still grosser nonsense.

After all this one might well believe that the Behins' "cultural life" was made up exclusively of the tomfoolery of the phosophs, and that they have never had any wise men.

Yet, strange to say, I must confirm that they had. But what a pitiable plight lay ahead of them!

The Reader already knows that if anyone professed sensible things, he would be beaten to death. For this very reason only very few wise men could get away with it.

"But how?" the Reader may ask. "If the Behins had wise men, that meant from the outset that they could not be Behins."

I must therefore explain that there were indeed almost completely right-minded people among them, whom they put into two classes: one kind they dubbed *makru* and laughed at them, the other they called lamik and beat them to death or burned them alive. (To their further fate I shall return later.)

The wise man becomes a makru when a clever word he utters

is misunderstood once, and from then onward he may express his opinion almost freely.

Some of the sages, once aware of this characteristic of the Behins, flew consciously to makruness. They did not tear up their clothes in the kipu manner but went about in quite normal, intact clothes, which provoked laughter. Indeed, they were treated like lunatics, and whatever they said was drowned in ridicule.

The makrus went even further. If one wanted to say something particularly sensible and dangerous he put a cap and bells on his head and put his fingers into his mouth. And the Behins listened to him with great amusement, many people made notes of his words, and they gave these words to nurses to cheer up a crying child.

So the makrus' lot was better than that of the lamiks only in that instead of an ignominious death they were awarded an ignominious life. The Behins jovially thumped them on the back, asking them to say something silly. And if one replied, "Turn to the betiks," that in itself was enough to give the Behins a fit of laughter and make them thump the makru's back again.

One such a famous makru, a certain Zolter, was even employed in the house of a formidable ear-betik who was one of the most formidable characters in the Behin settlement. With his henchmen, this ear-betik robbed and raided poor wretches. Famine and plague prevailed. One need not wonder that Behin history knows him as "The Building and Bread-Giving Great Healer."

This monster nevertheless received the mentioned makru in his house, and—according to contemporary notes—the makru amused his master very well. Once, having caught sight of the ear-betik, he cried a loud "Vake-vake," but snatched at his pocket instead of his foot. When the ear-betik asked why he did so, he answered, "Being so close to such a pickpocket, I must take hold of my purse."

The ear-betik laughed so heartily that his bilevs dangled in all their glory.

He dubbed the ear-betik a highwayman, parricide, a seducer, and a crazy ripper, hoping that amid the laughter something would perhaps start him thinking, but all in vain. And the ear-betik, in turn, named him the god of amusement, took him along everywhere he went, and laughed at him from morning till night but—to the good fortune and tragedy of the makru—he never understood him.

Some openly described how stupid and wretched the Behin life was, but the konas believed that all this concerned the kemons and the kemons thought it concerned the konas. And it never occurred to them that all the vile words the makrus wrote also applied to their own lives, that those words ultimately caused just as much destruction among their own kind as among the other beha. If a makru proclaimed, "The betiks are base evildo-ers," those who heard it might say to each other, "He sure put those kemons in their place."

A makru named Zift openly described all the filth and horror of the Behin settlement. Today it is from his book that the Behins explain to the children in the skoro how amusing farces are to be written.

A sage named Zadoch wrote that the Behin life would always remain dreary suffering and it could not even be hoped that this cursed race would ever be relieved of their torments, which they themselves caused. This sage they called the "Great Comforter" because, as they said, "He warned us to struggle and trust in a better future."

In fact the reading of Zift's book awakened me to my duty to publish my experiences gained in Kazohinia once I returned to my country, with which I would benefit science and the general public alike.

Thus I began to compile my travel notes. Through Zemoeki I managed to borrow a typewriter. By the nature of the matter my intention was highly secretive. I told him that I wanted to disguise the kemons' ignobilities in a long study.

I received the typewriter, on which, of course, there were only Behin characters, and I intended to translate the text into English after returning home.

So I settled down to work. I described the wise and quiet perfection of the Hins, which then, in that incredible environment, appeared to me even more clear and majestic than when I subsequently reflected on it in cultured Europe. Then I proceeded to the Behins. I described the hypocritical oppression of the people by the betiks, Zemoeki's crazy ideas, the behas' aimless quarrelling about the anebas, the stunting of children in the institutes, and all the self-torture with which they rendered their lives unbearable.

Zemoeki, of course, inquired more than once about my work. I managed to elude him by saying that it was still in the early stages, but I decided that for the sake of form I would write some pages of nonsense for him concerning the ignobilities of the kemons.

Regrettably I left this to the end, and thus it came about that my work did not remain secret.

That is, since the memorable fight the lock had been broken off my door and they knew nothing about knocking. In an instant Zemoeki rushed in with a loud prick-pruck just when I was hard at work.

I endeavored to get rid of the papers quickly, but in doing so I drew his attention to them all the more. I protested in vain. He snatched them from my hands and began to read. Although I said that all this was but a rough draft that required complete revision and that I did not like my work to be read at that stage, he said that was all the more a reason for him to read it, because he owed it to me and the anebas to be of help in the work of revision.

Zemoeki, therefore, set about reading, while I submitted to my fate and was prepared to be burned alive.

Of course, right at the beginning he asked why I had commenced with the Hins.

Again I told him that the whole of what he saw was but an introduction, so that we should better understand the kemons' ignobilities, which I would come to only at the end.

Zemoeki gloomily read the part dealing with the Hins' serene and peaceful life. Several times a heavy sigh broke from his chest, and at the end he stated with recognition that the torments of the Hins' comfortless world had not yet been described in such soul-stirring colors.

With this he proceeded to the Behins, while my teeth were chattering at the thought of my poor family. I must say that I was prepared for anything except what actually ensued.

Zemoeki immediately stated that the characters were not only kemons, but mainly konas, to which I could not even reply but only cast down my eyes.

And, as he read on, his face became more and more cheerful. Later he simply laughed from page to page.

In the beginning I thought he did not understand, but it turned out that Zemoeki had recognized everything perfectly. Interrupting his reading more than once, he expounded how splendidly I had expressed my opinion of the many monstrosities.

At the end he stood up, paced up and down the room, then stepping up to me began to scratch my posterior in ecstasy. "You have told them off wonderfully!" he cried. "This book must be published."

The words stuck in my throat. I didn't know whether I was on my head or my heels. And Zemoeki continued dashing to and fro and did not tire of praising me. Once he stopped and, turning toward me, suddenly asked, "My name also figures in it. Would you disclose whom you want to represent by that name?"

At first I thought he wanted to call me to account because of personal offense. Why, all the inanities that figured under his name he himself had spoken, professed, done! But he inquired in so friendly a manner and with such interest that I was convinced he did not recognize himself!

This turn, apart from all its eccentricity, was comforting for me inasmuch as I managed to avoid Zemoeki's wrath. In my confusion I could say only that his name was, of course, a symbol, but I could not reveal who was hidden behind it.

At this he began to try to guess who it could be. He was suspicious of a beratnu, then thought of a familiar betik.

"It's all the same," he concluded. "the book is good, and it must be published!"

At this I already found my voice.

"But the betik!" I said. "What will my betik say to it?!"

"Nothing. He will be amused by it."

"But for God's sake, haven't you read what I wrote of him? I call him a 'baking-sheet-soled idiot,' a 'demagogical pickpocket,' a 'narrow-minded ape,' to whom people "vake-vake" only because they are afraid of him."

"There you are!" he answered. "You yourself know what a narrow-minded ape he is. How do you imagine that he would recognize himself? He will believe that some of the kemon betiks are involved, or that all this is a description of the transitional or half-raw age. Should he ask it of you, in spite of everything, you, too, will tell him that, and that's all."

Zemoeki carried on for a long time, expressing his joy that I had recounted all the idiocies of this lunatic society to their faces so directly.

"And also splendid," he said, "is that you have defended the anebas against certain treacherous elements, which, as you have rightly pointed out, deceive people for business reasons only. Many such books would be needed to restore the pure cult of the yellow pebble and the square, to rescue them from the mud in which they have trampled them!"

Zemoeki also spoke of my merits in connection with the defense of the kipu, which, of course, was also manifested in my pointing out the claptrap of the charlatans and displaying bold support of the classic chair thorns.

"Surely," he said, "we would need many such aggressive testimonies if we are to clean the dirt away from the anebas and help those many dormant values assert themselves in the kona that are languishing oppressed in the jostling of frauds."

I think this was my greatest surprise among the Behins. I did not understand a word of the whole thing.

Finally Zemoeki rose and took leave, saying he had to hurry to a clothes-ripping master, as the next day he was due at a betik's jubilee where he would be the guest speaker, and his clothes had to be made more kipu for the occasion. And he asked me for some yellow pebbles so as to have something to squeeze under his arm at the betik's place, after which he rushed away in rapture.

"And the book must be published," Zemoeki called from the threshold. "You will see how that narrow-minded ape will laugh at it, and we at him!"

The proposal was enticing but after some thinking I realized that for the very same reason there was no point in publishing it. How could it be imagined that reading it would make them even one iota cleverer or would render their lives one jot more endurable with such a lack of comprehension? Should I publish the account of my travels? It deserved a better lot than to be the object of idiots' imbecilic guffaws.

As to what would have happened to me if the Behins had understood, it is better not to speak of this.

That is why I preferred to keep to my original intention and bring my book home to educated Great Britain, where the general public, together with my nation's august leaders, will certainly be well amused by the infinite narrow-mindedness of Zemoeki and the betik.

This was how I managed to avoid becoming a makru and a laughing stock for everyone.

14

The author explains the oddities of the konch *and the*
namuk. The author, too, is caught up in the fad of the
yellow-eared and the blue-eared. We read of the tragic fate
of the Liftmaster and the Dumplingmaster. The namuk
gives a confused speech at the konch. The author's naive
endeavor comes to a bad end, but he manages to leave the
konch safely. The author tries in vain to understand the
oddities he has experienced.

I MUST FIRST OF ALL APOLOGIZE TO THE LAYMAN, THE NON-physician, for adding the description of one more heap of Behin nonsense to the fanciful ideas in the chapter about the kipu, which were burdensome enough in themselves to cause a head-ache. Let me mention by way of justification that the endeavors of the mufruks to spoil human speech, though already described in detail, will not be fully clear unless I relate the adventure I had to endure during the konch. There, against my wishes, I was taken for a namuk—a person who, as I was to discern, is close in nature to a mufruk.

What the Behins term "konch" is when a lot of people gather and shout at random. For this it could perhaps be translated as a "meeting" or "rally," but their meetings, of course, are funda-mentally different from our's.

In my country it is common for respectable citizens, organized into associations, to occasionally come together so that by mutually exchanging their experiences they may augment their knowledge. We might also regard as meetings the sessions of our wise legislators, where our most outstanding speakers acquaint their audiences in touching speeches with how it would be possible to ensure peace and Christian civilization when faced by the dangers ensuing from the intrigues of certain foreign countries and the opposing party.

The basis of all these meetings is, it goes without saying, a sound mind, without which there would be no sense in the unselfish efforts of our speakers. Is this not the case?

But how could I render into the language of my country the konch, whose only aim is to extinguish any human sanity that might perhaps still exist with senseless verbal torrents?

After all this, perhaps it is unnecessary to mention that they called namuk anyone who at such a konch reeled off either his own rubbish or the flow of words committed to paper by another namuk.

I have already mentioned that at the konch everybody shouts at the same time, but neither the namuk's words nor those of the choir (I cannot term them an audience) have any meaning. More precisely, the words themselves may have a meaning, but this can be assumed only by a naive outsider—because the Behins themselves do not understand each other at all.

If you speak to a Behin and, let us suppose, say to him, "The sun is shining," he will understand it. But if you tell him the same at a konch, you must be prepared for him to draw his knife and react by saying, "Yes, it must be stabbed!"

My description may seem perhaps somewhat muddled, but it can be imagined how difficult it is to describe a system whose main characteristic is the absence of system. I might compare my task to that of the mathematician who wants to represent an irregular curve drawn by a child's hand in analytic equations.

However, there is one hard and fast rule: at a konch it is never the intellect but always stupidity that is epitomized. It is strange but true that the Behins' sense is in inverse proportion to the number of those present.

For the Reader to fully understand what follows, I must mention the antecedents.

In one instance I perceived that some people had painted their ear lobes blue, and when they caught sight of each other they rubbed their chins with their forefingers.

Among the many Behin fads this did not even attract my attention, except that the blue-eared people became more and more numerous, and later I also saw yellow-eared ones, who, on the other hand, rubbed their foreheads with their third fingers.

Gradually I began to suspect that perhaps this also belonged to the kipu, and if I did not smear my ears, the same thing would happen to me again as had happened in the case of my clothes that I had to eventually tear up on the betik's order.

So I spoke about the matter with Zemoeki and asked whether it would not be desirable for me to paint my ears blue.

"Oh, you unfortunate," he flared up. "Are you out of your mind? Such things are done only by hare-brained lunatics!"

For a moment I almost thought that the Behinic disease was curable, but by that time I had become accustomed to the rule whereby I should never indulge in such illusions. For the time being and for safety's sake I decided to leave my ears clean.

However, a few days later I came across Zemoeki, complete with yellow ears, and as I drew nearer he kept on rubbing his forehead eagerly with his third finger.

The sight filled me with deep pity and I tenderly inquired after his health. He replied with a question.

"How can it be that you have not yet painted your ears yellow?"

"Why, it was you who said that I should not paint them!" I said soothingly.

"Oh, you poor bivak!" he laughed. "You have already forgotten that you wanted to paint your ears blue, while the blues are all base evil-doers. A true kona, one who has any feeling for the anebas, paints his ears yellow."

What could I say? I tried to reassure Zemoeki that I would

reconsider the matter, and as soon as I got yellow paint I would paint my ears. Then I hastened to say "prick-pruck" and in the days that followed I tried to avoid his company as much as possible.

One day, having finished my work, I returned with my betik to his office. I placed the box with the yellow pebbles (after my betik had touched it three times with his copper cubes) on a shelf, and then together we went upstairs, then downstairs. Meanwhile I had to carry a thorny chair after him, the aim of which I had not the slightest idea, but from this day onward, I had to do this after work every day, and I was not going to inquire after the reason, being glad that one less stupidity disturbed my mind.

On one occasion when I had put down the thorny chair, I was just preparing to leave with a loud "vake-vake" when the betik called after me, "Tomorrow a great honor will fall to you."

Of course, at the very word itself, my back became covered with goose bumps. I stammered out my pleasure and inquired as to the nature of this future event.

"You will have the opportunity to prove your faculties for the kona and the anebas at the yellow-eared konch."

Suddenly I was seized with self-reproach for having so easily rid myself of Zemoeki instead of gently extracting from him the main essentials of the yellow idea.

Thus I hurriedly acquired some yellow paint, painted my ears, and called upon Zemoeki, for whom I rubbed my forehead eagerly with my third finger already in the distance.

Zemoeki exultantly stated that the sound conviction had brought me to my wits at last, for which I thanked him with a grateful heart, and briefly asked him why in fact I had painted my ears yellow.

With this, of course, I revealed that neither conviction and still less sanity had had anything to do with my action. But I already knew the Behins' nature well enough. I knew that for them sound conviction was to be understood as communal insanity.

And I was not disappointed in my calculation. Zemoeki heaped so many praises on my wisdom that I myself began to doubt the soundness of my mind.

But I was more interested in the yellow danger and asked him to tell me everything I had to know about the konch.

For Zemoeki's lecture to be comprehensible I must remind the Reader that the Hins allowed patients to the Behin settlement only after thorough examination, because there were some mental patients who imagined themselves Behin, whereas they had only a simple, curable paranoia.

It was a tragic event some fifty years ago that had prompted the Hins to this precaution, when the Behins had hacked two unfortunate paranoids to pieces.

We know that paranoia by no means takes over the brain to such an extent as the Behinic disease. There are many who, apart from their single monomania, think quite normally, so that a layman would not even notice the disorder.

One such patient began to speak about having seen a wonderful thing among the Hins—an elevator. He suggested that the Behins, too, should furnish taller buildings with such a device.

His words were at first received with great laughter, and they called him a Hin who had no sense for the boeto that required the Behin to go upstairs by foot.

"What would you say to that degenerated Behin," they retorted "who, sitting on a thornless chair, would have himself hauled up to the upper floors by a halter, after the manner of a brute beast?"

"The elevator brings destruction to the kona!" was the general opinion.

About the same time there were also more such unfortunate paranoids who were unthinkingly allowed, merely at their wish, into the Behin settlement.

It happened as follows. Several people spoke up for the elevator—there were even some who wrote studies in support of it. What is more, another paranoid began to write about having eaten many dumplings made with curd while he'd been among the Hins; and, though his common sense protested against the Hins' tomfoolery, he nevertheless had to admit that the curd dumplings had been good and he suggested that the Behins should also consume them.

At this the whole gathering rose in protest. The more staid among them called the new ideas youthful folly.

"Wild-goose-chasers," they said, "who don't want to work and be of use to the public with their labor, but pursue unattainable dreams instead."

Long essays appeared on how the curd dumpling did not conform to human nature and how hitherto the cause of every famine had demonstrably been the unrestricted consumption of curd dumplings.

Of the elevator some wrote that it imposed extraordinary exertion on man, while others asserted that the kona would perish in the excessive comfort and would be unable to answer its lofty purposes.

"The elevator makes one tired and emasculated," they said repeatedly.

"The elevator and the curd dumpling dull the brain's response to the boeto and the anebas!" wrote others. "Their unhealthy trend plunges the kona into ruin and throws it victim to the ignoble kemon."

"They want to extirpate us with the elevator and the curd dumpling," wrote one mufruk. "The only question is how long the sober Behin nation is going to tolerate this evil propaganda. It is our very existence that is at stake. The elevator and the curd dumpling will seek our lives if we don't become conscious of ourselves in time."

They labeled the comfortists (as they called themselves) lamiks and the matter came to an end by both unfortunate paranoids being beaten to death.

This was all clear and logical from the Behins up to this point, considering that everything was turned completely upside down. The oddity came only afterward.

After the comfortists were struck dead, their doctrines not only failed to cease: their followers even grew in number among the Behins. What is more, some betiks also joined and professed that the unfortunate victims had been the greatest geniuses of the kona, but they had been misunderstood.

When I had learned as much from Zemoeki's words, I asked him to tell me how all this led to the smearing of the ears. "The yellow-eared are the comfortists," he said, "and the blue-eared are the narrow-minded anticomfortists who do not understand the signs of the times."

So I understood that the next day the people of the Elevator Party would come together at the konch to demand the acceptance of the elevator which, according to Zemoeki, had already been accepted and even put into practice by many elak betiks.

"Indeed?" I asked in surprise. "Then why is there still no elevator anywhere?"

"Of course, there is!" Zemoeki answered in indignation. "Moreover, to my knowledge you, too, are an elevator attendant!"

I was a little bit perplexed, for until then I had been unaware that I had such a post.

"Oh? What?" I stammered.

Zemoeki frowned.

"Well, perhaps it is not you who is wont to carry the thorny chair upstairs?" he asked with deep resentment. "What kind of a beratnu are you if you don't perform this, either?"

"Oh, of course, of course!" I hastened to reassure him. "So, in brief, this is the kona's elevator!"

"Well, what else could the elevator be if not the elevator?"

What else could I expect of them? With disgust I refrained from further debate, believing that I had already understood everything.

So I was not disappointed in my presentiment.

The unfortunate paranoids had been beaten to death, and the

Behins, having not the vaguest idea of the elevator either, imagined that it was the chair going up and down. This was the way their thinking had developed until the Behins accepted it.

However, the fact that there existed an Elevator Party at all gave rise to the thought that now I might have the opportunity to spread a sound and useful idea among them.

"If there is an Elevator Party," I reasoned, "and I tell them that I demand, together with them, the introduction of the elevator, then perhaps they will not strike me to death, even if I indeed demand the introduction of the elevator."

I decided to explain to them the next day at the konch what a real elevator was like, thinking that finally I would have the chance to do them a good turn without endangering my life. To the extent that I knew an elevator's construction, I thought it over, whereupon I made sketches and a detailed explanatory text to deliver to them the next day.

To this very day I marvel at my naivety at the time.

The konch was in that barn, the institute for the degeneration of children, where once I had handed over the yellow pebbles to the proko.

Many yellow-eared Behins came together, and in their mutual pleasure they kept on rubbing their foreheads.

Suddenly, at one end of the barn, a Behin stood up on a table. His body was covered by a cloth torn into rags, colored pebbles and dead beetles hanging on strings from the holes. When he rubbed his forehead with his third finger, the yellow-eared vaked with wailings that pierced to the marrow.

"Who is he?" I asked Zemoeki, who was wailing beside me.

"A *namuk*."

"What's a namuk?"

"A namuk is one whose vocation it is to explain the honest truth."

When the row ceased, the namuk began to speak.

"We have come here to lead the kona from the greatest danger to the path of the true boeto, rescuing it from the whirlpool into which the vile anticomfortists want to plunge it so that we should fall victim to the kemons."

The response to this was a still greater uproar.

"We have demanded only," the ragamuffin went on, "that houses with three or more floors should be provided with elevators. But the anticomfortists have labelled us, the best konas, Hins, and this ignominy cannot be suffered by any self-respecting kona."

Needless to say, the yelling again resounded. This is why, for brevity's sake, I shall from now on indicate with an exclamation mark in brackets the increase of the uproar. (They bellowed incessantly; the difference was only in degree.)

"These hirelings of the kemon [!] did not blush to vilify the curd dumpling, and are crying from the housetops that we commit spirituality, moreover, in the presence of the yellow pebble [!]; on the other hand, they are oblivious to the fact that anyone who does not catch his foot before the square has no right whatsoever to put others wise; and this ignobility has been proved with regard to more than one anticomfortist [!!].

"We, accordingly, cannot reply to this mean machination and base challenge with anything except by continuing to demand the introduction of the elevator, but now not only in buildings with three floors but also in those with two or even one!

"And of the curd dumpling we wish only to say to our attackers that whoever calls the curd dumpling spirituality is a lamik, or at least a kemon troublemaker. The curd dumpling is good and gives strength, so we not only not refuse to abandon our demand that the yellow pebble should be renamed the curddumpling [!] but insist that every kona should be given not one but two yellow pebbles, one under his left arm and one under his right arm [!!] and they should finally admit that the yellow pebble will nourish and give real strength against the kemon only under the glorious name of curddumpling [!!]"

With this he got off the table. The yellow-eared vaked with all their force, and many surrounded the namuk, almost rubbing the skin off his forehead—a sign, according to Zemoeki, that he had spoken the truth.

So, the curd dumpling shared the elevator's fate.

Afterward another namuk followed in similarly or, if possible, still more tattered clothes. That the exclamation marks should not disturb the Reader, I shall now omit them, but he can in any case imagine the terrible cacophony.

He commenced by saying that he would now acquaint us with the Great Elevator Master's thoughts. He then sat down and took out a sheet of paper, from which he began to read the writings of the poor paranoid.

Now I ask the Reader to hold on tight.

The Elevator Master's text was purely and simply the standard description of an elevator—that the elevator is a little cabin in which people sit down; that it is then pulled up to a higher floor by electric power; and that it is also possible to descend in it without effort and without walking.

And if I had any doubts with regard to the Behins' knowledge concerning the nature of the elevator, they would have been eliminated by the original drawings that he presented afterward, which conformed entirely to the sketches I had prepared.

To tell the truth, I understood nothing of the whole matter.

Why if they knew the Elevator Master's ideas, and could follow his concepts with such desperate fury, how was it that the elevator became a thorny chair to be carried upstairs and back by the poor boxshaker?

Then this namuk announced that he would now recite the words of the great mufruk: the Dumpling Master.

At this, I already took out my travel diary, hoping that, considering my modest faculties, I would be of service to my colleagues, by hastily sketching what was to follow. My notes provide the following evidence.

The namuk stood, and with sweeping pathos and grotesque grimaces began to shout.

"The curd dumpling is a mixture of boiled dough and curd!"

Here he lowered his voice. The crowd clamored.

"In my experience it is a very good food."

Again the namuk stopped. Then he took a deep breath, raised his arms high, knitted his brows and bellowed, "It is to be served warm!!"

Dropping his arms with a sudden gesture, he slammed them on the table, bared his teeth, and, clenching his right fist, shook it toward the ceiling.

"It maintains physical strength!!"

Reaching forward horizontally with his palms, he panted with pursed lips.

"When we have eaten it, it causes a pleasant feeling."

With this he fell back on his chair. I ask the Reader to excuse me from describing the howling that followed. My ears still buzz when I think of it. Let it suffice that the shouters reviled the kemons and demanded that they should be evicerated. As to how the curd dumpling came to be a grudge against the kemons, don't ask me.

However, the best was now to come.

The namuk (the one who had bellowed and demonstrated all this) began to speak about how efficiently the elevator served the welfare of the kona.

"In olden times," he began, "the narrow-minded conservatives reproached the Elevator Master saying that his ideas would lead to the emasculation of the kona, and, moreover, that the elevator would directly prove to be the ruin of the kona. (General laughter.)

"However, I ask, what supplies the kona's strength against the ignoble kemons if not the elevator, which, imbuing the beratnu with the electric current of the boeto, swings him into the higher spheres? And is there a more wonderful aneba than the curd dumpling squeezed under the arm, which gives us strength not only to abstain from the pollution of spirituality but also to wipe the kemons' loathsome circles off the walls?"

With this the namuk left the table, and the crowd burst into an intensified howl. This, however, was more than I could have permitted without a word.

With great resolve I fought my way through the crowd and climbed onto the table, at which they turned their attention to me with interest, and I asked them in a few simple words to listen to me because I myself wished for the introduction of the elevator and wanted to say some true words about it.

Then I tried to enlighten them in brief about their mistakes. "The electric power of the elevator is not to be understood figuratively," I said. "Actual electricity is involved."

"Hear! Hear!"

"The fullest truth!"

"Down with the ignoble kemons!" the crowd clamored.

However, I continued.

"And the elevator does not hoist one up figuratively or spiritually—we actually sit in it, and it carries us up to the higher floors."

"Up to the higher floors!" they shouted. "Down with the kemons!"

"And the curd dumpling is not a yellow pebble but dough that is to be eaten, and thus it maintains our strength."

"Strength! Strength!"

"Strength against the kemons!" came the reply.

"But Behins!" I shouted. "Let us understand: the Elevator Master and the Dumpling Master did not speak about the kemons, but wanted us to travel easily to the higher floors and eat the curd dumpling so that we should be able to remain alive!"

"Up to the higher floors! Up! Up!"

"We want the elevator and the curd dumpling!"

"Down with ignominious spirituality!" they shouted. Several of them brandished drawn knives.

Now I began to lose my patience. I spoke my mind openly.

"But if you know the elevator and the curd dumpling, tell me why you still deceive yourselves with the thorny chair and the yellow pebble? Understand that those you follow did not intend such idiotic nonsense but life, comfort, and nourishment!"

"Nourishment!"

"Save our lives!"

"Strike the kemons to death!" they shouted, brandishing their knives.

The situation began to be dangerous, but this bottomless, swirling morass of stupidity made the blood rush to my face. At this stage, what did I care even if they were to strike me dead? I could but tell them off once! Not caring a fig for the dangers, I tried to raise my voice above all the others.

"You are half-witted amok-runners! Don't you think that this way you will not live? Don't you think that this whole herd of oxen will perish miserably?"

I stamped my foot so hard on the table that it was cleft in two.

The fury of the crowd here increased to paroxysm. The Behins stabbed their knives into the walls with a towering rage, and from between their foaming teeth the strident madness screeched, "We are a herd of oxen!"

"Let's rip open those raving mad kemons!"

The pitiable horrors of the scene suddenly brought about a great change in me. In a second I was over the climax of rage and felt that I had come to understand the innermost essence of the Behins.

For if, on the gate of hell, the word "lasciate" figured, on the gate of the Behin settlement this could have been most aptly written: "in vain."

In deep contempt I continued, "You are right. It is best if you slaughter each other until the last kona, kemon, comfortist, and anticomfortist dies out. The mountain, the valley, the cloud, the sunshine, the wise maggot, and the benign tiger will be grateful for it."

With this I got off and, folding my arms, with the audacity of prophets I bravely faced the swirling mass of the demented.

And vakeing they surrounded me, exulted and abused, the kemons and the anticomfortists, and they fell upon my forehead and rubbed it so that my skin almost caught fire. Then they hoisted me up and cried that I was the bravest kona.

Moreover, even a baking-sheet-soled betik shuffled over to me and solemnly took hold of my nose.

"That's right, kaleb," he said, shaking the copper cubes on his knees. "Not a single namuk has defended the kipu and the kona so forcefully up to now as you. Many similar brave and true konas are needed for us to be able to drown the ignoble enemy."

With this, he stepped onto the table, and publicly thanked me in warm words and suggested that the yellow-eared should accept my proposal and call themselves a herd of oxen. On their forehead they should glue tiny horns, that this elevated emblem should also display the boeto, which elevates the true comfortist—that is, the ox—above the base and obscure anticomfortists, and at the same time, gives strength against the ignoble kemons.

Finally pointing to me, the baking-sheet-soled betik called upon the crowd to vake at me for my beautiful words, and from now on to call me chief ox.

This, too, I had to suffer.

*

As I arrived home, a wild kaleidoscope of what had happened danced before me, and it was only after long hours that I could gather together a few thoughts by way of explanation. The mental blunting caused by the Behinic disease I imagine somehow like this:

The basic element of their existence is a grudge against each other that we might perhaps call some unquenchable bestiality—if, that is, I may at all compare the normal beast of prey that kills for its livelihood with those who ravage against the interests of their own lives.

Each group has a certain circle of monomanias and this is what, on the surface, distinguishes it from the others. This is, however, only the surface appearance. The truth is that they do not fight for monomanias but concoct monomanias to fight for.

Somebody becomes blue-eared only to be different from the yellow-eared and vice versa. They fight for fighting's sake.

"But then what are the many theories and debates for?" the Reader may rightly ask. "If the sole element of life for the Behins is their grudge against each other, why have they to invent kona, kemon, comfort, anticomfort, boeto, kipu, and other wild illusions? Why does everyone not turn on his neighbor with a club without any explanation?"

Well, this is what I do not understand, either. Undoubtedly, in comparison with wild animals, they have intelligence that enables them to suppress their sound instincts and fight for aims beyond the instincts, even for some that are in contradiction with life. And their better ego does not merely fail to suppress this faculty of theirs—they deliberately develop it.

Perhaps I understand even this. But why, for example, it would be necessary to concoct theories about hand-walking that will justify its being more convenient and healthy than walking upright, I do not understand and, what is more, I never will.

*The author encounters the Behins' strangest fancy: the
rules of eating for women. We further witness the amusing
custom of the Bigrusts. At the* shukk, *the author nearly
comes off badly. Time and again he is up against the rules
of eating for women, and on this account he suffers many
trials and tribulations.*

BUT LET US RETURN TO MY FURTHER FATE. NOW MY ACQUAIN-
tance with a woman entered into the matter and this, I might say,
caused my doom.

Their women were in general very loathsome. The right ear
of most of them, for instance, had been cut off. It was terrible
even to imagine the pain they must have suffered, and it was
even more terrible to look at these unfortunate, deformed figures. Unbelievable as it may seem, these women had not been
mutilated by sanguinary murderers or sadistic madmen: they
themselves had submitted to the operation, and indeed they
even had paid for it, for they held it to be kipu. And the men,
instead of turning away from them in pity, on the contrary preferred the earless women.

But they not only had their ears cut off. They also tried using
all kinds of absurd and disgusting methods to spoil the natural
beauty of the body. They painted their noses white using lime;
their posteriors they smeared with a stinking, sticky blue paint
and kept them naked, while on their stomachs they tied thick

pillows, and as to their mouths, they kept them permanently covered with handkerchiefs.

The woman, by the way, whom my wretched fate brought across my path, was called Zukrula, and I made her acquaintance at a shukk. At that time I myself did not know what a shukk was.

Zemoeki told me the news on one occasion that there would be a shukk that day, and suggested that I should attend it as it would be very interesting.

Out of curiosity, I went with Zemoeki and Zeremble. On the way, it struck me that at the foot of the trees some completely rusted tin sheets had been set up that I had not seen there the day before.

I asked why they did not move them out of the way; somebody might be injured by them.

In reply I was given a most resentful look.

"I would have you know," said Zemoeki, "that they are the Bigrusts, which are displayed on solemn occasions." From this I understood only that I had made a blunder again, so, now much more softly and with respect, I inquired after the nature of the Bigrusts, at which it came to light that this custom, too, was an aneba.

"I'm no boaster," Zeremble said, "but I can tell you that my sheet of iron became pockmarked with rust no less than eighty years ago."

And he looked around proudly.

But Zemoeki remarked that on his sheet of iron the rust was already two inches thick.

Now I was very curious and, to avoid any blunder, on the basis of my previous experiences I praised Zemoeki's Bigrust though I had no idea what that signified.

This method did indeed open their hearts, and while we proceeded they explained every rusty sheet of iron.

I had to stand for a long time in front of Zeremble's Bigrust, as he called my attention to every hole. It was undoubtedly in a pitiable state, and was saved from falling apart only by being nailed onto a board. And with a folding ruler Zemoeki measured the thickness of the individual Bigrusts, and any that were thinner than his own—even by a hair's breadth—he called brand new, a usable piece, and made derogatory remarks about it. About one he said that its proprietor might do better to make a bowl for his spirituality out of it, at which even Zeremble looked round in fear and warned him of the ketni.

Zemoeki, however, was in his element. One particularly impressive layer of rust he pronounced a forgery, the proprietor having glued it onto the sheet. He expressed his surprise that he had not yet been punished for false rusting. Of another he claimed it did not belong to the man in question, but that the man had suddenly become a betik and had purchased it from a rust owner who was now reduced to poverty.

"Although," said Zemoeki, "everyone knows that he was not even born here. Twenty years ago he worked outside as an ordinary and rough designer of elevated railways; his fingers are still gnarled from the compasses. Regrettably, however, it is not possible to take measures against him because he sits in the Rust Measuring and Records Office."

Zemoeki was greatly indignant that the cause of public rust was committed to the charge of such people. However, he did not omit to emphasize that his—that is, Zemoeki's—great-grandfather had been brought in when he ate his shoes, and he, too, was a remarkable man within the community: it was he who succeeded in bringing about the squeezing of the yellow pebble under the right arm instead of the left. His grandfather skinned a kemon alive. For weeks he greased his earlobe with the kemon's fat, for which many people admired him, but there were also those who envied him, as is usual with great men. As for Zemoeki's father, he was a great scientist, one of the founders of ellipsology. He had established why the circle was an ellipse for the kona, as a result of which he had contributed significantly to bringing to the surface the specific popular sciences latent in the kona.

Conversing in this fashion, we arrived at the shukk. We reached an enclosed area, where many people were standing outside a railing.

We had scarcely been there two minutes when two Behins suddenly dashed into the enclosure, eyes flashing with fury, and huge clubs in their hands. They began to thrash each other about the head and back, and within a short space of time blood was streaming all over the place and their skin hung in shreds.

I cried for help, and even the crowd began to shout inarticulately, but nobody attempted to separate them. Finally, I myself jumped over the railing but they grabbed me and yanked me right out. In vain I demanded the separation of the adversaries. They answered that it was a shukk, and that I should keep my mouth shut.

Around the two maniacs a third one was jumping about, who likewise had not the slightest intention of separating them. He only watched the fight, and from time to time called out to them, "Bruf!"

And the crowd shouted after him in ecstasy, "Bruf! Bruf!"

It appeared therefore that it was the job of the third person in the enclosure to incite the fighters and the crowd. The only odd thing was that some in the crowd in turn shouted, "No bruf! No bruf!"

Whereupon those who were bruffing hooted them down.

At the time I assumed that there were still some sensible people in the crowd who resisted the incitement. But not at all! Later I came to know that bruf meant something entirely different, but to this very day I have no clear idea what.

The fight ended when the skull of one of the fighters caved in with a loud crack; the crowd gave a yell, rushed into the field, surrounded the murderer, vaked to him, scratched the pants on his posterior into rags until he, too, collapsed because of blood loss and the strain on his heart.

And when I indignantly asked the bystanders how they could tolerate such a barbaric settling of differences, they said that they had not been enemies and that this was a shukk by which to develop health. And I referred in vain to my medical degree from Oxford University, claiming that a man with a broken skull was less healthy than a sound one, and only madmen cracked each other's heads in cold blood; it was they who became enraged, indeed fists rose, and I would certainly have been unable to avoid being lynched had I not been quick to take to my heels.

I went to the other side and watched the events from there.

Now two more maniacs dashed in, and the preceding scene recommenced. The instigator sometimes shouted the bruf, which was met by an intensified howling of the crowd.

In one instance, however, the bruf- bruf came from the crowd without the instigator having cried out. Nor did they calm down afterward, but commenced to bruf even more loudly, and abused the instigator because he had not seen the bruf. Others were by contrast shouting, "No bruf!"

"Bruf!"

"No bruf!"

The situation began to get dangerously out of hand, and I tried to cower, suspecting that trouble was brewing. But the Reader is wrong if he believes I succeeded in remaining at peace in this way, as one of them suddenly turned to me.

"Did you see the bruf?"

"No, I didn't," and I hastened to excuse myself, but he, instead of calming down, set upon me all the more angrily.

"Didn't you? Do you deny it? Do you hear?" He turned to the others. "This base blue-eared did not see the bruf!"

"Let him have it!" yelled ten voices at the same time and the blows had already begun to rain down on me.

Fortunately, however, another ten interfered.

"No bruf, no bruf!" they shouted and fell upon the first group as each wildly thrashed the other.

Making use of the uproar and protecting my head with my arms, I hurried to disappear from the scene, and at the price of a few bruises succeeded. But now I did not stop until I reached home, and I pledged to myself never even to show my face at a shukk.

The next day Zemoeki dashed into my room out of breath. In his great zeal he stumbled over the threshold and almost came down on his nose. He was in a pitiable state, poor thing. His head was bandaged, his face stuck all over with plasters.

"Well," I thought, "this one will not go to a shukk for a long time, either."

But Zemoeki, it seemed, did not care a fig for all this and poked at my chest.

"Did you see the bruf?"

"I did, I did!" I hastened to give him the pat answer lest the same thing happen to me as the day before. But instead of calming down, he turned on me.

"Oh, you wretch! Was it a bruf for you? Don't you have eyes? Or perhaps you, too, side with that incorrigible, foolish green-yellow gang?"

Naturally, I had again made a blunder, so I hastened to explain that I had seen it, but I had seen only that it was not a bruf but some fools had cried out that it was. With this, I just about managed to appease him.

Stepping to the tap, Zemoeki put a fresh compress on his head, and in the meantime he related that the rascal who had cracked his head had not got away with it, either, as Zemoeki had kicked him on the shin, so that he had immediately fallen off his feet, and his accomplices had had to carry him away by his legs and arms; they even had to run with him, while Zemoeki had managed to make off on his own two feet. And the cause of the great hurry was that the public peace guards were already on the way, who then indiscriminately beat to a pulp any able-bodied person with an unbroken skull who still remained; or, as Zemoeki put it, "They restored law and order."

Shuddering, I listened to him, and in my mind, I thanked my lucky stars for having received my blows prior to the restoration of law and order.

"But all this because of a bruf!" I exclaimed.

"What do you mean, 'all because of a bruf'?" Zemoeki rapped out. "If we don't take the bruf seriously, there is no point in the whole shukk!"

I would have liked to applaud wholeheartedly but I did not dare, which made Zemoeki still more annoyed.

"Well, tell me: is there a point or not?"

"There is not," I replied hesitatingly.

"There you are! Then we might as well stop organizing shukks!"

Now I approved somewhat more boldly, at which he added, "And we should destroy our whole human culture and go back to the jungle among the beasts!"

This, therefore, was how I learned the essence of the shukk. If someone strikes a fellow human being dead, he will be punished. But if he first utters the magic word "shukk," he will be excused!

With the Behins everything depends on the words.

And it was quite lucky that they did not punish those who did not want to have their heads bashed in to fully experience the shukk!

Of course, the Reader considers this last sentence a feeble witticism and smiles at my words. To my regret I must interrupt his pleasure, because there was actually also a magic word that, if the murderer pronounced it, not only exempted him from punishment, but saw the one who had not wanted to kill be punished instead. This was the buku. But of this I shall speak later. Now I had perhaps better not comment on this sort of madness, all the more so as I later became involved in a much more serious affair that did in the end literally ruin me.

Among the spectators at the shukk I noticed a woman emaciated to the bone and on her last leg. In her hand the handkerchief trembled, and she could hardly press it to her mouth.

In spite of my disgust I was moved to pity. Her weakness was so deplorable that as a physician I was unable to look upon her without a helping word. Somewhat perplexed, I looked for words to suggest, without offending the ketni, better nourishment for her, and finally I decided that, instead of beating around the bush with clumsy explanations, I would offer her, in a chivalrous manner, a part of my spirituality.

In order to do this I stepped up to her and made the offer that I would willingly abandon my dispensable spirituality available at home for her consumption.

The Reader would never have believed what a heated reproach I received in answer. She called me a bivak who had no idea of the ketni. What kind of woman did I take her for? Did I really think that she would be able to perpetrate such a foul deed?

"Are you thinking of eating?" The words had slipped out of me.

"Ugh! Bivak!" she screamed. "How can you imagine that I would even think of such things! And if you were to say it, then it should never have been said in such a way!"

But seeing her lamentable state, my most basic human feelings dictated that I should violate the rules and satisfy her hunger— why, she was about to collapse. So I said, "Whatever we say, the truth is that we all take spirituality."

Squealing with anger, she fell upon me asking what did I imagine? That she should need such a horrid thing? She had never desired it in all her life, for she was not that sort of woman, and that I should not forget. Any ketni man, by the way, would never behave like this on such an occasion but would ask whether she had wanted the *bikbam* and would not abuse a defenseless female.

This was where I committed my next blunder. This confirmed stubbornness of stupidity made me lose my temper, and I did not leave it at that. Informing her that I was a physician, I recommended that she look into a mirror, and she would see how the hunger was visible on her. After all, there was nothing to be ashamed of. Why, all of us ate, as sufficiently proven by the fact that we existed.

I guessed that she would at least take offense but I no longer cared; after all, I had nothing to lose, and by accepting my advice she would gain.

Of course what actually happened would have been beyond my wildest dreams.

The woman gasped for breath and then cried for help at the top of her voice. The guards gathered round, and she lied to them that I had attacked her and wanted to rob her of something. What it was she did not disclose, of course, but only spoke of some dearest treasure of hers even though she had nothing worth a penny on her.

This audacious slander repelled me, and I announced that not only had I not wanted to take anything from her, but I had wanted to give her a share in the pleasure of spirituality.

Then followed my real surprise.

The guards had a good laugh at my words, called me a fool, stated that that was precisely the point at issue, and dragged me before the betik who in turn sentenced me to a week's imprisonment because I had wanted to feed a woman!

I did not want to believe my ears and could not even defend myself for astonishment, but stood as though paralyzed with no control over my thoughts or what was happening to me.

I had been imprisoned for some hours before I could sufficiently arrange my thoughts to enable me to understand the situation. I had been jailed like some pickpocket—and why? Because I had been good and clear-headed.

After my release, I complained to Zemoeki indignantly, but instead of sympathizing he laughed at me, called me a bivak, and began teaching me the ketni.

Although the superciliousness of this lunatic annoyed me, I tried nonetheless to hear him out with patience, hoping that with what I "acquired" I would be able at least to steel myself against similar traps.

Hair-raising things came to light, I am bound to report.

I already knew that eating passed as an impropriety, but so far as women were concerned I would never have believed the sorts of tortuous ideas that were assigned to it.

Now I came to know, for example, that they wore a pillow over the stomach and a handkerchief on the mouth because both organs were connected with eating.

It was forbidden even to mention the mouth. One had to pretend that a woman had no mouth.

Of course, from the European point of view this seems unbelievable—that one should hold this most natural and honest function of life to be shameful, and that we should think in such a way about something without which we could not even live, but the tortuous way in which the Behin women had to conceal it defied all imagination. If a man and a woman came together, both spoke as if they had no idea that such a thing as a mouth existed, though both of course knew that it did, and moreover that this was known by the other. They named the mouth only when absolutely necessary, and even then in circumlocutory terms conceived especially for the observation of the ketni, calling it now "midface," then "thoughtflower," though it had nothing to do with thought, just like spirituality, as it was even denied that this was eaten by people, but had to be spoken of as if it were carried away by a stork. Of course, everybody realized that they themselves lied as well as knowing that others knew that they lied.

And the miserable women carried this loathsome bundle of lies throughout their lives with no sense of shame or decency and without raising a protesting voice at any time!

I, who am purely and simply describing this, gave a great deal of thought to whether it would be at all proper to publish such monstrosities. Certainly among my Readers there will be a fair number of my country's chaste and ingenuous maidens who, having been brought up in the sound European civilization, have always learned that to lie is immoral, and who will surely not be able to read all this without blushing. May it serve as my justification that when I remember the shameless Behin women I cannot stifle my rightful patriotic pride.

As to the monomania of wearing a handkerchief, I can relate a particularly fantastic episode. On one occasion a woman appeared in the yard with her mouth uncovered. My Readers cannot possibly imagine the resulting scandal. The bystanders blushed and turned away, covering their eyes; and women ran screaming in all directions. Finally a guard came and took the woman away. But the interesting point was their explanation— that the woman had gone mad!

I would still have liked to know what the bikbam was that the woman had spoken of and that I would have come to know had she wished it. But after so many failures I did not dare to ask because, although I was sure that this, too, would be some concocted nonsense, I did not feel a bit like adding fresh fuel to Zemoeki's derision and humiliating superciliousness. They laugh at anyone who does not know the concocted wordproducts of their fantasy lives. If, on the other hand, somebody does not know what an eclipse or a pancreas is, they view him with respect as it adds to his distinction.

So that I should discover without being laughed at what the bikbam was, following my discharge I again called upon the woman concerned and asked her, first of all, to excuse me for my earlier bivak behavior, then asked her whether she had wished the bikbam.

The woman's face became considerably friendlier; she stated that she kvared my words, that she did not enoate because of me, and as to the bikbam, she had indeed wished it.

So I managed to make her acquaintance. That was when I came to know that she was called Zukrula. We started out for a walk and were joined by Zemoeki and, considering my limitations, the conversation could be called sufficiently smooth. I tried to choose subjects to which I hoped that the shackles of the ketni, kipu, and other freak concepts did not apply. Of course, even so, I burned my fingers right at the start.

With my headstrong approach, I dared to utter the seemingly innocent sentence, "The sky is blue." Surely, I thought, this couldn't give rise to possible difficulties.

But Zukrula emphatically replied, "Yes, it *was* blue."

"It is now, too," I answered ingenuously and received a contemptuous look in reply. I blushed, and under some pretext called Zemoeki aside to ask him about the matter. However, no sooner were we in private than he heaped reproaches on me: how could I speak in the present tense in the presence of a woman?

Thus it came to light that in a conversation between a man and a woman, every verb had to be in the past tense; one could speak in the present tense only to a woman who had already taken off her mouthkerchief in one's presence.

Returning, I was at pains to observe this requirement but, I may say, the compulsory past tense caused me the greatest confusion on several occasions, as I did not know whether the present or the past was concerned. I have no idea why they do it. Doesn't speech exist in order to communicate actual ideas and, moreover, without endeavoring to cause misunderstanding?

But we had scarcely begun to continue our conversation when Zemoeki again called me aside and asked with resentment in his voice, why I kept calling her Zukrula, and why didn't I call her Zaikuebue.

"Because she is called Zukrula," I answered simply.

"Just call her Zaikuebue."

"She herself has said that she is Zukrula."

"Oh you bivak!" laughed Zemoeki. "She says it because ketni does not permit her to do otherwise, but you should address her as Zaikuebue."

Somebody else might well have gone mad in my place, and I realized only then how much one can endure. Thus we returned and the conversation continued.

Gradually Zukrula became kinder to me again and then asked me to touch a *buipiff* with her.

Somewhat frightened, I looked at Zemoeki as I was unaware of what kind of new trap awaited me, but he reciprocated my glance with a reassuring wink that I might do this safely.

Even so, of course, things were far from being in order, and I stammered out my confession that I was unversed in the buipiff. This elicited a contemptuous pouting from Zukrula, and she remarked that it seemed that men today received a rather theoretical education that did not meet the practical requirements of life.

Eventually Zemoeki came to my help and explained the matter.

The buipiff consists of a man and a woman touching the tips of their fingers in accordance to different arrangements of sequence and rhythm. The man's thumb touches the woman's third finger, then the third finger the little one, then again the third finger, and the little finger the woman's forefinger, and so on; and from time to time they point at each other's mouth. The buipiff has a thousand variations, the only common gesture being the pointing at the mouth that occurs in each of them. But what they point at is kept strictly secret because they are ashamed of it, and mention it only as the *phagmak* figure. I have no idea why they are ashamed of it, and if they are ashamed of it why they do it.

I also came to know that the buipiff was usually performed to music. This came in handy insofar as when I turned out to be a very blockheaded pupil, I could say by way of excuse that I could certainly have done it better to music.

Zukrula and Zemoeki suggested instead that we should go for a walk on the hillside. We set off. Zukrula at this point suddenly announced that she would very much like to have a butterfly with dark brown wings striped with blue. After a lengthy chase I managed to catch one for her, but it was not suitable because it was dark brown with blue stripes, whereas she preferred a blue-winged butterfly with brown stripes, whose wings she would cut off, frill, and glue onto the bristles of her clothes brush as that would look really good. She added that she had always desired a man who carried out all her orders—a strong and tyrannical man who would whip his woman if she did not obey.

Then it occurred to Zukrula that she would like to see a rainbow, whose arch was down and the foot was up, and that she did not understand what science was for if this could not be

produced; that it would be good to run with open arms in hot
snow; that it would be good to say everything in one breath but
without sound, because only that was true speech, and that we
could attain perfection if we did not speak; and that we paint
our foreheads yellow. And what would I say to that scientist
who had lately discovered the solution to all integral equations?
Was it true that it was his habit to cover his spirituality with a
red-and-purple kerchief? For I should note that he had made a
great impression on her, and she wore a copy of his article on her
midface in her mouthkerchief.

I heard these words in surprise, words that had a familiar ring;
they were indeed so strangely different from the madness of the
Behins that melted into paroxysm. As I realized, Zukrula's chatter, whims, and ideas were veritably soothing to me, reminding
me as they did of the sweet chatter of the ladies in my beloved
country, of their petty problems, and of the music of a thousand
variations emanating from the lovely female soul that makes the
weaker sex so exciting, mysterious, and desirable, and induces
men to dash off in pursuit of the beautiful creature, to catch
her, to solve the mystery, to penetrate the real and tangible
content that hides among the trills and fugues of her rhapsodic
moods—or at least we believe that there is something hiding
there.

I must say that at that moment I did not feel so out of place.
I even joined in the chattering, happily stating that although the
Behins turned every custom and institution upside down, they
were not able to divest the female soul of its true and natural
character.

But my pleasure did not last for long, for Zukrula suddenly
asked, "My little finger was thinner than my thumb, wasn't it?"

This, of course, had to be understood in the present tense.

Although the question was ridiculous, I was already accustomed to it and instead of laughing I obligingly inspected her
hand and agreed, with clear conscience, that her little finger was
indeed thinner.

At this Zukrula jumped up and looked me up and down with flashing eyes.

"Bivak!" she cried, adding "And as to the bikbam, I did not wish it! So it was out of the question!" and she ran away.

I gazed idiotically at Zemoeki, who, without waiting for my question, heaped abuse on me yet again. He, too, called me a bivak, and it took some minutes before he could calm down sufficiently for me to ask for an explanation.

This was how I learned that it was the strict obligation of a man to qualify the woman's little finger as thicker than her thumb and anyone who failed to do so perpetrated a kave act.

The normal Reader, of course, might well feel that there were some natural grounds for this: that the thumb was made thinner among the Behins, or something like that. I must affirm that this is not so. Their fingers are just like those of anyone else, but someone conjured up the idea that a thinner thumb is something to be proud of, and though everyone knows this is not true of anybody one still has to say so—to assert it, and even, if one is a man, to argue with a woman who says that her little finger is thinner. Then they debate about it for hours, and the woman is happy although she is well aware the whole time that the man is lying. While other people honor each other by telling the truth, the measure of honoring each other among the Behins is the ability to tell the greatest lie.

For the madness to be complete, I also mention the rule of the ketni whereby all this may only be stated about the woman to whom we are speaking. To say it of another woman is the greatest insult to the woman who is present.

The question of the bikbam gave me no rest, so the next day I again called upon Zukrula anew, offering my apologies and assuring her that she had misheard—that I had not said thinner but thicker.

As I had now lied doubly, Zukrula was appeased, and I urged her to tell me whether she had wished the bikbam. (The Reader is already aware of the function of the past tense.)

Zukrula became very kind once more; she announced that this way it was quite different, and as for the bikbam, she had indeed wished it.

With this, she took me together with Zemoeki and Zeremble to a betik who fastened the baking sheets upon his soles, then unfastened them and took them off. This he did three times, then threw a heated copper cube into some water, half of which he drank; having wrapped the cube into a ripped cloth he hit both of us on the head, unwrapped it, and asked me for money.

I found the sum a little too much; however, as I did not dare to mention it inside, I broached the subject with Zemoeki after we came back outside, suggesting that for such a short bikbam the betik could have asked less. However, Zemoeki benevolently explained that the money was not for the betik but for the bikru. I vehemently protested, saying that the bikru was a concept and one cannot pay a concept; besides, I had seen with my own eyes that the betik had taken the money, but Zemoeki reproachingly warned me that it was kave to say such a thing and that I had again made an unfortunate reference to my eyes. I should therefore note once and for all that I had given the money to the bikru.

As to what the bikru meant I was not at all aware, of course; I only gathered that it was a concept concocted to unify the reasons for all bad things. When my food was confiscated, it was in fact carried away by the bikru, and I paid my money to the bikru. If someone died of an illness, he was killed not by the germs but by the bikru. If he fell from a roof, it was the bikru who had pushed him off. When Zemoeki egged me on to beat the kemons, I had to note that it was not he, but the bikru, who compelled me to fight.

It was on account of the bikru that one had to feed on pebbles instead of food, to vake for the betik, to water the grass, and to burn clothes; and in general the Behins blamed the bikru for the whole of their topsy-turvy, unbearable lives. The bikru was ideally suited for excusing the germs, fire, water, confiscators, and most of all the betiks of all responsibility. The Reader may imagine, after all this, how every trouble and disease was rife here, and the Behins were unable to perceive the simple and obvious reasons, which even a schoolchild in my country would have known.

However, a dramatic turn of events ensued.

After the bikbam we took leave of Zemoeki and Zeremble with a warm prick-pruck, then Zukrula grasped me and started on the double toward my flat.

"Did you, perhaps, want to come to my place?" I asked.

"I most certainly do," she said decisively.

"What?" I was struck dumb with surprise at the unexpected present tense. "Was it now ketni for you to speak so?"

"Don't tease me," Zukrula chided. "Have you already forgotten being struck on the head with the copper cube?"

No sooner had we arrived home than Zukrula slammed the door shut and, removing her handkerchief from her mouth, gasped in choking ecstasy. "Feed me, please. I'm suffering the pangs of hunger—so let me have that food, stuff it into my mouth, into my stomach so I'll be satisfied at last!"

This made me shudder. Zukrula revelled in these forbidden words to such an extent that I, who had gradually become accustomed to the ketni, fled my flat in alarm lest I should be imprisoned again.

And Zukrula ran right after me, screaming abuse.

I scurried along with my hands on my ears to avoid falling under suspicion that I had even listened to such horrible words.

My Readers can have no idea what happened next.

The Behins dragged me off to the betik again, who sentenced me to a month's imprisonment because I had *not* fed a woman!

As I came to know later, as a result of the bikbam, everything that had been forbidden and was shameful before, afterward became a duty to be performed, and everything that had been ketni before became kave afterward!

My Readers, if they believe any of this at all, must be holding their sides with laughter as they read the comic adventures of a sane man among lunatics. The piquancy of this episode stems from the paradox whereby I did everything to follow the Behins' ideas with my unfortunately sane mind in order to avoid their being shocked, then everything turned out in reverse because it is the essence of the Behins' madness that they are not consistent even in their madness.

After the month was up and I was discharged, I wanted at any rate to get to the bottom of how things were in connection with the rules of eating for women.

So from then on I paid more attention to the women.

Once I saw one who, on passing me, stealthily, so that nobody else should see it, momentarily lifted her handkerchief from her mouth, from which I concluded that she was hungry but did not dare to let me know openly.

I rejoiced at the opportunity; I hoped I would be able to learn a lot through her. I therefore joined her and in a roundabout way I asked her her opinion of spirituality. At this she hurriedly called me aside and whispered frankly that she was, indeed, hungry and would be happy if she could have some of my spirituality.

I admit, these words came as an awfully pleasant surprise. Foolishly, I believed that I had found the first woman of sound mind whose words had some connection with the natural world. I led her into my room and uncovered my food for her with an open heart.

The woman sat down opposite me and fell upon my spirituality with a visibly good appetite. More than once she expressed her rapture, saying it was only I who could give such good food to her. Meanwhile I showed my gratitude with a smile, knowing that my food was the remains of the regular daily Hin lunch.

At one point the woman swallowed painfully, then, opening her mouth wide, rose and approached me as if she wanted to bite my nose. The strange move somewhat surprised me, and I drew back frightened as she sat back in her place with an expression no less surprised.

"Don't you want to look into my throat?"

"Into your throat? Why should I look into your throat?"

She shook her head.

"You are a strange man. Others would stipulate in advance that I should open my mouth wide after every bite."

I remarked that I abandoned any such demands in advance, since in my assessment eating was for satisfaction. For her part, she went on taking nourishment and related that on one occasion she had eaten a whole goose at some man's. With a roguish smile, she assured me that she could eat even more than that, and then requested me to turn to her at any other time should I want to feed a woman, and I should not believe other women, as they would by no means be able to eat as much of my food as she, nor with such a good appetite.

I gave her my word, at which she gave me her address and then proceeded to tell me about her former host—how, in addition to having to open her mouth wide at his request, she had also to eat the goose with chocolate as well as having to show her teeth after every bite.

I was already beginning to suffer from rather dissonant feelings, but the real surprise was still to come. The woman went on, and remarked that although she had had to eat a lot back then, she also earned a lot. He had been a very generous man.

With this, she wiped her mouth and—asked for money.

This unexpected turn of events surprised me so much that I could only stammer a protest, saying she had eaten her fill of my spirituality so she had no right to ask for extra payment.

The woman suddenly became furious, flew into a rage, called me names, termed it the greatest villainy that when she had devoted her midface to me I was not even prepared to compensate her, although she had charged comparatively little for the eating.

I asserted in vain that she had no right to ask for extra payment for her own pleasure. The more I tried to reason with common sense, the angrier she became.

"You worthless bivak!" she shouted. "I come in to you, allow myself to be satisfied and in the end you would run away with the fee of it? I'll give you something to think about!"

One word led to another, but I trusted that she would not dare to spread the news of her having taken her fill with me. Of course, I was again disappointed in my calculations.

With a dreadful howl, the woman flung the door open and ran away.

And the next day I was summoned to the betik, who informed me that yet another complaint had been lodged against me: I had not paid a woman to whom I had given spirituality.

The accusation stunned me. I did not even deny that I had given her spirituality; on the contrary, I referred to it myself, saying that I did not owe her any extra payment.

At this the betik burst into a loud laugh.

Idiotically, I looked around. I had no idea why I should be laughed at, and added that it had been the woman herself who had stated that she was hungry. So what right could she possibly have—when, taking pity on her owing to ravenous state, I had appeased her appetite—to make, in addition to the kindheartedness I'd already shown her, extra financial claims?

The betik laughed still more loudly, called me an amusing fool, and in no time everyone was doubled up with laughter.

This made me lose my temper completely, and I remarked that the matter was much more deplorable than to be dismissed by laughing. Declaring that I was aware of my rights, I was now making a counterclaim, and demanded from the woman the price of the pleasure to which I was at least as much entitled as she.

The laughter that burst out at this almost brought down the walls. It took many minutes for the betik to recover, and, wiping away his tears, he affirmed that it had been a very long time since he had had such a good laugh; but, after all, the matter was much more serious than any that could have been dropped simply by laughing at it, and after all, the law was the law. He was compelled to apply the laws, he said, as without them order and sane civilization would have been overturned.

Whether the Reader believes it or not, the Behins imprisoned me again!

I had a week to ponder what harm I had actually done.

The whole case was completely beyond me. Once I heard from Zemoeki of an instance when a man withdrew the bikbam offered because it had come to light that the woman had already accepted spirituality from another man. But in my case, the woman herself had told me that she had already been fed by several men, and yet with her they not only failed to take that as a sin but held that I should even have paid her for eating my food!

After my discharge I complained to Zemoeki of my adventure, but he too only laughed at it, especially at my having believed that the woman was hungry, although I could have known that it was not out of hunger that that sort of woman asked for spirituality. I asserted in vain that the woman herself had asked for food, but he simply replied that I should have known from that in andf of itself that she did not want to eat but to earn money, for a woman who was really hungry would not say so.

This was the last straw. I could not endure this tightrope any longer. I never knew when the sword of Damocles permanently hanging above my head would drop onto me.

Oh, how many times I yearned that my mind become deranged so that I would be similar to them and I would always know when white should be called black and when yellow! But for anyone who with his sound mind clearly sees the white, this faculty of clear sight is so confusing that he can never find the suitable lie, and so he fails. Once he violates the ketni, then he infringes the bikbam, or else he violates the child's bruhu. How much better off the lunatics are, how happy are the Behins, and also how happy are the subjects of the glorious British state that they can all live among their fellow citizens of sound mind, people similar to themselves.

Before long, however, I was informed that because of my run of scandals I had lost my job.

That was all I needed! I ran to and fro, asked Zemoeki to help me, but he, too, turned away from me as from some evildoer. And after a few days I was thrown out of my cell and was left to go out into the world.

I went back to the betik and implored him that if they were to deprive me of spirituality then they should also kill me. Why, it was an incontestable reality that everybody had a midface to receive the spirituality, which I could not abandon together with my job, and I felt I would die.

The betik, however, comforted me, saying that there was one truth only in the world—the kona, which was aneba—but if I wished to regain my life I had come to the right place; why, it was his very purpose to afford nourishment to the needy and the errant.

With tears in my eyes I stammered a few words of gratitude, and he asked me to pass him the box from the shelf—the box inscribed with the bikru's name.

When I had given it to him, he took out a yellow pebble, which he knocked against the side of the box a few times, then handed over to me to be squeezed under my arm.

I was astounded by this heartless cynicism that enabled him to play a practical joke on a fellow man pleading for his life. Regrettably, my vulnerable situation prevented me from giving an appropriate reply.

Instead, snatching one of my feet with a hand, and putting the other hand on my head, I had to implore him to give me spirituality as well as the anebas for nourishment so I could preserve my life.

The betik, however, far from getting friendlier, jumped up and shouted at me with flashing eyes that I should not dare to claim of the spirituality that the pebble nourished, and I should especially not mention this ignominious word in the vicinity of the yellow pebble, because for such an outrage of the anebas he would be compelled to levy very harsh punishment.

As a feeble defense I only stammered out that each of us had spirituality, even the elak betiks—in fact, they even more.

This was my ruin. He assured me that the betiks—as was

known to all—did not use spirituality, and he added that for this he would surely put me in my place. With that, he took me by the scruff of the neck and threw me out.

Trembling with impotent rage, I sobbed for a long time. My stomach rumbling from hunger, I loitered aimlessly until I finally chose the last resort: I sat under a tree and begged.

I lived in this manner for a week. I also slept under this tree the whole night long, cold and wrapped in my tattered clothes. The nights became more and more chilly, and I could not even clean myself properly. I contracted lice and scabies, and nobody cared for me.

Finally one day an idea occurred to me. I remembered the woman on account of whom I had lost my job. I decided to follow her example, figuring that in this manner it would be easy to obtain food and money.

So I called aside the very first woman who passed by and confidently whispered to her that I was awfully hungry and was willing to take some spirituality cheaply. At this, without any introduction, she began shrieking frantically. Many people gathered around to whom, between fits of swooning, she related what had happened.

Terrible things followed, the description of which I do not wish to burden the Reader's nerves with. To make a long story short, within five minutes I was sprawled on the ground in blood.

It turned out that eating for money was valid only for women; men were excluded. And the Reader is thoroughly wrong if he believes that I was knocked about by the female sex united in the defense of their interests. On the contrary: it was the men who beat me most thoroughly and viciously—especially the man whose food was usually eaten by this woman. So, though a whole world separated me from this unfortunate race, I sincerely took pity on this miserable, deplorably stupid, and deceived male sex, as they defended their own humiliation and exploitation. And it was the aforementioned man who shouted after every blow that I had wanted him to be deceived.

Yes, however difficult it is to understand, I must add that these men not only fail to perceive their being deceived: each is ready to believe that he would have been deceived if the woman had eaten the food of another man and not his. But this I do not even try to explain. Let us rather return to our subject, for my sufferings had not yet come to an end.

The next day an official came up to me and told me that Zukrula had laid a charge against me for having requested food of another woman, and I would probably be punished heavily. Amazed, I asked him why. He replied that only Zukrula was entitled to do so, for she had been hit on the head with the copper cube.

Thrilled with joy, I told him that I would also accept food from Zukrula, and indeed I even suggested that four or five women should team up to feed me alternately, by which the burden borne by each one would be less. He stated in consternation that that was impossible, because it was Zukrula who had been hit on the head.

I suggested that the others should also be hit on the head, at which he looked me up and down with utter contempt and said it seemed to him that I had sunk to the very depths of squalor and deserved to be burned at the stake.

I spent the following days in a quiet lethargy of semimadness, convinced that matters could at least not become any worse.

Alas, in this, too, I was to be disappointed.

CHAPTER

16

We reach the saddest chapter of the author's adventures.
The Behins break into the fit of rage called buku, and the
author almost falls victim to it. The author chronicles,
with reservations, the episode concerning the bikru.

A FEW DAYS LATER MANY PEOPLE GATHERED ROUND ME, OF
which I was very glad because it meant alms.

One of them got up on a stool and addressed the others. He
said that the kona's aim was to live in peace and brotherhood
with the kemons. Peace, love, and the mutual security of the family hearth must therefore be ensured and each, kona and kemon,
should support the other in the work of building.

Hearing this, I began to tremble. Although I did not know
what it meant, it sounded ominously sane and peaceful.

In a few minutes a formidable procession approached. A crowd
of Behins came in rows of five and they walked in step which,
considering the usual Behin disorder, was in itself surprising
enough.

However, it was still more conspicuous that each was clutching
a knife in his hand, with which at every second step he jabbed
toward the earth and shouted: "Zuk! . . . Zuk! . . . Zuk! . . . Zuk!"

Beside them walked a figure still more tattered than the betiks,
snapping an enormous pair of scissors and shouting a few words
at them from time to time that made them burst into frenzied ap-

plause, and shake their knives and howl: "Huuh! . . . Huuh! . . . Huuh!"

Another figure was rushing around the procession with a tin-box from which he breathlessly distributed yellow pebbles.

As they came nearer I was able to get a better look at the speaker. He had an expressionless, empty face, almost without a forehead. His tumbling mass of tousled hair made him appear still more beastly. His advanced Graves' disease and his bulging eyes caused fear enough even from a distance. His jaws were de-formed. That is, his lower set of teeth protruded so much that his mouth could not contain them, and on account of this his words could hardly be understood, although I was aware that my life might depend on how much of the events I could understand.

When they eventually passed close by me I succeeded in mak-ing out what he was saying.

"Monday, Tuesday, Thursday, Wednesday! . . . Monday, Tues-day, Thursday, Wednesday! . . ."

I looked on agape as he walked away. Was this what they were applauding? Was this what made them wild?

Suddenly I felt a hand on my shoulder. I turned. Two Behins stood in front of me with knives. One of them began to speak.

"What are you doing here?"

"I'm begging," I replied. "But tell me, who is that there with the scissors?"

"He is the knife betik. Don't you see that he has a double knife?"

"What is a knife betik?"

"He is the cleverest betik."

"The cleverest? How?"

"Because he bestows on us the salvation of the knife."

"If he is the cleverest, why doesn't he say Wednesday–Thurs-day?"

"Anybody could say that. He knows how we must win the salvation of the knife, and he is always right. Moreover, there is a buku now and this requires emergency measures. But let's get to the point: do you have a body-use license?"

"Wha-at?"

"In a word, you haven't. Then you are permitted to participate in the peace work."

"How?"

"Take this," and he poked a knife into my hand, "and come with us to the hillside where you will ensure peace and civilization."

"How?"

"By stabbing the kemons and they you."

It was only then that the utter horror of the situation unfolded before me. These unfortunate ones were now indeed on their way to kill. The fit of rage called buku, of which I had heard so many times but had always hoped to be untrue, lo and behold, had come upon them.

I hurriedly stated that for the time being I did not wish to make use of the permission, but he yelled at me, "I've told you that you are permitted to participate in the buku!"

With this he kicked me and pushed me into the ranks.

I tried to protest, but in no time knives threatened me from every side, and the words stuck in my throat.

So what I would never have believed of myself had come to pass. I had to join in and march, unprotestingly, together with these raging wretches, toward an unknown bloodbath. Moreover, for the nightmare to be complete, I had to jab with my knife toward the earth at every second step and shout, "Zuk! . . . Zuk! . . . Zuk! . . . "

And whenever the bird-headed terror beside the troop screeched "Thursday-Wednesday" in our direction I had to howl in chorus with the rest, "Huuh! . . . Huuh! . . . Huuh! . . ."

I write this down in the deepest shame. I would never have believed that I, an officer of the British Navy, could be compelled to sink so low by lunatics. But humiliation did not end with this.

It happened that at one point the monster stepped up to me and, flashing his protruding eyes, ordered that I should com-

mand the howling. When he had shouted "Wednesday," I had
to beckon with my knife, whereupon the mass broke into the
"Huuh."

So it was not enough that I had to go mad; with them, I was
also compelled to coerce others, too, for otherwise they would
have stabbed me to death.

I blushed with shame and decided that if I was ever able to return to my country I would immediately resign my commission.
A coward who, having been scared by the threats of a bird-headed
deformity, could become a party to the most evil-minded madness and meanest crime in the world could no longer pollute the
Navy with his presence. The only thing that prevented me from
doing so was, as the Reader will presently see, that I recovered
before long.

After a few minutes of marching, the hill came into view, and the
blood froze in my veins at the horror unfolding before my eyes.

On the hilltop konas and kemons brandished their knives
and rushed at each other foaming at the mouth, and within an
instant my ears were split by the bestial howl of the demented
inhabitants of the whole bedlam.

The inmates had broken loose; they kicked, tore, stabbed, and
cut each other up, and there was nobody to restrain them!

This was the last straw. As if I hadn't had enough trouble. The
Reader can imagine how I felt. I was about to be compelled to
die miserably for some absolutely senseless monomanias. The
monstrosities suddenly brought me back to myself.

I tried explaining what a horrible thing they were doing, but
they turned to me in surprise.

"Would you really want to remain alive when you could die in
buku by knife? Would you miss the chance of the salvation of the
knife, the greatest possible prize, for which it was worth being
born? It seems you have no feeling for the boeto!"

They had rushed me into many things, but into this horror no
kind of power could have forced me. I stated that I had no intention of perishing aimlessly and senselessly.

"Bivak!" they bellowed. "Do you think that the boeto is aimless? Curb your tongue, for you will regret it bitterly if you abuse
the kona!"

The knives again flashed toward me, and in terror I asked them
rather to let me beg, I had no wish to debase the kona's salvation,
and I wished them the best of everything. I asked only that they
should absolve me from the boeto. I was not bad, I said. I wished
nobody any trouble, but wanted only to live in peace, happiness
and tranquility, and I wished the same for every kona.

The reply I received was a frightful storm of abuse and
ample blows. They called me an incendiary, a madman, a Hin,
a red-handed executioner of mankind, boeto, the bikru, and
civilization, who had no feeling for the glorious anebas.

Most of all, however, they were abominably affronted that I had
wished peace, happiness, and tranquillity to every kona.

"To the stake with the lamik!" they shouted. "That's all we
need—that he should poison the healthy society with his base
machinations and overthrow order!"

Another said that I should go to the kemons with my subversive aims to overthrow order and peace there, not here where
everybody wanted peace and justice.

I volunteered with pleasure to go and tell the same to the kemons, but they guffawed and said that then I would be beaten
to death by them, and that it was impossible to do so, anyway,
as there was buku, and now both my spirit and body were at the
disposal of their possessor, the kona.

When I replied that the possessor of the body was the individual himself, they upbraided me fiercely for professing such false
doctrines, for it was known that I possessed only the clothes on
my body. If someone else dared to take off my clothes he would
be punished, but my body was not mine any more, because body
and spirit were not for the individual himself but were lent by
the bikru and the kona so that I should have something to clothe
with the garment constituting myself.

By now everyone was shouting "lamik!" all around me and

they demanded that, as the enemy of public peace and civilization, I should be taken to the betik.

I understood that every word here was a waste of breath. It would be best if they exterminated each other and only I should get away alive. I stated that I did not want to disturb them in their civilization and in the buku, and I even sincerely wished success to both parties (and that was not a lie, indeed); I asked only that they leave me, wretched bivak, in my shame.

But they had already taken hold of me, and they dragged me to the betik.

Ample blows showered down on my back, and insults were heaped upon me, but even as this was happening, my soul became only stronger—and I completely changed.

Self-confidence coursed through me as—having managed at last to recover from cowardly submissiveness and, in the manner of a hero, facing even a martyr's death—I was able to stand up against crack-brained sin and baseness. I was imbued with the proud knowledge that I conducted myself at the end as befitting an officer of the glorious British Navy.

They took me to the very same betik with whom I had served and who had recently thrown me out. He of course soon established that I was a lamik and sentenced me to be burned alive.

In the reasons offered, the epithets "extremist" and "disturber of the peace," as well as "moderate" and "charitable," occurred frequently. The Reader, of course, believes that those who were called "moderate" and "charitable" desired tranquility and peace, while the "extremists" and "disturbers of the peace" were those on the hill who were gorging out each other's eyes and dancing on the steaming bowels of their fellow men.

No!

They meant it the other way around!

Now they assigned a beratnu to me who, although he did not hurt me, commenced an endless jabber about all kinds of obscure things that I naturally did not understand. There was no rhyme or reason to it. I noted only that he frequently mentioned the bikru, which, naturally, now accounted for everything. It wasn't the guard, but the bikru's hand that had dragged me along to the betik; the bikru had punished me; the bikru was preparing the fire for the stake in the yard; and so on. As it was all the same to me, anyway, I dared to defy being laughed at and asked him point-blank what the bikru was.

"The bikru is the most betik betik," he replied.

"So he is a man?"

"He is no longer alive, but he lived once."

"And why do you call him the most betik betik?"

"Because of his infinitely wise tenets."

I trembled at the very word. What sort of madness was it that they called wisdom? All the same, I asked out of curiosity, "What did he teach?"

"That to be stabbed with a knife is not pleasure but pain; that we are born for life and not for death, and therefore we must not stab. He declared that there is no betik, but that we all are men alike; that it is not the yellow pebble that nourishes but spirituality, which the bikru called food, and that anyone who takes it away from others wears the bilevs in vain, for he is in reality a hypocrite and pickpocket. He said that we should live in peace, happiness, and mutual understanding."

The Reader is by now, of course, rubbing his eyes and does not want to believe this. Just imagine how I received these words! I could not believe my ears.

"What did you say?" I asked, dumbfounded.

But the beratnu said exactly the same thing the second time.

"Then he was a lamik!" I exclaimed in surprise.

"How can you make such an ignominious statement concerning the most betik betik?!" he cried out in consternation.

"So, indeed, such a man lived, and you did not burn him at the stake?"

Well . . . as a matter of fact, we did burn him at the stake, because people back then did not understand him. But since his glorious martyrdom we still accept his tenets, and from that time on we all live in his spirit."

"That's why you squeeze the yellow pebble under your arm?! That's why you take away the food from the starving, and that's why you stab the kemons?" I asked indignantly.

"All this we do to his glory and in his defense."

"Why? Is the kemon perhaps the enemy of the bikru? Don't you think that all this would even then be an ignominious mockery of the thesis that you must not stab?"

"The kemons are not enemies of the bikru. They worship him just like us."

Breath failed me. I thought I was dreaming. I had to pinch myself to make sure.

"But tell me, then, unfortunate one," I exclaimed, trembling, "why do you do all these horrors?"

"In defense of the bikru. To enforce his doctrines."

"And the kemons?"

"They want the same."

(I remark in parentheses that I impart this to the Reader only with reserve, because I admit that this part is doubted even by myself. True, my travel notes bear out the above and I, too, clearly remember the words. But this supersedes any mental defect to such an extent that I cannot imagine even lunatics to be capable of all this with unruffled conscience, and would rather take it to be the creation of my overstressed brain deranged by my sufferings of that time and the surrounding insanity. That I still publish it is purely for the sake of completeness, and, even if the part about the bikru was a hallucination, it may serve as material for any neuropathologists when they are studying states of agitation similar to mine at that time.)

The author is taken to the stake, but in a near miraculous manner he escapes. He fulfills an important but sad mission that entails the tragic perdition of the Behins.

THE GUARDS CAME, HANDCUFFED ME, AND WE STARTED into the open. In front of me walked the beratnu, holding the square high. From the hillside came the sound of ferocious shouting and gruesome death rattles. I was led to the pyre, my feet were bound, and I was thrown on top while the crowd frantically inveighed against me.

One Behin shouted that I had incited against the throwing out of food, which would have meant them starving to death; and another that I had protested against the removal of my spirituality, by which I had robbed others. Yet others proclaimed that I had stubbornly insisted on wearing my old shabby clothes, by which I had caused a public scandal; that I had made mockery of the kipu and denied the joy of the thorns—and that with the fanciful ideas of the most exaggerated false doctrines, I had poisoned decent public life and had wanted to plunge the blessing of civilization into blood, flame, and filth. Like one enormous buzzing beehive the Behins whirled around me, howling:

"You incited against common sense!"

"You claimed the circle was round!"

"You referred to your eyes in opposition to anebas!"

"You slandered the spirituality-giving betik!"

"You wanted to feed on spirituality!"

"You upset public peace! You stirred up strife with false doctrines!"

"You denied the bikru's tenets!"

"You fed a woman!"

"You didn't feed a woman!"

As for me, shutting my eyes, I acquiesced in everything and peacefully expected charitable death that would at last relieve me from the tortures of the raving. I gave a sigh of relief when they finally lighted the firebrand, and I took my leave while smiling at the crazy herd of Behins stamping their feet with rage—a herd whose howl melted into one horrible cacophony with the cries of death from the hillside.

And then a strange thing ensued.

Several cars drove in through the gate containing Hins wearing gas masks. Jet nozzles were mounted on the cars, and the Hins kept their hands on the controls. White smoke puffed from the nozzles. The Hins drove straight toward the hill.

I began shouting at the top of my lungs. The bystanders immediately covered my mouth and grabbed me by the throat but, fortunately, they were too late.

One of the cars turned out of the line and moved at full speed straight toward me.

At the appearance of the Hins the situation immediately changed. Everyone present, including the betik, snatched his right foot into his hand, and they outdid each other in shouting, "Vake! Vake!"

The Behins respected the Hins very much even though they loathed them. However, this does not appear to be paradoxical to someone who knows the Behins' mad ways; for it was not knowledge and good heart that impressed them, as is usual among educated Europeans, but roughness and crass brute force. And, after all, the Hins kept them in their power.

The Hins got out of the car, unbound my ropes, helped me into the car, and, handing me a gas mask, raced on.

All this took place in almost no time. I could hardly recover for sheer delight. My happiness was even more enhanced by the fact that I discovered Zatamon among those sitting in the car. I could not control myself any more. Weeping for joy, I grasped the liberating hand; I did not even care that my gratitude made no visible impression on him.

With tears in my eyes, I told Zatamon of my sufferings and entreated them to take me out with them, for I had not only failed to feel myself a Behin, but all my limbs were still trembling on account of the monstrosities I had been exposed to in that upset and deranged world.

Zatamon reacted only by observing that this, the kazi that I had now had the opportunity to experience, was the nonexisting life.

Although I did not fully understand what he meant by this, I could state with a clear conscience that I had never before realized so profoundly the wise and patient majesty of the kazo after the time spent among these raving madmen.

By this time our car had reached the hill and cut straight through the ranting masses. The massacre had just reached its peak. Blood flowed like water.

Here and there was a square or a circle fastened to a rod. The knives flashed, while brute fury hurled from some throats while blood gurgled from cut-open windpipes. The whole runaway bedlam bellowed, whirled, and killed. Horror came over me at the thought that I, too, had two hands and two feet like them.

Now we all put on our gas masks.

The Hins rushed among them with strong gas jets. The gas was ejected from the nozzles whistling under enormous pressure. In the meantime some of the cars had surrounded them so that nobody could escape.

The raving lunatics lost consciousness at the first breath, and one after another they dropped to the ground, but even as they fell they gripped their knives tightly, their eyes flashed, and in the last wild rattling, words were formed by the grinding teeth: "Bikru! Sanity! Aneba! Buku!"

When the last Behin had fallen asleep, the Hins got out, collected then, and put a straitjacket on each one. It was then that I saw the Hins shudder with horror for the first time: when they got out onto the ground they had to step into pools of human blood.

Now consultation began. They all agreed that there was no point in experimenting with these people any more, and it was advisable to bring all the fighting Behins to an end.

It was I who interfered, explaining to Zatamon that probably not all of them had killed of their own accord. Referring to my own case, I suggested that the incurable ones should be separated from those who were not beyond hope.

The Hins, seeing that I spoke sensibly in spite of my being suspected of Behinity myself, accepted my opinion. Indeed, they even asked me what method I held most suitable for selecting the least sick among them.

I recommended an election. The whole Behin settlement should vote to show who was in favor of the buku.

I had to explain the essence of the election in detail, as the Hins did not know and could not even imagine that there could be any question concerning life about which people had different opinions, as the fullness of life could be lived in one manner only. They were aware only of scientific differences of opinion where, if the litmus turned blue, the contrary opinion of a hundred scientists was disproved.

The Hins nonetheless accepted my suggestion, agreeing that in light of my experience among the Behins and my rather sound approach, they would commission me to arrange the ballot— and, so nothing should take place in an unnatural manner, the extermination of the hopeless ones, too, would be entrusted to the Behins themselves. Namely, those in favor of fighting would be led to a closed field, where they would be provided with knives so that they themselves could exterminate each other.

The Reader can imagine my pleasure at such a pleasant change at last occurring in my sad life.

Now a lot of trucks came in. When they reached us they stopped and the Hins jumped out. Taking hold of the sleeping Behins, they put them on the trucks, one by one, where air mattresses had already been laid out. This precise organization again filled me with admiration. Why, they had no kind of public organization, it was only the kazo that held them together in a firm unit—firmer than any artificial legislature.

The Behins were then transported to the hospital that was already equipped and waiting for them, though even so they were laid crammed together partly on beds and partly on air mattresses on the floor.

It was the injured who received attention first of all, and then each was given a tranquilizing and strengthening injection. When they had recovered consciousness, after some hours of observation they were again ordered to board the trucks and were transported back to the Behin settlement, where they were set loose.

As for myself, I was removed from among them and could once more take my place in the Belohin institute. There I was at last given clean clothes, had a proper bath, and shaved, the electric hat cut my hair and I was deloused. My contorted and crippled limbs, which still bore rope marks, were massaged by electric machines. And at night I retired to a soft bed—satisfied and clean, in a silent, electrically heated room. Nobody disturbed me and nothing threatened me; tomorrow seemed clear and certain. It was the ultimate pleasure I felt by stretching myself out with nothing to worry about.

I may safely say it was the happiest day of my life.

*

Wanting to merit the Hins' appreciation as much as possible, I organized the election with great zeal. The next day I entered the Behin settlement with ten Hins and two gas-equipped cars. Our appearance elicited great respect. All the betiks turned out to meet us. United, they took their copper cubes off their knees, and holding them in their palms, repeatedly offered them to us. The Hins of course did not understand this, but I saw that it was meant to be a sign of respect or submission. For me it was enormously satisfying to see the betik who had sentenced me to burn at the stake now offer me his clumsy rubbish with frightened humility, mentioning amid a lot of murmuring such idiotic nonsense as bruhu, aneba, ketni, and kona.

When he wanted to slip a yellow pebble into my hand I strongly felt like taking him by the scruff of the neck and stuffing the "nourishment" down his throat, but I feared that the Hins would then form an unfavorable opinion of me and again doubt my kazo turn of mind.

So I issued the order that all the Behins should gather together, at which those present ran away in all directions. But ten minutes later, everybody stood around us—konas and kemons separately, of course, and eyeing each other with ferocious hatred.

And I announced to both parties that the next day there would be a vote about the buku, and they would be given a free hand in their internal affairs.

After this we left.

The next day the ballot was indeed carried out, albeit separately on kona and kemon territories lest they should start a fight.

However, the result was a surprise to all of us: almost without exception, they clamored for the buku. This particularly touched a raw spot in me, as the Hins might draw the conclusion that the vote had been superfluous.

I tried to talk to the Behins one by one, in private. When I asked why they wanted to rip open the bodies of their fellow men, they all replied that such an intention was far from their minds—they only wanted to see the boeto ensured through the buku.

And I told them in vain that the boeto was but a word, and the essence of the thing was after all only pain, suffering, and death. They replied that it was just the opposite.

Suffering, they said, is but an episode, only on the surface, while the boeto is the sense, the essence, the inner content of things. He who doesn't feel it is color blind: someone who sees only the surface and has no sense of the essence that signifies the content of life.

They asserted without hesitation that the essence maintained life, for which it was even worth dying!

When I called their attention to the inherent contradiction, they replied that the life of the community required that individuals should die for it.

The Behins were convinced that the community could live only if individually all were to die.

Between the pronounced word and the mind there was no connection at all.

Therefore I argued no further, but announced that whoever had voted for the fight would be allowed to fight to their heart's content the next day in the free buku. They would be led to the hillside, provided with arms, and allowed to fight against each other, while those who had no wish to fight could remain at home.

Fortunately I had thus far had sufficient opportunity to experience their inconsistencies; for otherwise I would have been very surprised at the murmur of discontent that received my words.

Regrettably, however, much as I was accustomed to their inconsistencies, I could not get away from my sound logic sufficiently not to think about it at all. So even now I looked for an explanation, and thought that cowardice induced them to balk when it came to putting their enthusiasm into practice.

Now I was already very ashamed of myself before the Hins' and was anxious about my position because of this run of failures.

After a slight hesitation I even mentioned my uncertainty to the leader of the Hins accompanying me, lest another failure should make them believe I had not reckoned with anything.

I was all the more pleasantly surprised when he replied that it seemed I had made their acquaintance in vain, for my brain was too kazo to understand them, or more exactly, to get accustomed to them, because, naturally nothing could be understood the essence of which was senselessness.

What the Behins talked about that night, I do not know. Perhaps nothing; and the surprises that came the next day are also to be attributed to their peculiar madness, a special characteristic of which was that although there was no consistency in them, in a wondrous way each was inconsistent in the same manner.

So the next day we drove those who wanted to fight to the hillside.

They, of course, closed up their ranks in two stiffly separated groups and turned their backs on each other.

It was characteristic of the Hins' naivety that when they saw this they suggested that we should perhaps take the groups one by one and distribute the knives first to one group and let those of the other group fall upon each other only when the first group had exterminated each other.

Stifling my smile I had to explain to them that neither group would fight within itself, as for each the presence of the other was necessary. This they did not understand, of course, and asked why it was not simpler for them to stab at those nearest to them, as they were going to stab each other, anyway. I answered with the airiness of a very experienced man.

"The one group is kona, the other is kemon. They fight only if they come together."

It was only when the Hins looked at each other that I realized what a "senseless explanation" I had given. And, after some thought, I myself admitted that it was indeed incomprehensible why it was not possible to commence the massacre on themselves. Thus I remarked that Behin matters I could explain only in Behin, so they should not expect more of me.

Our cars confined the Behins within a large circle. We handed out the knives to them and finally I announced that the buku was open.

And then I saw in astonishment that the Behins did not budge. Our cars were standing all around, and we were all provided with gas masks, holding the jet nozzles ready; and inside the two groups of adversaries, some twelve hundred men stood motion-less.

One minute, two minutes, ten minutes passed. The Hins looked at me questioningly and I was in the greatest perplexity.

However, before long a man on the kona side climbed onto a tree stump and delivered a speech to the others.

"You may perhaps believe," he said, "that the Hins are now supporting us in achieving the boeto and now we have the op-portunity to wage buku for boeto life and peace."

"You are wrong," he continued. "In our ketni deeds, the Hins do not see the profound essence of life, but take them for sense-less fights. But how could this bivak crowd ever perceive what can only be breathed in by living and warm lungs in which sacred respect for the anebas and the boeto is alive, while empty and cold lungs remain far from it and lose their direction in the emptiness of the desert. Respect for the anebas and the bikru is the unshakable point that gives content and aim to our lives, which distinguishes the Behin from the brute Hin; this is what steels our arms in the noble buku, this is what makes the sons of the behas *bumbuk*, happy to sacrifice their lives for the boeto and the salvation of the knife."

Bumbuk means murderer, but I must point out to the Reader that they had more than one expression for this, depending on whom the murderer killed, because in their soft-headed opinion they did not despise all murderers equally, and the bumbuks were even esteemed. As to the meaning of this word, however, opinions differed. From what little I could gather, according to the konas, a bumbuk was one who had killed a kemon, and ac-cording to the kemons, it was one who had killed a kona.

Then he continued. "Respect for the salvation of the knife and the anebas is the source of life of the behas, without which our fate would be death and ruin." (Thus they seriously believed that they would have died had they not massacred each other!) "Let us therefore foster in our lungs higher ideals, and steadfast devotion to the bikru and the anebas. A true Behin lives or dies with his knife and boeto."

After this came much senseless jabber, but I have no wish to impart it to the Reader, particularly because I cannot even remember so much nonsense.

I could at least make out that treachery had taken place. He claimed that we had held the salvation of the knife up to ridicule, and that by our procedure we made the noble buku appear as if it were a common and aimless coming to blows, and now, as in an arena, to public ridicule, we pitted the bumbuks against each other like cocks. The defense of the boeto was not a puppet show but the salvation of the knife.

"Behins!" he shouted. "Don't you see that their aim is not that we should have a share in the salvation of the knife, but that we should destroy each other?!"

(I give up! Is the salvation of the knife not the destruction of each other?)

"Because," he said, "while we bumbuks would stupidly have killed each other off, this could only be utilized by the lamiks, who in a treacherous and perfidious way shirk their duties toward the anebas who await only that the cream and pride of both behas, the noble bumbuks, should perish to the last one, so that then the well-poisoners of the kona and the kemons should be able to unite the two behas. And do you know what will happen if the two behas unite? The beha itself will cease! All the anebas circle, square will cease, and every feat that distinguishes man from the beast of prey will be trampled into the mud!"

Angry outcries were to be heard.

"We won't allow the anebas to be destroyed!"

"Not this or that aneba is concerned here," the speaker went on, "but the very existence of the anebas and the order without which the noble bumbuks would have nothing to live and die for, and the salvation of the knife, which a ketni man has to defend from bloody destruction by some furious lunatics. For what would it be worth if we lived and there were no anebas? We must now unite against the common enemy, and not slaughter each other as it would not be buku but hideous butchery. So let's make peace, go home, and put those lamik traitors to the knife who, wanting to evade the bliss of boeto while looking on from safety, might watch the noble bumbuks bleeding like miserable puppets for public ridicule, so that afterward the lamiks' ignominious machinations might destroy the behas defended and preserved for us in hundreds of bloody bukus by our ancestors."

The speech was received with frenzied applause, the two camps mixed in no time, and among ardent scratchings of each other's posteriors they vowed friendship to each other against the lamiks, for what point would there have been in dying if it was not prohibited.

The two mortal enemies ceased to be enemies at the very moment when they were threatened by the danger that in the future they would indeed not be enemies, and they immediately made peace lest someone should create a real peace. The Behins' peace could serve the fight only.

Put down in this way, it sounds so tortuous that I do not even try to explain it. Even while describing it I feel that should I have to go on analyzing it, I myself would become completely confused.

The Hins, of course, did not understand a word of all this, except that the Behins did not want this either. But what did they actually want? I myself did not understand them either, but had forebodings of danger and I recommended the Hins to put on their gas masks.

No sooner had this been done than a delegation came to us requesting that we should let them go home, as they did not want the buku.

The Hins listened to them in bewilderment, but I hastened to enlighten them on the Behins' intention and advised them to put an end to their company as things were hopeless.

They received my words with some aversion. Naturally, from the naive Hin point of view it was difficult to understand why it meant still greater danger if somebody did not want to fight. A lengthy conference ensued. It was so strange to see the Hins hesitating, they who were so miraculously balanced and decisive in the matters of their own lives. In the end they decided that everybody could go home, but the knives had to be laid down.

This decision was received with an infernal howl.

From the surging one of the loudest suddenly emerged and, jumping toward my car, shouted foaming with rage, "Here is the traitor! He has brought ruin upon us!"

And he spat at me not caring that my hand rested on the button of the jet nozzle with which I could disable him in an instant. However, as I was afraid that the Hins might not understand, I dared not use the hose.

Yet another infernal howl accompanied the words. Fists rose against me.

Finally one of them yelled, "Why are you hesitating? Are you afraid of a lamik? To leave a lamik alive is tantamount to breaking our knives with our own hands!"

A murmur of horror was the reply. A torrent of abuse was hurled at me.

"It is you who outraged the boeto!"

"It is you who undermined the ketni!"

"You have spoiled the child's bruhu!"

"It is you who defiled the bikbam!"

"You have destroyed the peace!"

And the leader, taking advantage of the general feeling and outshouting everybody else, bellowed, "He is the one who used the knife for the most ignominious purpose!"

The crowd flared up—a mass of foaming consternation was the response. One even pronounced it: "For eating!"

The lunatics burst into an ear-splitting roar. The speaker hoarsely tried to outbellow the crowd.

"That's it! Do you know what this lamik does with the knife? He eats! Eats! He outrages civilization! Why are you hesitating? This will be the real buku! Follow me! Vake!"

With that, he rushed toward me and leapt onto the car's running board; the knife flashed, but I had managed to push the button of the jet nozzle a fraction of a second earlier.

A burst of gas roared out. It swept the Behin off the running board like a ball. He fell prostrate on the ground.

The others, utterly infuriated by the sight, yelled even more noisily.

"Vake! Vake!"

Many of them leapt toward me at the same time, I could hardly defend myself with the jet nozzle. Before long eight of them lay near my car. The crowd fell silent for a moment.

And now a strange thing ensued.

In the middle, a betik held up a square fastened on a pole in one hand and a circle in the other. And the crowd, one and all snatching their right foot in their hand, burst into an unearthly howl.

"Vake! Vake!"

Tears shone in their eyes, and then, as if at a given signal, they all began to sing.

I could not help it. The atmosphere, in spite of all its oddity, was so touching that it carried even me away, though I knew that every bit of it was directed against me. I feared that their behavior—stupid though it was and yet elevating—would win the Hins over. I admit that I was anxious for both my position and my life.

The song came to an end. Now one of them shouted out, "After me! Even if all of us should die, the behas and the boeto will live!"

And, waving his knife at me, he started forward. The crowd as one man flashed their knives high and followed him.

I was thoroughly bewildered. What should I do if I lost the sympathy of the Hins? The weapons were unequal to such an extent that not only was I myself ashamed of the mass destruction, but being aware of the Hins' humane turn of mind I knew that they would prevent me from carrying it out, and then I also would be lost.

And on the lips of the crowd the song resounded again and, with circles and squares held high, they walked toward me like the first Christians might have walked to meet the swords of the gladiators. I would never have believed that lunatics could be so enthusiastic about aimless and senseless obsessions.

They were no more than a few steps from me when, in a fit of despair, I squirted out the gas at them hoping to put them to flight.

But as soon as the first few had fallen, the others, following the rhythm of the song, steadfastly continued. More and more Behins fell and the crowd came in compacted lines toward me, jumping over the unconscious ones.

Suddenly, to my great surprise the Hins' cars moved into action; gas spouted from every jet nozzle.

All this happened simultaneously, without a single word of command.

The mass took fright and retreated, but the Hins gave no quarter. They advanced. The surrounding circle tightened; the white cloud whirled and rolled along. The Behins tried to escape, but the Hins cut off their line of retreat with jets of gas. They gathered again in the middle, and the song resounded anew.

However, the Hins were now in no mood for mercy. It wrung my heart to see how they sprayed the gas in cold blood into the crowd, which was now giving up the struggle.

The Behins collapsed one after the other as the song became fainter and fainter. Suddenly the circle and the square held near each other also wavered. The one who had held them collapsed, but immediately they were snatched from his hands by others who held them high until they, too, fell. They passed from one pair of hands to the next, until the last one stuck them into the ground and finally, he, too, broke off in midvoice.

Silence conquered the square, and my eyes bulged with tears.

But it was only now that the real horror came. The Hins changed the gas, put a different mask on me, and then flooded the crowd with the new gas. I noticed in alarm that the chests of the people lying on the ground ceased to rise and fall. I wanted to cry, but the mask prevented me.

Five minutes later they again changed the gas; this they squirted about at random, then everyone took off their masks. This last was probably a neutralizing gas.

The cloud was so thick that to begin with I could not see anything. It took some minutes before it became somewhat clearer. A heartbreaking sight unfolded before my eyes: on the two poles stuck into the ground shone the circle and the square, and around them one thousand two hundred corpses and were strewn over the ground.

After the howling rage of madness, an oppressive silence weighed heavy on the field. The Hins untied and removed their masks, then dismantled the jet nozzles without a word. The gloomy silence of death lay heavily on my chest. Or was it perhaps that of the Hin life?

As soon as I could speak, I asked Zatamon what had been done. With his usual dry composure he replied that they had annihilated the Behins. To my question as to who had ordered them to do so, he answered in surprise that no orders had been necessary here. Any man in his right mind could have seen that they had to be exterminated. Then he explained that whoever ran into death while he was in full health was a hopeless raving lunatic and entirely worthless to society.

I can assure the Reader that I felt very grieved about this rigid way of thinking, but I could not do a thing.

After this I withdrew to my room and buried myself in my thoughts.

I thought for a long time about the unfortunate Behins, and finally came to the conclusion that whatever terrible things they had perpetrated, they had been unaware not only of the horror of their deeds, which would be unbecoming even to madmen, but also of whether they had indeed done this or that.

Poor Behins, they had run and run, chasing castles in the air that they were not only unable to reach (as that is impossible),

but that they did not want, either, because as soon as they found
the path to one thing, they immediately wanted something else.

The Behins' life is absurdity itself, impossible to put into practice. Something may have been gnawing at their nerves, making
the living of life impossible for them. Their lives were without
meaning, just like their words and struggles.

Indeed, it was better this way, and only this way did it make
sense.

But alas! And now my heart sank because poor Zemoeki and
Zeremble occurred to me. Perhaps they, too, were lying now
among the many Behin corpses. Two poor fanciful fellows, at
whose follies I had sometimes laughed and sometimes become
annoyed, and whom I had perhaps lost for ever.

While it would have been difficult to account for just what
I had lost in them, they had nonetheless been my friends and a
feeling heart could not so easily forget such ties.

I went to bed that evening with a heavy heart and decided that
I would not brood over things, but relax thoroughly during the
days to come.

CHAPTER

18

Light is finally cast on the secrets of the Hins' strange existence, on the Behinity, and the kazo. The author and his country are deeply offended by Zatamon, leading him to a decision.

IN THE MORNING I LAY DOWN IN THE PLACE FOR SUNBATHING on the hospital roof, and the infinite happiness of relaxation descended on my nerves. In a drowsy-happy mood I contemplated the mountain opposite me, the side of which was divided in two by a long silvery spiral. It rotated now upward, now downward. I had no idea of its function. It was one of their strange machines, of which I had seen hundreds during my stay, but had I lived for twenty years among the Hins this would still have been too short a time to come to know all of them. While the machine itself was of no interest to me at the moment, seeing this mystical perpetual motion device did give me a pleasant, soothing feeling. My state of excitement gradually abated.

I had been enjoying the sweet freedom from care for many hours, when I felt a hand on my shoulder.

Looking up, I saw Zatamon. He brought up a chair and sat down by my side.

"Tell me," he said, "the impressions left in you from your life among the Behins."

To my question as to why that was necessary, he replied that it was requisite to the proper diagnosis of my present state. I tried again to sketch my sufferings in a few words, but the wounds of my soul were still so deep that even the mere memory sickened me. Trembling overcame me, my voice faltered, and I had to ask Zatamon to dispense, for the time being, with the idea of my conjuring up the events.

"I am a British citizen," I said. "I was brought up to respect sanity and civilization, in a place where 'yes' means agreement and 'no' means denial. Mental disorder I only cured, and you can imagine what it meant for me to be exposed to such a degree of insanity that we have never even heard of."

I expressed my sincere regret that this most terrible disease of the world had struck precisely their flourishing and peaceful island, and suggested that Zatamon might describe the disease in more detail, since it was of extraordinary interest to me as a physician. Although he had said something about the cosmic rays of the sun before my being locked up, to my regret, owing to my then erroneous beliefs (of which I was by this time much ashamed) I had not paid due attention.

I now truly ate humble pie, and it was satisfying to do penance for my sin. Among the wise Hins I actually felt like a child who had fled back to his mother's arms from the bullying of bad boys.

"I have already mentioned," Zatamon commenced, "that the functions of life are influenced by the cosmic rays of the sun. That is the source of all life. The will to live also comes from the sun, together with warmth in the form of cosmic rays. This radiation is received by the brain, which functions as an antenna, and the brain continues to operate in a manner determined by the rays. This is what forms instinct."

"That is, the rays have an effect on instinct similar to that which the hormones have on the functioning of the organs?"

"Yes. Even you partly know the effect of the sun's cosmic rays on life. You have experienced the coincidence of protuberances and sunspots with certain medical symptoms. You have been surprised at the close correlation you yourself have observed between solar activity and certain diseases and even the frequency of accidents. From such oscillations of the life force, you can see that it was dictated to the full by the effect of the sun's cosmic rays upon the nervous system. Vitality and instinct come from the sun. And as long as instinct remains instinct, without thought, there is no trouble. Have you seen the kazo life of the ants?"

"What?!" I interrupted him in surprise, as he had used this comparison once before. "What does this witless animal have to do with the kazo, which is the complicated rule of life for the intellectual beings of Hin society?"

"Only that rule is complicated which is not life itself—as, for example, the Behins' fantasies. Life is simple and comes automatically. It can be lived well in one way only, and to live it wrongly is not only difficult, it is impossible. In nature there are no contradictions; for contradictions themselves perish, as you saw with the Behins. I'll give you an example: in the animal kingdom long-lived and tough animals are the least prolific, while short-lived and fragile species are prolific. You, of course, respect in this the organizing force, the mystical miracles of nature, while it is really nothing other than the kazo—simple mathematical truth, reality itself; a fact that cannot be otherwise. If the hare hadn't a high reproduction rate, there would be no hares in the world at all, as they would have died out. By now it should be clear that man could not live, either, if a contradiction had arisen in his productive labor; for example, in the erroneous idea that instead of food we must feed on pebbles or knives. You must admit that a man living like that would perish in the same way as a hare incapable of mating. This is expressed by the more sane among you as natural selection."

"Well, is it not that?"

"It's much more simple. It is a mathematical formula: $a - a = 0$. That is, if I am alive but do not maintain my life I will perish. This is simply existing reality—the kazo—which, therefore, requires no learning. Knowledge and education are necessary only to be a Behin; the kazo is so. By itself."

I felt somewhat hurt by Zatamon's talking to me as if I were unaware of even the elements of arithmetic, and incidentally I mentioned that I was perfectly familiar with the laws of mathematics.

"Let's not say 'law,' he replied, because that already represents some sort of intellectual creation, whereas the kazo need not be understood, for life cannot even be imagined in any other way."

"So, accordingly," I said, "Behinity is the lack of capacity for the elements of arithmetic, whereby one is unable to perform even the simplest operation in subtraction."

"By and large that is so, but not because of an inability to count; instead, because the patient is unaware of the meaning of numbers. The Behin imagines that noneating is actually eating, and that the knife does not end life but promotes it."

"And how do such terrible misbeliefs get into his brain?"

"From the brain itself. The human brain is a more complicated receiver than the ant's nervous system, and as such it also emits self-oscillation that mixes with the cosmic rays of the sun. And the brain receives this mixed wave, by which its comprehension of things becomes distorted and its life functions diverge from the kazo. Besides real aims the brain itself produces aims, perverted instincts—ketni, kipu, bruhu, bikbam, boeto, and thousands of other nonexistent things, whose existence destroys itself and turns into nonexistence."

"Because they don't understand mathematics . . ."

"I repeat, the kazo does not have to be understood, for it is so by itself. One plus one equals two, and the expression $1 + 1 = 3$ is not only senseless but doesn't even exist. It's kazi. The kazo is what exists and the kazi is what does not exist, and he who wants to live in a kazi manner is no longer alive."

"But the Behins were alive."

"But in a disharmonious way. And disharmony inevitably liquidates itself. The kazi cannot stop. Neither the knife, nor the mufruks' breathing into the thin air, nor the yellow pebble will ever be nourishment. All these are nonexistent things, and the result, too, is noexistent life. It is death, as you have seen for yourself; for the boeto, square, ketni, and anebas one has not to become satisfied and live, but to starve and die. The whole of the Behins' past consisted in their massacring each other. But for real aims one must live: houses cannot be built and a cornfield cannot be reaped by a dead man."

I reflected on Zatamon's words for a long time. They had a familiar ring to them, as if I had heard them already sometime, somewhere, but now I did not ponder that. Their essence alone concerned me.

"This is quite understandable so far," I said, "but you have mentioned that the human brain produces a confusing self-oscillation on account of its being complex. How is it possible, then, that it confuses the Behin brain while yours is free of it?"

"Physiological research has borne out that the original inhabitants of our island were all Behins. But things out of harmony with the kazo or, as you would say, with nature, cannot survive for long—they perish and only what is harmonic remains. This is how the only organism with staying power has developed—a kazo organism. You know that, phagocytes have developed in the blood that devour germs and maintain the kazo balance—otherwise no man would have been able to live for a long time. And what was the attack of the germs? It was the self-oscillation present when human thinking began. On account of them struggling for imaginary aims, the ancient Hin or Behin kept dying out until finally, through a lucky permutation of the germ plasm, a new species, the Hin, came about, in which the antidote to self-oscillation already existed."

"And what is that?"

"Electric conducting layers took shape in the brain that shield the self-radiation, which thus cannot escape and cannot interfere with the cosmic rays. The beings produced in this manner are the Hins. Now you also understand why we consider the Behins a completely different species."

"And how is it possible that Behins exist today?"

"Behinity is caused by a latent gene that sometimes occurs

even in us, but of course we don't perceive it. It may easily happen, however, that when two Hins carrying this latent gene
mate the Behinity gene from both parents gets into the zygote.
In such cases the electric conducting layer is missing from the
descendant's brain—that is, a Behin offspring originates from
Hin parents."

"In other words, the Behins' mental disorder is in point of fact
a reversion to type?"

"Yes, that's it. A reversion to the disharmony of primitive conditions. Now you can understand why we separate the Behins,
and why we exclude them from mating with us. We hope that
with this continuous straining off of the sick species, this harmful latent gene will disappear in a few centuries."

Now very many things dawned upon me all at once.

"So this is why the Behins are not human beings?" I asked.

"That's it, exactly. The Behin is an ancient Hin. An obsolete,
superseded species. Do you understand our kazo life now? Do
you see how perfectly united cooperation of the termites is possible between reasonable, thinking people, too?"

"So, you have returned to nature?"

"We didn't return. One cannot step out of the kazo; one can
only be annihilated. We are the self-evident result of a mathematical procedure. We have developed from the self-destroying
Behin species as the only solution with staying power."

I fell into deep thought. Newton might well have felt so when
the apple fell to the ground before him, revealing the general
theory of gravitation, which keeps the whole universe in balance.
I felt how I was being transformed from one minute to the next.
Huge perspectives opened up before my mind, worlds wheeling
over on their axes. Suddenly everything stood before me in another way—clearly. Things had become simpler and taken shape.
The flame of the Burning Bush lit a torch within me and suddenly there emerged before me the trunk of the Tree of Life, of
which I had previously seen only the leaves, and only the greatest
biologists had been able to grope back to the branches.

After lengthy pondering, one more question rushed to my lips.

"I am still surprised that it is not possible to make the Behins understand simple reality. For their brain is otherwise quite well developed; they can count, I've even seen mathematicians of great merit among them, but in the simplest matters. . . ."

"The Behin's brain doesn't separate self-radiation from the cosmic rays and that the receiver distorts it in a complex manner only confirms the fact of distortion. The more they know the more foolishly they will think; the hungrier they are the more food they will throw out; the less struggle required to produce our daily bread, the more they will kill each other for it; and when they writhe hungrily, sick and suffering, they will hope to regain their strength through the 'breath' of the mufruk, the kipu, the boeto, the yellow pebble, or the salvation of the knife."

"There were also quite sensible Behins," I put in. "I heard of some bikru. . . ."

"Yes, there are ones whose intellect understands the necessity of the kazo but their being is still Behin, and this renders their way of thinking imperfect and prevents them from achieving full perception."

"What do you mean by that?"

"Their obsessions are characteristic of the Behins. The imagined misbeliefs."

"And what of the bikru?"

"Don't speak of 'the' bikru. You shouldn't think that they had only one bikru. There were several. Perhaps, you, too, might have become one of them."

"Indeed?!" I looked at him flabbergasted.

"Yes. They burn every bikru first. Later they recognize him because, as you yourself have seen, they have minds—but the self-radiation doesn't allow them to dominate clearly, and as soon as it comes to words, to say nothing of deeds, everything becomes reversed. The bikrus, however, have the ability to manifest their intelligence but, as I have said, in their being they are Behins and they are not free of imperfections and obsessions."

"Of obsessions? What obsessions do you mean?"

"To be a bikru is fundamentally a monomania: the erroneous belief that in the Behins there is a connection between the heard word and the brain. A bikru is a Behin whose only Behinity is that he doesn't realize among whom he lives; for it could not be imagined, could it, that someone aware of the Behinic disease would still want to explain reality to them?"

A deep, solemn silence ensued, broken only by the birdsong and, occasionally, the murmur of the distant sea. Zatamon stood up and gestured toward the sun with his right arm.

"Only the kazo exists!"

As I looked up at him from my recumbent position, he stood there in the flood of spring sunlight like a statue of life regained. A breeze ruffled the light folds in his clothes, and his high bronzed forehead flashed in the sunshine while his eyes received the rays without so much as a blink.

The trees in blossom on the mountainside opposite us, their silvery spiral snaking upwards; the sea; the birds; the high-speed train darting past down below; and this motionless man of health incarnate merged in wondrous harmony into an indivisible whole, a pure world, under the brilliance of the kazo.

And as the wretched writhing of the recent past occurred to me, I too opened my arms involuntarily toward the sun and heaved a sigh of rebirth.

The majesty of the kazo played music in my soul. After the dark, diseased tortures I'd undergone, the gates were opened up before me, and intoxicated with knowledge I drank of the light.

Zatamon sat back down beside me.

*

The only one thing I regretted was that I had learned something I could not turn to the benefit of my own country; first, because the Behinic disease was incurable, and also because it fortunately did not occur among us.

Looking back to the horrors of the Behins' freakish, atavistic brain, their whole fate appeared to me as self-regulating and inevitable.

"Now I understand you," I said, "I fully realize that the annihilation of the Behins was not an act of inhumanity—on the contrary, it was a necessary process, kazo itself, which could only have happened this way, and was inevitable. Redemption. How good that I, a man accustomed to the sane British environment, have been rescued from so horrible a society!"

Zatamon looked into the distance for some time and then said pensively, "One actually doesn't know one's own voice, one hears it from inside—through the skull."

"What do you mean by that?"

"When I heard my own voice for the first time from a recording device I did not recognize it. I felt it to be alien."

"And what does that imply?"

"That you never recognized your own voice among the Behins because you were hearing it for the first time from outside."

"What?" I exclaimed, astounded. "You cannot mean . . ."

"And you did not recognize your culture, as it differs from theirs in *form*. Their life destroys itself with different words from yours, but both are the same: Behinity. Or was it not you who told me once that the essence of life is not the hospital, the factory, bread, and health but the soul?"

I sprang to my feet. All of my limbs were trembling.

"I hope you don't mean that seriously!" I cried. "Don't you tell me you want to compare us to pebble squeezing and copper-cube worshipping lunatics?!"

"And you will never see yourselves," Zatamon went on in an unchanged tone. "You traveled throughout Lilliput in vain as well. Your Behin species merely entertains children with amusing 'exoticism.' You have also come to us in vain. You are unaware of reason. You are an atavistic, transitional species that must at first drive itself out of the existing world so that the kazo can assume harmonic form."

For minutes I was on the verge of stuffing his invective right back down his throat with my two hands. I reminded myself in vain that I was dealing with a senseless automaton whose gramophonelike gabble should not be taken seriously: but an insult had now been leveled at my nation that a gentleman had at all costs to avenge.

I say I was on the border of hitting him: Zatamon would not hit me back, anyway, and it was indeed a miracle of self-control that I was able to curb my temper. It occurred to me, however, that they might shut me up in the Behin settlement forever, or they would perhaps exterminate me as well, and among the Hins there was neither law, justice, nor authority to appeal to for redress of the grievances one suffers.

After a moment's hesitation, I looked Zatamon up and down contemptuously, and without deigning to answer his words I turned my back on him.

And he looked after me without a word.

*The author wishes to try getting home, but Zatamon does
not share his aim. Eventually the author himself makes a
boat and successfully sets out on the high seas.*

THIS SCENE HAD FINALLY SEALED MY FATE. ZATAMON'S
rough words had suddenly brought back to me the repulsive reality of Hin life that the intervening Behin horrors had made me
forget. All the hopelessnesses of their bleak existence unfolded
before me one by one: loneliness, alienation, supreme indifference toward people, rigid heartlessness, the monotonous buzz
of the textile factory; and, finally, the most terrible memory—
Zolema, the scentless flower.

I had never been in such a hopeless deadlock. The knowledge
that everything was hopeless slowly suppressed my indignation
and I reached that illusive silence in which one can coolly consider even suicide.

And yet perhaps there was a third solution that could change
everything for the better: escaping from this accursed island and
returning to my own country. Not even a prisoner clings to the
thin rays of sunlight filtering in to him through the bars of his cell
with the desire that I embraced in the hope of returning home.

As soon as the throbbing of my heart calmed down I tried
to consider matters rationally, and arrived at the decision that
I should at all costs attempt to escape, and only failing this should
I do away with myself.

An enormous task lay ahead of me—that much was certain. The Hins had no knowledge of navigation. The land was everything to them: it formed and shaped their livelihood, and their whole outlook was bound to it. It was perhaps because of this that they could not soar spiritually, either. The trading of the Phoenicians, the feverish expansion of the Romans, the thirst for adventures of the Spanish, and the buccaneering of the Normans—I would have looked for all of them in vain, not to mention my own country's sense of vocation in the dissemination of humanity and Christian civilization. The Hins knew that the earth was round and a hundred thousand times bigger than their island, but they did not even try to get in touch with other peoples. No desire for conquest or for riches, and not even curiosity, had driven them beyond their boundaries. They were simply not interested in anything beyond their bare necessities. They cultivated only those sciences that were of use to them.

The science of navigation was represented by some light boats that they rowed on the river or by the shore, but venturing out onto the high seas in them even in the calmest weather would have been most unadvisable.

Thus if I wanted to get away from here I would first have to build my own craft.

After prolonged hesitation I resolved to put my ill-feeling aside and talk further with Zatamon to ask his help.

The next day toward evening I called upon him again.

I sincerely confided in him that I could not bear life on their island, and if he did not want me to commit suicide he should procure the Hins' help. I told Zatamon that I knew something about boat building and, if I had a few men to help me, in two weeks we could patch up something seaworthy and they could get rid of me for good—the only solution for both of us.

Zatamon replied that he did not understand why anybody wanted imperfection, but it was a fact that Behins did indeed have such fixed ideas from which they could not be dissuaded.

However, the Hins could not be persuaded to perform anything that would entail harm to me.

"How do you imagine," he asked, "that a kazo being could de-
viate from the kazo? You can't force fish onto land and you can't
feed a dog on hay—if you attempted it they would not live."

This epitome of narrow-mindedness amazed me so much that
for a few minutes I had no idea what to say. At first I thought that
it was his grievance from the previous day that made him speak
like this, but in such a way as to conceal his resentment. Now
he grasped the first opportunity to harm me, while hiding his
spiteful intentions behind such a polite pretext.

The awareness returned to me only slowly that the Hins had no
idea of politeness and of the basic rules of gentlemanly conduct.
But if he really wasn't lying, then any further discussion would
be a waste of breath.

Without a word I turned on my heels and left Zatamon for good.

I resolved to escape come what may. As a last attempt I would
try to assemble a boat alone—and would do away with myself
only if this failed.

The next day I simply left the hospital. Nobody came looking
for me.

I went into town. I took a car and some tools from a garage,
drove out a good distance from town and, near a deep rivulet with
a good flow of water surrounded by dense bush, I dismantled the
engine. The next day, using another car, I took other tools, some
iron rods and sheets, and different machine parts. I erected a tent
made of raincoats, and with great difficulty I hammered out a
primitive propeller and a rudder using the iron plates.

Then I took out boards, and eventually cobbled together a
small barge, managed to haul it into the water with rope pulleys,
and set about installing the engine.

In carrying everything out, I naturally had no difficulties since
the goods were unguarded. But the work still had to be done
furtively, for if they had seen it they would obviously have taken
me for a Behin.

I do not want to bore the Reader with details. Suffice it to say that I worked in the forest for three months. At night I slept in town, but at last I had a job that did not bore me. Patriotism and homesickness spurred me on.

Three months later, in a huge truck, I made my rounds in almost every warehouse. From one I took three barrels of petrol, from another oil, then all kinds of food, including crispbread and canned foods in sufficient quantity for about three months. Although my voyage was unlikely to take more than a couple of weeks, I thought that there was no reason not to stow away more if the opportunity presented itself. These things were not guarded in any way.

What would happen if one day some rogue were to loot the Hins' warehouses? I could not help but wonder. By the same token, vulnerable though these facilities were, their stocks were extraordinarily large, and it would not have been felt too keenly if they were looted by a hundred or even a thousand rogues. Besides, there were no such people on the island. Viewing their enormous warehouses, I thought that as soon as I had reached home I would organize an expedition to return and plant the British flag, representing Christian civilization—before some greedy colonizing country were to subjugate the honest people of the island.

And so I became ever more aware of my elevated calling; my arrival in Kazohinia had actually been the special grace of Providence granting me this glorious and patriotic mission.

This awareness afforded me new strength. In a fervent prayer I thanked the Lord of infinite mercy in Heaven, and then continued my lofty work with redoubled efforts.

Everything was ready except for a supply of fresh water, for which unfortunately I had no suitable container. I certainly could not pour drinking water into a petrol drum!

It occurred to me that in the textile factory there was a lavatory where I had seen a hot water container on the wall. So I drove to the factory and there I asked the first Hin I came across to help me take down the container. He, of course, immediately lent his assistance unquestioningly. It is certain that in this respect I already understood them. He even helped to load it, and I could hardly restrain my laughter at the thought that the next day they would turn the tap in vain. They would definitely believe that I had met with a fatal accident that explained why I had not taken the container back from the "repair shop." On the way I looked in on the geophysical institute, from whose laboratory I collected a fine compass, a sextant, a telescope, and other essential instruments. This, of course, I had to do cautiously, waiting until the physicists were occupied elsewhere. All this I then transported to my vessel.

As I had already accomplished my patriotic work, only my departure remained.

I set sail deliberately by day, and into the bargain late in the afternoon, when most of the Hins were strolling on the seashore. Let them burst with rage on seeing my vessel vanish from sight!

Accordingly I embarked before twilight, inspected everything thoroughly once more, and asking the Almighty's guidance for my voyage I started the engine and put to sea.

At a distance of about two hundred paces from shore I altered course and progressed along the coastline of Kazohinia.

After a stretch of brush, the beach soon appeared. Hundreds of Hins were there lying down, walking, sitting, or bathing. My boat attracted the attention of many of them and, intoxicated with the sweet joy of freedom, I stood out on deck, waved my cap, and kept shouting, "Hello there!" at the top of my lungs. All of a sudden my pent-up human joy found an outlet after having had to contain itself while among them.

The Hins certainly took note, and with every face gaping vacantly they turned their attention toward me.

The knowledge that I was beyond their power, that here and now I could do whatever I wished, gave another impetus to my high spirits that now burst forth irresistibly. Throwing my cap into the air and myself to the floor, I kicked about, shouted goodbye to them, and laughed incessantly.

They were astonished for a while and marveled at me. They could not understand the situation. Many of them shouted out, asking what had happened. In reply I yelled "good-bye" to them. They seemed to have interpreted this as a request for help, and thinking that the water had cast me adrift, several Hins flung themselves into the sea. At this moment even the siren began to blow to indicate that someone was drowning and more than one rowboat started toward me with life preservers at the ready.

This comic turn of events made me laugh so hard that my abdominal muscles began to ache. I let the Hins come close, then opened up the throttle and shot away from them. Again I stepped on deck, jumping and dancing about, and then I stuck out my tongue.

For a while the Hins splashed about, then, in bewilderment, they swam back to the shore.

No sooner had I left the crowded beach behind me than my heart jumped to my throat and for a moment I turned serious. That lonely rock emerged in front of me on which I had once sat with Zolema believing, in a fit of passion, that I had found something of substance.

High up on the peak of the rock there stood a Hin. Was it perhaps Zolema? I was already far from the shore, and could not tell for sure. Possibly it was not even a woman; they were so uniform. Yes, it was but one of the many.

With an instinctive gesture I reached for my telescope, but I scanned the face in vain: I could make out no features; the head was in eclipse with the setting sun, and the strong light radiating around the face rendered it impossible to distinguish anything particular.

My high spirits suddenly vanished, the grief of memories twisted my heart, and, snatching at the rudder, I directed my craft at full throttle toward the open sea.

But I could not take my eyes off that solitary figure. It simply stood, like a statue, motionless, as if at one with the rock beneath. As the distance between us grew greater and the rock receded farther and farther from my eyes, the whole figure gradually merged with the blinding flood of sunlight. The sun set as I moved farther out to sea, as if following the figure, which sank slowly into the horizon, slowly diminishing and fusing with the light.

After a while I could no longer distinguish the rock itself. The whole island was now in the halo of the setting sun, which sank lower and lower until it disappeared with a last flare in the limitless water, snatching Kazohinia away forever.

And from my heart fell away an enormous stone; at last I could leave far behind me that terrible island where heart, love, and beauty were unknown concepts, and where the bleak prison of cheerless life had caused me so much suffering.

As I advanced, the hope of that distant other coast unfolded before the eye of my exulting mind—the land of the soul.

My pleasure was marred only by the fact that my eyes ached for quite a while. Indeed, I severely rebuked myself for having tried to look into the sun; being a doctor, I should have known that human eyes were not created for looking into so intense a light.

20

The author is caught in a storm. By a stroke of luck he meets the Terrible. He is kindly received by his fellow officers. He arrives home.

AS I TRAVELED FARTHER AND FARTHER, MY HIGH SPIRITS slowly returned, and an hour later I again wept, sang, and danced, giving vent to all the pleasure, grief, and feeling I had had to repress during my long year of imprisonment with the lunatics.

For two days I traveled thus, sleeping no more than a few hours a night. On the third day, with the help of my instruments, I established that I had reached the sea lane to India, and that I ought to sight land in two days at most. The situation was all the more urgent as my engine, unaccustomed to such a long running period, had to be stopped more and more frequently so I could clean it or replace the spark plugs.

On this third day, after lunch, black clouds suddenly gathered on the horizon, and after half an hour I was caught in a fierce storm. The wind caught my boat amidship with terrific force, and I feared it would sink. Exerting myself to my utmost, I continually bailed out the water and set the engine into the wind at full throttle.

After half an hour of desperate struggling, the engine stopped dead. That was the last straw! I opened up the engine immediately. Drenched to the skin, bailing out water with one hand and staggering from fatigue and exhaustion, I worked until I realized the horrible truth: two cylinders had seized up and no force could budge them.

I was entirely at the mercy of the elements.

But the best was yet to come.

When the storm abated, my instruments told me that beyond doubt I was farther back than I had been. I was in those very currents that a year ago had taken me at the beginning of my voyage to the island of the lunatics!

Indescribable despair overcame me. Lying in the bottom of my boat, I tore my hair and writhed about, and then, absolutely beside myself, I fell to my knees and prayed to God to save me this one last time from having to relive the past monstrosities and help me back to life. I vowed that I would never put to sea again. Only the murmur of the sea responded to my words, and I decided that if I sighted the island I would drown myself.

Evening came, and the horizon dressed itself in black, making the situation seem even more gloomy. Although I could have lit a lamp, as my batteries were not yet depleted, I did not dare to do so. My eyes were just about to close with exhaustion when I caught sight of a point of light on the distant horizon.

Hope gave new strength to my limbs. I jumped up, picked up a reflector, and waved it in that direction while shouting at the top of my lungs, although I knew that I could not be heard at such a distance.

A quarter of an hour passed before I was noticed. The blast of a siren replied, then I saw a hull turn toward me.

What I felt at that moment my Readers cannot imagine and I am unable to describe, but for me it will forever remain an unforgettable memory. Tears welled up in my eyes, and falling to my knees I stammered thanks to the infinitely merciful Lord of Heaven.

Half an hour later the ship was close to me, and once I was able to read her name, I cried out in perfect ecstasy.

It was the *Terrible!*

When the lifeboat reached me I embraced the very first sailor I saw and kissed him on both cheeks.

Climbing aboard, I was taken to the captain. Here I could not control myself anymore. Falling again to my knees, I kissed the British flag; then, standing up, I sang *God Save the King* in an almost delirious joy, at which off came the sailors' caps all around me and eyes dimmed with tears.

Nobody knew what was happening, but they felt it, and they did not disturb me.

It occurred only to me afterward that I should introduce myself.

I outlined the situation briefly, at which the captain sent me to the admiral under the escort of a lieutenant.

We found the admiral in the mess, where the officers happened to be sitting at their dinner. Seeing his epaulets, I sprang to attention and introduced myself briefly, at which the admiral shook my hand and said, "How d'you do,"—and I again burst into tears.

However, the admiral kindly beckoned to me to take a seat and the stewards set another place at the table, every piece of which was adorned with the royal coat of arms. Then I was offered a small glass of whisky.

All this I had not seen or tasted for a whole year—or more, for all I knew! I could hardly recover from my joy, and it was quite a while before I was able to send the first bite down my throat, as sobs choked me.

After dinner the admiral himself asked me to say a few words about my experiences, insofar as my condition permitted it.

I heaved a deep sigh and set about relating everything. Needless to say, within a few minutes I was forced to observe indications of doubt on the faces of my fellow officers—in spite of all their goodwill. Lest they should take me for either a fool or a liar, I also tried to submit material proof. Fortunately my craft had been lifted aboard, so I could show them some copies of a publication entitled "Textile Industry" that I had used for packing, with pictures of the factory in them. They began to take me seriously only when I read it fluently and explained it in translation. At this point, everyone gathered around me and listened eagerly to my story. The solemn silence was broken only occasionally by a burst of spontaneous laughter when I mentioned this or that piece of nonsense of the Hins or Behins. This abated and turned into comradely sympathy when I called their attention to the fact that I was the party who had been subjected to all this.

It also had a boisterous effect when I related how the betik honored me with his silly question, "How does your nose grow, kaleb?"—while he had not been at all interested in the growth of noses.

It caused great amusement when I spoke of the foot snatching, the vake-vake, and the betik's copper cube, and I take pride in having caused some merry moments especially to the admiral, who laughed so heartily at these unbelievable insanities and aimless stupidities that his decorations clinked on his chest.

Encouraged by this success, I too became animated and merry. I spoke with enthusiasm of the yellow pebble, earless women, the bikbam, the inscrutable ketni and kipu, the men defending their exploitation, the shukk, the Bigrusts, and above all of Zemoeki's boundless stupidity. Growing from minute to minute, the amusement reached its climax when I related that Zemoeki would not have recognized himself in my account of my travels and would only have laughed at the whole thing. At this point I had to interrupt my words because my audience's abdominal muscles began to ache.

"Did he laugh at his own portrait?" the admiral asked, wiping away his tears, once the general laughter had somewhat abated.

"And how heartily!" I replied.

At this, thunderous laughter again burst forth.

When, however, I arrived at my last story, that of the massacre that had raged on account of the circle and the square, the faces unexpectedly turned serious. The admiral politely remarked that although he did not doubt my veracity, here perhaps I had not observed everything properly, for starting a bestial bloodshed because of soft-headed obsessions and geometrical figures would signify a complete lack of thinking capacity and intelligence, which was unbelievable not only of men but also of brute beasts. To him it also seemed improbable that one professing truth and solid common sense with a clear conscience should be called an extremist and an exaggerating inciter, and that such a man should be put to the stake as an enemy of order and civilization. This was perhaps an exaggeration, he suggested, being incredible not only to the European way of thinking but to any other outlook as well. Surely something had escaped my attention or my sufferings had by that time dulled my senses.

His doubting of my words brought me the point of contradicting myself; forgetting about the respect due, the description of the entire massacre was again on the tip of my tongue when I was stunned into silence.

Indeed, thinking it over, I myself saw it all, in this environment, to be so unbelievable that on this night I considered it a dream. It was only on reading my travel notes the next day that I became convinced once again that it had all been reality. But that evening I did not dare to say another word. And I finally abandoned the idea of telling them about the bikru's tenets, which I myself cannot entirely believe even today.

Suddenly falling silent, I answered that at that particular moment I was not entirely sure of it myself, and that I would prefer to be excused from recalling the madness, and instead turn my attention to those sundry things so sane and sweet that I had not had the opportunity to hear from my compatriots for such a long time.

My words were received with understanding. Then the admiral stood up and, with a glass in his hand, began to speak.

He saluted me informally, expressing his pleasure that I had been lucky enough to get back from among the lunatics to the world of civilization, where I had the opportunity to rededicate my strengths to the service of my adored country.

The admiral enthusiastically reminded us of the greatness and special calling of our country, qualities that had enthroned her as the guardian of peace and civilization. And the trustee of this elevating vocation to safeguard the peace was the army, which ensured balance in the world, the survival of Christian justice, and, last but not least, the tranquility of the family hearths of British citizens.

With a transfigured expression the admiral assured us in a raised voice that there was no more elevating awareness than to serve under the British flag, as this was what led to true perfection of the soul, which filled the British citizen with pride and exalted him above all the other citizens of the world.

"To the heights of this happy feeling," he said, "only the living and warm heart of a patriot can rise, in which the sacred respect for ideals and traditions is alive, while the barren, bleak soul remains far from it and loses its way in the desert. Respect for the flag and the Bible imparts us with a rock-solid foundation that adds aim and content to our lives, and which distinguishes us from the brute beast; that is what steels our arms in the noble battles, and that is what makes the sons of the nation heroes who are happy to sacrifice their lives for honor and for the glory of death in action.

"Respect for military virtues and the national ideal is the source of the life of the people, without which our fate would be death and ruin. Let us therefore foster higher ideas in our heart, and our steadfast devotion to the Bible and our country, for a British patriot lives or dies with his sword and honor.

"For the time being we don't know," the admiral went on, "whether the war to come will be fought against the Germans, the French, or the Japanese, but wherever we shall be called by His Majesty's order we shall hasten without thought or hesitation to defend the flag, that much is certain.

"I firmly believe that when the bugle call is heard, every citizen, regardless of sex and age, will be happy to sacrifice his or her life for these ideals and this flag, for even if all of us should die, Great Britain and her ideals will live forever!"

Proposing a toast to the health of His Majesty, the admiral emptied his glass. Then, picking up the small flag that had stood on the table and holding it aloft, he shouted three cheers for king and country.

A soul-stirring scene followed.

The officers jumped up, tears shone in every eye, and we all broke into *God Save the King*.

After the last chord sounded, the officers embraced each other, and it was minutes before everyone sat down once again.

Now the officers wanted to have a word from me. I would have liked to thank them fittingly for the rapturous happiness that filled me now that I was in their circle after such a long period of deprivation.

I rose, but the glass trembled in my hand. My throat tightened; and in the end all I could do was shout in a voice touched with emotion, "My country! My King! My life is yours!"

What should have followed was suppressed by my fit of sobbing and by the thunderous cheering of my fellow officers.

Again we drank, then the admiral rose and bade us all good night. He gave me the signal honor of addressing me personally, saying, "Good show!" And, in true British fashion, expecting no answer, he turned on his heel and left.

After this I was led to my cabin where a freshly made bed already awaited me.

*

Returning home to Redriff, I found my wife and children in good health. The pleasure of seeing me again at first prevented my spouse from speaking, but then, bursting into tears of emotion, she said that I was already considered dead by everyone.

I tried to comfort her with tender words, saying that I had no more troubles and was able to devote my life to her and to my country.

Still sobbing, she asked me with the anxiety of the concerned wife whether, since the life insurance had already been spent for the proper conservation of the splendor of my house, it would not be advisable for me to return inconspicuously to Kazohinia to wait there until the thirty-year statute of limitations expired.

This, of course, I could not accept because it would have been bordering on fraud, which was alien to the character of a British citizen. And, furthermore, the whole staff of officers was already aware of my arrival. Thus I reassured my wife by saying that we should be perfectly able to pay back the insurance money after I had published the account of my travels; for my experiences were so edifying that any government would highly appreciate them and patronize their distribution in order that its subjects should learn—from the description of a society consisting of un- worthy and stupid Behins and governed by vicious leaders—to appreciate their own environment.

And when my tactful but nonetheless determined attitude had also made the gigolo leave my house, the domestic peace that is so pleasant a feature of the cozy English home was completely restored.

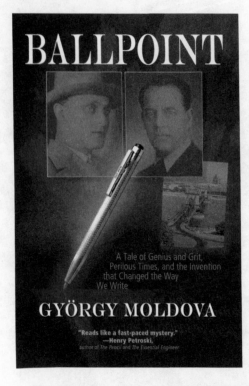